THE END OF ALL THINGS

THE DIVINE APOCALYPSE

R.D. Schwarz

PublishAmerica
Baltimore

First printing

All characters in this book are fictitious, and any resemblance to real persons, living or dead, is coincidental.

PublishAmerica has allowed this work to remain exactly as the author intended, verbatim, without editorial input.

Hardcover 978-1-4560-4207-3
Softcover 978-1-4560-4208-0
PUBLISHED BY PUBLISHAMERICA, LLLP
www.publishamerica.com
Baltimore

Printed in the United States of America

Dedicated to my father, Richard D. Schwarz, Jr.,
without whom this completed book may have never come to fruition;
and to every homeless soul who dares to imagine, just like me.

Acknowledgements

In the completion of my writing, I would like to acknowledge Dr. Ilo Soovere for his seemingly infinite encouragement and three simple letters that would serve as the foundation for my thoughts: C, C, and T; to Dad, for your invaluable insight and ability to work alongside me despite having stage-four colon cancer; for teaching me the difference between good and evil, and the timeless importance of the truth; my heart is forever with you; to Dr. Faye Lari, for guiding me in the first and perhaps the simplest step to personal success: accomplishing something; to my best friend Joseph Domiano, for being what he always has been; to Dan (you know who you are) for being the first person to tell me my story was worth telling, and for standing by me through the hard times; for the long conversations of physics and politics we shared over coffee, and to all the hopes and dreams a man without a home can have; to Owen and Olivia, with all my love, hugs and kisses; to my sister, Emily Schwarz, for always serving as someone to talk to even when circumstances were difficult; and to all my family at VA Perry Point, The Helping-Up Mission, and The Baltimore Station for giving me the running start and wisdom I needed just to be able to recognize the absolute beauty there is to be seen in the midst of disaster; and last but not least, to Publish America, for giving a man a chance to put his words out in print.

CONTENTS

"After this I looked, and there before me was a door standing open in heaven. And the voice I had heard speaking to me like a trumpet said, 'Come up here, and I will show you what takes place after this.'"

Revelations 4:1

THE END OF ALL THINGS

THE DIVINE APOCALYPSE

PROLOGUE

The Reign of Man

It was called the Age of Absolution, a period of time in mankind's existence where the advancements made in the fields of mathematics and medicine had become unequivocal; gone were the days of question and philosophical thinking; gone were the days of religious thought. Random occurrences within the human body and nature had been solved. All of mankind's answers had been ascertained through the discovery of an absolute one particle known as the mota, and through it a golden era of booming financial progress and the mastery of medicine came to pass. Through the implementation of logic, mankind discovered seemingly everything there was to discover about human anatomy and physiology; psychological disorders and all known viruses and diseases were pinpointed and eliminated when mankind discovered how to biologically engineer human genetics through the use of logic-based machines. Discovering the exact function of every individual neuron within the brain, scientists mapped out quadrillions of conduction sites within the organ; they attained all of the characteristics of neurological transmission and also exacted the correlation between the brain and the spinal cord.

Using newly discovered high frequency electromagnetic radiation, scientists and physicians worked side by side to manipulate the genetic matter within each individual neuron of the human brain. They were able to completely modify and repair neurons through these finely tuned frequencies, programming each neuron to work according to their will as technology intertwined with biology. And as soon as they had discovered the exact flow of information within the human body, scientists applied this knowledge in manufacturing machines that mirrored their own neurological anatomy. For the first time in mankind's history, their ability to restore and create had become equal to their ability to destroy.

A certain scientist by the name of Xar was born with exceptional abilities and was responsible for the recent advancements made by mankind. He was considered their saving grace; he was the cure for the dying; he was the perfect human mind. Because of his amazing capabilities, Xar rose to the level of Captain in the navy at the meager age of ten. While working in the naval laboratories, Xar discovered that the human body had once been able to live for hundreds of years at a time. Through advanced electronic engineering, Xar surpassed these limitations by allotting mankind the ability to live far longer through the modulation of neurological transmission to block harmful electromagnetic radiation. However, population control and finances were a major factor with the advancements made by Xar and his colleagues. Frustrated by his obvious superiority, Xar realized that only he seemed to have the answers to the problems mankind faced. He had no equal. An artist, Xar illustrated what mankind could be if they followed a certain order. He was a master painter and sculptor, and he created a series of mixed artwork called "Eden." A mockery of the idea of a god, Xar used a combination of paintings and sculpture to give the rest of mankind a vision of what they could become. It served as a vision for a Utopia, and became mankind's greatest desire.

At the age of fourteen, Xar was elected ruler of the European nations. It was during this year that Xar became aware that his abilities were not limited to his mind. He found that he could control the physical elements around him without the aid of machines. But for several years, he kept his power hidden from public knowledge. His papers on the discovery of mass as a part of the electromagnetic spectrum were the foundation for a book we would later publish. At age fifteen, he determined that the smallest particle on the mass portion of the electromagnetic spectrum was the mota. That foundational particle could only be disintegrated further into energy. Xar found that this particle could be manipulated on a broad scale in order to attain greater control of all matter in the universe. He united the European nations with the remainder of the inhabited earth at the age of sixteen. It was during that time that he established universal trade and optimized communications through the neurological linkage of human minds. Data transfer was instantaneous, one person able to see what another was thinking once he or she had been programmed to do so. At his young age, he seemed an unbelievably perfect leader. His government combined elements of a democratic republic with socialism and monarchy. All trade was based on credit, and everyone was allotted a fair share based on their occupations. The outcome of this reform in government and trade was the absolute freedom of mankind to do as he willed. As business boomed in the trade sector, Xar financed the creation of stasis chambers in the province of Ordren. This location was just outside the city of Jerusalem in Israel.

At seventeen, Xar began a massive cutback on homelessness and general crime. These stasis chambers served as holding locations for vagrants and miscreants, who he deemed "misdirected nature." However, he did not have a perfect grasp on all of mankind's ills as crime remained a viable factor. In order to establish advancements toward his utopian vision, Xar engineered a technological masterpiece. It was called "the perfect enforcer of harmony." In one month, Xar completed what was hailed as the greatest advancement for peace in human history. It was known as the Ventari Project. The ventari would serve as peacekeepers for a world in perfect order. One of the ventari assigned tasks would bring in the vagrants and place them into stasis. The captured would then be subjected to neurological reprogramming. Data was copied from a socially acceptable individual and written into the brain of one who was deemed unacceptable. Xar called for all of humanity to follow his benevolent commands in the continued establishment of his new government. And as they had been doing since the beginning of time, humankind followed the new king.

Xar's vision of a Utopia never came to fruition as he had wished it to. He was frustrated by portions of humanity who resisted his orders. Some cities throughout the world would not heed to his declarations. As a whole, the nation of Israel would not submit to his will. For this reason, Xar became enraged. He declared war on the nation, sending masses of his creations into the city of Jerusalem to capture it. The war did not last long as Xar's forces were unequaled and unbelievably powerful. He took the city of Jerusalem in two days, killing almost every resident of the city and doing everything within his power to keep this war from public knowledge.

He declared himself High Lord of Jerusalem at age thirty-one, when he came into contact with another brilliant mind. A master physician, a man by the name of Alune came to know High Lord Xar when he was discovered to have unusual powers which seemed to parallel Xar‘s. He could control nature itself, able to bring on lightning storms at will and control matter around him at a young age. Like High Lord Xar, Alune's memory was impeccable. He could recall every second of every day in his life, and predict events about to transpire using advanced probability and mathematics. And to High Lord Xar's great surprise, Alune was genetically and physiologically unaltered.

Alune stated that he had the answers to High Lord Xar's problems with achieving his Utopia, and the two united as one over the course of a year. During this time, the two became the political leaders of a newly established order: The Scientific Magisterium; this political system worked just as Xar's original political order, but added hefty punitive recourse for any who did not follow the scientific endeavors of Xar and Alune. Directly after having established the Scientific Magisterium, High Lord Xar had a visit from a most unexpected source. It was yet another visitor who seemed to have capabilities even beyond that of Alune and Xar. This visitor had commands for the two in demonstration of his own superiority. Xar kept the news of this newly found visitor quiet; he kept the communication between himself and this visitor secure. This visitor demonstrated supernatural power, and Xar trusted that Alune, he and this entity were the sovereign elite; he was led to believe that he and his companion were gods. Upon the command of this new figurehead, High Lord Xar handed over his power to Alune and stepped down as high lord. He was then made Vice Lord of Jerusalem. High Lord Alune rebuilt the pyramids of Egypt, reigned over Rome and began what he called the "Babylon Project" after having been instructed by the visitor to do so. Under High Lord Alune, society seemed to be moving perfectly. But there were still unexpected issues arising around the area of Jerusalem. Even Vice Lord Xar had no explanation for them. High Lord Alune addressed the world and issued a decree in an attempt to put a stop to the resistance in the city of Jerusalem and the suburbs of it. This order would be the very one to spell out the beginning of the end for all of humankind.

CHAPTER ONE

Out of the Darkness

This evening would forever be known as the Doomsday Affair. It was a dark and stormy night on the evening of their death. Lightning cracked across the blackened sky. High Lord Alune had ordered that the refugees of the city of Adriel be placed into the stasis chambers in the province of Ordren, about two miles outside of the world capital of Jerusalem. A suburb of Jerusalem, Adriel was once a great city, with intricate towering buildings and grandiose works of art as far as the eye could see. The Adrielians were known for their artistry and sculpture, and they were also known for peace. But once Alune had become High Lord of Jerusalem, the city was cut off from all trade. The reasoning behind Alune's decision was to allocate the funds necessary to fortify Jerusalem's defenses, that he may ensure his safety as high commander of the known world. The ventari peacekeepers were on the move, their bodies flying through the air in a blue and white stream of flame.

There were seven hundred peacekeepers that descended upon the city of Adriel, their artolium bodies impenetrable to nearly all forms of resistance. There was a great crash of thunder when the first peacekeeper landed, and behind him came a rain of reinforcements. About three thousand men were gathered in the streets of the city, crying out for mercy as they were defenseless against the ventari's ruthless arsenal. The first ventari to land stood out from the rest of his counterparts as commotion was stirred up amidst the fearful refugees of Adriel. This ventari carried a brown leather satchel on his left hip. Homeless and clothed in rags and tattered cloth, the exiles called out to the ventari for mercy. But their pleas would come to no avail. The ventari were silent, as they always are. Their bodies glistened in the light of the moon, and their metal frames made them seem almost human. But these men, these soldiers of Alune, were far from what they once were. Although entitled as such, they were anything but keepers of peace. Their minds had been reprogrammed, and their bodies were shaped in the form of a human. They had articulated eyes, ears, noses, lips and uniformly bald heads—a precise portrayal of a noetic terrestrial being. But their external shell demonstrated their true nature. Possessing translucent armor, the peacekeeper's insides could clearly be seen from without. Their inner mechanisms were powered by a very potent particle charge known as ethalon. The ethalon they contained could be seen from within the confines of their chest, and appeared as a ball of fire with particles gravitating around it like many electrons orbiting the nucleus of an atom. The ethalon flowed like blood to an artificial blue artolium shielding that closely resembled a muscle. As the ethalon was pumped into it, the ribbed shielding would contract and protract.

These machines were built with the design of the Roman gods of old in mind, bearing an anatomy of a male's lean muscle mass. But they were purely machine, built to sustain a rain fire of bullets, immune to the effects of most heat and radiation, and virtually impenetrable to the sword. Their inner workings were intricate and finely tuned to a state of perfection, designed to allow them to survive, process, kill and fly. Their speed was insurmountable to anything mankind had ever developed. Capable of moving at mind-numbing speeds and able to swiftly move in and out of the earth's atmosphere at will, their engineering made them nigh unstoppable.

The ventari who stood out from the legion of ventari behind him held out his hands and spread his fingers. Out of the ventari's palm, what some refer to as "the eye" opened. The eye was comprised of five blades of metal shaped in a circle which opened to unveil a blinding light. Within a ventari's hand, an amplifier increases the ethalon's potency several thousand times. The outcome is a concentration of particles known as a sterai beam. The beam can be manipulated by the ventari into the shape of a one and a half inch straight beam, a wave, or a cone. Below the peacekeeper, a man dropped to his knees and begged for leniency from the ventari's threatening hand. The peacekeeper then closed the eye of his palm and drew a scroll from the satchel at his side. He held it high in the air, and as he did, a vizedrone dropped from the sky like the dragon he is to the roost. Vizedrones are fearsome monstrosities, originally designed by the artist Hendur. Their mouths greatly resembled a bearded dragon, with faces that were rounded. But their eyes were closer to the center of their face. Like a metal Mohawk, they had horns from the tip of their nose to the very end of their tail. The horns varied in length, but appeared to be the sharpest and longest around the tail. Their arms and claws were bulky, and their general size was comparable to that of an aircraft carrier — overwhelmingly enormous. Scales covered the whole of their body with a partially artolium shielding.

Artists after Hendur had followed in his creative footsteps, creating machines that served various purposes in the forms of different animals. Shaped like a full-bodied medieval dragon, these militaristic tanks of war were initially meant to be used only when necessary to maintain order. And order was the name of the game on this night. High Lord Alune had guaranteed all of mankind that they were one step from Utopia, and that Adriel's acquisition was a half of a step in that direction. The scroll in the peacekeeper's hand was a decree from High Lord Alune that all the refugees of Adriel be removed at once and placed into stasis for a period of one year so that the city of Adriel may be destroyed and rebuilt.

From the crowd, the vagrants began to move into the custody of the peacekeepers quietly. In one large mass they came, each man moving to a ventari for transport back to the province of Ordren where they would be kept and processed. The peacekeeper held his scroll in the air, his arm remaining firm in place like a pillar of stone until all of the men in the streets of Adriel were in the arms of the ventari behind him. All of them that is, except for two. In the center of the city an old man sat down near a broken sculpture. He was clothed in all white robes, and held an old, dusty book in his hands. He twirled the ends of his long, white beard as if he was in great thought. To his left, near a fractured stone fountain that no longer functioned, another man sat holding a white cat in his hands. He would pet the cat ever so often. He was cleanly shaven, and had long, flowing gray hair that reached down to the middle of his back. The man near the sculpture was silent, and stared at the forward ventari with great focus. The ventari held his scroll up in the air, still offering for the two men to move. The great vizedrone near the ventari opened his jaws, unveiling a mouth full of razor sharp teeth.

"Why do you hesitate? Time is being wasted here," the vizedrone spoke as he growled at the men who remained still in the streets, his voice slithering like a snake. Neither one of the men responded to the vizedrone's inquiry, but instead remained silent and set their eyes on the peacekeeper that held the scroll. "Are you fools? Do you not value your lives?" At this, the man near the sculpture took a stand, grabbing hold of a cane that was positioned next to him to help him to rise to his feet. He paused for a moment, twirling his beard as he had before. He then held up the old book in his right hand in the same fashion that the ventari who stood ten yards away from him held its scroll. Looking the ventari straight in the eyes, his weakened old arms held the book in place as steadfastly as the machine held the scroll. At this, there was an outbreak of laughter from the crowd—the vagrants who a moment earlier had stood by the side of the two men. The vizedrone joined in the laughter, and took a step toward the man who was holding the book. "You know what we must do here. Your prerogatives are not your own. All of you are the property of the new order, and this day shall be the last day mankind will know resistance. Tonight it ends." The man who stood near the fountain gently placed the cat he was holding on the ground. He then took a stand and walked alongside the man who held the aged book in the sky. The refugees all became silent when the man near the fractured fountain walked next

to the unmoved old man with the tome. "We offe
and you refuse? I offer you the world. You need o
will come to you." The bearded man then began t
sturdy as a diamond.

"We are not of this world. We have an offer for you, and it is in m hand. You were once human as we are. You have the spirit in you to choose yet. This is your last chance, for the end of days begins now. What I hold in my hand is my answer to your inquiries, and it is my only offer."

"You must be joking," the vizedrone hissed, grim in his tone. "Surely you do not still hold to the philosophy of that foolish religion of old! You have caused much dissention and have been granted leniency. Is it so much to ask that you abide by the law?"

"There is only one law I hold to, and it is this one," the bearded man said, still holding his arm in place. "You will all feel the repercussions of this night, for it has been written before the point of time began. Remember my words, for they are not my own. They come from a higher power." The vizedrone nodded.

"Very well, then," the vizedrone began as he glanced behind him. "Set up mobile cameras where they die. The world will enjoy looking upon what remains of these pests."

The ventari dropped his scroll and reached his arm out in front of him. As the five metal blades in his hand opened, a great wave of white light pulsed from his palm. The light swept the bearded man and the man that stood beside him away in a blinding blast that left the refugees' ears ringing. The vizedrone approached the place where the men stood, his massive claws crushing the concrete ground with every step he took. And when the vizedrone reached the place of the flare, he looked to the ground. A pool of blood swirled around something that survived the detonation against all odds. Reaching into the blood with his claws, the monster withdrew the book the old man had held. The vizedrone's eyes grew red, a laser scanning the surface of the book and removing all of the blood from its surface. The monster growled when he saw the words that were inscribed into the frayed book's surface. And the words read, "The Holy Bible." As

.vo hovering cameras descended from the air and moved into position near the vizedrone, a bolt of lightning flew across the restless sky—a welcome to the end of all things.

In a dark room, a man sat before a sixty-inch projected image of a newscast. His hands were crossed in front of his unseen face as he watched a female newscaster report.

"Today, just outside the city of Adriel, a great earthquake has shaken the very foundation of Jerusalem. The two refugees who died during what is being called a routine patrol are said to be the perpetrators of this heinous crime. Their bodies were noted to have somehow returned despite the condition of their deaths. Eyewitnesses say they stood in the very place they were killed and proceeded to ascend into the clouds. As High Lord Alune's top scientists continue to investigate the matter, the Chief of Science in Jerusalem has issued a report. In his report, Chief Scientist Olar states that first contact may have been made with an alien species. We will continue to update you with the news on this matter as intelligence continues to be gathered. This is…"

The dark figure shut the image off by pressing a darkened button to his side. He then returned his hands to their original position in front of his face.

"Nazere? Nazere?! Awaken!" The cold cell in the holding chambers of Ordren was dimly lit by moonlight from a window to the right of the cell when Nazere's sleeping eyes opened. An ion shield covered the window and kept insiders from escaping. Nazere's sandy-blonde hair glimmered in the moonlight that was peeking in from the window. Nazere was tall, a good six-foot and three inches in height. Above him, a much taller being in a large black shroud stood three feet beside where he was laying in his bunk. The figure was wearing a black hood that hid his face, and he stood within a twenty by twenty foot space that consisted of all artolium walls and a door about five feet deep. Other than a spiral toilet in the corner of the space, the room was completely empty. Nazere rubbed his eyelids with his hands, jumping when his eyes met the dark figure standing in his chambers. His alertness was peaked when the dark figure took a step toward him.

"The time has come, my son," the dark figure began in a voice as deep as the bottom of the dark-blue ocean. "We must make haste to depart from this place in time. And time is of the essence." Nazere's eyes widened as he held tightly to his steel bunk, displaying an evident sense of fear as the dark figure spoke.

"Who are you?" Nazere asked nervously, astounded by the appearance of the apparition before him. "And how did you get in here?!" The dark figure remained still.

"That is unimportant at this time. What is important is that we take flight from this place at once. The ventari are coming for you." Nazere displayed a puzzled look on his face as he carefully listened to the words of the benighted figure.

"Why would the ventari be coming for me? They have me! I'm scheduled to be put into stasis tomorrow at noon. What do you want from me?" The dark figure laughed crookedly.

"Perhaps this will answer your questions." The dark figure placed his hand into his shroud and withdrew it slowly, placing a piece of paper in front of Nazere. The figure's hands were as gray as slate, and his finger nails were long and sharp. Hesitant to reach out and receive the document, Nazere slowly inched his arm forward and snatched the paper from the figure's hand. Once he had received the manuscript, Nazere's eyes immediately widened in amazement at the writing on the paper's surface. The inscription was written in black ink.

"This is a letter from my father," Nazere began slowly, his voice drained at the sight before him. "I never knew my father. How can this be possible?"

"Read it carefully," the dark figure instructed. Nazere read out loud.

"'My dear son,

I hope this letter finds you well. The time has come for me to leave this place, but before I do, I have a message for you. A vision came to me last night, and I saw the end of all things before they came to be. You have been chosen by the Master to finish the work He has willed to be completed. There will be a messenger who comes to you in the night. He will take you from the darkness and into the light, and you will see things you have never seen before. Follow him closely. You are the first to come and bring forth the judgment. Know that I am your father in that I know that your mother was Eliza. Your hair is sandy-blonde, and your age will be twenty-four by the time you receive this letter. Know that I am going on to a better place. Tomorrow at dawn I depart from here to go to Rome, where I will be executed. My only regret is in not being able to say goodbye to you in person. Heed wisdom my son. Keep the word of the Master close to you wherever you may go. What you do not know now, you will learn.

Love always,

Richard.'"

Nazere paused for a moment in shock and awe at what he had read, an endless torrent of thoughts flooding the shallow end of the pool that was his mind. After spending so much time in isolation and seclusion, an outside message was something he could scarcely place his trust in. He had trouble placing trust in just about anyone, let alone a hideous stranger. He was hasty and demanding in his words, as if something were clicking in his head that he didn't expect — something real. Mania overtook him. "How did he know that I would be twenty-four upon the arrival of this paper? What is going on here? I need answers!"

"They will come to you. But first we must leave this place. We have but a moment before the ventari discovers my presence."

"And just how do you suggest we get out of here?" The dark figure laughed a deep, dark laugh.

"Take faith, my son. I will show you the way." The dark figure reached out his arm in Nazere's direction. "Take my hand." Nazere hesitated, his eyelids tightening at the image of the gray, scaly hand outstretched in his direction.

"How do I know I can trust you?" With one swift motion, a great pair of white-feathered wings spread out from behind the dark figure's back. The wings were enormous, the bottoms of them dropping to the floor of the cell in their full expanse. The dark figure reached his hand out further toward Nazere.

"What is your name?" Nazere asked.

"My name is a name that surpasses the lapse of time. I am called Keldrid. Come!" Nazere reached out his hand, and the moment he did Keldrid drew a sword bearing a golden hilt with his left hand from behind his shroud. Nazere cowered in fear as Keldrid lifted his blade in the air. And all at once, he swiftly struck the wall of the cell. Sparks flew throughout the room like a million little dancing flames, and a great circular hole was cut in the wall. And the moment the blade blew through the thick, artolium barrier in a great white light, alarms began to sound throughout the complex. "On the wings of eagles we shall fly from here." Keldrid returned his sword behind him, where it seemed to disappear into thin air. Nazere laughed subconsciously in amazement. He had never seen anything quite like this. Keldrid continued in his dark tone as to explain his condition.

"Every angel needs a blade. Mine was named by the Master before time began. It is called Entryu." After grasping Nazere's hand firmly and pulling him up on his back, Keldrid's wings began to flap. Immediately the two of them took flight through the hole in the wall and into the darkness of the night. As soon as Nazere hit the air, he knew that something was amiss. This was no ordinary being, and he couldn't help but wonder if all the old stories he was told were true. The stories were muddled in his mind, but he could vaguely remember his childhood memories. Moving at an astounding rate of speed, the two of them flew over the towering buildings that surrounded the Ordren jail. Amidst the buildings below, vehicles were flying in all directions in specialized traffic patterns. The whole of the province of Ordren was illuminated by architecturally sophisticated buildings. And far below, Nazere could see the stasis chambers in the center of the surrounding structures. The very chambers he was doomed to if this unthinkable turn of events hadn't transpired. They stood a mile high in the sky, and were thin and oval shaped at the top. The stasis chambers were clear, and inside humans hung suspended from spine-like machines surgically attached to their heads from above. There were millions of men and women in the stasis chambers, and there were exactly one thousand stasis buildings clustered together in the center of the province.

"So you are an angel?" Nazere asked mid-flight as the wind whipped through his hair. "My mother read me stories about you when I was a child, but I was never sure until now." Maybe I'm not even sure now, he thought.

"There are many things you have to learn," Keldrid replied. "And I am the one who will teach you. Days will pass, and with them, your understanding." Nazere glanced behind him, and as he did, he noticed a great multitude of blue flames in flight rapidly approaching Keldrid. "It is time to speed things up a bit. We need to get you to safe haven." In one instantaneous motion, Keldrid took on a metamorphosis and became a cloud of shadow accompanied by the strong scent and appearance of smoke. And as soon as he did, the blue flames that were the ventari following close behind them disappeared as the shadow became faster than light itself. No mass known to man can move faster than the speed of light.

"Where are we going?" Nazere asked nervously as he held on for dear life.

"To Undrum. It is one of the final hiding places of the refugees." And within a moment's time, Keldrid came to a mighty halt. A shockwave penetrated the air molecules that surrounded Nazere and himself in a wide radius. Nazere hopped off of Keldrid's back and took a brief look around. The two of them were nowhere near Ordren. There were evergreen trees and snow as far as the eye could see. There was frost in the air, and a frozen lake off to the left side of a towering log cabin. "This is the place," Keldrid spoke as he pointed his long, right fingernail straight ahead. The towering log cabin spiraled upward, and had five windows cascading down the front of the building. Below the windows was one massive oak door marked with the white portrait of a knight's chess piece. The pale oak logs that made up the body of the cabin were twisted and coiled all the way to the top of the edifice. The foundation of the cabin was extremely wide, spanning for the distance of over fifty yards. The top of the gigantic building had a silver crown, and at the top of the crown there was a statue of a silver horse with its front hooves in the air. To the right of the cabin was a stone courtyard, with a simple stone foundation that was one-hundred by one-hundred yards long. It was immense, and an immediate eye-catcher for Nazere as he looked upon it. The stone courtyard was filled with life sized stone horses with wings, and bits of grass that sprouted out of the snow between the crevices of the yard. All of the horses had their hooves on the ground and their wings unopened at their sides, and were equally spaced out in ranks and files. There were about one hundred horses in total. Nazere didn't have the time to count them all. "Come!" Nazere hesitated once again.

"Where are we exactly?" he asked.

"Undrum, as I said. Or what was once known as Norway. It is far from the reaches of your adversaries."

"Wait a minute, now," Nazere began as disbelief filled his already dumfounded brain. "Adversaries?"

"You have many of them," Keldrid replied. Nazere was overcome with shock, his eyebrows locked down in frustration as he considered who might be after him.

"So we're just going to enter this building?" he asked nervously with his eyes wide open.

"You are being expected."

"Well, I think I'll knock first," Nazere replied with a skeptical look on his face. He approached the door and knocked on it precisely three times. Keldrid followed shortly behind him. As if exactly on time, the door creaked open as soon as it was knocked upon. Behind the thick wooden door, a woman with black hair, a beautiful snow white face and a thin body came to the entrance. She was wearing a white sweater and tan pants, with plush black snow boots. She smiled as she looked upon Nazere for the first time.

"He's here, Ryan!" she exclaimed, turning her head to the right and calling into the cabin.

"Hello," Nazere said, his nerves now completely wracked. "I hope you aren't frightened by my angel." The woman's attention was immediately redirected to Nazere's face.

"So this is the one," the woman said, grinning to unveil a brilliantly white, pristine set of teeth. Two men came to the door and stood behind the woman. One of the men was tall with blonde hair, wearing a black sweater with denim jeans and black boots. The other man had black hair, and wore a hooded sweatshirt with boot-cut jeans and tennis shoes. Keldrid leaned over Nazere's shoulder.

"They can't see me," Keldrid whispered in Nazere's ear with a dark twist to his voice. "It is to your benefit not to make mention of my name."

"My name is Elle Winstrom," the woman began as she smiled. Her voice was light, sweeter than the taste of raw sugarcane and as mild as a warm blanket to Nazere's ears. Nazere was immediately captivated by her natural beauty as it instantly projected itself both inside and out. "This is Ryan Galeheart," she said pointing to the man with the black hair. "And this is David Sendrick. And what is your name?"

"Nazere Roivas." Elle cracked a greater smile.

"It is just as we expected. Please. Come in and get out of that cold! Nice jail get-up by the way!"

"Thanks a lot," Nazere smirked, aware of Elle's sense of humor. "I just got out of the Ordren province."

"Out of the Ordren province?" David asked with a look of wonder and fascination on his face. "No one has ever escaped its prisons — or any prison like it for as long as I can remember. To break free from it is an absolutely unheard-of feat!"

"Until now," Ryan interjected, his voice deep and consistent. "It appears that things are changing at long last."

"Well, come in," Elle said. "Come in and join us. We have much to discuss."

To discuss? Nazere thought to himself. What could we possibly talk about? Perhaps my life thus far on the streets of Baltimore or in Ordren?

Nazere and Keldrid entered the cabin's door, and Elle shut the large, creaky body of oak firmly behind her. The interior of the cabin was luxurious, with a large crystal chandelier hanging from a very long chain in the center of the room. The entire floor was made of sparkling, white granite that glistened like the sands of the Caribbean. There was a kitchen in the left hand corner of the room. The kitchen consisted of oak cabinets, a white granite countertop, and a hovering, stainless steel combination oven and stove. Everything in the room smelled like a blend of cinnamon and freshly baked apple pie. A subtle hint of delectable perfume followed Elle in a trail, and Nazere was enticed by the intriguing scent of it. There was a large, unmarked oak table under the chandelier. There was also a sizeable blue sofa to the right of the chandelier and a red sofa to the left. To the left of the blue sofa, a holographic display hovered over a black bar on the granite floor. The bar simply served as a projector. Under the projector there was a white carpet with the black insignia of knight's chess piece sewn into the fabric. On the table in the center of the room was a hovering orb. The orb was completely black, and had a blue light on the very top of it. Twelve pine-oak chairs sat around the table, each evenly spaced out. The chair at the head of the table stood out from the rest as it was slightly larger than the others. Next to the entrance, there was a seemingly endless oak staircase that spiraled up to rooms on the upper floors.

"Take a seat, big guy," Elle said as she lay a hand on Nazere's shoulder. "Come sit in these chairs over here." David and Ryan immediately took seats toward the front of the table. David took a seat on the right chair nearest to the entrance of the cabin, and Ryan took a seat on the left chair nearest to it. "Hayden Luminquire will be down in a moment." Elle took a seat next to David, and Nazere took a seat next to her. Keldrid rested himself on the red sofa on the left side of the room and closed his white wings.

Hayden Luminquire? Nazere wondered.

"You have a raiditor, I see," Nazere noticed as he looked at the orb hovering over the table.

"Yes we do," David began. "I do all the electronic maintenance around here. I've tweaked the raiditor out so it can detect ventari in addition to the usual vizedrones and phantoms. We are very safe here."

"So you said you were expecting me. How is that possible?"

"We are prophets," Elle responded, her eyes lighting up as she looked upon Nazere. "We have foreseen your coming for quite some time."

"Prophets?" Nazere asked with a confused look on his face. "You mean to say that you can see the future?"

"We can see what that which is willed to be seen," Ryan interjected.

"Yes," Elle added. "There is much going on right now that is beyond your understanding. But it will come to you in time." Elle briefly glanced at Ryan and then turned back to Nazere. "Tell us a little about yourself, Nazere."

Here we go, Nazere thought to himself. A red flush consumed Nazere's pale cheeks as embarassment set in completely. He started slowly, speaking every word with the utmost sincerity.

"There isn't much to tell. I was an outcast in the Western States. The ventari killed my mother because she refused to move into stasis. I became a dezium addict after she died. I went into seclusion for a year. And allow me to elaborate on my definition of seclusion. I became homeless, sleeping on park benches in Baltimore wherever I could find them. I ate out of trash cans, and lived off of anything I could find." Nazere paused as he recalled that he had been an active thief in Baltimore, but he made the decision not to make mention of this humiliating reality. Otherwise, the truth seemed to flow from Nazere in a way it ordinarily wouldn't. "Eventually the ventari peacekeepers caught up to me. I was destitute when they finally arrested me. I had nothing but a few pills of dezium left over when I went to prison. I've been there for two years now. In the end, I suppose I got what I deserved."

"Dezium," Elle began slowly. "That's a very addictive drug. You will be safe here, but one rule I must stress upon is that there is to be absolutely no drug use. You can leave that life behind. You are free now. And I have safety in mind as well. The ventari can sniff that stuff out from miles away. We don't want any unexpected encounters."

Free, Nazere contemplated. I suppose as free as I'll ever be. But here? Why?

"Let's get down to business," a voice echoed from the spiral staircase. "The work of the Master is our first priority." Nazere looked up, and about mid-way on the staircase was a man in clean, white robes. He was slowly advancing downward with a slightly curved, light-oak staff in his right hand. The man had a long white beard, a long white mustache, and long pearly-white hair. The wrinkles in his forehead and upper cheeks exhibited the fact that he was quite an elderly gentleman. He walked to the bottom of the staircase, advancing to the table and taking a seat at the head of it in the largest chair.

"Nazere. Allow me to introduce you to Hayden," Elle began, opening her left palm in the direction of the old man. "He is the high prophet of our gathering."

"We are called the Gathering of the White Knight," Hayden began as he first set eyes on Nazere. "We have been given a mission, and you have been chosen to carry out our objective." Nazere looked around at everyone sitting at the table in absolute disbelief at the strange turn of events unfurling.

"Chosen? Who chose me? Whoever it was, they must not be very good at making choices."

"On the contrary," Hayden replied. "You are the only one for the job." Nazere turned around to look for Keldrid. Perhaps the angel could give him some form of guidance. But he had disappeared from his place on the red sofa. Nazere then redirected his attention to the table.

"So you call yourself prophets," he began as he exhaled the turbulence in his mind. "What are you prophets of? What is your purpose?" The rest of the table remained silent.

"This is the purpose," Hayden replied softly as he gently placed a book on the table.

"The Bible?" Nazere questioned, almost laughing to himself. "Are you kidding me? They disproved any existence of a god over fifty years ago! I'm no genius — granted, I am homeless — but I keep up on scientific advancements. They have discovered an absolute one. It is the mota, and the foundational building block of all things. Is this all some sort of scientific experiment?"

"No, Nazere," Elle said shaking her head with a solemn look on her face. "We are true prophets, and we have foreseen the ending of the world. The Master has chosen you to pioneer the last battle. I know that you may not believe it now, but it's true."

"The earth is nearing its final breath," Hayden said as he looked deep into Nazere's eyes. "Mankind's final attempts at establishing a Utopia will destroy the world as we know it. The Master is returning to carry out his final acts very soon. Now all that matters is that we prepare you for the inevitable. The seals of the final judgment are upon us at this very moment. When they are revealed within the confines of time, the signs will be evident."

"It is true," David added. "You are the ultimate key in carrying out the Master's final judgment." Nazere's face carried with it a strong aura of shock and disbelief at this point.

Perhaps these people are mad, Nazere thought. This must be some form of experiment.

"How can you prove to me that what you are saying is true?" Nazere asked, a demanding look in his eyes. Hayden smiled.

"Like Thomas, you doubt," Hayden started. "But your mother taught you all you need to know. All you need to do is believe. Have a little faith. And that's where your first test will come."

"What are you saying?" Nazere asked.

"High Lord Alune has fortified the city of Jerusalem," Hayden replied. "In order for the end times to come to pass, Solomon's temple must be penetrated. As it stands now, the temple has been rebuilt, and High Lord Alune has taken his seat on the throne of the temple."

"Jerusalem?" Nazere asked, laughing to himself. "That's beyond impossible to penetrate. There isn't a chance." Hayden shook his head, a quite serious look on his aged face.

"Nothing is impossible."

"We need to intercept a set of ventari armor," David said, looking directly at Nazere. "The main processing plant for the armor is in New York City. Ryan has elected himself to accompany you on your journey."

"Whoa, whoa, whoa," Nazere began, swinging his arms in the air. "I didn't say I was doing anything for you people." Hayden sighed in his own frustration. "Even if we were to retrieve a set of ventari armor by some random chance, who do you propose is going to wear it?" The whole room set their eyes on Nazere.

"You are," Elle encouraged in a voice like silk, smiling. Elle reached her hand across the table and softly placed her smooth palm on top of Nazere's. "You can do this, Nazere. I have seen it." And at that very moment, a vision appeared before Nazere. He was standing in the air above New York City, a blue sky and a field of tall structures in the distance. As he glanced around, he noticed that phantoms were flying on all sides of him and infesting the air in a dark swarm. From below him, their sixteen, steel, blue-ringed tentacles reached up at him from all angles. The phantoms grabbed a hold of him, wrapping their tentacles around his body as if each one was a boa constrictor, one of the phantoms moving its pitch-black face close to Nazere's body. He watched as the six-eyed machine prepared to fire the blue firestorm cannon enclosed in its enormous face. The machine's six eyes were a neon blue, and its head was shaped identical to that of a crab's. Trying to hold on against the oncoming tide, Nazere reached his arm out in front of him in resistance. He was able to push through the steel appendages that held him back, instantly noticing that his hand was no longer ordinary- it was the hand of a ventari. He unleashed a bolt of pure white light as if it were completely natural, and the phantom in front of him dropped to the city below like a brick being thrown from atop a tall building. Nazere inhaled a deep breath of fresh air as he returned from his vision, and David looked directly into his eyes.

"Are you alright, mate?" David asked, leaning over in Nazere's direction.

"I'm fine. I guess it's just been a long day."

"Do you know why you were named Nazere, my boy?" Hayden asked slowly, squinting as he leaned toward Nazere.

"My mother said my father named me."

"That is correct. You are named after the place of Nazareth in Israel," Hayden said. "I knew your father long before he was taken away."

"So," Ryan began. "What say you, Nazere? I will stand by your side if you will go with me to retrieve the armor."

"Ryan!" Elle exclaimed. "We can't risk losing you. He was prophesied to go! Not you!"

"I'm sorry, Elle," Ryan replied. "Nazere will need some support to get on his feet. What say you, Nazere? I will escort you to where you must go." Nazere paused for a moment as the memories of the jail cell he left behind returned to him. There was no turning back now. He thought to himself for a good minute or two, considering his options.

"Alright," Nazere told Ryan as he nodded. "I am with you." Hayden clapped and smiled, his smile soon after breaking out into laughter.

"Splendid," David began as he grinned. "I'll get the Redeemer ready for takeoff. I've been putting a lot of work into her, so hopefully it pays off."

"The Redeemer?" Nazere asked. He had never been so puzzled in all of his life.

"The Redeemer is the flagship of the Gathering of the White Knight," Hayden replied. "It has been especially designed to fend off a vizedrone in a worst case scenario."

"I'm not sure it could battle two vizedrones at once," David began. "But she's the fastest thing in the sky right now. All the systems have been updated and are up to speed. She's at least efficient enough in her engineering to take out one dragon should the occasion arise."

"Very well," Hayden began. "Our meeting here is adjourned, then. Elle, if you would, please settle Nazere into his new home."

"New home?" Nazere asked. He hadn't known a sense of home for quite some time.

"For now," Elle said. "The Council of the White Queen should decide where you go from here. You'll learn more about the council when the time is right. Right now, let's get you upstairs and settled into your room. It has already been prepared for you." Elle got up from her seat and took Nazere's hand, guiding him to the bottom of the spiraling staircase. "It's just this way."

"I'm coming behind you," David said as he got up from his seat, joining Elle and Nazere at the bottom of the staircase. Together, David, Elle, and Nazere ascended the staircase to the third floor. Once there, Elle opened the door to Nazere's bright new room. The room was quaint, with chocolate-brown painted walls, a cute little brown lamp on an oak nightstand to the right of Nazere's bed, and solid pine-oak floors. A far cry from his bunk in the prison, Nazere's bed was lavish and color coordinated with the rest of the room. He could feel the warmth of the white blankets and thick, brown comforter on his mattress without having to lie down in it. A window, no longer covered with an intrusive ion shield, granted Nazere a grandiose view of the great outdoors just below him. David excitedly walked over to the window and waved for Nazere to join him in looking out of it.

"Look out here," David began excitedly. "There she is!" Outside the window and sitting in the snow, an orb shaped ion shield covered the Redeemer. Built in the form of an eagle, the Redeemer was designed to move and function according to its bird counterpart. About a third the size of the cabin, the Redeemer was a behemoth of a machine. The color of the bird was coordinated, its white head a precise reflection of a bald eagle's. Its feathers were made of metal, but each individual strand of every feather appeared lifelike and soft. Even its eyes were exacted, black pupils enclosed by dark brown irises. Nazere and Elle huddled close to the window as they peeked out. For Nazere, the sight was both vindicating and intriguing- a long departure from the view he was accustomed to. He was confronted once again in the Undrum cabin by a sight that he had never had the pleasure of viewing. The Redeemer was flapping its wings and crying out akin to a living eagle. "She's built of thirty percent artolium alloys. That's a higher ratio than the phantoms. Unfortunately, it isn't higher than a vizedrone or a dreadnaught."

"Not to mention," Elle added as she continued to look out the window. "A dreadnaught is about one hundred times the size of the Redeemer. But I like our big bird. She's pretty." Elle walked over to the doorway. "Are you hungry, Nazere? I'm heading downstairs if you want me to cook something for you."

Access to food, Nazere thought. This could be a good thing after all.

"I'll be alright," Nazere replied as he looked Elle in the eyes. "I think I'm going to get some rest. I'm out of the darkness of the cell now. It really is nice to be back in the light of day again."

"Here," David said as he placed a book on Nazere's nightstand. "Read this book. It will be your foundation as a prophet."

A prophet? There must be some mistake.

"Thanks, David," Nazere said as he took a seat on his bed. "I think I'll read a bit as I fall asleep." He picked up the book David had left for him on the nightstand, beginning to scan its pages with his eyes.

"That's a boy," Elle said, smiling. "Have sweet dreams, okay?"

"We're out of here for now," David said. "We'll be praying for you. Operation Maelstrom begins in the morning. We can't afford to wait any longer, so rest up."

Operation Maelstrom? I think I'll just go with it. I'll figure out what's going on with this mad house in the morning.

"Goodnight, Nazere," Elle said as she shut off the light switch to his room and gently closed the door.

As Nazere began to read, a strange feeling overcame him all of a sudden. And at that very moment, Keldrid appeared before Nazere. His shadowy figure was motionless in place like an iron statue. "So you are the real deal after all, aren't you?" Nazere asked, trusting that there was a method to the madness that had played out during the day.

"I will not leave you," Keldrid replied in his twisted voice. "Wherever you go, I will go also. You will not be alone. Fall asleep now, and know that you are under the guard of Entryu." And for the duration of that night, Keldrid remained in place, and Nazere continued to read. While Keldrid remained in the room with him, Nazere became more comfortable with the idea of having his angel by his side. And finally, in the wee hours of the morning and after much reading, Nazere fell sound asleep. It had been quite a long day, and much longer days were coming. Much sooner than Nazere could possibly expect.

CHAPTER TWO

The House of Arthur

Deep in sleep, Nazere began to rock to and fro in his bed like a ship on the turbulent seas as a vision came to him in the night. He was suspended in midair, standing in an all white room that glistened like sun reflecting off of the waves of the ocean. His vision came to him slowly, and his eyes began to adjust as the image of an innumerable count of figures dressed in radiant white robes stood in a circle around what appeared to be a lamb. The lamb was right in the center of the great white void of a room. Underneath the lamb was a great golden circle, shining like the blinding light of the sun. And as Nazere focused his eyes in a little closer, he noticed the lamb was laying down on its side as if it had been fatally injured. But as he looked even closer yet, he noticed the lamb bore unusual characteristics. As the lamb lifted its head, he noticed it had seven eyes. And on its head were seven golden, spiked horns. Nazere attempted to move his right arm, but was unable to do so; he couldn't move anything. All of the figures surrounding the lamb were kneeling. All of them bowed down except for one who stood holding a great, long scroll of untainted parchment paper in his hands. He had flowing, radiant black hair, and his skin shimmered like there were a thousand stars on the surface of it. A noise like a clash of thunder reverberated throughout the void as the being began to speak.

"None are worthy to read the scroll," the being said. "The time for the final judgment has come, and none can read the deed to the earth that is the rightful possession of the lamb." A figure stood from the crowd and approached the being holding the scroll. He had long silver hair, and was equal in height to the being that held the scroll.

"Gabriel," the figure with the silver hair began. "The time has come for us to unleash the first seal, for none can read the scroll but the lamb that was slain." There was another great clash of thunder as the lamb lifted its body and rose to its knees.

"Micheal! Amass your forces," Gabriel replied. "Behold! The Master has spoken!" And as the lamb fully came to its hooves, a blinding light consumed the entirety of the void before Nazere. As Nazere's eyes came to, a new vision was presented before him. It was the image of a man riding on a white horse with a black bow at his side, parked directly in front of the earth. The earth looked small before the rider as if it were but a globe, a scaled-down recreation of the original. All of the stars fell from the sky around the living sphere like bright crystals dropping out of sight as the rider took an arrow from his quiver and placed it in his right hand. The rider then took aim at the earth, and as the horse began to gallop forward at full speed, the rider fired a rapid and precise shot. There was a great explosion on the face of the earth as if many volcanos had erupted at once, and the waters of the world became red like blood when the arrow penetrated them. And again, there was a great peal of thunder.

Opening his eyes, Nazere adjusted to his normal, cozy atmosphere as he rose from his bed. The light from the window beside his nightstand illuminated his old-world fashioned room. He lifted his soft, brown quilt from his body as he sat up in his bed and placed his feet on the hardwood floors beneath him. He sat in quiet contemplation of the dream he had experienced while he slept. He looked to the corner of the room where Keldrid had stood the night before. Keldrid had disappeared. Nazere stood up and walked outside of his door to the spiral staircase beyond it. Looking down the spiral staircase as he took his first step down it, Nazere saw Elle, Ryan and David sitting on the blue sofa in front of the holographic display. Their eyes were glued to the screen. "Good morning," Nazere said as he called downward to Elle, Ryan and David. Elle turned her head and looked up at Nazere.

"Come down here," Elle told Nazere as she motioned to him with her hands. "There is something you need to see." Nazere advanced down the stairs, still wearing the gray jail outfit he had for days before. Nazere took a seat next to Elle, looking on as images were displayed before the four who sat watching. "Let me replay this for you," Elle insisted. She pushed a red button on the black electronic bar below the holographic image, rewinding the show they were attentively engaged in. Nazere watched as Elle leaned over, pressed the green play button on the bar and returned to her comfortable position on the blue sofa. "Listen carefully." An announcer stood before a crowd of over a million men in the city of Rome, and read from a square holographic script that was displayed before him in red lettering. And the man spoke:

"On this day, March the thirtieth, High Lord Alune has issued an order to execute the men and women now placed in stasis in the province of Ordren. In addition and in accordance with the mandates set forth by Vice Lord Xar, all religious movements are to be discontinued immediately. This day shall be forever known as the day mankind established Utopia, and High Lord Alune shall continue his reign upon his throne in the Royal Temple of Jerusalem. Peace shall be enforced and maintained. All normal festivities are encouraged and are set to continue as scheduled in celebration of the rule of the great scientist, High Lord Alune." Elle reached over and clicked the blue stop button on the black control bar.

"Vice Lord Xar?" Nazere asked. "The last I heard he was the commander of the Western States' naval operations. After that he became lord over Jerusalem."

"That he was," David said. "But he has handed over his authority to High Lord Alune. Much has changed in the past year."

"The first seal has been unleashed," Elle began. "High Lord Alune will rule for seven years from this day."

"The first seal?" Nazere questioned. "Funny that you should mention that. I had a strange dream last night, and I heard something about a seal being released."

"What?!" Ryan asked excitedly, nearly jumping from his seat. "You had a vision? What did you see?"

"I don't know if it was a vision," Nazere replied. "It was a dream, and there was a lamb in the center of this massive, glowing white room. The lamb looked like it was dying, but as my dream ended it rose to its hooves."

"That is wonderful news!" Elle exclaimed. "You have seen the Master then! He is the lamb that you have seen." Elle's eyebrows tightened as she slowed her speech. "What else did you see?"

"I saw a man riding atop a white horse with a bow in his hand," Nazere replied slowly as he focused on remembering exactly what he saw. "He fired an arrow at the earth, and the earth turned as red as blood. That was the end of it."

"I too have seen the vision," Hayden called down the stairs as he began to descend them. He walked with his large, curved wooden staff over to where the four in the gathering were sitting on the large blue sofa. "The end is nigh. Death is coming for us. We have only to pray for the grace to complete the work we know we must." Hayden walked downstairs and sat in his chair at the oak table, drinking from a mug of tea that rested on the table before him. "Excellent tea," Hayden began cheerily. "Earl Grey is a favorite of mine. The oil of bergamot truly gives it a magnificent flavor. Would you like a cup of tea, my dear boy?" Hayden asked Nazere.

"No thank you, sir," Nazere replied.

"Very well, then." Hayden took a few sips from his mug, and then paused for a moment. "Oh! I nearly forgot!" Hayden exclaimed as he stood from his chair, leaving his mug sitting on the table. "Follow me this way, Nazere. We can't have you walking around in those prison clothes when you venture out today. I have some clothing upstairs for you." Hayden presented a great smile as he walked past Nazere toward the staircase.

"Thank you, sir," Nazere replied to Hayden as he rose from his seat in the chair and proceeded to follow behind him. Hayden ascended the spiral staircase to the fifth floor with his staff by his side. Once at the top, Hayden opened the door to the room on that level.

"It's just in here," Hayden said, still smiling. On the bed of the room was a white t-shirt with the outline of a lamb printed in black on its face. Below the t-shirt, a pair of sand-blown, denim jeans was placed on the bed. "These should suit you just fine. There is a pair of black shoes under the bed. You'll find socks in your nightstand. Go ahead and get changed. There is much to take care of today!" Hayden shut the door and Nazere began to change into the clothes that were placed before him on the bed. Nazere stood in his room and looked out his window at the Redeemer as he threw on his cotton shirt. The eagle sat in the exact spot it had a day earlier, still perching in its ion shielding. Once he was dressed completely, he took a few steps back from his window. Overwhelmed with everything that was going on around him, Nazere dropped back on his bed and sprawled himself out across it. Only a moment later, there was a knock at the door.

"Who is it?" Nazere asked.

"It's me. Elle."

"Come in," Nazere said as he sat up from his bed. Elle opened the door and walked in.

"I just wanted to talk to you. I know that the next few days are going to be long, so I made you a little yoralium to keep you awake. A cup of coffee would do, but yoralium does seem to work better. Just take this cup and drink up."

"Thanks, Elle," Nazere replied. "This stuff can keep you up for days."

"Yes, and it's completely harmless. I just want you to be awake and aware when you leave this place and go on your venture with Ryan. You know I won't be there, but I'll be praying for you." Nazere smiled at Elle.

"I appreciate that. When will we be leaving?"

"Well, that was the other reason for my coming up here. David has requested your presence downstairs."

"Alright. I'll be right down." Nazere arose and walked behind Elle down the winding staircase to where Hayden, Ryan and David all sat in their respective seats at the oak table under the chandalier. Elle walked to her seat and Nazere took a seat in his chair beside her's. Hayden went straight to work.

"Welcome, friends," Hayden began, smiling before his gathering. "Before us we have a task that is going to be near impossible to complete. But I know that nothing is impossible for our Master. I trust in your abilities to work as a united force to put the working of the will of the Master into motion." Hayden turned to his side. "David, are you prepared to take flight?"

"The Redeemer is ready for flight immediately, high prophet."

"And Ryan," Hayden started. "I understand you are undergoing the unique task of accompanying Nazere to his destination? I simply want to confirm that with you."

"I am," Ryan replied. "But we will not go unprepared. I have readied a few of my own items with the Gantor Pinnacle's defenses in mind." Hayden nodded.

"You are going to Baltimore, then," Hayden said. "You must seek out the household of our dear comrade Arthur before you travel to New York City."

"Yes, teacher," David responded. "We are going to need the talents of Owen to prepare ourselves properly for the operation. We know what must be done."

"Then you are all, indeed, prepared," Hayden said, glancing around at everyone at the table. "No matter what happens, know that the Master is close to you wherever you are. Keep the faith, and do not falter. And may the Redeemer carry you in safety." Hayden closed his eyes as if in a trance. "Go now, for time is short. I can feel the presence of evil growing stronger by the moment."

This guy has got to be insane, Nazere thought. Maybe I'm still in a dream. I can't make heads or tails of anything!

"Are you ready, Nazere?" Elle asked.

"As ready as I'll ever be, I guess," Nazere replied as he sighed.

"Then let's head outside," Elle said. "Everyone grab your shields at the door. We're going to need them." Rising from their seats, Elle, Nazere, David and Ryan headed to the large oaken door. Next to the door, on a four-legged steel podium, there were four bracelets. Each one held the capacity to hold an ion shield around a body for up to twelve days. However, the capabilities of the weaponry wielded by the phantoms, vizedrones and the ventari far exceeded the ability of the ion shields to defend against such energy. Each bracelet that lay on the podium had its own individual color. Elle placed her bracelet, especially colored pink for her own personal taste, around her forearm. The bracelet automatically fastened around her wrist. A quick flash of many tiny sparks covered all of Elle's body, indicating that the ions were active. David followed behind Elle, grabbing his golden bracelet from the three that remained. Ryan then picked his bracelet up. Like the others, it automatically tightened around his wrist. Its silver surface glimmered as it beeped and activated to the touch of his skin. The last bracelet was blue, and sat alone on the podium. Nazere looked down and grabbed the bracelet from off of the podium. Though it looked too large for him, when he placed it on his forearm it tightened up to his wrist for a perfect fit.

"State of the art," David commented. "Let's get to the bird. We're heading to Baltimore." The four of them all walked out into the snow together, and David pulled out his remote trentorod for the ion shield around the Redeemer. Snow was falling like one hundred thousand tiny feathers from the sky, and as the flakes of snow would hit the ion shield they would melt upon impact.

"Lower the shield," David spoke into his remote. The remote extended into a longer rod, and the ion shield deactivated. Snow began to fall on the metal casing of the great eagle and accumulated quickly. "Wings up!" David yelled to the bird. The Redeemer instantaneously flapped its wings into the upright position and held them there, exposing the entrance to the Redeemer in the belly of the bird. Holding the rod in his hand, David inserted the device into a hole in the circular door at the stomach of the Redeemer. The Redeemer made a loud shrieking cry, and the door pushed in and rolled open. The door was about fifty feet tall in and of itself. "Activate the controls, babygirl." When Nazere walked in, he looked around the immense interior of the bird. There were four holographic control panels in total, all of them colored blue and green and suspended in the air. Each of them were rectangular in shape. In the center of the Redeemer, there was a great schematic diagram of the bird's engineering suspended in midair. It displayed engine information, shield status, core temperature, and the condition of the trillions of processors built into the bird's metal cells.

Off to the right of this diagram there was a large holographic image of the bird's exterior. It displayed the bird's exterior as blue, which indicated its hull was at its maximum integrity. The image rotated slowly in a circle. Below it in front of a central chair were two green holographic control panels. Below the panels were eight other chairs, each of the seats adorned with a plush covering. The covering was a scarlet red color with the emblem of a horse symbolizing a knight imprinted on its back in silver. There were three stairs leading up to the chairs, and David quickly advanced up them and hopped in the center seat. First, he pushed a red button to the right of his chair. Next, he then began manipulating the two green holographic panels in front of him, pushing buttons on the panels and twirling the suspended images in order to activate the bird's lift-off process. And suddenly, the door behind Nazere rolled back into place and pushed forward to shut.

Elle walked over to the seat on the far left side of the room. Ryan took a seat on the far right side of the room, pulling a disk out of his pocket and inserting it into a metal slot in front of him on a long rectangular steel pane. Ryan then placed a wireless earphone into his right ear and began shaking his head.

"Music," Ryan said as he turned to Nazere. "It'll get you through."

"Come here, Nazere," Elle said as she waved Nazere over. "The Redeemer is about to lift off. You won't want to be standing there." Nazere walked over to where Elle was sitting and took a seat directly next to her.

"Get ready," David said as he pushed a large button in the center of the holographic panel he was operating.

Two crimson colored straps flew out from behind each occupied seat and crossed to form an "X" as they strapped each person in. The engine then began to run, and as it did, the bird let out yet another loud screech. And on the holographic panel in front of David, blue numbers that suspended in the air signified a countdown from ten. And as the timer hit three, the bird's talons began to move. Running forward, the eagle's wings flapped downward in one swift motion.

"Here we go!" David exclaimed as he continued to work the panels in front of him. "Throw on the ion shield!"

The bird lifted off, and as it did, Nazere looked at the display in front of David. The right display expanded before the entire group, showing the outsides of the Redeemer in the fashion of an ultra-thin widescreen television. The cabin, the snow and the frozen lake below soon became a distanced view as the bird's wings flapped in the air. All of the occupants of the ship were headed upward quickly as the eagle‘s immense wingspan elevated them into the sky. And within seconds, the Redeemer was high above the fluffy, white clouds; it was flying higher at an astounding velocity as it continued to pick up speed. "We'll be concealed when we hit free space. That will keep the vizedrones and phantoms off of us. Fortunately for us, they aren't a prominent force in Baltimore."

The Redeemer flew to the highest point in the sky, its ion shielding scorching the earth's atmosphere as it rose into the blackness of space. Leaning over, Nazere looked on in amazement as the stars became visible all around him. "There she is," Ryan began, looking down at Earth and pointing with his right hand. "Everything we fight for is right there."

"Set your destination to the House of Arthur, Baltimore," David said as he spoke once again into the control panel in front of him. Nazere watched as the Redeemer spread its magnificent wings in the blackness of space, his sense of marvel growing as he looked down at the torn face of the earth far below him. Structures below illuminated the whole of the world, making it glow brightly from afar like a heavily decorated Christmas tree. The Redeemer spoke back to David with a female voice.

"Acquiring target now," the Redeemer said. "How has your day been, David?"

"Same old, same old, my dear," David replied. "I've got a long one ahead of me. A bit stressful if you comprehend what I am conveying."

"I understand, captain," the Redeemer replied. "Target now acquired. Preparing to descend upon the destination of the House of Arthur, Baltimore, The Western States." The Redeemer let out a loud shriek that sent a shockwave out into space. The Redeemer then closed its wings together in parallel to one another and began to drop like an anvil off a ten story building. The drop kept the skin on Nazere's face flapping upward as microgravity took over.

"Whoa," Nazere blurted out as he his body was driven downward with the Redeemer.

"Don't try to talk," Elle said as she giggled uncontrolably. "Now you have me talking! Thanks a lot! Too ironic!"

The Redeemer blew through the atmosphere in a ball of flame, and as the city of Baltimore came into view, the majestic bird spread its wings. The display before David exhibited the many buildings and structures of the city.

"There's the National Aquarium," Nazere noted, a spark of excitement lighting within him as he looked down upon the city he knew so well.

"It's not much of an aquarium anymore," Ryan commented as he removed the headpiece from his ear. "Vice Lord Xar converted it into a scientific research facility for marine life. He used it in the development of his stormdivers. They are fully genetically engineered. Funny, though. The vice lord is convinced man has discovered all there is to know now. According to him, science is the answer to all of man's problems."

"I'd prefer if we not talk about him right now," Elle said with a straight look on her face. "We're far from the homestead. If he senses us here, he will send every force he has to intercept us."

"If he senses us?" Nazere asked slowly.

"He is far more powerful than you know now," Ryan replied. "You will understand in time. Just be patient, and everything will come to you. We are here to help you see things the way they are meant to be seen."

"Get ready people," David started as he again began to manipulate the holographic controls in front of him. "We're near the landing zone." The Redeemer flew down at the street level, flying by a number of elaborate row homes. "We're going into dangerous territory. Ryan, I'm going to need you to screen us."

"I got the block, buddy," Ryan replied. "No one will know who we are."

"How is that?" Nazere asked.

"Ryan's gifts are in being able to infiltrate and control the thoughts of others," Elle replied. "His real gift lies in being able to move matter. Hayden has taught him well."

"On these streets, we'll need a bit of a mind screen," Ryan commented. "I'm still training in my prophetic skills, but I am well attuned to the minds of others around me. The real test will come when we hit the Gantor Pinnacle in New York. My mind control abilities don't stand up well against enemies who have already sensed our presence."

"Approaching the destination of the House of Arthur," the Redeemer began. "In three. Two. One." The great eagle came to a stop that sent a gust of wind flying in all directions, causing dust on the street to zoom through the air in miniature tornadoes. The Redeemer then set its talons on the ground, and opened its wings to the upright position. The sun was high in the sky, shining down on the steel rooftops of row homes and reflecting off of the Redeemer and the intricate glass architecture of nearby structures. "Landing complete."

"Well done, babe," David said and he put his hands behind his head and leaned back in his chair.

"Please, David," Elle started with a smug look on her face. "It's a machine. Not in front of Nazere."

"Love you, Redeemer," David said, smiling in sheer defiance of Elle.

"Love you too, Dave," the Redeemer replied. "I hope my flying was satisfactory."

"It always is," David said. "I'm sending you into standby mode now, babygirl. Deactivate your ion shield and open the entrance." The circular door then pushed back and opened for the four on board to exit. Climbing outside of the Redeemer, Nazere looked for the largest glass building. He then climbed out of the Redeemer and started walking toward it.

"Where do you think you're going?" Elle asked as she climbed out of the Redeemer with Ryan. "The House of Arthur is this way. Didn't expect anything too lavish, did we?" Elle pointed to an old dilapidated row home sandwiched between four row homes on both sides of it. She began walking toward the door to the building, shaking her head and smiling as Nazere followed behind. "Come on, Dave!" Elle yelled back toward the opened ship as she made her way to the stairs of the House of Arthur. "Pay your final respects to the Redeemer and then get in here!" Hopping out of the ship, Dave stood next to the Redeemer for a few minutes. He looked it over as he always did when he was finished flying it.

"Good ride," David said softly as he patted the metal exterior of the Redeemer gently. He then withdrew his control rod from the door of the Redeemer, turned around and walked toward the row home where Ryan, Elle and Nazere were waiting to enter.

"Hurry up, David," Ryan said. "It's windy out here and we have business that needs attending to."

"I gotcha man," David replied as he hurried his step. "Here! I'll knock, okay?" David knocked on the door three times, and the door was answered by a woman with blonde hair wearing black high heel shoes, a red and black striped dress and rose red lipstick.

"David!" the woman exclaimed as she reached out and hugged David. "How are you?"

"Fantastic as usual. How are you Sara? You look well."

"She always looks well," Ryan whispered to Nazere. Elle gave Ryan a stern look.

"I've seen better days," Sara replied. Sara then glanced over at Nazere. "So this is the one?"

"It is," David replied with a grin.

"By all means, come in," Sara said as she waved for everyone outside to enter in. Once Elle, David, Ryan and Nazere were inside, Sara shut the door and activated a holographic alarm that was suspended out of a black box sitting on a wooden stand to the right of the door. The aroma of sweet, fragrant dark chocolate permeated the house's atmosphere like a candy shop. Absolutely everything inside of the home was colored red and black, a strange coordination to say the least. The rug at the foot of the door was red with the black outline of a lion printed on its surface. The banisters that led upstairs were painted black, and the floor was marble, colored red and black in a chess pattern. A solid gold bust of a lion on the ceiling stood out sharply from the rest of the room. There was a red sofa in the left corner of the room, and two black ones sitting next to one another on the right side of the room. Chessboards with red and black pieces were spread throughout the room on small red tables. A few of the tenants of the household sat playing games with one another. But they didn't use their hands to move the pieces. The pieces moved on their own. There were a few men and women walking around in the foyer of the house, paying no mind to the new arrivals standing at the entrance to the household. They appeared busy, and seemed to lack the time to stop even for a moment. But out of the commotion, a certain man with black skin and dreadlocks walked up to Sara; she stood stationary next to the gang still standing at the door. He had a lean, muscular build, and a warm and welcoming smile that was as genial as a host to an opulent restaurant.

"Welcome to our humble abode, brothers and sister," he began.

"Good to see you again, Adrax Braver," Ryan replied, smiling. "How goes your training?" Adrax laughed.

"Arthur is a tough cookie. But his teachings are immortal. I have been seeing to my students and their training for battle. It is truly good to see you again too, brother." Adrax took hold of Ryan's hand and pulled him close to his chest, patting his back but for a second and then stepping back. "I keep in the Word as much as possible, but when I am distracted, Arthur can sense it. He helps me when I need guidance the most." Adrax glanced at all at the entrance for a moment. "So you have heard the news I suppose?"

"The first seal of judgment has been set loose," Elle interjected.

"Yes," Adrax replied. "We are all watching and waiting, making our preparations for the time of the last war." Sara turned to Ryan.

"I'm unable to tell," Sara began. "Who is it you are here to see first? Oh, and allow me to fully introduce myself to you, Nazere. I am Sara Maple, shield maiden of the Gathering of the White Lion."

"You knew my name?" Nazere asked, as stunned as ever.

"We are prophets," Sara replied. "We all knew you were coming. My abilities are limited, so I need assistance from time to time. But my gift of foresight is increasing with every passing day. I can feel the evil in this city rising with great vehemence."

"I have felt it too," Adrax added. "But don't let me keep you. I have much practice to perform. We are battling forces not of this world, and constant training is essential." Adrax smiled and walked to the corner of the room where black stairs descended to the basement of the house. Nazere glanced at Elle for a second, thinking deeply to himself. For a reason even he didn't understand, he trusted her.

Perhaps these people are not mad after all, Nazere thought without eliciting a hint of an external expression. He was good at hiding his emotions when he wanted to. There's something strange about everything around me. There must be some explanation for it all.

"How is this house so small from the outside but so large within?" Nazere asked Elle in a whisper.

"The Master has allowed it to be this way," Elle replied back in a whisper. "There are few places for the prophets to hide from our enemies."

"We're here to see High Prophet Arthur," Ryan told Sara.

"Please follow me this way, then," Sara replied. "Up these stairs is the Roundtable of the Lion. Arthur awaits your presence." Elle, Nazere, David and Ryan followed as Sara ascended the staircase to the left of the house. At the top of the stairs, an old man with a gray goatee and short gray hair sat in a red and gold chair near a furnace smoking a pipe and reading a book. He wore a black suit with a white shirt and a patterned red tie. The furnace behind him was black and had an emblem of a lion's face embossed in gold above it. The fires of the furnace burning at the lumber within made a minor crackling noise that spread throughout the room. Directly in front of the man there was a great round table, and the man's chair was positioned behind it. Another man was sitting in a chair at the table, and his back was facing the entrance to the room. He had long blonde hair, and wore a red leather jacket and red leather pants with red dress shoes. The table was immense, with exactly forty-five black-iron chairs circling around it. The table was made of iron, and had the imprint of a full lion's body in black. There appeared to be a demon with a tail within the lion's opened mouth. There was a raiditor hovering over the center of the table where the imprint of the lion's body was.

The upstairs was wide and open, with redwood bookcases that reached the ceiling encompassing the entire perimeter of the room. They were completely filled with books of all sorts and sizes. At the head of the table, a Holy Bible with a red leather covering sat next to a long sword. The sword was placed directly to the right of the man sitting with his back facing the entrance. It was a silver blade, with a gold hilt much like Entryu's. The main difference was that the hilt of this blade had a lion's open mouth on both ends of it. In the right corner of the room there was an hourglass that reached to the ceiling filled with black colored sand. The hourglass slowly passed sand through its small center, but there was a great deal of sand on the bottom of the hourglass.

"Come in," the old man in the chair said as he lifted his eyes to the captive audience at the entrance to his chambers. "I welcome you to the Gathering of the White Lion. Please come and take a seat at the roundtable." Ryan walked in first and took a seat to the right of the man dressed in all red. Elle walked in next, sitting next to Ryan. David followed, sitting on the left side of the man adorned in red leather. Nazere hesitated.

"Come sit with me," Sara said, the mascara on her long eyelashes gaining Nazere's immediate attention. Taking Nazere's hand, Sara guided the lost man to a seat next to her's. She took her seat next to David. Nazere then sat next to Sara. Elle's eyes met Sara's with a hint of competition in them; she wondered why Nazere hadn't sat next to her.

"We are all here for one reason," the old man began as he sat his book on the table. "Operation Maelstrom has begun. As has been foreseen in the dreams of the chosen and those who have come long before him, the first seal has been set loose upon the earth. My name is Arthur Nedrem. I am the chief ambassador from the Council of the White Queen to the Gathering of the White Lion. I am also the Gathering of the White Lion's high prophet. My dear friend Hayden Luminquire, as most of you well know, is the chosen ambassador from the Council of the White Queen for the Gathering of the White Knight. He sends his greetings to those of you who have departed."

"High prophet," David began. "We have come to seek wisdom and gather the tools necessary for the operation we are set to carry out. As you can see, we have brought…"

"Say no more," Arthur interrupted. "Tell me Nazere. Why have you come?" Nazere looked at Arthur like he was an advanced equation, immediately trying to find an answer to his query.

"I have seen enough evidence to go forth, I suppose. I trust that these prophets I have come into contact with will carry me through to complete what they have said I was chosen to do." Arthur leaned closer to the table.

"Trust is a valuable asset, indeed. But I am failing to see a key connection here. There is an element that you lack that you must gain in order to proceed. Otherwise, you will fail. Do you know what element it is that you lack?"

"Strength? Willpower, perhaps?"

"What do you know of faith?" the high prophet asked. The room was as calm as an abandoned chapel, with all eyes at the roundtable set on Nazere. He took a moment to collect a wise response as he turned his eyes to the red, iron surface of the table.

"I was taught long ago that it is the key to eternal life. My mother taught me all about it."

"Do you hold to it? How strong is the faith that you carry?" The old man pulled a pen from his suit's breast pocket and tossed it on the table. He then set his eyes firmly upon Nazere's. "Try and pick that pen up." Nazere reached out and picked up the pen.

"Give me the pen back," Arthur commanded. Nazere tossed the pen back across the table to Arthur. "Now. Really try to pick it up this time." Again, Arthur threw the pen on the table. And again, Nazere picked up the pen instinctively. Sara nodded. "This is why you fail," Arthur began slowly. "You do not try to do anything. You simply do. That is where faith comes into the picture. Faith is nothing without action. But when accompanied by action, faith has immeasurable power. It is said that faith can move mountains, but the Master has chosen you to move far more than tall mounds of rock. You will find through your own personal development what exactly defines the boundary between good and evil in this world, because as it stands now I can tell you that you do not know. Nevertheless, you are the great spark of hope for mankind, despite the fact that you have emerged from the most unthinkable circumstances."

"What I don't understand is why He chose me to carry out his work," Nazere began. "Out of all of the people in this world, I am the least qualified. My faith is mediocre at best. I falter at the simplest of temptations. I was a homeless outcast for years. All of this begs a simple question. Why has He chosen someone who can barely take care of himself?" Elle looked into Nazere's eyes and smiled. She wanted to speak, but she held back.

"There are some things the Master has not given me the understanding to comprehend. But your destiny has been seen, and it has been written. You will be tempted, and you will falter." Arthur leaned over and looked deeply into Nazere's eyes. "We all falter, and have all fallen short of what we were designed to be. It isn't the falling down that is the miracle. It is in gaining the strength to rise back up again." Arthur pulled the pen across the table to his hand, exhibiting his own astonishing ability to move matter. "I have been given gifts from the Master, and you will learn that yours are far greater than you can possibly understand now. There is much dissension in the world right now, although the politicians who command it have convinced mankind to drink and be merry for victory has been attained. What mankind has failed to see is that all of our successive actions have caused irrevocable damage to the earth. We continue to move our pawns forward while awaiting response from a full set of queens on the opposite side of the table."

"What would you ask of me?" Nazere asked fervently.

"Take faith, my son, for these are black days. And the end of all things comes with great haste. If you take but a moment to believe in what cannot be seen, you will become immensely stronger. Take refuge in the arms of the Master no matter what wicked thing may cross your path, and you will prevail. More understanding of what I am trying to convey will come with time." Ryan moved to the edge of his seat.

"High prophet," he began. "We seek weaponry for our assault on the Gantor Pinnacle. What can be done to see to it that we are well equipped?" The man dressed in red laughed. Turning his head, a gold earring could be seen hanging from his ear.

"Behold my blade," the man began as he raised his sword into the air. The sword was pristine, crafted by the hands of a master blacksmith and shining in the ambient light of the room. Its double-edged tip appeared immaculately sharp, as if it could pierce anything. "I have made four in its likeness for those who are traveling into the fray."

"Jentaru," David began, looking on the blade in awe. "The closest thing to an angel's blade man could ever attain. Its design is heaven-sent."

"You say you have made four in its likeness?" Ryan asked.

"Indeed," the man replied. "And each one is as potent as the first."

"What do you call yourself?" Nazere asked, curious as to who this man was.

"My name is Owen Candlefire, master blacksmith for the Gathering of the White Lion. I have crafted blades that have cast lesser demons into the bottomless pit. The only thing my blades cannot penetrate is ventari armor."

"Where is Drake at the moment, Owen?" Ryan asked. "I am in need of a gunblade. Drake could see to its construction." Owen nodded.

"Drake has been busy working on the Deliverer in the basement," Owen said. "He has nearly completed its construction."

"Go there now," Arthur commanded. "This meeting is over. Sara will see that all of you are given rooms for the evening." Arthur smiled. “I do so hope you enjoy your stay in our humble abode.” Arthur picked his book off the table, and continued to read. As soon as he adjourned the meeting, all of the people in the room other than Arthur made their exit and began walking downstairs. Elle quickened her step so that she could walk alongside Nazere.

“This way to the base floor,” Sara said. “Your rooms will be down here as well. Please follow me.” Sara led the group to the corner of the foyer and opened a door that led to a winding staircase that twisted downward. The staircase was dimly lit by red candles on both sides of it. And at the bottom of the staircase, there was a massive opening. There were seven black doors on one side of the opening, and seven black doors on the other side. In the very back of the room, there was one unique room, the door painted red rather than the black that covered the rest of the room. Each door bore the emblem of the lion’s head, and was made of sturdy iron. In the center of the room, a man wearing a protective steel mask stood welding metal on the exterior of a lion the size of the Redeemer. The lion was as accurately crafted as the Redeemer. It had a full mane and thousands upon thousands of golden hairs exactly like the actual animal. Everything was precise, and the only way to differentiate the machine from the animal was its sheer size and the glow of its red eyes. The eyes had irises and pupils that were illuminated by a powerful red light from within. Its nose was black, and its ears were a precise mixture of white and pink. Blue sparks flew everywhere as Drake welded the front right paw of the behemoth. The downstairs smelled like a bit of gasoline mixed with the fumes of the dark chocolate from upstairs.

“Drake Winterbane!” Sara called out. “There are some men here to see you.”

“I know,” Drake replied as he discontinued his welding and removed his face shield. He had a red goatee, long red hair tied in a ponytail, and wore a white t-shirt and black cargo pants. “Good to see the Gathering of the White Knight in our midst again. How have you been Ryan?”

“It is so good to see you, brother,” Ryan said as he reached out and embraced Drake. “It looks like you’re nearly finished the Deliverer.

In fact, it looks absolutely fantastic right now."

"Yep," Drake replied as he looked up at his advanced work of technological art. "She's nearly ready to run."

"Impressive work, Drake," David commented as he walked closer to the Deliverer and looked at it from a close vantage point. "Did you implement a built-in raiditor?"

"I most certainly did," Drake replied. "I tweaked the engine for ground speed to outmatch the Redeemer." David laughed.

"None can outmatch the Redeemer," David said, a competitive edge to his voice. "But I truly respect your efforts."

"We'll see about that," Drake said cackling. "So what brings you to my workshop? Going to bed so soon?"

"No," Ryan said with a straight look on his face. "I am in need of your particular skills. Operation Maelstrom is about to be underway."

"Let me guess," Drake began smiling. "You want a gun for your blade?"

"Oh, here we go," David sneered, his eyes rolling to the back of his head. Electronics and mechanics were his speciality, but Drake was a proficient gunsmith.

"The arsenal is in the back room. You can take your pick. The new guy can come along too." Nazere and Ryan followed Drake to the red door in the back of the room. "Access code: Lion Heart." Once Drake had spoken the password, the iron door creaked open to reveal a dark room. "Activate the lights." The lights in the room immediately elucidated the entirety of the space. "Just as a side note for you, Nazere," Drake began as he glanced over his shoulder at him. "Passwords are necessary to enter certain doors, but you won't need passwords to leave any room in this house. Or any other gathering's house for that matter. They're all formatted the same."

Within the room, large photon hand cannons hung suspended in the air in a variety of shapes and sizes. Altogether, there was a selection of at least fifty different guns. Ryan walked over to a mid-sized photon cannon and pulled it out of its place in the air. Constructed with three holes in its barrel, this particular photon cannon was capable of triple the standard rate of fire with the push of a small button on the side of the cannon. The button was lit by a small, red, light-emitting diode line segment on top of it. The remainder of the cannon was covered with a wavy, red light-emitting diode pattern.

"This will do," Ryan said as he looked over his newly chosen weapon. Nazere looked around the room. Nothing in sight seemed to catch his attention.

"I really don't know what I want," Nazere said as he glanced around the room. A look of excitement overtook Drake's face.

"By all means," Drake started. "Let me show you a little trinket that may prove even more potent than any of these cannons." Drake walked to the back of the room and approached a long steel box that seemed to be welded to the floor. "Withdraw: Scepter," he spoke into the box. Out of the box popped out a scepter with three blue rings around its tip. The scepter was thin, and by the look of it constructed of pure white artolium. "If you are savvy with your arms, this weapon will prove a valuable asset to dual wield along with a prophet's sword." Nazere grabbed the scepter with his right hand while it was still suspended in the air. It was incredibly light-weight, and as Nazere swung it a smile crossed his face.

"This thing swings like a dream," Nazere commented as he continued to maneuver the scepter before him.

"It is capable of immobilizing just about anything," Drake said, his eyes lighting up with excitement as he watched Nazere move the scepter around. "One hit with that scepter and your enemy will be paralyzed in his tracks. It is especially useful against machines. Up until now, it has been the only defense against the ventari." Drake paused for a moment, watching Nazere as he maneuvered the scepter in the space in front of him. "The question is, do you know how to fight? How skilled are you in using the sword? And here," Drake began as he picked up a sheath from a pile on the floor. "Take this sheath for that scepter. You wouldn't want the end of it touching anything." Drake threw Nazere a black sheath that had two slots, and Nazere threw the strap of it around his back. Nazere dropped the scepter to his side where the sheath hung at his hip.

"I have actually never had to use a blade," Nazere responded.

Drake smiled.

"Well then," Drake said as he crossed his arms before Nazere. "We will have to better acquaint you with Adrax. He is the chief battle prophet of our gathering. Ryan and I need to fuse Owen's blade with the cannon. Go now and ask Elle to take you to Adrax's quarters. It is the last door on the left. She knows where it is." Ryan pulled a small dime sized black square out of his pocket and held it in his palm. He then held out his arm and dropped his palm, the square becoming suspended in the space before him. The square then lit up a bright green, and a number of holographic panes came popping out of the square. A rotating image of the sword designed by Owen rotated in green on one side of the square, and an image of the photon cannon selected by Ryan rotated in blue on the other. Drake began pressing buttons on the floating holographic pane on his side, and Ryan pressed buttons on his side. Nazere walked out of the room as Ryan and Drake continued their work in crafting their weaponry. Elle was waiting just outside, in a quiet conversation with David.

"Excuse me," Nazere interrupted. "But Drake said I should have you escort me to Adrax's quarters, Elle." Elle refocused her attention to Nazere.

"Blade training time, huh?" Elle asked as she smiled. "Just follow me." Elle began walking to the corner of the room, and Nazere followed directly behind. "Adrax is a great guy, and he has a lot of experience in spiritual battle," Elle said as she walked, glancing slightly over her shoulder. "He may be able to help you with more than just the sword training." Elle approached the door closely. "Password: Healing Grace." The lion's face on the door took on a pink glow, and the door came flying open. This room was barren except for a white light taller than Nazere flaring in the center of the room over top of a carpet identical to the one at the entrance to the house. The walls were all painted black like the rooms before it. "You go first," Elle said as she signaled for Nazere to walk into the light.

"You want me to walk into that?" Nazere asked with a confused look on his face.

"Right into it," Elle said. "Come. I'll help you." Elle softly took

Nazere's hand, smiling as she walked alongside him into the light. A great flash of white light blinded Nazere's vision for a moment, but within seconds his vision became clear. There was forest surrounding Nazere and Elle as far as the eye could see. Directly in front of the couple there were three towers that reached into the sky. They were taller than any skyscrapers designed on the earth, constructs of a seldom-imaginable proportion. Each tower was made of concrete-sealed ashlar, built akin to the medieval turrets of old, much taller and far wider than their ancient twins. They were arranged in a triangle formation, two of the towers in parallel while the middle tower stood fifty yards behind them. On the central tower, there was a thin, wooden bar protruding from several inches below its peak. Each tower had the same curved black door, accompanied by rusted iron handles. Nazere's eyes glanced up at the wooden bar on the central tower. He noticed that Adrax was crouched upside down on the thin wooden plank. His eyes widened and his mouth opened every so slightly in shock at the unusual acrobatic display.

"I've been awaiting your arrival, Nazere," Adrax called down, still defying gravity as he was crouched on the wooden plank. He then dropped to the ground below in a blur, moving at an inhuman speed. Nazere was completely confounded. Crouched on the floor, Adrax looked at Nazere for a moment and smiled. He then became a blur again and advanced a distance of about forty yards instantly. There he stood in front of Elle and Nazere.

"Where are we?" Nazere asked Elle as he leaned to her right ear and whispered.

"This is the spirit realm," Elle whispered back. "It is all a manifestation of Adrax's faith. He created it through the Master for training purposes." Adrax made a courteous bow before Elle and Nazere. Behind Adrax's back was a sheath with a wide black hilt towering out of it.

"Welcome to the training ground of the white lion's warriors," Adrax said as he returned to his erect and upright position and confronted Nazere face-to-face. "The towers behind you are our training turrets. Inside, prophets practice combining the physical reality with the spiritual one, manipulating weaponry to gain an advantage against our mighty opposition." Adrax pointed behind him. "The right-most tower is for the most advanced prophets. The central tower is for intermediate combatants. And to our left, there is the beginner's tower. That is where you will start, and I would be delighted to be your guide." Adrax took a step back and waved to the two. "Please. Follow me inside." Walking behind him at Elle's side, Nazere watched as Adrax pulled the door of the left tower open with his right arm. "After you," Adrax said as he signaled for Elle and Nazere to enter in.

The view inside the left tower was incredible. There were about thirty men and women scattered about the room, all wearing goggles with four light-emitting diode segments encircling each eye. A great coat of arms with a lion's head on it hung from the tower's back wall. Purple flags with lions on them protruded from every corner of the tower about eight feet up. Each one of the men inside carried a unique sword, and every soldier was swinging at holographic images of sentinels, dreadhunters, and bloodguards. Adrax put his hands behind his back as he walked about the large room, glancing around at the men and women battling the projected images. The room was as loud as a rock concert, the constant clashing of swords and the realistic sounds generated by the reflections of enemies generating an ear-breaking melody. "Sentinel and dreadhunter combat!" Adrax yelled out over the noises resounding throughout the turret. "This is the first phase of training!" He turned and put his pointer finger in Nazere's face. "One must first be able to overcome the sentinel and the dreadhunter!"

Adrax led Elle and Nazere over to a young woman who was in a heated duel with a sentinel. The woman was swinging her sword as if the image of the robot were real, taking great care with every advance she made in attempting to destroy the image. "This, as both of you should know, is a sentinel," Adrax said as he pointed to the holographic image of the machine. "A twelve foot tower of a machine, the sentinel has a nigh impenetrable exoskeleton. The sentinel has a monstrous chest, with bulky arms and shoulders. As it is often used for security purposes, the sentinel attacks with his fists. His face, however, is its one and only shortcoming. Behind it is its primary wiring and a fully exposed central processor. Unlike the vizedrones, bloodguards and ventari, there is no human component to the sentinel or the dreadhunter." Nazere took a close look at the sentinel's face, which mirrored ancient Roman silver face busts. Its face had a high shine, and its eyes were sterling silver with an amber light where the pupil should be. The rest of the sentinel's body was a metallic amber color and also reflected light with a high shine. The sentinel's arms and chest were humanlike, but its legs were slow to move and thick all the way around. They were clearly heavy, and as wide as tree trunks from the foot to the upper thigh. Adrax withdrew his blade from his back, which was a very large sized, curved saber that took on a red glow as soon as he took hold of its hilt. Curious as to the saber‘s capabilities, Nazere paid careful attention to Adrax‘s every movement. "May I?" Adrax asked the young student battling the projected image, stepping next to her and grasping his saber in his right hand.

"Destroy it, teacher!" the student cheered. To Nazere's amazement, Adrax increased the size of his saber sevenfold; it appeared to be unbelievably heavy. Adding to the astounded expression on Nazere's face, Adrax then lifted the holographic image by the neck with his left arm and drove his saber through its face. There was a wide, gaping hole in the holographic image of the sentinel's face. As holographic sparks came flying from the face like a sparkler, the sentinel came crashing to the ground. Adrax resized his saber and returned it to its sheath as if this sort of combat were routine for him. He made it look like child's play.

"That is how a sentinel is destroyed," Adrax said as he turned to Nazere and Elle. He then walked around the large room to the yet another student. This one was a male with black hair, and his full focus was on the task of defeating the image before him. "Our next subject is battling a dreadhunter. A dreadhunter is quick and agile, with reflexes and agility that has been magnified many times over. It is an intricately genetically engineered panther with a thirst for prophet blood. It is tragic that these animals have been used to serve this purpose, but we cannot change that reality. The only way to kill it is to strike it directly in the heart. Its other engineered skin cells are extremely resilient, able to withstand a great deal of damage. But the cells around its chest are penetrable, making the kill possible." Adrax turned to the student. "May I?" Nazere focused in on Adrax's next process very closely as he watched the projected panther move like he had never seen a cat move before. It seemed the animal was highly intelligent, with swift and precise swipes that appeared unavoidable.

"Finish it," the student replied as he took a step back.

Adrax withdrew his saber and increased its size sevenfold once again. Nazere's pupils widened as Adrax then lifted the holographic image of the cat from afar by lifting his left hand ever-so-slightly. The dreadhunter struggled as it was lifted twenty feet in the air, growling, swiping, and trying to get down from its exposed position. In one well-calculated strike, Adrax leaped under the dreadhunter's location and drove his saber into the panther's heart by lifting his blade above his head. Landing across the room, Adrax kneeled down at the opposite side of the stone turret and sheathed his blade. The dreadhunter moaned and fell to the floor, completely motionless.

"Impressive!" Nazere exclaimed as he watched Adrax rise to the upright position and turn around. Adrax then walked to yet another student. "Come over here, Nazere," Adrax commanded. Nazere and Elle continued to follow Adrax around the room. "This is where you will start. Our next target is the bloodguard. Before I go any further, I want you to know that killing humans is to be avoided as much as possible. But when the time of wrath comes, bringing death to the soulless will become a necessary part of survival. You should know that bloodguards are completely processed and devoid of any soul." Nazere knew all too well, looking at the modified humans with the same sense of distaste as he had when he was on the streets. He had lost close friends to their barbarous hands more times than he could count.

"As you can see," Adrax began as he pointed to the student next him. "Bloodguards are well armored. They have anti-radiation masks and wear purely spidersilk armor. The spidersilk armor is as hard as steel and resistant to sword attacks, but not impenetrable. They have the nocturnal eyes of a cat within the eye openings on their mask. This gives them an advantage in the dark." Nazere looked at the mask of the bloodguard and noted that it looked like a smiling, ceramic theater mask. The mask was white and the eyes underneath it could be easily seen from without. Each guard wore a red cape and the outline of a red heart on their silver, spidersilk uniforms. "The photon cannons they carry won't penetrate the tri-layer ion shield around your body in the first shot. However, their finger blades have been designed with heavily concentrated particle charges. They can slice right through the ion shield. Their hand-blades are what you want to avoid. All things considered, bloodguards are flexible, but they are the simplest kills to make. Please allow me to demonstrate."

"Go right ahead and show him, teacher," the student said to Adrax, standing back as Adrax took control of the fight. Adrax held his saber in front of him, but this time he didn't increase its size. The bloodguard focused its attention on Adrax, extending each finger's blade to the length of an ultra-thin dagger. The hand-blades were gunmetal gray and had a slight flicker to them. This flicker demonstrated the concentration of particles on the edge of each finger. The image of the bloodguard slashed its right blades forward with great force when Adrax stood up to the plate. Adrax countered the attack by lunging his saber toward the bloodguard. The blades clashed together, and the bloodguard threw its left hand forward in an attempt to hit Adrax. Using his saber, Adrax threw the blades on the bloodguard's right hand down to its side. He then countered the left attack, driving the left arm of the bloodguard back as he lifted up on his saber. As the image was now fully exploited, Adrax drove his blade into the bloodguard's chest. The bloodguard fell to his knees, collapsing on the ground as its image dissipated.

"Now," Adrax started. "It is time for you to practice." Adrax threw Nazere his saber, and Nazere managed to catch the sharp weapon by the hilt. When Nazere caught the weapon, the saber lost its red glow. Looking down at the blade with a puzzled look on his face, Nazere wondered why the glow was extinguished when he held to the hilt.

"Excellent catch," Adrax commented as he smiled. "Are you ready, Nazere?"

"As ready as I will ever be, I suppose," Nazere replied, still looking at the saber in confusion as to why it would not glow for him.

"You can handle this, Nazere," Elle said, providing him a bit of confidence. She was prepared to watch his every move. "I fully know what you're capable of."

Adrax nodded. "Generate a bloodguard!" Adrax yelled out. A new bloodguard's digital reflection was instantaneously generated in front of Nazere. As immediately as it came, it lashed out at him with its right arm. Nazere countered with the saber, and drove the bloodguard's hand back. The bloodguard then attacked with his left arm, and Nazere countered by driving that arm back as well. Nazere drove his saber forward, but just as he did, the bloodguard raised its right hand again and drove the saber away. Knocked back, Nazere raised his saber in defense. Within, Nazere felt ill-prepared for this sort of combat. "Breathe. Take control. Think wisely," Adrax slowly counseled Nazere. The bloodguard advanced toward Nazere with its hand-blades, waving both arms viciously as if it were desperate to obliterate Nazere. Holographic sparks flew throughout the room like white fireflies as Nazere held to his saber tightly. And just as the bloodguard was about to drive his left hand down into Nazere's chest, Nazere inhaled and drove his saber upward with all his might. The saber had penetrated the bloodguard's stomach. The bloodguard stepped back and took a look at the hole in his chest as Nazere withdrew the saber. The image then fell to his knees and collapsed on the floor, fading away in a few short flickers.

"Well done," Adrax commented. "You have much to learn, but that was a good start."

"Good show, Nazere!" Elle exclaimed, smiling and clapping.

"I would ask you for a duel," Adrax began, smiling. "But I think that should wait until later. I am confident in your ability to defend yourself. I have nothing more for you right now. I simply wanted to introduce you to what you will be facing in the Gantor Pinnacle." Elle turned to Nazere, still smiling.

"Let's head back to the house," Elle said. "It's getting late."

"One last thing," Adrax said as he turned to Elle as to hold her up for but a moment. "I have a gift for Nazere. Something I've been saving for quite some time. I prepared it months ago for the moment of his arrival." Adrax pulled a small black cube out of his pocket. He then turned to Nazere. "The Master commanded me to build a little something special for you. He should serve as a good companion in times of trouble." Adrax extended his arm and held the cube out in his palm. "Come to me, Verus!" In a ball of white smoke, a figure appeared before Nazere's feet. It was a German shepherd with light-hazel eyes, and it looked up at Nazere as soon as it was brought forth. "The device I hold is a summtorent," Adrax began as he set his gaze upon Nazere. "It is used to call upon Verus whenever you should need him. He is no ordinary dog," Adrax began as he kneeled next to the German shepherd and began to pet him. "This dog has been genetically modified to be your saving grace in times of need. I think he would give even the ventari a good fight. He won't leave your side, and he can fight like the best of them."

"Amazing," Nazere said as he too knelt down next to the dog, petting his fur. "He's a beautiful animal."

"He's very cute," Elle said smiling. "He'll make a nice little friend for you, Nazere."

"Take this," Adrax said handing Nazere the cube. "It's yours." Nazere recieved the cube and handed the saber he was gripping in his right hand back to Adrax. Nazere then took to his feet.

"Come, Verus," Nazere commanded his new associate. Verus walked directly up to Nazere and sat down. Nazere leaned over and pet the dog as he panted, Verus' tongue hanging out of his mouth.

"I won't hold you any longer," Adrax said as he set his eyes on Nazere and Elle. "I pray you both have a safe journey when you depart from Baltimore. I'm sure I will be seeing you again." Adrax paused for a moment. "Summon: Gate!" A great white light like the one that brought Elle and Nazere into the spirit realm appeared before Adrax. Before departing, Elle gave Adrax a hug.

"Thank you for your help, Adrax," Elle said.

"It was my pleasure," he replied. "I look forward to more training with Nazere in the future."

"Come on, you," Elle began as she stared down Nazere. "We're heading back."

"Would you take my hand again, Elle?" Nazere asked. "The light makes me a bit nervous."

"Any time," she replied as she approached Nazere and looked into his eyes. And together, the two of them passed through the gate and back to the room from whence they came. Verus followed closely behind, jumping into the white light after his new master. When they passed through the gate, Elle walked up to the door leading to the workshop. The door automatically opened. Following behind Elle, Nazere walked out into the workshop where Ryan, David, Sara, Drake and two other men stood talking. One of the men was of medium height; he was older, bald, cleanly shaven and wore all black robes. The other man was dressed similarly, except that he had a hood that accompanied his black robes. Under his black hood, you could see his black mustache, twisted black beard and a tattoo of a lion's head on his forehead. He looked to be considerably younger than the man that stood next to him. As for Ryan, he now had a thin hilt protruding from a green, leather sheath on his back.

"How was it?" Ryan asked Elle. "Did he do alright?" Elle smiled.

"He needs more practice," Elle started as she briefly turned her eyes up at Nazere. "But I have a feeling it will come to him when the time is right." Ryan nodded.

"Sword mastery doesn't come overnight," Ryan began. "Unless, of course, the Master wills for it to be so."

"So this is the chosen one?" the bald man asked as he walked up to Nazere and took him by the hand, smiling. "It is so good to finally make your acquaintance. My name is Endarius Darkhand, and I am one of the members of the Gathering of the White Lion." The man spoke slowly with a dark tone to his voice. He looked to the man in the hood and pointed his arm, extending his finger in a gradual fashion. "This is my apprentice, Ferris Shadowpath. Together, we are members of the Ministry of the First Death. Our job is bringing judgment on the wicked. Our secondary obligation is to defend the members of the White Lion from any and all harm." Ferris formed a very malevolent smile upon his face, his eyes set directly on Nazere.

"Arthur has invited us to join him for a drink upstairs," David announced to the group. "He wants to consecrate our mission before we depart in the morning." David's eyes then caught a glimpse of the German shepherd who was now between Nazere's legs. "Nice dog you have there, Nazere."

"Thanks," Nazere replied as he patted Verus on the head. "I think I'm already growing fond of him." Ryan glanced over at Nazere with a twinkle in his eyes.

"Would you like to see the gunblade?" Ryan asked, a hint of pride in his voice.

"Sure," Nazere said as he walked closer to Ryan. Ryan reached around to the green sheath around his back. He then grasped the thin, silver hilt and pulled out his gunblade. The cannon's barrel had been infused into the midsection of the sword. The wavy pattern on the photon cannon now had a gray luminescence about it, and the eyes of the lion's heads on the golden hilt of the sword bore a green radiance. The blade of the sword jutted out from underneath the cannon about two feet and took on a fully green essence.

"Very impressive," Nazere commented excitedly. Verus barked as if he were concurring with his master. "I've never seen anything like it."

"Well, gentlemen," Elle began. "I would love to sit around and talk guns and stuff, but the high prophet is awaiting our arrival upstairs. Let's not keep him waiting, okay?"

"Very well, your heinous," Ryan smirked at Elle as he reseated his sword in its sheath. Together, everyone in the workshop climbed the stairs of the house in a single file line. They remained silent as they ascended the staircase to the roundtable at the top of the building. Glasses were all neatly arranged around the table, perfectly spaced out from one another before each chair around the roundtable. Their round, reflective surfaces glimmered in the orange light generated by the furnace of the room. Sitting on the chair closest to the entrance to the room, Owen held a sword out in front of him with both of his hands. Behind him on the table, there was a bottle with a paper label glued to its surface and a cork on its top. The bottle read "Arthur's Vintage Press: 2076." Adrax sat with ten of his students on the right side of Arthur. Arthur sat in his usual spot, taking a puff from his pipe as smoke drifted into the air. The scent of the rising vapor immediately informed Nazere that Arthur was smoking a cherry flavored tobacco.

"How did you get up here so fast?" Nazere asked Adrax with a startled expression on his face.

"I have my ways," Adrax replied, a wide smile from cheek to cheek. "I couldn't miss the chance to toast to your first excursion into enemy territory." In front of Nazere, Owen took a stand from his place at the roundtable. He then turned around and looked him directly in the eyes.

"Nazere," Owen began slowly. Owen took a knee before Nazere, bowing his head before him as he held out the sword with both of his hands. He held it as if it were an offering for a king, and he was slow and sincere with each word he spoke. "I present you with your first sword. Use it well, and may it serve to be your protector when you walk through the valley of the shadow of death." Arthur set his eyes on the bottle on the table, pulling the bottle across the table and popping the cork without the use of a corkscrew. He then began to pass the bottle around the table. The group that had entered from the workshop all took seats to the left of the round table. Elle was closest to Arthur, with an empty chair next to her. She was saving a spot, and Arthur knew it. He turned to Elle for but a moment and smiled. He then watched as Nazere reached out and gripped the hilt of his blade with his right hand. As he did, the blade began to take on a radiant blue glow. "This is for you. This is for the one who has been chosen. You are our great hope." Owen continued to kneel his head before Nazere. Nazere looked at the sword with great fascination as the light of the blue blade seemed to come to life before him. After examining the blade thoroughly, Nazere tucked the sword away into the second slot in the sheath on his back.

"Come take a seat, my boy," Arthur offered with a smile rounding his dimpled cheeks. "Tonight we celebrate the beginning of the end." Nazere walked up to the roundtable and sat next to Elle. After he had taken a seat, Owen took to his feet and returned to his chair at the end of the table. Verus climbed under the table and worked his way between Nazere's knees with some clever maneuvering. Elle dropped her hand under the table and took hold of Nazere's. Nazere began to blush as she did, but he most certainly didn't want her to see. His heart jumped in his chest as she took hold of his hand for the first time. "Someone fill that man's glass. Oh never mind," Arthur said laughing. "I'll do it." Arthur picked up the bottle without using his hands and slowly poured the contents of the bottle into Nazere's glass.

"I enjoy this wine," David commented. "It's a good merlot. It has hints of chocolate and raspberries. It is so very yummy in my tummy!" Ryan shook his head, scoffing at David.

"For shame," Ryan sneered.

"Tonight we toast," Arthur began as he lifted his glass. "To the Master, and that His will be carried out in the days to come. May our gatherings emerge victoriously! Cheers!" And all of the people at the table lifted their glasses and drank their wine down at one time. David had his drink down first. Elle sipped at her wine as she held her glass with one hand, burping after her first drink.

"Excuse me," Elle said as she blushed.

"That's okay," Nazere said as he laughed. "It happens."

"And now," Arthur began. "for dessert, we have something very special in honor of our new guest." Arthur clapped his hands, and as he did, gold lined black plates appeared before everyone on the table. And on top of the plates, very fluffy bread resembling pound cake was miraculously manifested. David reached out and stuffed the whole piece of bread into his mouth.

"Oh my goodness," David began with a mouth full of bread. "Manna! This is quite the delectable treat! It the best food in heaven or on earth!"

"Thank you," Ryan told Arthur as he pulled his manna apart, preparing to eat it.

"Thank the good Lord above," Arthur said. "He sent it. But I can say that I do enjoy manna from time to time myself."

"Oh, yes," Elle said, hints of excitement chiming in her voice. "I can bake, but absolutely nothing compares to manna." Nazere picked up the bread and took a bite. Immediately, his taste buds exploded with a combination of flavors he had never experienced before.

"This is amazing!" Nazere exclaimed, speaking with a bit of the bread in his mouth.

"Mind your manners, now," Elle told Nazere, smiling at him while gently rubbing his hand with her thumb. Verus barked under the table.

"Here boy," Nazere said as the dog looked upon the food with eager eyes. "You can have some of mine." He handed Verus a chunk of his manna, satiating the dog as he immediately began to devour it.

"Aww," Elle began. "That's sweet of you, Nazere. Do you want some of mine?"

"No," Nazere replied. "By all means, you enjoy yours. But thank you for the offer." Nazere looked across the table at Endarius, who slowly and methodically picked at his manna. He noticed Endarius was looking directly into Nazere's eyes. Nazere turned his head close to Elle. "He seems strange," Nazere whispered to Elle, hoping Endarius couldn't hear what he was saying. "There's just something about him." Elle chewed and swallowed her remaining manna as she leaned toward Nazere.

"Many people think that," she whispered back. "Be careful what you say in here. Endarius has startling senses." Nazere nodded and returned to eating his manna.

"So what time in the morning do you plan to leave?" Adrax asked David as he ate.

"First thing in the morning," David replied. "We are on schedule as it is, but time is running and it isn't going to stop for anyone. We need to accomplish our mission."

"Be careful out there," Adrax said. "And that includes all of you. Elle, Ryan, David and Nazere, please know that my prayers will be for you."

"I'm quite confident they will be successful," Arthur interjected. "None can stop the will of the Master."

“Are we quite sure what that is, high prophet?” Endarius asked in his sinister tone as he turned his gaze to Arthur. “Have you foreseen the accomplishment of the events to come?” Arthur paused for a few moments, staring at the table before him as his eyebrows became tightened.

“It has been a good evening,” Arthur said as he turned his eyes up, smiled, and took a stand. “I would love to remain here with you, but I must be off. I have imminent business to attend to.” There was a silence about the table as Arthur took hold of his cane and quickly walked out of the room.

“Hey,” Elle whispered to Nazere. “Let’s go to the roof. The view is beautiful up there. I want to talk to you for a bit before we leave tomorrow.”

“Alright,” Nazere replied. “You’ll have to show me the way.” Elle took Nazere by the hand and pulled him out of the room, leaving the rest of the group to their drinks and their manna. Verus climbed from out of under the table and followed behind his master. Elle led the way, taking a right out of the entrance to the roundtable’s room to where there was yet another door. Like the others in the house, it had the emblem of a golden lion’s head on it.

“Password: Healing Grace,” Elle spoke into the door. The lion’s eyes came to life with a pink glow and immediately opened for Elle. Beyond the door was a black winding staircase that was illuminated by the light of the moon above. The staircase appeared to be made of iron, and its stairs were made of pure silver. Elle, who still held tightly to Nazere’s hand, guided him up to the top of the roof. Once they were there, they were met by a stone surface with a black railing around it. There were two red-cushioned chairs sitting near the edge of the railing. Elle let go of Nazere’s hand, waving for him to follow her. “Come sit with me,” she said as she walked toward the chairs. Elle took a seat in the left chair, and Nazere on the right one. Verus walked over and sat down by Nazere’s side. Below them were towering buildings, and above were radiant stars and elucidated flying vehicles moving swiftly throughout the atmosphere. Altogether they lit up the blackened night sky. The whole of the city of Baltimore could be seen from the roof of the House of Arthur.

"It's beautiful out here," Elle said as she looked up into the distance. She gently leaned her head against the red cushion behind her. "My father used to take me up to the rooftops on our flat in London. We used to sit up late at night and just look at the stars." Nazere's eyes were set to the sky, the same one he had slept under for years. He glanced down briefly, noticing a park bench he used to sleep on in the dead of winter. He suddenly remembered the cold. Trying to forget his past life, Nazere set his eyes to the heavens above. "He would point up at that star there," Elle began as she pointed to the corner of the big dipper. "And he would tell me how beautiful it was to him. But as he held my hand, he would always say that it meant nothing to him, because I was his favorite star." Elle paused for a moment as she just gazed upon the stars in the night sky. The air was cool, a slight breeze creating a seemingly perfect atmosphere for sitting outdoors. "Do you have a favorite star?"

"If you look up there," Nazere began as he pointed into the sky. "My favorite is the tip of Taurus' horns. It seems to shine so brightly against the backdrop of the rest of the stars in the constellation." Elle smiled as she turned and looked at Nazere.

"I agree," she said, exhaling a withheld breath. The two were as nervous as any new couple could be, their chests rising ever so often in response to simple spoken words.

"I just want to admit something, Elle, because I feel like you're the one woman I can talk to," Nazere said, his eyes glued to the stars.

"What is it?" Elle asked.

"In the beginning, when I first came into contact with you and the gathering, I thought you were completely insane," Nazere began, speaking boldly but hoping Elle wouldn't take his openness the wrong way. "I thought there had to be something wrong. I guess I'm just analytical that way. But I can tell you now that my outlook has changed entirely. I feel like I can talk to you, and I hope you don't mind that I thought you were a little out in the deep end initially." Elle turned to Nazere, her cheeks glowing at the truth she knew he was communicating. That truth meant something to her.

"I don't mind at all that you thought I was nuts in the beginning, Nazere," Elle began, laughing a bit. "I can't blame you. I'm just glad that you feel that you can talk to me and be open now. I'm always here to listen whenever you need someone to talk to. Okay?"

"Okay," Nazere replied. The two shut their eyes in continued, complete relaxation.

"Can you answer something for me, Nazere?"

"Anything," Nazere replied.

"Are you afraid of what's to come? Do you fear what's going to happen?"

"A little, I guess," Nazere replied. "I've definitely been thinking about it."

"I'm afraid for you," Elle said as she took Nazere's hand.

"You shouldn't be," Nazere replied. "I've handled myself on the streets for years. I think I can withstand what is to come." Nazere paused for a moment as he leaned his head back on the cushion behind his neck and let the comforting atmosphere soak into his body. He held Elle's hand and looked over to her. "You have a sweet heart, Elle. And you're completely beautiful to me." Elle's eyes lit up like a candle as they turned to Nazere. "It has been a long time since I've had someone to talk to. I guess I got lucky when I met you. You're something unique to me. There isn't much left in the world that is really special. But your heart is something that I've never come by before. I can see where your father was coming from. No star's brilliance could compare to the beauty I see in you."

"I like talking to you, too," Elle replied softly with a grin on her face. "You are fascinating to me. I could sit out here and watch the stars with you forever. It's nice isn't it?" Nazere nodded, his heart dancing in his chest.

"It's wonderful," he replied. The two sat out in the chairs for a few minutes, holding each other's hand and looking into the sky above.

"Hey, Nazere," Elle began in a whisper.

"Yes, Elle?"

"I'm thankful for you, too." She turned her head toward him. "I guess we both got lucky," she whispered. She then looked deeply into his eyes. "I want you to know that I am behind you no matter what happens. I believe in you." His eyes gleaming, Nazere started to lean toward Elle as their hands grazed one another's. And just as he did, the door behind the pair opened.

"Hey there, you two," Sara Maple began. "We're locking up! Nazere, I need to take you to your room."

"We were just talking," Elle said as she was alerted of Sara's presence. "I'm off to bed, Nazere. We'll talk more later, okay?"

"Okay," Nazere replied, his heart still flying around within him like a little jet. He quickly glanced over at Elle and whispered, "I enjoyed spending this time with you, Elle." Elle couldn't hold back her glow.

"I did too," she replied. Nazere then released her hand. She then got up from her seat and walked inside. Sara walked over to Nazere.

"I need to show you where your room is," Sara said. "Please come this way. Your pup looks tired too." Nazere looked to his side and noticed that Verus had down on the roof. He hadn't even been paying attention. "You both need some rest." Nazere got up from his chair.

"Come on boy," Nazere began. "We're going to sleep." Nazere followed Sara back down the staircase with Verus getting up and following right behind them.

"Password: Shield Maiden," Sara spoke into the door. The door's eyes took on a purple glow and came flying open. Sara crossed the workshop and walked to the second door on the left. "This is your room," Sara said as Nazere and Verus stood before her. "Allow me to unlock it. Oh! And you do know that once a door has been opened you don't need a password to exit, correct?"

"Yes," Nazere replied. "Drake informed me." Sara smiled.

"Very good, then. Let's get you settled in. Password: Shield Maiden." The door's eyes again took on a purple glow and the door came open with haste. Inside, there was a bed with a red comforter and a nightstand with a red, leather Holy Bible on top of it. The floor was like the floor in the foyer, made of red and black checkered marble. Sara walked into the room. "Before you go to bed, I want to know that you are not to venture out into the night. Is that understood?"

"Yes," Nazere replied. "I won't be going anywhere. No worries, Sara."

"Alright," Sara began. "Well in that case, I wish you a good night. Sweet dreams." And with that, Sara stepped out of the room and shut the door softly behind her. Verus walked to the side of the bed where he lay down and closed his eyes. Nazere shut off the lights and lay down in his bed, pulling the thick blankets over him. He hadn't felt so comfortable for ages it seemed. But there was a small issue. Several hours passed, and as they did, Nazere realized the yoralium Elle had given him had not worn off. He was utterly restless. And as he lay in his bed, the thought of venturing out to the Lone Wolf Pub at Fells Point entered his mind. He knew he could get some dezium there, and the thought continued to agitate him. I'll just slip out for a moment, he thought to himself. He quickly formulated a scheme to allow himself to escape for a bit. Nazere arose from his bed and opened the door, tip-toeing out of the house with the greatest of care. He moved as if he were attempting to evade the ventari peacekeepers. Once he was out of the front door, he began walking down the empty street. It didn't take him very long to reach his destination. Within a half-an-hour, he was in front of the Lone Wolf Pub. This bar was characterized by the wooden bust of a wolf protruding from above the top of its steel doors. Nazere approached the door nonchalantly and opened it. Inside, the bar was busy with intoxicated customers. It is at night that the vampires come out to play — the genetically engineered vampires of a city filled with people who could take on various, altered forms if they decided to do so. And most did; werewolves and witches were not uncommon in the society of the new order. But as Nazere had been incarcerated, he was not enlightened on current events. Vice Lord Xar and High Lord Alune had given the people of every nation the power to modify their own bodies through the allotment of free biological engineering. Any man or woman could modify their nature in any form they wanted to. Inside the bar, men dressed in street clothes were shooting pool, drinking and smoking. The stale scent of alcohol enveloped the air, lingering smoke adding to the characteristic scent of the establishment. Nazere approached the bar, and behind it a bartender covered in tattoos met him with a strange look.

"Excuse me, sir," Nazere began. "I need some dezium pills. I want ten. I have a credit card." Nazere reached down into his sock, where he had hidden his credit card before he was jailed.

"I'll be happy to oblige you," the bartender replied. "I just need to see your mark first."

"My mark?" Nazere asked with a look of confusion on his face. He knew nothing of a mark. All of a sudden, all of the noise in the bar came to a sudden stand still. There was absolute silence as everyone in the bar looked at Nazere. It was as if their hearing was peaked, and they heard every single word Nazere spoke.

"Yes," the bartender began with a smug look on his face. "Your mark. Where is it?"

"I don't have one," Nazere replied. At this, all of the customers in the bar drew their swords. A certain man stepped up from out of the crowd. He was quite muscular in build, and had the tattoo of a barcode on his exposed right shoulder. His eyes spelled anger, and his clenched fists presented a clear danger.

"I smell prophet blood!" the man yelled, opening his mouth to expose two razor sharp fangs within. Everyone in the room soon began moving toward Nazere. Nazere began backing up toward the door in an attempt to get outside, but the man with the fangs beat him to the punch. He held the steel door shut with his muscular right arm. He then pulled his sword out from a sheath that hung at his waist. The man then swiped downward with great force. It was at that very moment that another blade clashed with the attacker's. Nazere looked to his side, and to his great surprise, Keldrid stood countering the man's sword with Entryu. The man with the fangs tried to lift his blade back up. The veins on his muscular biceps strained heavily, his face turning red as blood pumped throughout his body. But despite the man's greatest efforts, he was unable to free up his sword.

"Stand back," Keldrid instructed Nazere. Nazere stood as motionless as a cornered deer behind Keldrid at the entrance to the Lone Wolf Pub. With one swift motion, Keldrid cut the man with the fangs in two from the torso. The whole upper part of his body fell backward as blood covered his torso's resting place on the bar's linoleum floors. Everyone in the room immediately drew their guns, standing at the ready as they were able to see Keldrid. And all at once, the whole of the room began to open fire. Keldrid held out his right hand, and the white flares that came down like a rain of fire in his his face were collected in one radiant ball in front of him. Keldrid then pushed the ball forward, where it remained still and suspended in the air. Within three seconds, the ball exploded into multiple blasts and was repelled back upon those who had fired upon Keldrid. Everyone in the entire room fell to the floor, blood pooling up all over the ground. Keldrid then placed Entryu behind him where it disappeared into thin air. Nazere looked around the room, his eyes widened at what he had seen. Every man in the room lay dead on the floor, including the bartender who had drawn his own personal photon cannon.

"Run!" Keldrid commanded Nazere. Nazere ran out into the streets, and men from a neighboring bar who had heard the blasts in the Lone Wolf began to make their way towards it. Nazere saw them sprinting out of the corner of his left eye as he glanced behind him. As he continued to run away from the bar, he watched briefly as they all began drawing blades. And as soon as they did, Keldrid started cutting them to pieces. Keldrid's swipes were perfect, unmatched by anything Nazere had ever seen. Maintaining his focus on returning to the House of Arthur, Nazere turned his head away from the bloody scrap. Out of the blackness of the night, a man flew down and descended upon Nazere as he ran. Nazere came to a complete stop, frozen in his footsteps and overtaken by fear. The man had long blonde hair and wore a leather jacket, with tattoos covering the entirety of his body. One of the tattoos was a barcode identical to the other Nazere had seen.

"Where do you think you're going, boy?" the man asked as he hissed and exposed his fangs. "I'm going to eat you alive!" The man drew a sword from a sheath at his side. Nazere looked behind him in a panic and watched as Keldrid continued to cut down the men from the bar that was now in the distance. As he watched, he briefly witnessed Keldrid knock a man to the floor and drive Entryu through his chest with both hands as if his actions were second nature. Nazere turned back toward the man in front of him in a panic. He noticed that the man who stood in front of him had his blade in mid air about to strike down. At that moment, everything seemed to slow down to a crawl. Out of the shadows of the night, an enormous figure emerged and tackled the man with the long blonde hair to the ground before he could lash out with his attack. As Nazere glanced to his side, he noticed that the figure was Verus. Like a hungry wolf, he was tearing the man's face off with his fangs. The man attempted to move, but he was completely pinned. His only hope was to struggle to survive on the black pavement. To Nazere's continued surprise, Verus had increased his size tenfold. The dog relentlessly drove his fangs into the man's face as his hands attempted to gain control of Verus. The man cried out in agony, and Nazere sprinted forward to get out of the area. Once Nazere had made his way back to the house, he was puzzled as he tried to open the door. It was locked, and he had no way in. He had no key, and he had no password to gain access. Without any options, Nazere decided to knock. The door came open after about a minute or so of consecutive knocks.

"Nazere?" Sara asked. "What are you doing outside? Get in here!" Sara pulled Nazere into the house and shut the door behind her. "What were you doing outside?" she asked with her hands on her hips.

"I just went for a little walk," Nazere replied, trying to hide the fact that he was catching his breath. He felt as if he were about to have a heart attack.

"You can never go out after dark in these parts," Sara said. "It is far too dangerous. The citizens of this city and all of the cities of the earth carry the mark of the beast. Come inside and get downstairs."

"What is the mark of the beast?" Nazere asked before he took a step.

"It is necessary for the buying and selling of anything," Sara replied. "It can be seen on anyone in the form of a tattoo of a barcode. The barcode is scanned at any place of business. The numbers must match the number of the beast, and his number is calculated to be six-hundred and sixty-six." Nazere walked inside and began walking to the corner of the foyer. "And stay there this time!" Sara shouted as he began to descend the staircase. Nazere returned to his room, and took a paranoid look around. He still felt there was something following him. As his heart rate decreased, Nazere climbed under his red comforter and turned to get as comfortable as he could. All the action of the evening had worn him out. He thought of Keldrid and Verus as he drifted into a deep sleep.

Flash. All of a sudden, there was a great blinding light. And as Nazere came to, he noticed he was outside on the streets of Baltimore again. He looked around, and noted he was a few houses down from the House of Arthur. He began to walk down the street. "Verus!" he called out. "Keldrid! Where are you?" Nazere began to walk further down the street, and in the distance he saw smoke rising into the sky. He began to run down the roadway in front of him, and as he neared the spot of the spoke he made an alarming discovery. The House of Arthur was on fire, and the flames covered the entirety of the building. And just as Nazere was about to cry out in alarm, the image of the burning building disappeared. There was nothing but blackness and a dark void all around him. And out of the void, the face of a dragon with red skin and razor sharp fangs appeared over Nazere's body. The dragon had a long face, with spines all over it. The dragon's face was within arm's reach, and its eyes were set directly on him. "I have you now!" the dragon called out.

Nazere awoke in a deep sweat. He popped up from his bed and saw Keldrid standing in the corner of his room. He looked to the left of his bed in a fright, his dream so realistic that it made him question whether or not he was still in the middle of it; the sight before him made him calm down a bit. Verus had returned to his normal size, and was curled up with his tail near his face. The dog was twitching his eyes, sound asleep.

"Sleep well?" Keldrid asked in his usual tone of voice.

"Am I still dreaming?" Nazere asked Keldrid.

"No. You are quite awake," Keldrid replied.

"How did Verus and yourself make it back without alerting any of the ventari?"

"With the greatest of ease," Keldrid replied. "You underestimate the gravity of the circumstances you have unfurled. You should not have gone out last night."

"I apologize," Nazere replied, sweat dripping from his forehead.

"You are human," Keldrid returned in his sinister voice. "You are weak. It is to be expected. But if you are to accomplish the tasks of the Master, you must choose wisely."

"What were those creatures? And why did they look for a mark on me?"

"They were vampires," Keldrid replied. "They frequent city bars and revel in evil. They are of superhuman strength and long to drink of the blood of the prophets. They have become inhuman through their own choices. I would not advise to pursue services of any kind in any city."

"I suppose I missed a lot during my imprisonment at Ordren. So what happened last night? How did you escape? Why did I dream that the House of Arthur was burning?"

"No more questions!" Keldrid demanded. "Only know that you are safe, and it is my duty to see that you remain that way. There is a long day ahead of you. Speak nothing of what transpired. Rather, prepare your mind for what is to come." At that very moment, Elle opened the door and came walking in, wearing a pink t-shirt and jeans and carrying something in her hands. Nazere glanced at Elle for but a moment. When he looked back to the corner of the room he noticed that Keldrid had disappeared.

"Did you hear what happened last night?" Elle asked with a stern look on her face, holding something red in her right hand. Her arms were crossed.

"No," Nazere replied. "But I might have an idea."

"Over three hundred men were killed," Elle said. "They were cut to pieces and butchered in the city late last night. Sara said you went out, but she knows it wasn't you who completely obliterated them. What exactly is going on here?"

"Nothing," Nazere replied. "I just went for a walk."

"Uh huh," Elle replied with a crystal clear look of doubt upon her face. "I know there is something you aren't telling me. I just wish I could see it!" Following behind Elle, David made his entrance into the room.

"Good morning you two," he said with a smile on his face. "Did you hear what happened last night?"

"Yes," Elle began. "I was just discussing it with my dear friend here, who alleges he went out for a little stroll last night." Elle gave Nazere an angry stare.

"Three hundred vamps, ripped to pieces!" David exclaimed. "That's quite an impressive count!" Verus raised his head, sobbed, and then returned to sleeping.

"Yes," Elle began sarcastically. "It's all quite 'impressive.'"

"What time is it?" Nazere asked as he turned in his bed and placed his feet on the marble floor beneath him.

"It's time to go," David replied. "Ryan is bidding adieu to Drake downstairs. We need to get moving post-haste this morning. Hayden contacted me on my cell phone last night. We have little time to dilly-dally around." Elle nodded.

"Come on, Nazere," Elle said. "Get up and get dressed. And here," Elle said as she tossed Nazere a red t-shirt with the black outline of a lion on it. "There's a little gift from Arthur. Meet us upstairs when you are ready." It was evident that Elle wasn't enthused with Nazere's lack of communication. As Elle and David left the room, Nazere began to get changed. He took off his shirt from the day before and quickly changed into the red one. He then began walking through the workshop and upstairs to where the gathering was waiting for him.

"Good morning, chosen one," Adrax said as he greeted Nazere with a smile. He was standing next to Ryan Galeheart, David Sendrick and Elle Winstrom. In front of the entrance to the house, Arthur Nedrem, Sara Maple, Adrax Braver, Drake Winterbane and Owen Candlefire all stood together near the door. Owen approached Nazere with a hopeful look on his face.

"Good luck, my friend," he told Nazere as he gently took hold of his hand. "I hope Jentaru aids you in reaching your goal."

"Thank you for your services," Nazere replied. "It was my pleasure meeting you."

"Nazere," Drake said as he stepped up to him. "I prayed for you last night, my friend. I know you are in good company. Remember to use the scepter I gave you with the utmost care. It will be your comrade in a clinch situation." Drake smiled as Nazere shook his hand.

"It was good to meet you," Sara Maple said to Nazere. "Remember to use wisdom in all that you do. We all have faith that the Master will deliver you from the Gantor Pinnacle. Just listen to advice, okay?" Elle gave Nazere another angry gaze.

"I'll keep that in mind," Nazere replied. Adrax walked up to Nazere and put his hand on his shoulder.

"You have much to learn," Adrax began. "But I don't know the plans the Master has for you. I trust in your abilities. Just be careful out there, my friend." Adrax smiled as he withdrew his arm from Nazere's shoulder and stepped back. Finally, Arthur approached Nazere and wrapped his arms around him in a firm hug.

"The hour glass pours on," Arthur began. "It was truly an honor to have you in our household. Remember, faith is your greatest asset. Use it with wisdom and you will be delivered to safety. For if the Master is for you, who can stand against you?" Arthur smiled as he looked into Nazere's eyes. "You have all my prayers and all of my heart as you venture forth." Arthur looked around to the Gathering of the White Knight. "All of you. I know you will accomplish what the Master has set forth for you to complete." David bowed courteously before Arthur.

"Thank you, high prophet," David said, grinning cheek to cheek. "We go with the blessing of your household. And thanks for the gifts!"

"Well," Ryan began as he glanced at David. "The time has come. Does everyone have their blades?"

"Yes," Elle replied with her pink hilt jutting out of the pink sheath at her side. "We are ready."

"Very well then," Ryan continued. "It is time for us to depart, high prophet. All our best wishes. Thank you for your assistance and kindness."

"It is always a blessing to have you," Arthur replied. "God speed my brethren." And with Arthur's final words, Elle, Ryan, David and Nazere stepped outside. Arthur started to close to door. As he did, he took one last look at them and smiled. He then shut the door completely.

"Alright, babygirl!" David yelled as he walked toward the Redeemer. It was parked right where he left it in the center of the street. "Time to get this show on the road! Wings up!" The Redeemer then flapped its wings out and moved them to the upright position. David pulled out his trentorod and walked up to the circular door to the Redeemer. He then inserted it, causing the door to pop back and roll open. The Redeemer let out a loud shriek. "Everybody in!" David exclaimed.

"Roger that, wing commander," Ryan said smiling. The group walked inside and immediately took the seats they had the day before. The belt straps on each seat flew out into the air as if they were alive and strapped each one of them in. David pushed the red button next to his chair, which activated the holographic controls of the ship. David then punched a few buttons on the suspended controls in front of him. The Redeemer flapped its wings out to the flight position. "We're going to make a good running start before we take off," David said as he continued to hit points on the holographic control scheme before him. The Redeemer started moving one leg forward slowly. It then moved the other. The gradual pace of placing one talon before the other continued as the countdown timer popped up before David. And as the timer reached two seconds, the Redeemer was running full speed ahead.

"Current speed is set to three hundred and two miles per hour," the Redeemer said as it continued to accelerate. "Preparing to take flight."

"That's my girl," David said as he smiled. "How you feeling today, my beautiful?"

"Excellent as always, David," the Redeemer replied. "I do hope your stay at the House of Arthur was pleasant."

"It was, my dear," David replied as the timer hit zero. "Let's take to the air." The Redeemer began to flap its wings and fly above the many towering buildings below it. "We're going to stay inside the atmosphere this round, girly."

"Time for some music," Ryan said as he put in his earpiece.

"What is the next destination, captain?" the Redeemer asked.

"New York City, The Gantor Pinnacle," David replied. "Keep us at a medium altitude."

"Affirmative," the Redeemer replied as she continued to increase speed. Watching the display in front of David, Nazere noticed that the buildings below now appeared small like a bunch of little toy models. "Speed increased to four-hundred and fifty miles per hour. Preparing to enter the state of Pennsylvania. Our current checkpoint is Philadelphia." Nazere watched as the city below became distanced. The new view was now a cluster of small houses and structures. Elle reached out her hand and grabbed hold of Nazere's. She then leaned her head over toward his ear.

"Be careful," she whispered.

"I will be," Nazere whispered back, thankful that Elle was no longer upset with him. Elle then returned her head to its original position.

"We should be in Philadelphia in about three minutes," David said as he circled his hands in maneuvering the control plot before him. "There should be nothing but smooth sailing from here."

Far below the Redeemer on the ground, three vizedrones waited in an opening surrounded by tall rocks and trees. One vizedrone on the ground in front of the other two, its massive tail moving and eagerly awaiting action. They could sense movement in the skies as they turned their eyes upward. The Redeemer flew directly above them, fluttering its wings in the air as it passed the clearing. The foremost vizedrone raised its head as its eyes lit up a crimson shade of red. "Target acquired," the vizedrone said as it pushed down on the ground and threw itself upward. As it lifted off, its tail twirled behind it like a cyclone. The other two vizedrones behind him pushed off the ground and followed in pursuit, the ground crumbling underneath their mighty claws.

Ryan took the ear piece out of his ear and looked closely at the radar in front of him. His eyes displayed a look of sheer shock. "David!" Ryan exclaimed, almost stumbling over his word.

"What's up, Ryan?" David asked as he turned in his direction.

"Check your radar!" Ryan yelled, still looking at the image in front of him. "Do you see what I see?!"

"I'm not seeing anything," David replied.

"Is everything alright?" Nazere asked nervously.

"In the rear," Ryan said. "Three unidentified vessels moving toward our trajectory fast."

"I see them," David said as he looked deeper into his radar. "Redeemer, scan all targets within range now!" A new holographic image colored red popped up in front of David.

"Scan complete," the Redeemer said. "Three vizedrones identified within range." David began punching buttons rapidly.

"Throw up the ion shield!" David yelled. "Begin emergency evasive maneuvers!"

"Now attempting evasive maneuvers," the Redeemer replied. The Redeemer began to spin around in the sky, changing its course repeatedly in an attempt to avoid the vizedrones rapidly approaching the eagle from behind. The vizedrone in front was quickly approaching the Redeemer, its extremely long tail flailing and coiling in the air as it flew.

"The evasive maneuvers aren't working," Elle said as she leaned forward and looked at the radar in front of David.

"There's no way we can take three at one time," Ryan said as he pulled up a holographic imaging screen in front of him. "We need to send this bird into cloak, David. I'll handle the rest."

"Very well," David replied. "Let's give this a shot. Cloak the ship, Redeemer!" At David's command, the Redeemer disappeared into thin air. The vizedrone quickly approaching from behind threw its wings out to their full length, increasing its speed dramatically. It then flew to a higher altitude, its tail twirling in the sky behind it.

"Follow my lead," the front vizedrone commanded the two following him. The other vizedrones expanded their wings, increasing their speed. They trailed closely behind the leader. "We have them now!" The leading vizedrone flapped its wings violently in the air once it met a certain altitude, sending a mighty shockwave for miles.

"Alert! Damage to ion shield sustained," the Redeemer said as it embraced the impact of the enormous shockwave. The holographic image of the circle surrounding the Redeemer on the deck of the ship began to glow red.

"Keep maneuvering," David commanded. "We have to elude these monsters or we're done for." The Redeemer continued to fly in a swerving pattern, and as it did the whole of the deck shook aggressively. Elle held to Nazere's hand tightly as the entire bird vibrated. The leading vizedrone opened its nostrils, and as it did it caught the scent of the Redeemer. It flew down to the level of the Redeemer and opened its eyes fully. The eyes projected two red lasers and scanned the air the Redeemer was flying through quickly.

Nazere looked at the display in front of David and noticed large structures and skyscrapers within view. "Checkpoint: Philadelphia now reached," the Redeemer said as it continued to swing from side to side in the sky.

"Prey within range," the frontrunner vizedrone said. "Preparing to fire ethalon cannon now." The vizedrone opened its jaws to their widest point, exposing a large, black cannon within. And from the cannon a great orange light began to flare up. The vizedrone continued to hold its jaws open, and as it did, the orange light within its mouth accumulated into an orb. That orb soon consumed the whole of the contents of the vizedrone's mouth. Within the vizedrone, its computer systems had begun to take aim. Its display set its crosshairs directly on the Redeemer. And all at once, the great orb of orange light was released, the vizedrone's head thrown back in response to the kickback of the powerful shot.

"Ethalon incoming!" the Redeemer exclaimed. And as soon as it had spoken the words, the ion shield around the Redeemer fell completely. The holographic display of the Redeemer's circular ion shield disappeared. The ship went spiraling out of control, sirens echoing throughout the deck of the ship.

"The ion shields are down!" Ryan yelled out. "The cloak isn't working! We need to return fire now!" David pushed a couple of buttons on the holographic images in front of him as the ship began to stabilize.

"We're not going to make it are we?" Elle asked, her hand quivering in Nazere's.

"Chances of survival approximately twelve percent," the Redeemer replied.

"That's not very comforting," Elle said as she gripped Nazere's hand harder. A look of fear overcame Nazere as he looked at the display next to David and saw the three vizedrones flying behind the Redeemer within a not so distant proximity.

"God help us," Nazere said as he gripped the armrest to his right side. And in a wall of shadow and smoke, the dark figure that was Keldrid made an appearance beside Nazere. He placed his gray, scaly hand on Nazere's shoulder. Verus cowered and barked at the sight of Keldrid. "Keldrid!" Nazere yelled out in astonishment at his appearance.

"Who are you talking to?" Elle asked with a confused and nervous look on her face.

"No one," Nazere said, holding his tongue.

"Redeemer!" David exclaimed. "Fire a proteon defensive flare at target number one. I've marked it for you."

"Affirmative," the Redeemer replied. Out of the fantail of the Redeemer, a large cannon raised up. It then began to glow purple. And within seconds, a large orb equal in size to the ethalon ball that hit the Redeemer had accumulated. "Now firing," the Redeemer said as it released the massive purple orb. The vizedrone flying behind the Redeemer put its head down in an attempt to brace itself against the oncoming discharge. The blast came head on and hit the front of the vizedrone's circular ion shield, forcing him into a back-flip. The dragon shook its head and rallied with the other two vizedrones behind it, increasing its speed once again in pursuit of the Redeemer.

"Direct hit!" Ryan yelled out. "I'm scanning his shields." Ryan pressed a few buttons in front of him on the steel panel. "They're down!" The outline of the Redeemer came soaring across the city of Philadelphia, and the three vizedrones flocked directly behind it. All of the vizedrones locked on to the Redeemer.

"They are ours now!" the center vizedrone exclaimed. "Fire everything you've got!" All three vizedrones came to a halt over the city, throwing out their wings and sending three small shockwaves over the buildings below. They then began to open their jaws in preparation of orange ethalon blasts.

"We're going to have to go one on one with the center vizedrone," David said. "Redeemer! Turn us around!"

"What?" Elle asked nervously, pointing at the display with her left hand repeatedly. "The vizedrones are preparing to fire on us!"

"I'm going to drop the left and right ones," Ryan said to Elle. "I have to hold the other two back if we have any chance to survive. David, you have to keep this thing moving!"

"I've got it," David replied, hastily pressing buttons on the Redeemer's control scheme. Ryan closed his eyes and kneeled his head.

"Aaaahhhh!" Ryan screamed. The left and right vizedrones were driven down by Ryan's empowered focus. They were shoved forcefully backward and fell to the city below. A pedestrian on the streets below looked up into the sky and screamed as he saw the vizedrones dropping straight down over top of him like a couple of enormous boulders.

"Incoming!" the pedestrian yelled. People on the streets screamed and scattered in all directions. The vizedrones came crashing down, temporarily immobilized by Ryan's dominating abilities. As they fell, they cascaded down the sides of two separate buildings. One hit a building on the right of the street, and the other hit a skyscraper on the left. Glass shattered and dust flew through the air in a million little particles. Concrete was eradicated, and several vehicles flying high in the city were slammed. The entire area below was crushed by the twin vizedrones' epic fall.

"Hold them Ryan!" Elle yelled.

"Aaaahhhh!" Ryan continued to cry out. "I can only hold them for so long!" The Redeemer came full circle, flying directly at the vizedrone that remained. The vizedrone's cannon was beginning to flare up, growing as every moment passed.

"Engage the storm-boosters, Redeemer!" David yelled out. The Redeemer opened two jet engines under each wing. The engines began to expel fire, the exhaust glowing a neon shade of green. "We're about to hit it!" David yelled out. "Go now!" The vizedrone's blast was at full charge, and just as it released it the Redeemer blinked past the vizedrone and screeched as it flew out of range of the blast. The great charge from the vizedrone flew into the distance and detonated into an explosion twenty times the size of the initial flare. The two vizedrones on the ground attempted to get on their feet but were knocked back down every time they tried to do so by Ryan's continued control over them. They struggled to move their wings, but every time they would lift one it would fall back down to the street, crumbling the ground beneath it.

Coming full circle again, the Redeemer set its sights on the back of the vizedrone still posing in place in the blue sky. Inside of the Redeemer, David set the ship's crosshairs on the vizedrone.

"Brace for impact!" David yelled out. The Redeemer lengthened her talons to five times their normal size, the edge of each talon sparkling in the light of the sun. With everyone's eyes set on the display, the Redeemer flew directly into the vizedrone. The vizedrone flipped around, the two becoming intertwined in a ball in the air. Sparks flew everywhere as the Redeemer and the vizedrone tore at each other's outer hull. The two interlocked vessels rose higher in the air as they attempted to gain an advantage in pinning the other down. The vizedrone withdrew its tail from the twirling ball, and out of the tail came a long, artolium blade. The vizedrone then began to swipe at the wings of the Redeemer like a scorpion, penetrating the bird's wings and leaving holes throughout it.

"We can't take too much more of this," David said as he looked at the diagram of the Redeemer spinning to his left. The diagram displayed red marks all over both of the Redeemer's wings as sirens continued to sound throughout the deck of the ship. The two beasts continued to spin and rend and tear at each other. The Redeemer drove its razor-sharp talons through the hull of the vizedrone again and again, sustaining additional damage from the dragon's wicked tail. After repeatedly scratching at the dragon's face, the Redeemer finally drove the vizedrone underneath of her.

"We need to fire now!" Elle yelled. "Hit it, David!"

"Redeemer," David began calmly. "Fire your ethalon cannon now!" Nazere engaged his vision in at the diplay as the Redeemer set its crosshairs on the vizedrone's head. The Redeemer opened its beak and exposed its own ethalon cannon within. As the cannon began to charge, the vizedrone struggled to open its mouth. But the Redeemer's talons kept the vizedrone's mouth shut tightly. Within seconds, the Redeemer had a fully readied white ethalon flare. And as the two span around in the air like two fighting cats, the Redeemer let the fully prepared charge loose on the vizedrone's face. There was a great explosion, the Redeemer flocking upward as a result of the aftermath. It opened its wings, and as it did the vizedrone that was intertwined with it went plummeting to the ground below.

"Target neutralized," the Redeemer reported.

"Aaaahhhh!" Ryan yelled. "I can't hold both of them anymore! I need to let one go!" Keldrid looked down at the display as one of the vizedrones freed its wings. The dragon balanced itself on its feet and rocketed up in the air at full speed. The vizedrone then spread its wings to full length. The Redeemer stood hovering in the air directly across from the vizedrone. It then spread its wings to their full length, revealing a sharp blade at the end of each feather.

"Round two," David began. "I don't know how much more the Redeemer can take before we fall." David hit a few buttons on the control panel. "Fire now, Redeemer!" Face to face in the air, the Redeemer and the vizedrone began to amass the ethalon charges from their mouths simultaneously. When the two released their blasts, there was a great light in the space between the two of them. The discharges had exploded, neutralizing each other. "Fire again!" David yelled. The vizedrone across from the Redeemer began to prepare a second charge, its mouth lighting up with orange fury.

"Preemptive fire commencing," the Redeemer said as it fired an early shot. The ball hit the vizedrone's ion shield, causing a tremendous detonation that shoved the vizedrone backward and warded off its attempt to fire.

"Its ion shield is down," Elle said as she eagerly watched the display next to David. "We need to wrestle it down! It's our only chance."

"Redeemer," David began. "Fly full force ahead and drive that beast into the ground!" The Redeemer let out a great screech and began zooming forward at an uncanny speed. As soon as it collided with the vizedrone, it curled its wings and leeched them into the head of the vizedrone. The vizedrone's eyes closed and its body became inanimate as its internal processors were destroyed. But as it slowly began to fall to the ground, the vizedrone's tail whipped upwards and hit the Redeemer in the chest.

Inside of the Redeemer, the spike of the tail was driven through the deck behind Elle's chair. It appeared as a silver thorn in the heart of the Redeemer. The spike held for about two seconds and then retracted. The vizedrone plummeted onto the center of a tall building below it. Tier by tier, the building collapsed under the weight of the immense vizedrone. A great cloud of smoke and fire amidst a cluster of rubble was all that remained of the building after the fallen vizedrone dropped upon it.

"Target neutralized," the Redeemer reported. "Weapon systems are now offline."

"Damn it!" David yelled as he looked at the wounded holographic image of the Redeemer. It flickered in and out due to the extensive damage done to the bird. "There's no way we can do anything to resist the next one." David turned to Nazere with a look of sympathy in his eyes. "I apologize, Nazere. I have failed you."

"And I can't hold the last one any longer," Ryan said, exhaling as he opened his eyes and looked up. The vizedrone propelled itself up into the sky like a phoenix rising from the ashes, its wings springing outward and its wide jaws opening up. Keldrid looked down at the display again.

"We're a sitting duck," Ryan said as he hit the steel panel in front of him in frustration. "So much for making it to New York."

"Take faith," Elle said as she watched the display nervously. "It isn't meant to end here." The vizedrone's opened mouth had a great orange charge that had already begun to swirl violently from within it. The charge grew greater and greater, until at last it was full-fledged.

"Can we maneuver around it?" David asked the Redeemer.

"All flight mechanics have been disrupted, captain," the Redeemer replied.

"So that's a no I suppose?" Elle asked.

"Yes," David replied, sighing. "There's nothing we can do." Verus whimpered as if he knew what was occurring all around him. Nazere looked to his side where Keldrid stood staring at the display. Keldrid lifted his hand from Nazere's shoulder. He then drew his right hand out, exposing his gray skin and his long, black fingernails. He placed his hands evenly in front of his chest, positioning the two parallel to one another. He held that position for a moment. A thousand racing thoughts were flying through Nazere's head as he switched his eyes' focus between the display and Keldrid. It seemed unavoidable; the charge was at its full capacity. The vizedrone fired the great ethalon blast it had charged at the Redeemer, and as the bright orange light approached the ship everyone onboard closed their eyes. Keldrid then clapped his palms together. He held that position tightly. Directly in front of the Redeemer, the ethalon blast came to a miraculous and instantaneous halt. The light from the blast blinded everyone on the Redeemer, but David opened his right eye momentarily to see what had happened.

"How is that possible?" David asked with a puzzled look on his face. "The blast has stopped dead in its tracks."

"There is hope yet," Nazere said, opening his eyes and smiling. Keldrid then opened his hands widely, spreading his arms out fully and positioning his extended fingers at shoulder height. The ethalon blast slowly began to be driven backward in the direction of the vizedrone. Keldrid held his stance perfectly, as if he were an immovable object. There was a good eighty yards between the Redeemer and the vizedrone. The vizedrone in front of the Redeemer struggled to move, flailing its tail around like a fish that had just been caught. Keldrid closed his fingers, and the vizedrone's jaws were yanked apart as if someone were pulling them open. As the complications piled up for the dragon, the vizedrone now struggled to close its mouth and move out of its position. The blast slowly moved toward the captured vessel. It floated like a bubble through the air until it finally stopped, suspended several feet in front of the vizedrone. Keldrid then clapped his hands together, and there was a great outburst of lightning across a cloudless sky. Everyone onboard the Redeemer watched in awe as the bolt subsided and the orb of concentrated particles sat motionlessly before the dragon. And like a ball being tossed into a basket, the sphere of ethalon dove into the vizedrone's mouth. The vizedrone thrashed around for a moment as its face lit up like the tip of a candle. And all of a sudden, the vizedrone's head exploded, sending molten fragments of its face into a thousand different directions.

"What just happened?" Ryan asked, his eyes sealed to the display. "I have never seen anything like that occur before." David stared at the display with a look of shock and awe on his face. Elle clapped and cheered for a moment. She then returned to holding Nazere‘s hand, rubbing Nazere‘s hand gently with her thumb. What remained of the vizedrone fell directly in the middle of the street, collapsing in a cloud of sparks and ashes.

"Thank the Master!" she cried out as she attempted to stand up out of her seat in excitement. "We're safe after all! Take that you stupid vizedrones!"

"A miracle," Nazere said as he turned to Keldrid. His hood no longer facing the display, Keldrid dropped his hands to his side. The Redeemer hovered in the sky, with exposed holes in all sides of the eagle's wings. As it hovered, it retracted the neon green jets from its wings.

"The Redeemer needs repairs," David began. "We're going to need to land it here."

"We'll be delayed if we do that," Ryan replied. "We need to get to New York City immediately!"

"We can't risk another vizedrone attack," David said. Keldrid slowly leaned his hood down to Nazere's ear.

"Tell him there will not be another attack," Keldrid whispered to

Nazere. Verus barked at Keldrid again.

"What is your dog barking at?" Elle asked Nazere.

"Don't land the ship," Nazere said, looking to David. "I'm sure there will not be another attack."

"How can you be so sure?" David asked.

"Trust me," Nazere replied. David looked at Nazere for a moment in quiet contemplation.

"Redeemer," David began.

"Yes, captain?" the Redeemer replied.

"Get us to New York City. We have a suit of armor to retrieve." David turned and nodded in Nazere's direction.

"Very well, captain," the Redeemer replied. "Setting the primary destination to the Gantor Pinnacle now."

"I do hope you're right, Nazere," Ryan said, putting his earpiece back in his ear. "I've got a migraine." The Redeemer flapped its wings and floated around in a circle, redirecting itself in the direction of New York City.

"Increasing speed now," the Redeemer said. The Redeemer released a loud outcry as it began to fly swiftly forward. As the great eagle flew through the skies, Nazere watched as the smoking city below him gradually faded out of sight. After only a few minutes of flight, the Redeemer was within range of New York City. The myriad of distant lights came up on the display, and when they did Keldrid pointed.

"Tell them to park it there," Keldrid whispered in Nazere's ear.

"Where is that?" Nazere asked quietly. Keldrid paused for a moment as the bird came flying closer into the city. Below, sky touching buildings highlighted the constellated metropolis. Directly underneath him, Nazere's eyes caught a generous glimpse of the enormous target he was aimed to enter. The display was overtaken with the view of a monstrous silver pyramid that reached to the clouds. It was surrounded by exactly six sterling silver spines that were evenly spaced around its perimeter in perfect parallel. The spines reached to the very tip of the silver pinnacle. The Gantor Pinnacle towered over every other building in the city, the innumerable lights on the side of the structure causing the wonder to refract like a diamond in the sunlight. The Redeemer flew around the Statue of Liberty in a loop, flapping its wings in the air as it circled the outside of the city. The once great iron statue had been completely defaced by the High Lord Alune's seemingly omnipresent empire. The statue was completely intact except for the face. The face was scratched and marred to the point that it was unrecognizable. It appeared to be a freak against a backdrop of unadulterated works of architectural art. To the right of the Redeemer, a rectangular tower stood parallel to the Gantor Pinnacle.

"There," Keldrid said as he pointed to the tower. "Tell them to land the Redeemer there."

"David," Nazere began, following Keldrid's instructions. "Land the Redeemer on that tower over there." Nazere pointed to the tower, which was constructed of black glass with an artolium frame.

"Are you kidding me?" David asked with his mouth gaping open in question. "That is the Contemptys Tower! That is only the most unsafe place in the city to land."

"Do it," Elle told David. "I trust Nazere's judgment." David hesitated as the Redeemer circled around the Contemptys Tower.

"Alright," David replied, nodding in agreement. "Redeemer, take us down on the Contemptys Tower. We'll complete our repairs there."

"Affirmative, captain," the Redeemer said. "Initiating landing sequence in three… two… one." The Redeemer swept down and landed on the barren, stone surface of the tower, closing its wings behind it when it landed. Nazere noticed a bridge connecting the tower with one of the metal spines that was erected around the immense pinnacle. David took in a deep breath of fresh air.

"Okay," David began. "Here we are. My monitors are picking up about a thousand phantoms, but for some reason they aren't pursuing us. Strange." Ryan reached into his pocket and pulled out a small, red, triangular disk. The disk was reflective, appearing to have a high-gloss plastic covering.

"I have the plans ready," Ryan began. "We're fully prepared to go forward with the operation."

"Redeemer," David started. "Begin your shell repairs now." There were a number of beeps within the deck of the Redeemer. Everyone's ribbon belts came flying off, and the ribbons retracted into their slots behind each seat.

"Deploying atrons," the Redeemer said.

"Wings up!" David yelled. The Redeemer threw its wings to their upright position. "Open the doors," David said as he took a stand. The door to the Redeemer pushed inward and came rolling open. Everyone then made their exit from the eagle. Standing outside, Nazere looked on curiously as a hundred little pod-shaped robots with four legs climbed all over the Redeemer. Each one was painted a shade of light-blue and shot a dark blue laser at an exposed area, repairing the damage done to the Redeemer instantly. The sky was turning an amber hue as the sun was about to set, and the wind blew fiercely on the rooftop of the Contemptys Tower. "We'll hold the fort down," David said as he put his arm on Ryan's shoulder. "You three be careful out there. That includes you, Verus." Verus remained close to Nazere's side, as did Keldrid.

"Good luck, Nazere," Elle said as she reached out and gave him a hug. "When you come back, you won't be the same as you are now. It'll be a whole new you." A tear began to well in Elle's eye, her left hand wiping it away as she smiled over her emotion.

"Yeah," Nazere replied slowly, an inflection in his voice. "A whole new me." Ryan turned to Nazere and smiled.

"Do you have your weapons ready, Nazere?" Ryan asked.

"Both of them," Nazere replied, smiling back as he tried not to think about the unforseeable change that was about to confront him.

"Then we're ready," Ryan said. "Keep the Redeemer cloaked, David. The time has come for the beginning of the end. We can take the bridge over to one of the spires. From there, we'll have to work our way down to the center of the complex." Ryan held the red, triangular disk out in his palm. "Show us the routes," Ryan commanded. The disk projected a holographic image above it, showing the basic floor plans of the tower they were standing on. Ryan looked at Nazere for a moment and then shut off the holographic image by pushing a button on the side of the disk. “Wherever we may be, this disk has the potential to serve as an entry route should we need one. We need to take the utmost care in whatever we do. Our first step is entering the bridge straight ahead.” About twenty yards from where they were standing there was the opening for the bridge to the first spire. The bridge was rectangular, with an onyx exterior. A reflection of the long road to come for Nazere, the bridge was at least one thousand yards in length. “Let’s go,” Ryan said, walking toward the opening in the bridge.

“Goodbye, Elle,” Nazere said as he began to follow behind Ryan.

“It isn’t goodbye!” Elle yelled as Nazere began to walk away. “It’s hello to a new beginning!” Elle paused for a moment. “And Nazere!“ she yelled. Nazere glanced back. “You’ll be right here!“ Elle smiled as she pointed to her heart. Nazere smiled back at Elle, forming his two hands into the shape of a heart in reply. He then turned his face toward the bridge. And together, Ryan and Nazere walked toward the bridge. When they finally reached it, a dark tunnel illuminated by blue light-emitting diodes on the ceiling unveiled the long stretch ahead of them.

CHAPTER THREE

Infiltrating the Core

The bridge of the Contemptys Tower had an eerie silence about it, the side walls of the bridge consisting of large tanks that cascaded down to the very end of the tunnel. Bubbles rising from the tanks, the water had a neon-blue glow to it. Inside of the tanks, creatures that greatly resembled bats meandered about in the water. Amongst the animals were human skeletons. The skeletons floated freely in the water, deprived of all of the flesh on their bodies. These bat-like creatures within the tanks had an extra long gray dorsal fin, perhaps three times the length of a dolphin's. These bats were abnormally muscular, with an immense wingspan. They also had four eyes on either side of their face and a razor sharp horn on the top of their heads. As they swam around in their tanks, bolts of electricity would arc across the bubbling water. Verus looked up and whimpered at the very sight of them. They span around in the water as if they were performing for their guests. They seemed to be aware that Nazere, Verus and Ryan were walking across the bridge as they locked their many eyes on them. These bats were far from blind.

The ground beneath Nazere's feet was made of steel and colored an ocean blue, and there were flags hanging from the ceiling. The ceilings' flags were black, and bore the red emblem of a dragon's head breathing flame on them. The flags hung by the hundreds all the way down the bridge into the distance. As Nazere and Ryan advanced forward down the tunnel, they turned to notice living humans were being dropped into the water from a space above the bridge periodically. What is dropping the humans in? Nazere wondered. The creatures would swarm around the humans dropped in the water and devour them immediately upon their being tossed into the water. They would take initial bites, and then rend and tear at any remaining flesh on the body. A horrific sight, Nazere kept his eyes straight ahead of him. In the far distance, a studded-iron black door with bone spikes surrounding its perimeter and a large bone skull on its surface marked the entrance to the first spire.

"Disgusting abominations," Ryan commented at the creatures in the tanks.

"What are those creatures?" Nazere asked Ryan, fascinated as he glanced to his right and watched them move about in the water once they had finished their feeding.

"Those are stormdivers," Ryan replied, a slight look of fear in his eyes. "They are incredibly agile. They are able to move swiftly in the water, on land and especially in the air. They are the workings of Vice Lord Xar's research at the former National Aquarium in Baltimore."

Nazere, Keldrid and Ryan walked all the way down the long bridge to the large black door, Verus following right along. Ryan pushed the skull forward, and the skull popped out toward Ryan. The eyes of the skull then began to gleam red. A loud creaking sound echoed in the halls of the bridge as the door to the spire came swinging open. Ryan reached into his pocket and pulled out what appeared to be three large bracelets. One of the bracelets was colored green, one brown, and the other blue. Ryan took the green one and put it over his head, where it settled near his neck and immediately fastened to it. The bracelets were in fact collars. He held out the blue and brown collars with his right arm and handed them to Nazere.

"Take this before we go on," Ryan instructed Nazere. "The brown one is for your pup. It is a cloaking device. We need to remain hidden while we are in the spire. There are sentinels and bloodguards everywhere inside." Nazere took the over-sized collar and placed it around his neck, where it fastened tightly.

"Sit, Verus," Nazere instructed his dog. Verus walked up to Nazere and sat down before him. Nazere then took the brown collar and fastened it around Verus' neck.

"Hey," Nazere began as he smiled and looked up at Ryan. "I can still see you."

"That is the trick with these little trinkets. No one else can see us, but we can see each other. They also silence your footsteps and voice. The one catch is that certain enemies are able to see through the cloak. Once a dreadhunter or stormdiver has set its eyes on you, it is able to track you wherever you may go and alert nearby sentry men." Ryan walked through the door and looked both ways cautiously. Nazere, Verus and Keldrid followed close behind. Inside of the spire, there was a winding pathway that led to a circular platform three miles below them. There was a long neon-blue banister that accompanied the pathway that led to the bottom platform. On the various levels of the spire, Nazere noticed bloodguards on watchful patrol. Each bloodguard carried a photon cannon that was colored red and silver. Far below them, on the bottom level, Nazere could vaguely make out the large outlines of sentinels also on patrol. Their silver faces moved from side to side as they stood watch against outsiders.

Nazere realized that this was not the simulation he had encountered at the House of Arthur. This was tangible reality. He had dealt with quite a few bloodguards in the city of Baltimore, and had witnessed their entirely merciless nature time and again. Once anyone had violated the law, the bloodguard was the executioner that immediately awaited them if a ventari wasn't there to intervene. And their tactics in bringing death were both brutal and barbaric, the slain cut to pieces by the bloodguards' hand-blades and left to rot in the middle of the streets. Of course, there was no recourse for this form of vicious law-enforcement from a blinded society of equally corrupt politicians and bureaucrats. The value for human life had become only as good as its economic status. Through the experiences of his life on the street, Nazere had witnessed the perversion of minds gone wrong and captured a portrait of the unseen harvest that mankind had sown for himself without even knowing it. Even he could smell the winepress of wrath slowly drift into the air without the need for the repeated sight of man's folly. All of mankind's darkest ideations had become a legal reality, the fiction of yesteryear transforming into the haunting actuality of the current day through furtherances of science and technology. The bloodguards were only a part of what he remembered. And although he wanted to spit the memories of the gross perversion of society out of his head, the realities he now faced had in truth become all too typical to him over time. Every witnessed instance of death on the streets was just a part of yet another day. And although he always wanted to, there was never anything he could do to stop the silent killings. He only had the power to do his best in avoiding becoming one of them.

There were over one-hundred bloodguards patrolling the vast length of the staircase. The spiral led upward, but the entrance to the Gantor Pinnacle could be clearly seen far below. Ryan, Nazere, Verus and Keldrid moved in the direction of the platform on the lowest level. There, the emblem of a giant black skull encompassed nearly the whole of the floor. A giant, glowing red ring surrounded the skull in a wide circle. To the far right of the platform at the bottom of the seemingly unending staircase, a door with twenty steel blades protruding from its dreadful face marked the group's target destination. On the surface of the giant steel door, there was the solid imprint of a black arrow being driven through the black outline of a human head. The door as a whole seemed to scream "Keep out" through such a simple illustration.

"We have to walk very carefully," Ryan said. "If we happen to bump into any one of these bloodguards, we're going to have a heavy fight on our hands."

"How do you suppose we sneak by them?" Nazere asked. Ryan pulled yet another small trinket from his pocket. It was a thin, oval shaped electronic device that was no larger than a quarter. It was colored black with a purple-lit dot in the center of it.

"This is an attenurant," Ryan began. "I'm going to give you five for now. I have a couple on me. One throw at the ground and the bloodguards will be immobilized. The attenurant immobilizes all enemies within a five-hundred yard radius for about three seconds, which should be enough time to make it past a bloodguard without alerting any others. They don't remember anything after one has taken affect over them either. Remember that these devices are rare! Use them wisely! And unfortunately, sentinels are immune to attenurants. Don't bother trying to toss one toward them." Ryan handed Nazere his five attenurants and began to advance down the winding pathway. Together, the group of four walked about thirty yards before they were within range of the first bloodguard. The soldier blocked the pathway, and was walking in the same direction that the group was.

"Alright," Ryan began. "Just keep walking behind him. The plan is to get to the bottom of the pathway without attracting any attention from these bloodguards. We can finish off the sentinels at the bottom and high tail it out of here if we're wise."

"What about the alarms?" Nazere asked as he continued to walk forward.

"I have one attenurant that lasts for about two hours. The problem is that I don't have a battery to power it. I'm going to have to cut one out of a sentinel and attach it to the attenurant before giving it a toss. That should hold all of the bloodguards in this spire in place." As soon as Ryan had completed explaining his strategy, the bloodguard ahead of the group began to turn around.

"Alright," Ryan began. "This is…" Nazere tossed an attenurant at the feet of the bloodguard. The attenurant blinked in a small flash of light as it hit the floor. The bloodguard stopped dead in his tracks, one leg locked in the air as he was in mid-stride. "Okay, then," Ryan began as he looked at the bloodguard. "Run!" Together, the group hurried past the bloodguard by means of a sprint and continued to advance down the pathway. Keldrid moved to the rest of the group's position by means of smoke and shadow, weaving past the bloodguard and reappearing by Nazere's side. "We made it," Ryan said, leaning over with his hands on his knees and panting from his first, heavy sprint. "I guess that's all that matters. Now we just rinse and repeat." Ryan noticed yet another bloodguard walking toward them. "I've got this one," Ryan said as he tossed an attenurant at the feet of the bloodguard.

"Nice toss," Nazere commented as he sprinted past the bloodguard. Verus barked as he ran beside his master.

"Thanks," Ryan said after reaching a secure location on the staircase. "I try." Again, Keldrid smoothly weaved around the bloodguard in a stream of black shadows and smoke. Nazere glanced back and noticed that the first bloodguard that had been stunned had continued walking as if nothing had happened.

"This is working pretty effectively," Nazere said as he smiled. "I think we'll be at the bottom of the spire in no time."

"Maybe so," Ryan said as he continued to walk forward slowly. "But it's best to take your time when you're doing this sort of thing. We don't want to risk any harm." The group continued to walk about fifty yards until they were confronted by yet another bloodguard. This one was walking quickly in the direction of the group.

"This one's mine," Nazere said. "Are you ready, Ryan?"

"On your mark," Ryan replied.

"Get set," Nazere said as he looked at Ryan and smiled. "Go!" Nazere tossed the attenurant at the feet of the bloodguard. The group raced past the bloodguard, Keldrid streaming behind them. The bloodguard stood immobilized, stuck in place like an insect caught in a spider's web.

"Good show," Ryan said, leaning over after sprinting twenty yards past the bloodguard.

"I try," Nazere smirked as he too leaned over. "Let's keep walking." Nazere took a few steps forward when, all of a sudden, Verus began growling. Nazere glanced down at Verus with a look of deep concern. "What's wrong boy?" Verus' eyes were set to the wall, and he began barking at the sight before him. When Ryan glanced up, his eyes widened and his demeanor came full circle.

"Dreadhunter!" Ryan exclaimed. Nazere looked up, and crawling on the wall was a fierce looking dreadhunter with its fangs fully exposed. It began to growl as soon as soon as Nazere set his eyes upon it. "Jump!" Ryan yelled anxiously as he climbed up on the balcony.

"Straight to the floor!" Nazere didn't hesitate. He climbed up on the balcony beside Ryan. Verus jumped up with them, glancing back at the dreadhunter and taunting it with fangs and growls. "Go now!" Ryan yelled. Together, Ryan, Nazere and Verus jumped off the balcony and into the center of the air. Bloodguards on all levels began opening fire as soon as they made the plunge. The fire continually missed Ryan, Nazere and Verus as they dived down parallel to one another in the direction of the center of the floor.

"Draw your blade as soon as you hit the floor!" Ryan exclaimed while in mid air, his heart beating in his chest like a thousand drums in unison. "We have to get the battery and toss the attenurant before they sound the alarm!" Verus, Nazere and Ryan tumbled across the floor once they hit it, their ion shields flickering and saving them from what would have been certain death. Keldrid weaved his way down to the center of the room, where he drew Entryu from behind his back and stood at the ready. The dreadhunter dived right behind them, landing upright on the floor with the utmost agility. Ryan rolled across the room, stopping directly in front of the poised dreadhunter. Looking up, the dreadhunter snarled in Ryan's face. Crouching in the pounce position, the dreadhunter prepared to attack. And just as it was about to ambush Ryan, Verus sprang upon the dreadhunter from the side. The two animals went rolling into the corner of the room, where a sentinel looked down upon Verus and began to target him. The sentinel put his hand to the side of his amber-colored head and activated a heat seeking yellow laser.

"Canine target acquired," the sentinel said as it extended its arm in the air, prepared to smash Verus with his devastating fist. While the dreadhunter was pinned to the floor, Verus proceeded to increase his size tenfold. Nazere was at the opposite end of the room, directly in front of two sentinels. They both lifted their arms to the sides of their heads and activated their heat seeking lasers. Just as the sentinel in front of Verus was about to annihilate him with a downward thrust, Ryan jumped to his feet. He darted over to the sentinel and raised his sword over Verus' body in his defense. The sword hurled out green sparks as the sentinel's furious fist met it head on.

On the opposite end of the room, Nazere gathered himself together on the floor. He quickly jumped to his feet and gripped the hilt to the sword within the sheath at his side. As soon as he withdrew it, the blade took on a bright blue essence. A sentinel was directly above Nazere, with a second one directly behind him. As the sentinel attempted to pound Nazere, he raised his blade in order to fend off the heavy blow. The blue blade blocked the attack, and sparks flew in all directions. But as soon as Nazere had blocked the first attack, the second sentinel had raised his fist. "I need a little help over here!" Nazere yelled out with a tone of panic in his voice. Keldrid turned his hood in Nazere's direction, watching as he stood in the middle of two gigantic sentinels. Ryan twirled his blade around, freeing it from the hand of the sentinel that stood over Verus. Taking advantage of the opportunity, Ryan stabbed the sentinel directly in the face with his sword. The sentinel grabbed its face with its hands and came crashing to its knees. It then collapsed, a loud smacking noise reverberating through the air as its heavy body hit the ground. Ryan glanced up and noticed that bloodhunters on all levels were sprinting toward the bottom of the spire. He then quickly drove his blade into the heart of the fallen sentinel, cutting a hole in a circular fashion. The green gunblade seemed to have a great deal of ionic potency to it as the cut seared the metal around the circumference of the hole.

"I'm a little preoccupied over here!" Ryan yelled in reply. "Do your best to hold them back!" Verus struggled next to Ryan to pin the ruthless dreadhunter to the floor, but fire from above began to hit Verus in the back. Yelping in pain, Verus rolled off to the side, letting the dreadhunter take the upper hand. Once on top, the dreadhunter increased its own size tenfold to overcome Verus' resistance. Ryan reached down into the sentinel's center and pulled off the amber shell that had sunken into the hole in its chest. He then began to cut a series of wires that were attached to the round portion of exoskeleton he had retrieved. "I only need a few seconds, Nazere!"

The second sentinel on Nazere's end of the room drove his hand down to attack. Nazere quickly blocked the strike with his blue sword by swinging it from one sentinel's hand to the other. Nazere then pulled up on his sword and twirled it around to the striking position. The first sentinel put both of his fists behind his head, and as he did, Nazere drove his blade into the dead center of his face. The smitten sentinel swung blindly, and Nazere dodged his miscalculated attack as the sentinel came crashing to his knees. As the second sentinel raised both of his hands, Nazere drew his scepter. The sentinel's arms came thundering down in unison, and as Nazere blocked the hand blows with his sword, he struck the sentinel in the chest with the end of his scepter. A ball of electricity consumed the sentinel's frame, and the blitzed sentinel dropped to its knees. Taking advantage of the opportunity, Nazere drove his sword through the center of the sentinel's silver face. Both sentinels collapsed on their chests simultaneously, generating an ear-shattering, smacking noise. Nazere then returned his scepter to its sheath at his hip.

Once the wires were severed, Ryan held his hand above the opening in the sentinel's shell and pulled its inner battery out by utilizing his limited power to move objects. Ryan hastened to find the long acting attenurant in his pocket. In the mean time, the dreadhunter was clawing and biting at Verus as he was pinned to the floor. Verus barked and growled at the dreadhunter's relentless attacks. Yet another sentinel stepped up to Ryan from behind him. Unable to find the attenurant in time, Ryan was forced to engage in combat with the machine. He whirled his blade around and struck at the weakest part of the machine, driving the edge of the gunblade into the sentinel's face.

On the other side of the room, the first bloodguard had reached the ground floor. Nazere looked off to his right and noticed an alarm behind a plastic cube to the right of the enormous bladed door. The bloodguard ran to the alarm, and Nazere sprinted fearlessly in an attempt to intercept him. Noticing Nazere, the bloodguard raised his photon cannon. "Stand back!" the bloodguard yelled out to Nazere. Ignoring his commands, Nazere ran full speed at the bloodguard. The bloodguard fired his weapon and Nazere pushed the blast off to the side with his right hand as it didn't faze his ion shielding. Nazere only saw the memories of the bloodguards he had seen in the city, knowing that this guard was no different. There was passion in his footsteps as he sprinted forward, the faces of the dead a constant reminder of what these soulless humans were capable of. As the bloodguard fired a second round, Nazere collided with the bloodguard, tackling him to the floor. In the process of doing so, he threw out all five attenurants at an oncoming wave of eight bloodguards who had reached the bottom of the staircase.

"Now would be a good time for the two-hour attenurant!" Nazere yelled as he lunged his sword into the heart of the bloodguard beneath him, knowing he had but three seconds before the guards would reawaken.

Finishing the sentinel before him, Ryan returned to his task of finding the long-acting attenurant in his pocket. Sheathing his blade behind him, he reached inside his jacket and began searching with both of his hands. "Oh, where is this thing?!" Ryan yelled out in frustration. He continued to reach around, desperately searching for its location in his jacket. After much searching, he finally pulled it out of his right pocket. Taking the cartridge shaped battery in one hand and the attenurant in the other, he clicked the two together. The eight bloodguards on the ground began to charge Nazere with their hand-blades fully extended, his eyes widening as they neared his location over the dead bloodguard he had just finished. There was a great white blink that came from the cartridge colliding with the attenurant in Ryan's hands. Verus yelped as he was sustaining bite after bite from the dreadhunter on the ground, blood covering the floor under the dog in a small pool. "I've got it!" Ryan yelled as he threw the attenurant on the floor. And all at once, every bloodguard in the room became paralyzed in their tracks. The eight who had reached the bottom of the stairs were only inches from Nazere when it happened.

"Good work!" Nazere yelled as he glanced over at the spark of the long-acting attenurant on the floor. His blue sword was positioned toward the frozen bloodguards in front of him.

Ryan pulled out his gunblade and immediately took aim. He then began firing at the dreadhunter ripping at Verus. The automatic fire of photon bolts didn't even faze its skin. The dreadhunter continued to violently maul Verus on the ground, the panther thrashing around in a desperate attempt to make the kill. With his imminent threats now paralyzed or dead, Nazere glanced to his side and locked his eyes on the dreadhunter that was on top of Verus. Remembering what Adrax had taught him, Nazere sprinted toward the dreadhunter at the other end of the room, his blue sword glowing brilliantly in his right arm.

"Ryan!" Nazere yelled. "Pick that dreadhunter up!" Ryan held his hand in the air and closed his eyes.

"Aaaahhhh!" Ryan screamed. The dreadhunter then began to lift off of Verus, its claws tearing additional skin from the dog as they were slowly pulled into the air. Verus lay on the ground motionless, blood now covering him completely. The dreadhunter struggled as it was picked up into the air completely, the panther growling and swiping its enormous paws in pure angst as it attempted to finish Verus. Nazere walked up to the mutant beast with his blue blade out in front of him. The panther then began to swipe at Nazere, but the dreadhunter's attacks were out of range.

"I can't hold him much longer, Nazere!" Ryan yelled. "Aaaahhhh!" Throwing his arms to his side, Nazere pulled his sword back in exacting preparation to strike. And in one quick motion he catapulted the blade into the dreadhunter's chest. The dreadhunter's pupils dilated as it dropped its arms and legs, its body still in suspension. Nazere withdrew his sword when the deed was done. Ryan then dropped the dreadhunter to the floor, where it lay in a pool of its own blood. Nazere immediately turned his attention to Verus, who was whimpering on the floor in pain from a multitude of exposed wounds. He then knelt down and touched his hand to Verus' fur, two of his fingers dripping of the German shepherd's blood. Verus then began to slowly close his eyes.

"No!" Nazere yelled, looking hopelessly at his companion. "Verus!" Nazere turned his neck and moved his eyes in Ryan's direction. "Ryan! He is dying!" Ryan ran up to where Nazere knelt next to Verus. Ryan dropped to a knee and set his gunblade on the black skull-imprinted ground. He then reached into his pocket and pulled out a clear plastic vial filled with a very small amount of neon green fluid. The vial had a silver cap on it in the shape of a knight's chess piece. Ryan removed the cap, revealing a blotter underneath. He then pried open Verus' right eyelid with his left hand and kept it open with his right hand. He landed a single drop of the green fluid in Verus' eye.

"Kazium," Ryan began in a soft voice. "They call it Angel's Blood. It is the rarest drug on the face of the earth." Ryan released Verus' right eyelid. Immediately, the cut areas of Verus' body began to seal. Keldrid turned his head and watched the commotion on the floor near Verus. Nazere ran his hand through the soft fur on Verus' head gently, and just as he did, Verus opened his eyes and began to rise up on his feet. His first attempt to rise failed. Verus limped and collapsed on the floor. Nazere quickly returned his blue sword to the second slot in the sheath at his side. He then opened his hands widely before Verus.

"Come on, boy," Nazere said, watching Verus anxiously. Verus looked up at Nazere, and as he did, he came to his feet. His tail then began to wag, and the dog barked at Nazere. "That's a boy!" Nazere exclaimed as he knelt down and gave Verus a great hug. Nazere then set his eyes on Ryan.

"It fully healed him," Nazere blurted out softly out of astonishment at the potency of the chemical. Ryan looked around, ensuring that all of the bloodguards in the room were fixed in place.

"Yes," Ryan said as he picked his gunblade off the floor and returned it to its green sheath behind his back. "Kazium can heal anything that has not been completely killed. It is useful in times of dire need. But there isn't even a full drop of it left in the vial. It is impossible to come by." Ryan looked to the bladed door as Nazere took a stand. A blue, square holographic panel to the left of the steel door was suspended in the air at a forty-five degree angle. The panel leaned against the artolium wall and had several sub-panels within the confines of its blue, square perimeter that were colored in red. "Follow me," Ryan instructed as he began walking toward the panel. Nazere, Verus and Keldrid all grouped up behind Ryan as he stood in front of the blue hologram and pulled the red, triangular disk from his pocket.

"Quite a useful gadget that device has proven to be," Nazere commented as Ryan held the triangle out in his palm, his arm fully extended. Ryan then dropped his arm, and the triangle became suspended in front of the holographic panel near the door. The triangle opened up tri-fold and became triple its original size as soon as Ryan released it. The new triangle then projected an image of the Gantor Pinnacle's exterior above it.

"This is the key to the complex," Ryan began as the holographic panel's red buttons began to blink. "It has been ascertained at the cost of many men's lives in the Old Battle of Jerusalem. It now serves us as the only means of access to the Gantor Pinnacle." The holographic image beeped, and as it did, the image on the door changed from the arrow and head to a black image of a skull. The skull then became three-dimensional, reaching its neck out of the door and looking at Ryan, Nazere and Verus. The skull carried an aura of shadow as it turned its head from side to side, scanning the space in which Nazere, Ryan and Verus were standing. The skull could not detect Keldrid, who towered over Nazere. The skull set its eye sockets directly on Nazere himself, and the dreaded image appeared to be completely full of life.

"Only he who holds the crusader's key shall pass this gate," the visage spoke with a deep, dark tone to his voice. The skull extended its smoking neck out in the direction of Nazere, positioning it directly in front of his face. "All who do not present the key shall be devoured."

"Behold!" Ryan exclaimed as he took hold of the triangular key and threw it to the floor. "The key to the Crusader's Steeple." The skull looked to his right as the triangular key melted into a puddle of copper on the ground. In this pool of liquid, the copper then became animate and began to reshape itself. It took on the form of a conventional key on the floor, with the symbol of a knight's helmet embossed at the end opposite of the typical notches and grooves. Ryan looked at Nazere. "Go ahead," he urged. "Pick it up." Reaching down, Nazere grabbed the key with his right hand and returned to his upright position. He then held the tool out in the center of his palm. The skull's eye sockets then constricted at the sight of the rusted copper key, ardently looking it over. There was a brief pause as the skull's eye sockets remained locked in place at the image of the key in Nazere's hand.

"So you have it, then," the skull said, his eye sockets widening as he withdrew his neck from Nazere's face. "The Crusader's Steeple's champion himself dare not enter this domain, for it is filled with gloom and destruction. You shall pass from this place into the oblivion that awaits you. I forewarn you that no man has entered the complex and left its confines without embracing death. Welcome, fated ones, to the Gantor Pinnacle." The skull then retracted back into the door, returning to its original form as a black emblem of an arrow piercing through a man's head. And within two seconds, the door came swinging to the right like a guillotine flying sideways. And as the door opened, the copper key in Nazere's hand returned to its original shape.

"Do you need this?" Nazere asked, holding the triangular disk out to Ryan.

"Yes," Ryan replied, taking the disk and slipping it into his jacket pocket. "It may come in handy later."

"What is the Crusader's Steeple? And who was its champion?" Nazere asked.

"The steeple is a still-existent battle site in Jerusalem where hundreds of men lost their lives fighting against Vice Lord Xar's newly introduced ventari. Its champion was the only prophet that managed to escape the Old Battle of Jerusalem with his life. He downloaded the necessary information to enter the Gantor Pinnacle to the disk in my pocket after fighting his way into some high-security offices in Washington, D.C. He later programmed the disk to demonstrate the key's place of origin, and to fulfill a prophecy. It was foreseen that he who touches the copper key shall be the first one to reenter the Crusader's Steeple. That is why I had you pick it up."

"I don't see myself going to Jerusalem any time soon," Nazere began, nodding his head. "But thanks for allowing me to be the one to touch the key."

"Not a problem," Ryan replied with a smile.

"I'm sure it wasn't," Nazere said, still nodding and contemplating the idea of the possible curse he just unleashed on himself.

"Let's go forth," Ryan said as he veered his eyes toward the open entryway and patted Verus on the head. Nazere briefly looked around as he and the others that accompanied him stepped foot into the next room. The ceiling was no where in sight. There was a great space like the center of a stadium in the room before them, and there were no guards within range of the group. The room was shaped like one massive cylinder, with a solid gold lift in the center of the room. The lift was suspended in the air over a wide, black, circular gap in the center of the floor. The golden lift had a square shaped limestone perimeter, with the limestone bust of a demon's head and arms on each side of the inside of the lift. Each demon's head was characterized by two short horns, sharp fangs, and a devilish beard. One of the demon's heads was laughing, its hands opened at its side. The next demon head covered its eyes. The next held its hands to its ears. And finally, the last demon had its hands covering its mouth. At the floor of the lift was the embossed image of a ventari set into an iron rectangle. The ventari had its arms extended to its sides, and its legs were connected together with the toes beneath them pointing downward. Surrounding the illustration of the ventari was a pattern of equally spaced-out spades, exactly like the symbols on a deck of playing cards. There were thirty spades altogether, ten embossed on the right and left sides of the ventari. There were five on the top and bottom.

Nazere looked down and noticed that the ground below his feet was comprised of tiles. Each tile produced a pattern throughout the room through the use of an image of a skull that was artistically engraved into every other tile. The skulls were accurate portraits of actual human skulls, with great detail placed into each engraved image. Above him, as far as the eye could see, were glass pods clustered together like one massive tube lined with salmon eggs. As he looked a bit closer, he noticed that these glass pods were the holding cells of humans. Each human floated in a bright, neon green fluid. All of them were in the fetal position, and each had an black electronic arm resembling a mechanical spinal cord attached to their brain stems. Nazere couldn't see where the electronic arms led to as they extended out of sight above the glass cells. He only knew that each was surgically attached to every person in the green pods. These cells were absolutely countless in number- a jaw-dropping visual to behold. Setting his eyes to ground level, Nazere walked up to the glass encasing closest to him. It was the cell of a boy who was curled up in an seemingly extra-tight fetal position. The boy's eyes and lips were closed, his hands positioned by the side of his temples. He put his hand against the glass surrounding the boy, his heart dropping in his chest at the very sight of him. Nazere knew isolation, but not like this. The boy was considerably young, his blonde hair floating in the water that surrounded him like a million, little golden threads.

"Who has done this?" Nazere asked in disgust, turning to Ryan with the crystal-clear appearance of anger consuming his face. Keldrid stood behind Nazere, also looking into the glass container.

"This is the work of High Lord Alune," Ryan said as he walked to where Nazere was standing and placed his hand softly on his shoulder. "This is only a sample of the army he is amassing for the last war." Nazere stared for a moment with a look of disbelief at the sight before him, slowly withdrawing his hand from the glass. "Come," Ryan said, beginning to move in the direction of the lift in the center of the room. "We must make our way downward."

"Our objective is not within the upper portion of the pinnacle?" Nazere questioned as he turned around and began to follow Ryan.

"I'm afraid not," Ryan replied. "In order for us to secure the ventari armor we must infiltrate the core of this place. The lift ahead of us will take us down there. Now that we‘re all out of attenurants, I hope we don‘t face too many more bloodguards." As Nazere approached the lift, the large, circular gap between him and the lift brought him to question.

"How do you suppose we are going to cross this gap?" Nazere asked Ryan as the group stood on the edge of the black, gaping hole surrounding the lift.

"I'll take care of that," Ryan said. "Hold on." Ryan closed his eyes, and as he did, Nazere felt his legs lift off the ground. He looked to his right to see Verus flying next to him, the dog barking as he was moved through the air by means of Ryan‘s gift. Keldrid became a haze of smoke and shadow, weaving on-board the lift to Nazere‘s right side. Ryan then opened his eyes.

"Well how do you suppose you are going to get over here now?!" Nazere yelled with his hands open at his sides in question.

"Look here, man with little faith," he began, smiling. "My gifts are well attuned." Ryan took a few paces back. He then sprinted toward the gap and took a massive leap, becoming a blur in midair. He made his providential landing where Nazere, Verus and Keldrid were all standing together in a bunch.

"Excellent performance," Nazere said to Ryan. "I suppose I won't question you next time." Turning his eyes to the limestone perimeter of the lift, Nazere leaned over and stared at the face of the laughing demon with a look of great interest sparkling in his ever-curious eyes. "What do these busts symbolize?" Nazere asked. "They look nightmarish. Their faces closely resemble gargoyles."

"These are the access panels for the two tiers of the Gantor Pinnacle," Ryan began, pulling out the triangular disk held within his green jacket pocket. The triangular disk then projected a diagram of the two floors beneath the lift without the necessity of a push of a single button. Ryan held the disk out in his right palm, allowing ample room for the storage device to project imagery. "The right password must be used in the right sequence in order for the lift to become operable."

"What happens if we use the wrong code?" Nazere asked curiously.

"We die," Ryan replied, making eye contact with Nazere as a sincere look overcame his face.

Ryan then typed a couple of hidden keys on the disk. A holographic image of the demon with its ears covered was projected in front of the group, spinning in midair above the disk. Below the rotating demon, the phrase "HEAR NO EVIL" popped up. Ryan looked confused.

"It can't be that simple," he began out loud, questioning his own judgment. He paused for a moment, and inhaled a deep breath of calming air. The projected image then returned to the disk, and Ryan held the disk at his right side. "Here we go," Ryan began. "Get your blade ready, Nazere. This is the only clue we'll be getting, so we'll have to find the password to the tier beyond this one on the next floor." Nazere drew his sword from the sheath at his hip, and it immediately took on its radiant, blue glow. "We're about to go onto the first tier. If my memory serves me correctly, I do believe I remember foreseeing the walls of this place in a vision." Nazere turned to Ryan.

"I'm prepared," he began, swinging his blade lightly in the air. "I'm beginning to grow very fond of my sword." Ryan nodded, putting his disk back in his jacket pocket.

"Hopefully you won't have to use it much where we're going. This is primarily a processing and manufacturing plant, so I would wager we will see little more combat." Ryan exhaled a nervous breath. He gripped his gunblade tightly in his right hand and anxiously moved his fingers his left. "Here goes nothing," Ryan began, leaning his face down to the bust of the demon covering its ears. "Password: Hear no evil." The demon's bust then came to life, the red demon letting out a terribly loud scream as it attempted to climb from out of its stone prison. Its arms pushed against the limestone perimeter as it tried to free itself from its captivity as best it could. Ryan leaned away from the demon, taking two cautious steps back. The demon's body stood out three dimensionally, but was sucked back into the stone seconds before it could pull itself from its rock-solid confines. When the demon returned to stone, its hands were gone, and its eyes were exposed. There was a pause for about one minute.

"Nothing's happening," Nazere said as he glanced over at Ryan.

"Fear not," Keldrid whispered as he leaned over and whispered in Nazere's right ear. "This is only the beginning of your journey." All of a sudden, the lift began to rattle, and Nazere and Ryan held firmly to the limestone perimeter of the lift. The lift then began to drop at full speed, flying through the air so fast it left a trail of visible gust and wind behind it. As the lift picked up speed the eyes of the demon who had reached out began to glow a brilliant shade of red.

"What's happening?" Nazere asked nervously as he turned to Ryan, experiencing the full effect of micro-gravity.

"We're taking to the first tier," Ryan said calmly as he held tightly to the stone wall in front of him. The great lift continued to fly at full speed, dropping like a free-falling elevator as it approached its destination.

"I smell something odd," Nazere noted as he opened his nostrils. "It smells like iron." Out of the darkness, a dark red room came into view as the lift came to a tremendous stop. The stop of the lift sent a shockwave of electricity arcing in every which direction, the lift's tremendous halt resounding with the noise of mighty thunder. Nazere only had a fleeting moment to look around at the disturbing view that encompassed his entire field of visibility. And as he did, his startled eyes grew wide and his silent mouth opened in awe. The room's walls were covered in crimson blood, the blood slowly dripping down the wall's metal surface. This room was even larger than the one before it, and there were many large columns evenly spread out in ranks and files throughout it. The columns were made of black marble, and solid gold identified the fluted tops and bottoms of every pillar.

At the top of the room, dead men with limp necks that hung over the rest of their bodies were bonded to the walls by means of a spider-like machine that hid their entire torso in black. The spider had a rounded abdomen and six arms that were grafted to the blood soaked, artolium walls. Every immobile spider was spaced out ten feet apart from one another, and there were over three hundred of them in the room. Each man was being drained of his blood by means of the spider-like machine, the blood dripping down the walls into large, stone pools. Sentinels with cylindrical, green tanks on their backs were siphoning the blood that ran into the pools, their attention solely on their task at hand. They accomplished the collection of blood by sucking the crimson fluid into their large, metal tanks via clear vacuum tubes at their sides. The clear vacuum tubes were linked directly to the tanks on their backs. Bloodguards covered the entirety of the room, numbered in the hundreds. Combined with the blood on the walls, this large presence of scarlet caped soldiers gave the room its dark-red ambience. It wasn't the sentinels or bloodguards on all sides of the room that brought Nazere to fear. It was the stormdivers clinging to the walls that drank of the blood that slowly poured down them. A certain stormdiver leeched its thick tongue to the side of the wall. Nazere veered his eyes up at the bat, and the creature slowly glanced its eight eyes back at him.

"The Sanctum of Blood!" Ryan yelled in horror as he realized where he was. "Nazere! Take my hand now!" Nazere reached out and took Ryan's hand at once. Ryan then jumped and propelled the two of them off the lift in a blur. They landed behind the column that was closest to the lift. The enemies were all quite aware of the presence of the few imposters that had made their way into their dark chambers. Bloodguards on all sides of the room drew their photon cannons immediately. They began to open fire rapidly in the direction of the column that served to shield the group. Loud pops and booms enveloped the air like a series of conventional, old-fashioned cannons being fired in unison.

"Imposters in the…," a bloodguard began to speak into his mask, attempting to alert other floors of the group's presence. Ryan aimed his gunblade precisely and fired a single shot into the bloodguard's chest, leaving a gaping hole in it the size of a Frisbee. The bloodguard dropped to the floor in response to the direct hit. Ryan then began firing at any bloodguards within his sight. In turn, they continued to fire a barrage of photon bolts back at him.

"Stay down!" Ryan yelled at Nazere, crouching down behind the column.

"Where is Verus?!" Nazere yelled out, crouching alongside Ryan behind the column. On top of the lift, Verus began to growl and expose the large fangs within his jaws. He was looking up at a stormdiver on the wall, who stared back at Verus with its many eyes precisely directed at the dog. Verus increased his size twelve-fold as he made a massive leap from the lift and onto the stone floor beyond it. Electricity began to arc across every wall in the room as the stormdiver looking at Verus dropped to the floor in front of him. The stormdiver opened its jaws and let out a deafening shriek, exposing six layers of razor sharp teeth.

"There must be twenty stormdivers in here!" Nazere exclaimed as he looked around. "I think we're in trouble!"

"You could say that!" Ryan yelled back as he continued to peer around the column, firing and periodically dodging bolts from the blood guards in the room. The bolts from the bloodguards were hitting the column in succession, crushing its surface and weakening its thick foundation. The sentinels draining the blood in the stone pools on both sides of the room were alerted as soon as the first shot was fired in the sanctum. Each stopped what they had been doing and began activating the lasers on their heads. They walked in the direction of the column Nazere and Ryan were seeking shelter behind. Their legs slowly dragged forward as each sentinel placed one enormous leg in front of the other. Keldrid stood atop the lift, his unseen face keeping a watchful eye on Nazere and the exchange of fire before him. "This column is going to collapse!" Ryan yelled as he reached out to fire at a bloodguard. "Take my hand, Nazere!" Nazere took Ryan's hand as the first column came crashing down, breaking into three pieces after having withstood so many consecutive photon blasts. Before the column hit the ground in pieces, Ryan had propelled himself and Nazere behind a column to the right of the fallen pillar.

"I'll cover your back," Nazere said as he drew his sword, his eyes taking notice of nearby enemies. "Those bloodguards are facing us!" Two bloodguards behind Ryan and Nazere began firing at them, missing as they were firing from a distanced range. Nazere jumped to his feet and ran in the direction of the two bloodguards, fending off oncoming fire as best he could with his blazing blue sword. As Keldrid continued to watch, he noticed four additional bloodguards to the left of the two Nazere was charging. He then became a stream of shadow and smoke, moving in the direction of Nazere in a swerving motion that closely mimicked a sidewinder.

Standing before Verus, a great stormdiver hurled a concentrated bolt of lightning straight at the over-sized German shepherd. This sent Verus flying hundreds of feet backward, directly under the broad legs of a towering sentinel. The sentinel slowly raised its arm, and just as it did, Verus jumped up and ripped the face of the sentinel off. Yellow sparks flew everywhere as the sentinel came tumbling down, its head‘s internal processor and wiring torn asunder by the dog‘s vicious bite. Verus then set his hazel eyes on the stormdiver that had attacked him. He growled angrily and ran full speed at the bat, taking a confident leap into its body. Once the bat was pinned, Verus ripped at the stormdiver's face mercilessly as it struggled to move its outstretched wings underneath him. As the stormdiver became motionless, many of the stormdivers drinking from the blood on the wall began to shift their many eyes. They set them on Verus, who readily awaited their attack on the floor below.

Charging into the two bloodguards before him, Nazere directed his sword as nimbly as an impala through the first bloodguard's chest. He then swiped his blade around, and in a circular blue wave, he chopped down on the remaining bloodguard's arm. This sent the arm, which was cut off from the shoulder, falling on the floor in a bloody puddle. Without delay, Nazere then drove his glowing sword through the bloodguard's chest. From behind, four bloodguards took aim at Nazere and fired. Each blast hit Nazere's body-tight ion shield, his shield gleaming as it withstood the full extent of the photon discharge. Each of the four bloodguards then drew their hand-blades, their fingertips becoming twenty times longer. The noise of their blades' extension was like two carving knives' sharpened edges been rubbed against one another. The guards began to charge Nazere straightaway, a sentinel's bulky frame appearing out of the corner of Nazere's alert eyes. He was quickly becoming overwhelmed. Coming forth in a wall of smoke and black next to Nazere, Keldrid drew forth Entryu.

"Stand down!" Keldrid commanded Nazere. Nazere ducked his head down, alarmed as Keldrid lifted his sword above Nazere's body. Holding Entryu by the side of the hilt, Keldrid threw Entryu out toward the bloodguards like a boomerang. The blade cut all four of the bloodguards who had been charging forward in half with superb accuracy. Every one of them was cut precisely in half, as if they were measured for doom before it ever struck them. Entryu then returned to the right hand of Keldrid, where the angel caught it by the hilt. As he did, Nazere drove his blade through the sentinel standing over top of him. However, the blade missed the face and penetrated the sentinel's neck. And Nazere failed as he attempted to withdraw it. He threw his right leg up on the lower abdomen of the sentinel and attempted to yank from the hilt with all of his might. But so much as he tried, he could not pull the sword out of its lodged place.

"It's stuck!" Nazere yelled at Keldrid, still straining to pry the blade from the sentinel's neck.

The sentinel propped its right arm back in preparation to hammer Nazere with his unstoppable fist. As it did, Keldrid stepped alongside Nazere. He then raised Entryu above the sentinel, cutting down on the sentinel's head until Entryu met Nazere's blue blade. Nazere fell back on his rear end when his blade was released from the sentinel. The machine's metal frame became molten as the impact from Entryu splintered its face and generated a rippling effect that melted through the rest of the machine's body. Running from across the room, eighteen bloodguards appeared in front of Nazere and Keldrid. Each of them stopped in place and took aim with their cannons. When they opened fire, one of their photon bolts hit Nazere in the arm.

"Ion shield currently at thirty percent strength," Nazere's wrist reported in a feminine voice. Keldrid looked out at the oncoming bloodguards, his sword in front of him, blood dripping from the edge of it. The bloodguards began to move closer slowly, but the majority of their shots were missing Nazere. The group of guards continued to walk forward, quickening their steps as they endeavored to improve their accuracy. Their nocturnal pupils constricted as they moved within thirty yards of their target. They only continued to miss. Dropping their photon cannons, they all drew their hand-blades in preparation to engage in melee combat. Keldrid turned his hidden face toward Nazere and sheathed Entryu.

"Unitedly now," he said softly and slowly as he cupped his hands together. Nazere nodded, trusting that Keldrid had a plan devised. And as the eighteen bloodguards ran in, Nazere span his blade in a preparatory circle off to the right of his unmoved stance. Time slowed to a snail's pace as Nazere cut into the side of the first oncoming bloodguard. As the second bloodguard was about to land a blow on Nazere's head, Keldrid unclasped his hands. Out of his hands came a black monarch butterfly, fluttering its wings as it lifted itself up to a higher space. The elegant insect flew gently above Keldrid's head, and Keldrid directed his unseen face up at the ostensibly insignificant creature. As the butterfly hovered in the air, Keldrid mumbled something out loud that Nazere couldn't understand. And at that very moment, all of time stopped. But the butterfly flew yet.

"Cut them down," Keldrid said to Nazere in his twisted voice as he turned his face to him. "Your time is short." The butterfly landed on Nazere's shoulder. As soon as it did, the heart within Nazere's chest began beating like a rabbit thumping its foot. As an adrenaline rush overcame him, he dashed through the ranks of bloodguards before him like a bolt of lightning. All he had to do was think it, and he had rushed through the soulless guards with perfect precision in seventeen pinpointed strikes. At the end of the ranks of bloodguards, the butterfly on Nazere's shoulder faded to black ashes as he came to a halt. Glancing over his shoulder, Nazere noticed all of the bloodguards that had stood before him had been butchered. Cut into pieces, blood covered the floor underneath them.

"An eye for an eye," Keldrid began slowly, subtly. "And a tooth for a tooth. They were long overdue."

Glancing to his left and right, Nazere noticed that many more bloodguards were now racing in his direction from all sides like souped-up motor vehicles bent on retaliation. He set his eyes on his blue blade, now covered in the blood of his slain enemies. He kept his eyes there. Now there were two voices in his head. One told him that he was about to die, about to embrace the morbid fate that he had just dealt to those that stood against him. The voice told him he was delusional, that he was lost, and that he could not possibly change what was all around him. But there was another voice, and its tone was identical to Keldrid's.

"Ask yourself this, human," the voice said as Nazere looked upon the reflections of steadily approaching bloodguards on his glowing, blue sword. "What have you observed in this world that is normal? You think that you are out of your right mind, but in fact you are now more in it than you have ever been. I tell you that everything over and under the sun is unique. Your condition is no different, but it is unique. And in so much as it is, embrace the change that it brings forth. Do not ever worry."

"Good coverage!" Ryan yelled as he glanced at the dead bloodguards for but a brief second. He didn't notice the bloodguards barreling in on Nazere from the right and the left. His eyes were preoccupied with taking accurate aim and firing at multiple targets at once. He was busy fending off bloodguards with his gunblade yards away, and had no idea that any intervention had occurred.

Turning his dark hood upward again, Keldrid closed and opened his right palm above his head. A small, shiny bubble appeared on top of it. As Keldrid dropped his palm, the bubble took flight and began moving in Ryan's direction. The guards were racing, Nazere's adrenaline hitting its peak point as he looked at his blade and remained in place despite his darkest fears. As the bubble popped on Ryan's back, his gunblade fired a thousand shots at once in a rain of photon bolts. The bolts took on a mind of their own, seeking out all of the bloodguards that remained it the room.

"Forget doubt," Keldrid said as he placed his scaly, gray hand on Nazere's shoulder. Nazere's eyes widened as he realized that Keldrid could hear his every thought. "Believe that you will be carried through, and your vision will become reality." Several guards sought to elude the consecutive stream of fire, but none could be fast enough. When the bolts hit the guise-wearing guards, they ended the masked upon impact. The repeated blasts ignited all of the guards charging Nazere to the left and right, disintegrating them into dust. The dust softly floated away in the scarlet room, and with it flew Nazere's uncertainty. "Whoa!" Ryan exclaimed as glanced around with a stupefied look on his face. He smiled and clapped in a burst of excitement. "Did you just see that, Nazere?!" Nazere was preoccupied, his eyes now set on the ceiling.

"There's something over here in this corner," Nazere said as he lifted his pointer finger straight above his head.

Ryan looked up inquisitively at the left corner of the room. There, he noticed something that stood out like a sore thumb. In the left corner of the room there was a great "V" etched into a marble square. As he looked across the room to the area Nazere was pointing at, he noticed an "E" carved into another marble square.

"I think this is a clue. We need to get to the other end of the room,"

Ryan said as he climbed to his feet. "The ceiling bears the password for the next tier. I have foreseen this."

In the mean time, electricity wrapped around Verus' body like a small storm as four stormdivers climbed all over him. Peering around the column, Ryan noticed sentinels with active heat seeking lasers still moving in his direction. Ryan charged over to the sentinels growing closer to him, positioning his gunblade in front of him. He was thirsty to finish the machines in melee combat.

"I'll cover Verus!" Nazere called out as he set his eyes on his dog. He charged toward the stormdivers that were crawling all over the German shepherd with his sword in his right hand. While moving, he watched as Verus jumped out from the violent fray and ended one of the stormdivers by launching his teeth into its neck. A stormdiver came directly behind Verus and landed on his back, wrapping its muscular arms around the dog's immense body.

"Ion shielding currently at twenty-two percent," Nazere's bracelet reported as he neared Verus' location. The electricity from the stormdivers began to strike Nazere repeatedly. Ignoring the warning signals, Nazere drove his blade into the back of the stormdiver who had pursued his companion. He then pried the stormdiver off of Verus by pulling back on his sword. Verus flipped around acrobatically after making his most recent kill. He then tackled the next stormdiver with terribly spry speed. The bolts of lightning from the bats continued to hit Nazere. As they did, Nazere drove his sword into the face of the stormdiver next to the one Verus had tackled. He wanted to gain the tactical advantage, eliminating all nearby stormdivers quickly in order to secure the area. The stormdiver fell back, sprawling its wings out as it lay dead on the ground.

"Ion shielding currently at ten percent," Nazere's bracelet updated him.

"Ryan!" Nazere yelled as he stabbed an oncoming stormdiver. "I can't keep this up for much longer before my shield fails!" Ryan withdrew the tip of his gunblade from the face of a sentinel he had just defeated, hearing Nazere's pleas for aid. He stopped for a moment, pondering a scheme he was formulating in his head. He then smiled.

"I'm making a run for it!" Ryan yelled to Nazere. He then darted across the room and out of sight. In a few short moments, he came sprinting back with eight stormdivers following closely behind him. "It's an 'I' and an 'L'!" Ryan shouted as he came running across the room.

"An 'I' and an 'L'?" Nazere asked with a confounded expression on his face as Ryan neared him.

"Yes, man!" Ryan yelled, his eyes widened in horror as he sprinted. "I need a little help here!" Ryan turned around with his gunblade at the ready once he had reached Nazere at the opposite end of the room, panting heavily. Verus continued his assault on his enemies by pouncing on the stormdiver closest to him. Nazere then looked around the sanctum for Keldrid as he drove his sword through yet another stormdiver. Keldrid was nowhere to be seen.

"Live?" Nazere asked, puzzled as he swiped at the stormdiver in front of him and missed. The stormdiver let out a great shriek as bolts of lightning were launched into the air. Lightning was flying everywhere throughout the room, and Nazere knew he didn't have much time before his ion shielding would give out.

"Evil?" Ryan asked back as he thought about what the password could be. He then stabbed an oncoming stormdiver through the chest.

"I can't concentrate on the problem," Nazere said as he drove his sword through the neck of the stormdiver he had missed.

"Ion shield currently at four percent. Please recharge," Nazere's ion shield requested as it began to blink red.

"We've got no time!" Nazere yelled anxiously. "My ion shield is down to four percent and dropping!" A hand touched Nazere's shoulder, and a black hood leaned down to his right ear.

"The tongue is vile," Keldrid whispered.

"Vile?" Nazere questioned.

"Vile?" Ryan questioned back. Nazere thought deeply for a moment as a sentinel walked up behind him.

"Wait!" Nazere began as he turned and confidently drove his sword through the sentinel's face and swiftly withdrew it. "I have the answer! Get us to the lift now!" Nazere reached out his hand, and as soon as Ryan finished off another stormdiver he took hold of it.

"Follow my lead, brother!" Ryan yelled as he took a split second to glance at Nazere. Beginning with a running start, Ryan transported Nazere and himself onboard the lift in a blur of inhuman speed. Verus came sprinting behind, lunging his oversized body onto the lift. A flock of stormdivers descended on the lift directly behind Verus, hovering overhead in a black mass of about thirty and growing. "Password: Speak no evil!" Nazere exclaimed as he leaned down to the limestone image of the demon covering his mouth. The lift began to shake as stormdivers continued to accumulate above the lift.

"I pray you're right," Ryan said as he looked at the flock above the lift. In the blinking of an eye, the stone bust of the demon with his hands over his mouth came jutting out of the stone perimeter around the group. The demon then let out a great breath of flame above the perimeter of the lift, igniting all of the stormdivers that surrounded it. One by one, the burning bats fell to the floor. One dropped on the lift, its body overtaken by potent flames and smoke. The demon then attempted to lash out at Nazere with its right hand, but was sucked back into its stone prison before it was able to reach him. Its hands were no longer present when it began became two dimensional, and its eyes waxed a brilliant shade of amber.

"We're about to find out," Nazere replied as he held to the stone around him. The unstable lift began to shift and shuffle, and as it did Keldrid hovered above the lift with smoke and shadows rising from his figure. The lift then dropped at the speed of light, leaving a trail of electricity and static behind it. Keldrid flew directly behind the lift. His hood was clearly visible to Nazere as he held to the side of the limestone perimeter and glanced up.

"Well," Ryan said to Nazere as the lift dropped, blackness and bolts of light flying in the air just outside the perimeter. "I must say, for having so little experience with the sword, you proved quite impressive up there."

"It wasn't all my doing, I assure you," Nazere replied.

"That's the spirit," Ryan said smiling and holding to the stone wall in front of him. "Give all of the glory to the Master." All at once, the great lift came to a substantially mighty stop, sending a shockwave of visibly disrupted air molecules flying in all directions. The demon's eyes then became colorless, and the wall with the demon covering his eyes crumbled to the floor in a cloud of dust. Nazere's eyes squinted as he looked out into the room before him. There was absolute silence in the room, except for a strange noise coming from underneath the lift. It sounded like an arching object in motion accompanied by a barely audible pulse. Nearly a mile below, inanimate ventari were positioned in ranks and files by the thousands. Nazere peered under the lift and noticed a great sphere with the reflective appearance of glass straight below it. Within it was a gigantic, blue ethalon charge, producing the subtle sound of a pulse as its energy oscillated. Circling the sphere were four large artolium rings, and their swings penetrated the wind and shattered air molecules in the zone, generating a loud swooping sound. From the encircled sphere, thousands of illuminated blue cords ran to each of the spines of the inanimate ventari. Ryan anxiously withdrew the traingular disk he was carrying from his jacket pocket. He then hit a hidden button on the surface of the disk.

"Gantor Pinnacle Core reached," the disk reported.

"That's it! We're finally here!" Ryan exclaimed. "Below us is the core that empowers the ventari armor spread throughout this room. Its power exceeds even that of a core of a dreadnaught, which is also powered by ethalon." Ryan pointed to the ventari suits below him. "As you can see, Nazere, all of the ventari are powered by the sphere in the center of this room. It is a blue ethalon charge. The one here is also the most powerful one in the entire world." Ryan paused for a moment. "The curtain is calling you, Nazere. You do understand what you must do now, don't you?"

"I just enter the ventari suit, right?"

"These ventari are unprocessed and unmanned," Ryan began. "The password to engage them is 'Bringer of the Blue Flame.' Simply speak those words and the ventari suit will become operable." Ryan paused for a moment as he turned and looked Nazere deeply in the eyes. "There is one catch, though. Once you enter a suit, your body cannot be restored. It is gone forever."

"Gone forever?" Nazere asked, a look of resignation on his face. "I have to give up my body?" As soon as Nazere asked his question, a stack of stone tablets piled on the floor below near the core began rising up one by one. Ryan looked straight forward and watched as the tablets began to form a winding bridge to the bottom of the room.

"It must be done," Ryan replied as each tablet continued to rise into the air. In the center of the tablets, there was a circular section the size of a small room. It rose up and connected to the bridge. The circle served as a midpoint between the lift and the bottom level.

"You must do it," Ryan started. "You have been chosen. This is only the beginning. I know the concept may seem difficult to accept. But I believe in your ability to see it through. I'll be right here with you. I'm by your side all the way." Nazere looked at the bridge before him. Then all of his memories began returning to him. The very thought of losing the body he had always known made him sick to his stomach.

"Let's get out of here while we still can," Nazere said, shaking his head. "I don't want this anymore. I thought I was ready to make this change, but I was wrong." Ryan looked at Nazere with stern eyes.

"You must go forward!" Ryan urged as he looked at Nazere. "Without you, Operation Maelstrom will fail." Ryan looked deeply into Nazere's eyes once again. "Remember Elle! Remember David! We are relying on you!" Nazere took a look around him.

"I'm staying here," Nazere said as he sat on the lift. "You go ahead. There's nothing stopping you from attaining a suit of armor."

"You must…," Ryan began. Suddenly, there was a great crushing sound that reverberated throughout the room and muted Ryan's voice. Crumbled stone fell from the ceiling to the lift below. As Ryan looked up, his eyes grew wider than they had ever grown. Taking a stand, Nazere veered his eyes toward the ceiling. Above them, a Goliath of a creature had taken a step with his muscular right arm. The creature had midnight black skin, four gigantic arms, and four nocturnal eyes. His eyes were a blood red shade, and all of them focused in and out as they beheld their prey- endlessly threatening. His nose was like that of a snake, and his body was covered in scales. He was a brute, with enormous muscles from head to toe. His neck was excessively thick, with a choker made of sharpened teeth around it. His mouth was open, exposing a fearful set of fangs. A forked tongue slipped out from within his open mouth as he looked down upon Nazere, Ryan and Verus. Orange venom dripped from his toxic lips.

"What is that thing?!" Nazere cried out. The creature laughed.

"I am the keeper of this place!" the creature began in a booming voice, his mouth full of layers of fangs like a great white shark. "My name is Archiron the Breaker, and your presence here has sealed your fate!" The creature then dropped to the lift below, all four arms pounding the golden floor of the lift. The creature was tremendous, standing taller than three stacked sentinels as it outstretched his back and hissed at the group standing before him. The creature's heart beat out of its muscle-ripped chest, thumping and pounding as it took a step toward Ryan. Nazere drew his scepter and hit Archiron in the abdomen with it. The scepter simply bounced back as if Archiron's abdomen were rubber. It had absolutely no effect on the hideous monster. Nazere then prepared by unsheathing his sword. He lashed out at the creature, driving his blazing blue sword into Archiron's chest. Archiron laughed as Nazere fell backward, the sword unable to penetrate Archiron's tremendous scales. Verus growled at Archiron, growing to his maximum of twelve times his normal size.

"To the bridge!" Ryan yelled as he picked up Nazere with his hand. "We must move! Archiron is a legendary manifestation of Vice Lord Xar. His armor is too strong for our weaponry." Ryan propelled Nazere and himself to the bridge in a long jump that appeared as a blurred wave. Tablets were still rising from the ground past the room-sized circular tablet. Keldrid remained in place, simply watching as Ryan and Nazere began to descend the stone staircase that led to the floor as fast as their legs would carry them. Archiron moved forward like a mammoth sized ape, his four arms crushing the floor into pieces as he advanced. Ryan and Nazere sprinted into the circular plane in the middle of the bridge just like their life depended on it. Archiron followed in hot pursuit, the bridge crumbling behind him as he stepped on the first two tablets.

"There's no going back now," Ryan began as he reached into his pocket. "Take this, Nazere. If you don't get into the ventari suit we are dead anyway! This is a therum drop. Suck on it. It will make your neurons immune to the ventari takeover."

"The ventari takeover?" Nazere asked, in a panic as Archiron made a massive leap in their direction from behind them.

"Yes!" Ryan exclaimed. "The suit will overtake your mind without this drop. It is a part of the initial processing! Just take it!" Ryan handed Nazere the therum drop, and Nazere immediately put it into his mouth. It tasted like licorice root to Nazere's tastebuds. When Archiron landed, he stood directly in front of Ryan, Nazere and Verus.

"What have we here?" Archiron began, cackling and hissing. "A few intruders trapped like little insects! I eat intruders!" Archrion grabbed Ryan with his upper right arm and picked him up into the air. Verus jumped up and launched his jaw into the creature's bulky arm. "Humorous," Archiron said as he held Ryan in front of him, squeezing his hand around his neck. He was completely ignorant of Verus' attacks. "Such petty creatures humans are."

"Jump!" Ryan yelled, his face reddened by Archiron's firm grip. He was barely able to speak. "You will make it! Thrust the cord of the ventari into your back! And remember, the password is 'Bringer of the Blue Flame'!" Archiron squeezed harder and grabbed Verus with one of his left hands, flinging him off the platform and onto the ground below. Verus quickly shook himself off and returned to his feet, running full speed up the now completed bridge in an attempt to rescue Ryan. Nazere squinted at Ryan's face, Ryan struggling to breathe and his face growing crimson red as his capillaries filled with blood. Archiron continued to squeeze it mercilessly. Taking in a breath of much needed air, Nazere took a dynamic leap into the air. Nazere rolled in a ball as he gradually came to a halt at the floor of the installation.

"Ion shield currently at one percent," Nazere's wrist reported.

Barely, Nazere thought to himself as he exhaled. He then looked up and sprinted to the closest ventari suit, pulling the cord out of its back. The cord had one sharp, spear-like tip to it like a very large needle. As he looked at the needle, a wave of memories completely overtook

Nazere. He flashed back to the memories he had of being a young boy. He recalled his mother reading to him before he fell asleep; he remembered his mother pinching his cheeks and always telling him how much she loved his smile, and how much that mattered to him. She always made the extra effort at every one his birthdays to make him elicit that smile. Those were the recollections of a time he could never bring back, although he would always cling to the memory of the only woman he ever had in his life. His mother was taken away, and he was now alone. And there were many memories of being alone that Nazere never wanted to relive; falling asleep on the streets of Baltimore was like second nature to him. How he longed to be cared for like he used to. The face his mother loved would be gone, replaced by the generic face of a killing machine. Nazere couldn't help but wonder, Who could love a ventari? Glancing up at Ryan, who was suffering in the arms of the dark abomination, Nazere's heart pounded in his chest. He looked down at his hands one last time. He then focused on the needle in his hand. Closing his eyes, Nazere grabbed hold of the tip and drove it into his back. As soon as he did, his body immediately fell to the ground like a limp play-thing.

With Archiron about to snap Ryan's neck with his second arm on his right side, Keldrid began to blow visible breath into the air. And from Keldrid's invisible mouth, a swarm of locust went flying in the direction of Archiron. Archiron had just placed his second arm on Ryan's skull. Ryan braced himself as Archiron took a lethal hold, about to snap his neck. And just as he did, the swarm of locust cast out by Keldrid descended upon Archiron like the plague it was. The swarm attacked Archiron's face, completely covering its scaled surface. Archiron dropped Ryan and began attempting to scrape the amassed locust off of his face with all of his arms. Ryan fell to his knees, holding his neck and gasping for breath. After breathing steadily for a moment or two, Ryan glanced up at Archiron. From Ryan's vantage point, Archiron appeared to be battling with nothing. Confused by the creature's defiant behavior, Ryan jumped to the ground near to where Nazere's human body was ing face-down. His ion shield flickered as he hit the floor after jumping from such a height. As soon as he did, the locust swarm disappeared completely, and Archiron set his eyes on Verus. The dog stood straight before him, and was unafraid with his fangs fully exposed. "I will eat you alive, little beast!" Archiron screamed angrily as he lunged forward toward Verus.

Nazere's eyes opened to a blue holographic display in front of his face. The display then began to flash "INDICATE PASSWORD." Nazere was completely unable to move. But he was able to speak.

"Password: Bringer of the Blue Flame," Nazere replied to the display's prompt. The display then began to pull up a targeting system. The targeting system instantaneously set its crosshairs on Archiron. Archiron picked Verus up by the collar with his right arm and clobbered his face with his muscular left fist. Verus fell to the ground, driven temporarily unconscious by the vile creature's devastating punch. Ryan lay dizzied on the ground, trying to get his bearing as he took to his right knee. And just as he did, he saw it. A great blue flame flew through the air in a giant arc, headed directly toward Archiron.

"Now I kill you, little mut!" Archiron exclaimed as he picked up Verus with his right arm. He opened his mouth, about to take a nice bite of the dog with his many venomous fangs. Ryan took to his feet and began to run full-speed up the winding stone staircase, now moving with all his strength to come to the aid of the German shepherd in distress. Before he reached the top, a deafening shockwave exploded throughout the chambers of the core. It shook the stone room violently, and originated directly above Archiron. Bits and pieces of cracked stone fell to the floor in the wake of the triumphant outburst. His ears ringing from the potent wave, Ryan glanced up.

A ventari stood above Archiron, with his right arm fully extended in the abominable creature's direction. Archiron veered his many eyes up to the ventari's poised location hovering above him. "You will listen to the voice of your master, machine!" Archiron demanded. A smile rounded the ventari's face. The black creature's eight eyes widened, his pupils dilating as he looked upon the right hand of the ventari. The creature had just enough time to drop Verus to the floor. The sterai beam came upon the huge creature in a brilliant, white flash. Archiron came plummeting off the platform and onto the floor. His head was gone and his neck was on fire, smoke rising from the newly made cavity. Ryan laughed in sheer amazement.

"Nazere!" Ryan yelled out as he glanced up at the ventari. Nazere's arm was still extended in front of him in the air. "You have done it!" Returning to consciousness, Verus climbed to his legs and shook himself out. He then looked down at Archiron's slain body, and as Archiron's heart beat, he noticed that it began to glint red. Archiron's heart continued to beat, but with every beat the rhythm became slower. Verus began to growl at the pounding heart, as if he knew something was out of order. Nazere flew down to his own slain body, which lay sprawled out on the floor with the cord still attached to its back. He then reached over and pryed the capsule that was used to contain Verus out of his own lifeless hands.

"Come, Verus!" Nazere yelled. Verus came running down the bridge and returned to his summtorant in a sphere of smoke. Nazere held the summtorant tightly in his hand. Archiron's heart continued beating, until at last it stopped. And when it did, his heart began to glow a bright red. Alarms throughout the building immediately began to sound. "Come, Ryan," Nazere said, glancing over at Ryan with his newly attained blue face. His body was now that of a ventari, possessing the muscular build of a Roman god. "Let's get out of here." Ryan maintained a smile.

"I'll fly right behind you," Ryan said as he lifted himself off the ground.

"You can do that too, huh?" Nazere asked as he smiled.

"I can," Ryan began. "Aerodynamics need not apply when you are a well-trained battle prophet. But don't fly too fast. I may not be able to keep up."

Together, as alarms sounded throughout the complex, Ryan and Nazere flew up through the great black space that the lift had dropped them through. Keldrid caught up to the two men in a comet of shadows and smoke. The three then flew in perfect parallel.

"Well done, my child," Keldrid said to Nazere as he flew alongside him. "But you will want to make haste from here. They will be coming for you." Nazere nodded his head as he kept flying, Ryan ascending from the depths by his side.

In a building to the right of the Gantor Pinnacle, a structure towering nearly as high as the pinnacle itself, a man sat with his hands crossed in front of his face. The man had a red flashing holographic image in front of him. The room he stood in had a long black and gold carpet leading up to his chair. The room was dimly lit, with the light pouring in from the window to the right of the man's chair serving as the only source of light for the room. The remainder of the room was darkened. The man had gray hair of average length, brown eyes, and a cleanly shaven face. His eyes were set on the red holographic image before him, an emotionless look on his face. Suddenly, a man entered his room from beyond the door at the end of the black and gold carpet.

As the man entered the room, he knelt before the man who sat in the chair. The man who entered the room was young and wore no mask. His head was shaved, and he bore the tattoo of a barcode on his neck. He had a suit of artolium armor on and carried a helmet by his side.

"Explain something for me, Lieutenant Galen," the man with the gray hair said as he looked at the lieutenant. "How is it that someone has managed to reach the core of the Gantor Pinnacle?"

"There was something else…," the lieutenant began.

"You can't explain it!" the man with the gray hair yelled in interruption as he took a stand from his chair. "Now," the man began as he toned down his dialogue and returned to his seat. "I want you to deploy everything we have in this city to put a stop to this disorderly conduct. Is that clear, Lieutenant Galen?"

"Yes, Commander Entril," the lieutenant replied, bowing his head before the commander. "I will ensure that whatever is inside of the pinnacle is destroyed." The old man leaned toward the lieutenant, staring him down.

"You will," he began calmly. "Or I will have your head on a plate." The lieutenant stood up and turned around, making his exit to the dim room. The man in the chair leaned back, returning to looking at the flashing display in front of him with his hands crossed in front of his face. Outside of the commander's window, a wave of phantoms began to swarm around the apex of the pinnacle like a bunch of flies with blue-ringed tentacles.

Inside of the Gantor Pinnacle, Nazere continued to fly upward alongside Keldrid and Ryan. They had just passed the Sanctum of Blood, and were heading straight through the roof. In the distance, Nazere could see the cells of humans in the green water. "All the way!" Ryan exclaimed. "We can break through the top and rendezvous with the Redeemer!" Nazere, Ryan and Keldrid continued to fly straight up, shattering the glass of cells in a circular fashion the further they advanced. Green water poured to the ground below, the shockwave of the group's sheer speed breaking the sound barrier. Nearing the top of the pinnacle, Nazere reached out his right hand and released a single beam of concentrated light above him. The light left a gaping hole in the roof, the molten metal of the surface of the roof dripping like sludge. Nazere took to the skies, taking a liberating look at the city around him. He had made it.

"There they are!" Elle yelled to David from within the Redeemer, looking over in the direction of the three flying in the air. Her heart pounded in her chest as she took a look at Nazere. Her heart cried out as she watched phantoms surround him in the sky. Phantoms began to swarm around Nazere by the hundreds, and their tentacles began to extend in his direction.

"You must move!" Nazere yelled to Ryan. "Get back to the Redeemer now! I will handle these machines."

"May the Master be with you," Ryan said.

"He will be," Nazere replied. "Now go!" Heeding Nazere's advice, Ryan flew back in the direction of the Redeemer. But three phantoms followed closely behind him. Nazere extended his left arm, and the three phantoms that were following Ryan were locked in place by the gravitational pull of the radiant, opened eye of his palm. The blue-ringed, silver tentacles of two phantoms reached up toward Nazere from beneath him as he kept his arm extended. Nazere watched carefully, and as soon as Ryan had reached the platform holding the Redeemer he released the phantoms in front of him. The leading phantom turned around and flew in front of Nazere, its six tentacles wrapping around him. The second phantom then closed in on Nazere's head, looking him directly in the eyes. Its six eyes lit up a bright neon blue in preparation for its attack, a cannon showing itself from within the black phantom's crab-like mouth. And as the phantom charged its firestorm particle cannon, Nazere opened his arms, sending a shockwave of torn molecules rippling through the air.

The phantoms' tentacles came flying off of Nazere, flailing upwards in all directions. He dropped to a point in the sky where he was below most of the phantoms striving to attack him. From inside of the ventari suit, Nazere's crosshairs locked onto all of the phantoms above him. He then raised his right palm, the blades of the eye of it coming open as soon as the thought of retribution entered his head. And a great white sterai wave in the shape of a cone consumed all of the phantoms before Nazere as soon as he willed it to. The concentrated blast was so great that it could be seen from space, penetrating the earth's atmosphere and flying well beyond it.

Lowering his hand, Nazere flashed back to the vision he had of destroying the phantoms that had appeared before him. "The prophecy is complete," Nazere spoke into the air, in full realization that the events of this day had been no dream. From below him, a swarm of hundreds of additional phantoms amassed around Nazere in the sky. Raising his arm, he fire three consecutive waves at the swarm. "One. Two. Three," Nazere spoke calmly. His deepest fears began to fade away as he experienced first-hand how well attuned he was to his new body. And when the light subsided, none of his enemy war machines were left flying. Not even a hint of their presence remained in the wake of the three sterai beams he projected. Nazere then charged into a blue flame. Fire covered the whole of his body as he looked down at his unscathed hands and smiled in amazement. The flame that consumed his being had no affect on his artolium skin whatsoever. He then glanced over his shoulder at the ones he left behind. He flew over to the Redeemer in a split second, a long trail of ocean-blue energy painting the sky.

The Redeemer removed its cloak, and its outer shell became

visible to Nazere. He stood suspended in the air relatively close to where he knew it was waiting, only a foot off of the tower's surface. The Redeemer's wings were in the upright position, and Elle, Ryan and David all came climbing out of the ship as soon as he had stopped in the air. David and Elle gathered around him in sheer amazement at his accomplishment. They smiled as they touched his transparent skin while he remained firmly in place.

"Startling," David began, closely examining Nazere. "I've never been this close to a ventari."

"Me either," Elle said, smiling into Nazere's face. "I missed you, Nazere. You look so much different. But please know that that means nothing to me." She wrapped her arms around Nazere tightly, elated that he had made it back safetly. In her heart of hearts, that's all she really wanted. Nazere landed his feet on the surface of the Contemptys Tower and held Elle softly in return. As Nazere released his embrace, Elle looked him in the eyes.

"I didn't have to use my sword!" she exclaimed as she smiled up at him.

"Good," Nazere replied. "I wouldn't want you to ever have to do that."

"You completed what you set out to do," Elle said softly as she hugged him again. "I'm proud of you." Nazere smiled. He then dropped his hands from around Elle and looked over to see Ryan standing by himself, staring at the ground. As Elle backed off of Nazere, Nazere walked up to Ryan and embraced him like the family he had suddenly become to him.

"Thank you for standing by me," Nazere said as he hugged Ryan firmly. "Changing wasn't quite as horrible as I thought it would be."

"That's what true friends are for," Ryan said as he pulled back and looked Nazere in the eyes. "I would stand by you to the bitter ends of the earth. We are brothers, Nazere. And we are in this together." David looked up to the sky, his eyes beginning to show signs of immediate shock as his jaw dropped. A vizedrone hungry for battle was flying face-first in the direction of the Redeemer.

"We've got a problem!" David yelled as he pointed to the vizedrone in the sky. Nazere turned around as if he didn't have a care in the world, focused on the dragon and put his right hand in the air. He then opened the eye to his palm, sending a perfectly precise one and a half inch beam at the dragon's head. There was a short detonation of sterai energy as the machine fell headless to the streets below like an insect after being shocked by an electrical lamp.

"I guess that issue is solved," Ryan said as he looked at David with a smirk on his face. "The ventari are truly unparalleled in their prowess. And we have a ventari on our side now!"

"We still need to get moving," David said as he began walking toward to the Redeemer. "These airways are extremely dangerous territory. Are you coming with us, Nazere?" Nazere shook his head.

"I'll fly on my own," he replied. Elle's demeanor changed as she demonstrated a bit of disappointment in not having Nazere next to her on such an eventful occasion.

"I'll join you," Keldrid said as he appeared next to Nazere.

"If you insist," Elle said, almost somber in expression as she also moved in the direction of the Redeemer. She glanced back over her shoulder but for a second. "I'll see you back at the house, Nazere! Okay?"

"Okay," Nazere replied.

The house, Nazere thought. For the longest time he hadn't had a single place to call home. It seemed that all the damage in his life was slowly coming undone. As soon as the gathering boarded the Redeemer, the bird flapped its wings out and began to get a running start. Nazere ran along side the Redeemer, and they both lifted into the air at the same time. The Redeemer let out a great shriek as it flew over the city of New York. Becoming a stream of blue fire, Nazere flew along side it. Keldrid twisted his flight pattern together with Nazere's, creating a spiral of black and blue across the sky. The Redeemer cried out again as it picked up speed, and Nazere and Keldrid followed close behind.

Within minutes, the gathering had returned to the house. Nazere and Keldrid came to a mighty stop in front of the huge door to the Undrum cabin, sending shockwaves flying outward from their broken momentum. Nazere turned to Keldrid and smiled while David parked the Redeemer in its normal spot to the left of the cabin.

"Keep your ion shields up," David said as he stepped out of the Redeemer. "I hate snow on my beautiful girl."

"Please David," Elle smirked, putting a finger inside her mouth as to signify she was going to puke. She climbed out of the Redeemer behind David. "You're making me sick." When Ryan stepped out of the Redeemer, he stretched his body out by reaching his arms high above him.

"I'm getting pretty tired," Ryan to Nazere as he walked inside of the cabin door and yawned. "Let's go get some rest, buddy. It's been a good day." As Nazere opened the creaky entrance, he noticed Hayden was sitting in his usual spot at the table, drinking a cup of tea.

"Just in time," Hayden began. "Please come in, my children." The gathering walked in, taking their usual chairs around the table. Keldrid took his seat on the red sofa as he had before. Once comfortably seated, the gathering attentively awaited what Hayden was about to say. "You look very inhuman, Nazere,“ Hayden said as he got up from his chair and walked to where Nazere sat. He then wrapped his arms around him and looked him in his eyes with a smile on his face. "But I am so very proud of you. You have accomplished something, and that is the first step toward your necessary change.“

"I have a new companion,“ Nazere reported as he held out his summtorant. "Come, Verus!“ he commanded. Verus came out of the summtorant in a ball of smoke and sat before Nazere. Hayden reached down and gently ran his hand through the dog‘s brown and black fur. Nazere leaned over and embraced Verus as the dog sat panting. As Nazere released his arms, he watched Hayden sit back down in his chair. A look of seriousness crossed his face. Everyone at the table remained quiet and still as they set their eyes on High Prophet Hayden.

"There is some business I have to discuss with all of you. You have completed your task today, and there is much to be said of that. But as you all well know, Operation Maelstrom is not complete. Tomorrow, you will rally with the forces of the Gathering of the White Rook; they await your arrival. High Prophet Baun remains a captive, and is now in stasis in the province of Ordren."

"Ordren?" Nazere asked with a puzzled look on his face. He didn't want to return there. "That place is crawling with ventari. It will be one against many."

"That is why you will seek aid. The Gathering of the White Lion has already committed to joining in on the operation. Baun must be rescued in order for the Master's tasks to come to fruition. And so it will be done." Hayden paused for a moment as he looked around at the group and smiled. "I want to let you each of you know that I am very proud of your ability to unite as one. You have proven to be outstandingly resilient as a team. But there is much work to do yet. So go now, and rest. For in the morning, the rally of the gatherings begins."

The gathering all began rising from their seats at once; the majority began walking up the spiral staircase. Ryan lay his hand on Nazere's shoulder as he passed him. "It was truly a good day, today, Nazere," Ryan said in walking by. "I was glad to have you by my side — honored, in fact."

"As was I," Nazere replied. "You're a good friend, Ryan. We made a few memories together, side by side." Ryan glanced back at Nazere as he reached the staircase and winked as he walked out of sight.

"Good show today, mate," David said to Nazere as he walked by him, smiling. "I'll see you in the morning, then?"

"Of course," Nazere replied. "Excellent flying, David. I wish I could do what you do." Finally, Elle walked up to Nazere.

"I told you that you could do it," Elle began as she walked close to Nazere. She looked deeply into his eyes as she had before. "I just wanted you to know that I'm so very happy to have you around. I thought about you the whole time you were gone. I had a wonderful time with you in Baltimore. It was nice just to be together with you. And I really did miss you." Elle wrapped her hands around Nazere's neck. "I'm so proud of you," she whispered softly, a tiny smile cracking across her face. The two looked at one another as all thought seemed to fade away, and as if all that mattered was that they were in a soft embrace. And just as Elle was about to lean into Nazere,

Hayden coughed.

"Ahem," Hayden began as he spat the contents of his tea out on the table. "Do excuse me. The tea is quite hot this evening." Elle smiled completely, still looking Nazere in the eyes.

"I'll see you in the morning, Nazere," Elle said as she reached up and kissed him on the cheek. Elle then ascended the stairs, her eyes set on Nazere as she slowly walked. Nazere paused for a moment. He was waiting for a moment when Hayden wasn't paying attention. Once he had the opportunity, he signaled to Keldrid to follow him upstairs. Keldrid stood up from his seat. He then walked up to Nazere, and leaned close to him.

"I've never said this to any human," Keldrid began. "But I think I'm growing quite fond of you."

"You aren't so bad yourself, Keldrid," Nazere whispered under his breath. And together, Keldrid, Nazere and Verus walked upstairs. Once back in the room, Verus curled up next to Nazere's bed and began drifting off to sleep. The dog snored loudly as soon as he had fallen asleep. Taking hold of his brown comforter, Nazere slipped into his bed and got comfortable. Keldrid stood in the corner of the room. About to pick up the book on his nightstand and begin reading, a thought crossed Nazere's mind. He looked over to Keldrid.

"Enlighten me," Nazere began. "I've read of the great war in heaven. You were there weren't you, Keldrid?"

"I was," Keldrid replied.

"Tell me the story. Tell me how it all began."

"Very well," Keldrid began with a sinister tone. "I shall tell you of the first war. Before time began, God and his angels lived in harmony. There was peace, and all of existence was made perfect. However, one of God's perfect beings drew the special attention of the Lord. He was a mighty musician, and day in and day out he played on his harp for the Lord. He far exceeded the abilities of all the other angels, and with every passing day God gave him more power. This angel continued to play for the Lord and God was pleased with his perfect performances. God loved this angel with all his heart. But after some time, God had given this angel so much power that the angel's eyes became opened in entirely new ways. The angel looked on God and became jealous of his great might and power. 'Lord,' he said to him. 'My power is great, but I can never be what you are. Will you grant me your power that I might sing you a greater song?' The Lord declined, stating that He alone could hold the ultimate power in heaven. Discontented with the Lord's reply, this angel walked out of the Lord's presence and began stirring dissension in heaven. He called to the angels that looked up to him, and he beckoned them to join him in dethroning the King. Knowing he could not do it alone, the angel was joined by a third of heaven's assembly. Together, they walked into the throne room of the great King of all things. And one by one they drew swords. And war broke out in heaven. God's angels battled the angels dedicated to the great musician's cause. Unable to overcome the King, God's angels surrounded the betrayers. And one by one, the betrayers were cast from the heavens into the abyss. In the darkness of the void, the angels called out for redemption. But there could be no salvation for them. The great angel I spoke of is called Lucifer, and God was deeply saddened by his loss."

"So what of the earth?" Nazere asked. "Why was it created? What great purpose does it serve?"

"I cannot speak anymore tonight," Keldrid said as he looked at Nazere. "Sleep now, for tomorrow is going to be another long day. Rest well, human." Nazere lay back in his bed and turned to his side. And within a few minutes, he had drifted into a deep sleep.

CHAPTER FOUR

The Gathering of the White Rook

And everything faded to black. Suddenly, out of the darkness came a thick, hazy mist. The mist expanded in a full circle around Nazere, bursting into flame before his very eyes. Before Nazere stood three dark figures, all of them standing in parallel to one another. These figures appeared to be the silhouettes of men. The center figure came out of the shadows, walking forward toward Nazere. The man's rising from the darkness brought him into plain sight, and he took on the appearance of a towering red dragon in the incandescence of the fire. Scales and sharp spines covered the dragon, its stomach reaching Nazere's eye level as it began to take to its hind legs. The dragon lifted its body high over Nazere, moving its massive tail as it erected itself to its ultimate height. Reaching his arm out, Nazere attempted to fire a bolt of energy from his mechanical hand at the dragon's gargantuan, armored chest; his attempt only failed. The dragon then leaned his face close to Nazere's and opened its massive jaws, sharp teeth accompanied by a sharp tongue. Beginning to speak, it uttered the words, "You are utterly hopeless."

Awakening from the nightmare, Nazere arose from his bed filled with fright filling his unsteady mind like a quart of orange juice being poured into a paper pitcher, gandering around in a mental collapse of paranoia. Keldrid remained in his usual position in the corner of the room, quiet and in-situ. Looking down at his hands, Nazere checked to ensure the events that had transpired the day before really had. Reaching his arms out, the light from the window to his left reflected off of his newly attained transparent armor. His arms carried the luminescense of a thousand shining stars, with the intricate mechanisms within his suit shifting as he moved about like a busy factory in absolute motility. While still in his bed and within seconds of rising from his sleeping position, a holographic display appeared before his eyes. There were panels in blue that displayed his core temperature, armor condition, and weapons' targeting systems. In green, a panel was flashing "System Dominance Offline." This indicated that the trillions of cell processors throughout his body had no control over his actions. He had successfully overcome the takeover process of the machine and had become the first man to maintain his mental faculties while transitioning into a ventari suit. However, from his vantage point, a purple panel indicated that nervous system sensations had also been maintained. Capable of tracking all neurological input, it flashed, "Sleeping Process Discontinued."

The pumps, wiring and pistons within Nazere's new body exploded into motion as he pulled his brown comforter off and rose from his bed. He felt as light as a feather as he moved, but he no longer felt the inclination to stretch as he had after every night's sleep for as long as he could remember. The words "Unidentified Canine" spread across Nazere's field of vision as he looked at Verus on the floor. The dog was still sleeping soundly.

"Good morning, human," Keldrid greeted Nazere as soon as the ventari had stood up.

"Morning, Keldrid," Nazere replied. "How are you feeling this morning?"

"I feel nothing," Keldrid replied.

"To my astonishment, I am happy to admit that I can't relate," Nazere said, smiling as he adjusted to the new body he had acquired.

The idea of the transfer hadn't truly penetrated Nazere's mind until he had awakened, the reality of his metamorphosis becoming tangible as he began to feel every sensation exactly as he had in his human body. Nazere wondered how his essence had been able to fully transfer into this new technological wonder that he had so suddenly become; his mind seemed the same, as his likes, dislikes and memory still remained. Is this my soul that has been transferred — my spirit? he wondered. He could feel the newly-found power of his ventari body, along with an ever-present, low-intensity background noise; it was faint, a small humming vibration that he couldn't seem to shake. Is this so much a noise or an idea? he continued in thought. This noise was not his own; it was clearly stifled, but very persistant. He concentrated on the thought intently as his waking mind became more alert. What is it? The subtle vibration was like something faintly calling him — whispering his very name. This was the signal of the Scientific Magisterium, the very same signal that controlled every last one of the other ventari; but it remained only a faint background signal to Nazere. As Nazere concerntrated on it, however, it took the form of what he used to consider a temptation. Ever so slight, and easily controllable, he guessed, because of the therum drop that Ryan had given me. Nazere felt uneasy about the presence of this urge nonetheless; there was a temptation he felt to surrender to the signal and allow all of his choices to be made for him; to be controlled and fellowship with the collective that the signal represented and not have to make the hard choices he knew would be ever before him because of this temptation. He had a strong feeling that this insidious signal would continue to be an ever-present problem and an eventual source of conflict for him — much like the temptation he had for drugs were in his other body; it seemed the problems for him would never end. Fear ran throughout his mind like a lab rat on a wheel, so he made the conscious and deliberate decision to focus on something else.

Nazere looked at his hands as he held them out in front of him, zooming his internal cameras in on the artolium eyes on his palms. The five blades of the eye were closed, a round blue circle surrounding the eye gleaming a neon blue. Looking at the internals of his arms, Nazere noticed the intricacies of the wiring attached to his hand. The wires were numbered in the thousands and colored in various shades of blue, all of them linked to a small, cylindrical pump cannon in his forearm. The cannon was made of sterling artolium, and was eight inches long and two inches wide.

Testing his ability to move matter, Nazere leaned over and reached his arms under his bed. He then lifted. The bed was constructed of heavy oak with a solid steel frame, but Nazere's arms felt as light as air as he held his own bed ten inches from his chest. Suddenly, a knock came at the door. Nazere turned his head to the left, still holding the bed in front of him. Without time for Nazere to speak in response to the knock, Elle walked into the brown room. A wide smile covered her face as instantaneously as she stepped foot into Nazere's sleeping quarters. She stared as Nazere held the bed in front of him as if it were weightless. Elle put her hands behind her back, beginning to laugh as she continued to watch Nazere. From outside of the door, the fragrant scent of something pleasant being cooked downstairs touched down on Nazere's nostrils. He could also smell the rich, aromatic scent of freshly brewed coffee wafting in from downstairs.

"I'm sorry," Elle began as she laughed to herself. "I'm just trying to imagine what possessed you to pick up your bed. Men always have to test their own strength, don't they?" Embarrassed, Nazere slowly dropped the bed down to its original position. He then turned to Elle and smiled.

"Yes, that's it," Nazere began as he looked at Elle, trying to hold his natural smile back. "I regularly test my bed-lifting strength in the morning. It's my normal routine." Elle held her hand to her face, her cheeks blushing a vibrant pink as she attempted to hold back a laugh.

"Well, come downstairs and get something to eat when you're ready," Elle said as she began to step outside of the door. A look of confusion overtook Nazere's translucent face as he glanced at the door's entrance.

"Do you know if my new body can even take in food?" Nazere asked. Holding her hands on the frame of the door, Elle peered in and smiled again as she looked at him.

"Of course you can eat food," she began. "In fact, you need to eat much more food than you did before. I have eggs, pancakes, French toast and sausage downstairs. Come down and look at your plate."

Elle released her hands and walked out of the door. Nazere continued to examine his chest and legs closely. He then thought about going downstairs, and his eyes were immediately confronted with an internal display prompt.

"Blink now?" the display questioned. Elle silently sneaked back to the door and peered in to watch Nazere. It appeared as if he was staring into space, but he was very much aware of Elle's presence. He turned his face in her direction.

"Hurry!" she demanded, a bit embarrassed that she was caught watching him. "I've been slaving over a hot stove all morning for you. Get your butt downstairs!" Nazere nodded.

"I'll be down," he replied. Elle walked away from the door, and as she did, Nazere heard her footsteps slowly descend the winding staircase of the Undrum cabin. On Nazere's visual display, a map of the entire cabin and the area outside was shown before him. He could see the Redeemer's wings moving subtly outside of his window without needing to physically peer out of the glass pane. He watched the outline of Elle's body walk down the winding stairs, and the figures of three men downstairs near the table. Nazere began to take a step, and just as he did a prompt appeared before him again.

"Blink now?" the display questioned. The internal computers of the ventari suit were anticipating Nazere's desired movements. Nazere turned his head slightly as he thought to himself for a second in quiet contemplation.

"Blink," Nazere replied. In less than a split second, Nazere appeared at the bottom of the winding staircase directly next to Elle. Looking to her side at Nazere, Elle shook her head.

"Well, well," Elle began as she smiled at Nazere. "How fancy. Are you trying to impress me?"

"Not at all," Nazere replied with a straight face as he looked into Elle's eyes. "I was actually aiming for the kitchen. I missed." He wasn't aiming for the kitchen at all.

"Uh huh," Elle replied as she walked over to where David and Ryan were standing. In her direction, the table was adorned with pewter plates and silverware placed out evenly with the greatest of care. In the center of the table next to the raiditor, a large black pan was laid out with pancakes stacked high and sausage piled in a large bunch. In Nazere's seat next to Elle's, breakfast was stacked on an especially large pewter plate. The pancakes seemed to pile to the ceiling, and sausage was piled neatly next to it. In front of Nazere's seat, a utensil he had never seen was set underneath a forest green cloth. The ends of the silver utensil had a blue incandescence to it, and the item greatly resembled a wand. At the end of the table, Hayden sat slowly eating his pancakes and sausage. Elle walked over to the hovering stove off to the left of the table and continued to flip French toast that was already in another pan on top of it. The stove's silver shine seemed to reflect off of all the dinnerware on the oak table. Suspended above the ground, its center fire heated the stainless steel pan that was on top of it as Elle continued her finely-mastered craft of preparing food.

"Good morning, sunshine," David greeted Nazere as he stood around the table piling his plate high with food, his fork in one hand and a plate in the other. "I suppose my prayers were answered last night. Your face! It looks so much better now." David laughed and nudged Ryan. "That other one was scaring me." Ryan, who was standing next to David, smiled at David's smart remarks. Elle turned around with a stern look on her face.

"I, for one, happen to think he was pretty cute," she said as she loaded another large plate of food and set it next to Nazere's chair. Elle leaned over in the relative direction of Ryan and David's faces as she set the plate down, her eyebrows stern and her face quite serious. "You two leave him alone, you understand? He's been through a lot."

"Yes, your heinous," Ryan replied with a smug look on his face, preoccupied with the plate of food in his hands and the mug of steaming-hot coffee that awaited him at the table. Ryan then took his normal seat on the left, nearest to the great door of the Undrum cabin, digging into his food as soon as he sat down. Hayden looked up, and he smiled as his eyes met Nazere's.

"Good morning, my boy," Hayden began as he finished his last bite of food. "Did you rest well last night?" Nazere shook his head.

"I keep having the strangest dreams," Nazere began. "I'd never had them in the past. They just keep coming. And I'd swear they were real." David continued to stack his plate, which was already quite full. But as he heard Nazere's words, he turned his head in his direction.

"What was your dream of this time, Nazere?" David asked curiously, his face filled with wonderment. Hayden raised his hand in the air.

"That is not for you to know, David," Hayden instructed. "His revelations will come to be made known in time. For now, please satiate your hunger for food. Concern yourself with the day ahead." David turned to Hayden and nodded.

"I didn't mean to be a bother," David said as he took a seat.

"You are no bother at all," Hayden replied. "I just don't want Nazere overwhelmed with unnecessary questions so early in the morning." Hayden turned his eyes to the sun-soaked window to his right. "It is a beautiful day, by the way. We are blessed to have it." Hayden waved his arms and signaled for Nazere to come a little closer. "Take a seat, my boy. My dear Elle has been hard at work preparing your meal for the day." Hayden smiled at Nazere as he walked over to his seat and sat down. Nazere then unveiled the utensil sitting to the side of his seat by removing the forest green cloth wrapped around it. Elle walked back to the stove, turned it off, and then came to take her seat next to Nazere.

"What is this thing?" Nazere asked as he held the wand looking device in front of him. He looked upon it as if it were some sort of alien specimen.

"It's a tespord," David replied, speaking with his mouth open and full of food.

"A tespord?" Nazere questioned as he continued to examine the wand looking item. The end of the tespord had a bulb that contained a swirling blue charge of what appeared to be ethalon while the rest of the item was silver and had the outline of a ventari embossed into it. The emblem of the ventari pictured the machine with its arms and legs extended with two rings surrounding it.

"A tespord is a ventari utensil," Ryan spoke across the table as he took a brief break from eating. "They aren't hard to come by."

"I had one especially ordered before your coming," Hayden began. "The consumption of energy is quite important for a ventari. You must keep your charge at full capacity in order to remain offensively and defensively effective."

"So how do I use it?" Nazere asked as he looked around him at everyone at the table. Elle took Nazere's hand and gently drove Nazere's hand and the tespord's lit end into the pile of pancakes in front of him. As the tespord made contact, the pancakes were incinerated before Nazere's very eyes. The food lifted up and gravitated toward the utensil, and as it did the tespord's internal charge began to glow brighter. Looking down at his chest, Nazere noticed that the machinery within his body was converting the food into blue pulses of light. The pulses of light flowed steadily into his chest, which began to glow a brilliant shade of light blue as Elle continued to assist him in driving the tespord into the food in front of him. Within seconds the entire plate in front of Nazere had been incinerated and sucked into the tespord. Nazere's display began to flash words as the energy was taken in.

"Replenishing Energy Now," it read as Elle continued to guide Nazere in consuming his food.

"Do you have it now?" Elle asked as she leaned over next to Nazere like a mother would to her child, her hand on his back. Nazere nodded as a strong hunger suddenly emerged within him. Nazere moved the tespord to the plate next to him and consumed all of the contents of the plate in a few short seconds.

"I can actually taste the food," Nazere commented as his body received the steadily flowing energy from the tespord. Nazere moved the tespord over to the giant stack of sausage next to the pancakes.

"Fascinating, isn't it?" David asked, looking across the table at Nazere.

"This is how you will eat from now on," Elle started. "It will take some getting used to, but in time it will become second nature."

"I'm more thirsty more than anything else," Nazere said.

"Well," David began. "Your body cannot drink anything. Your artolium skin cells absorb moisture from the air. You require so little that you can go months without any moisture at all. It is normal to feel thirsty for the first few days, though. You just have to adjust."

"How are your senses, Nazere?" Ryan asked. "Have they adapted yet? Can you feel anything?"

"I feel everything as I normally did," Nazere replied, turning his eyes to Elle. "Thank you for the breakfast, Elle." Elle blushed and smiled.

"I thought I'd give you a welcoming start for your day. I want you to feel at home, and I want you to be happy."

"As 'the day' is brought to my attention," Hayden began. "I do believe we are to begin our travels to the Bastion of the Lights' End. I have decided that I will be joining you."

"The Bastion of the Lights' End?" Nazere asked.

"It is the castle of the Gathering of the White Rook," Ryan replied as he slowly continued to eat.

"We must rally greater company in order to ensure High Prophet Baun's rescue from the well guarded province of Ordren," Hayden said as he leaned forward in his chair. "The Bastion of the Lights' End is our first and foremost destination. There we will meet with the Gathering of the White Lion, as I had indicated yesterday. It is essential that the appropriate route of action be taken in order for us to invade the enemy's territory with any chance of success."

"High prophet," Elle began, still standing. "Have you any idea of when we will begin our offensive on the city of Ordren?"

"We will need quite a few days of preparation," Hayden replied. "James Featherwing, the chief battle prophet of the Gathering of the White Rook, has been in contact. He sent me a message on my cell phone late last night. He has all of our rooms at the castle prepared for our arrival. Once there, we will have to devise a strategy to infiltrate the heavily fortified province." Hayden looked across the table to a man with a mouth still stuffed with food. "David. When will you have the Redeemer ready for flight?" David dropped his fork and looked up at Hayden.

"I have to go work a little maintenance on the weapons' engine," David began as he chewed and swallowed his breakfast. "It should only take me a few minutes. The damage it sustained the other day has thrown the targeting systems off a bit."

"Very well," Hayden replied. "In the mean time, let me show Nazere a bit of our tower that I haven't yet. There are some items of importance that I need to bring to his attention."

"May I come along?" Elle asked excitedly. Nazere sat with his chest gleaming brightly, his body fully charged with energy as he had emptied every plate in front of him.

"Man, that French toast was good," Nazere commented as he leaned back and patted his own stomach.

"Certainly," Hayden replied. "I assume that both of you are done with your morning meals, then?"

"Yes," Nazere said, his stomach glowing like a fully illuminated lightning bug.

"Then come. Follow me up the stairs. We are going to the Hallowed Adytum."

"The Hallowed Adytum?!" Elle asked, an excited tone to her voice and a visual expression of amazement to her face. "You have never allowed any of us to go inside of it!"

"Where is it?" Nazere asked.

"It is at the apex to our home!" Elle exclaimed, her face becoming an aspect of exhilaration. "It is sacred ground, and I've been dying to go there for the longest time." Elle veered her eyes toward High Prophet Hayden. "Let's go up there now!" Hayden nodded.

"We shall go now, Elle. Patience, my dear," Hayden said as he arose from his chair, holding to the light-oak staff at his side as he made to his feet. "Follow closely behind me. Both of you." With an elated look on her face, Elle leaned down and wrapped her hands around Nazere's bulky arm.

"Let's go, big guy," Elle said to Nazere. Hayden had already begun to walk up the spiraling staircase, lifting his staff upward as he ascended the pathway. Nazere stood up from his chair and smiled as he walked alongside Elle. She continued to talk to him as they stepped up the coiled staircase. "The Hallowed Adytum is the temple at the pinnacle of this place. No one has ever stepped foot within its confines except Hayden. This is a pretty major occasion."

"We're making our way to the very top," Hayden said as he kept his eyes set straight ahead of him. "Try to keep up with an old man," he said smiling. Climbing the spiral past Nazere's room, Hayden walked to the very top of the cabin. Nazere and Elle looked down at the bottom of the cabin together. The table and sofas that made up the den of the house seemed so very minuscule from where they were. At the very top of the stairs, a door with the symbol of a knight's chess piece set in iron marked the very last room in the cabin. Nazere and Elle stood directly behind Hayden as he pushed his hand forward in the space in front of him, never physically touching the door. The eyes of the chess piece took on a white radiance, and the door miraculously came swinging open. "After you, my dears," Hayden said as he smiled and waved for the two to enter before him.

Nazere took the first step in, and Elle followed right behind. Both of them looked around the room in awe at the view from the entrance. The room was made of solid gold, floors and ceiling alike. The floor had the intricate imprints of fully armored knights holding spades at their right sides spread throughout it in a checkered pattern. The imprints were approximately five feet in length. There were two pillars in the middle of the room, and between them was an old, black-iron box that was collecting cobwebs and dust all around it. Protruding from the pillars were two life-sized seraphim statues with long, lifted wings. Both of them were blowing into curved horns they held in their hands. Their faces were exposed, but a hood and a great robe covered the rest of their bodies. The statues were solid gold, gleaming amidst the glorious radiance of the golden room.

"This place is brilliant!" Elle exclaimed as she glanced around in all directions, her eyes widely opened. Nazere walked within a foot of Elle.

"What is the significance of the Hallowed Adytum, exactly?" Nazere whispered to Elle.

"This is the sacred temple of our humble cabin," Elle replied in a whisper of her own. "It holds holy relics that have been preserved over the ages. This is my first time seeing it in person, but it is just as

I dreamt it would be." Nazere and Elle continued to look around the room. To the right of the webbed, iron box were eight staffs in different shapes and sizes. They were colored in varying shades of white, black and brown. They all leaned to the right of the room against the solid gold wall. To the left of where Nazere was standing, a large gold-framed painting of a well armored knight dodging the flames from the breath of a dragon caught his attention. The knight carried a sword, and his steel shield was blocking the flames the dragon spewed from its mouth. The painting of the dragon immediately made Nazere recall his most recent dream. The appearance of the dragon was exactly as he saw it in his nightmare, the dragon having many spines and red-scaled armor. As Nazere peered to his right, he became deeply captivated by the astonishing observation he made there.

Walking toward the left of the room, Nazere closed in on yet another gold-framed painting that had caught his attention. Nazere focused his internal display in on the details of the artwork. This painting was one of a three-headed dragon, the dragon bearing gray-scale armor, and each of his heads breathing a bright green flame. Before the great dragon stood a ventari, with his right arm held up in the direction of the dragon. A sterai flare was beginning to charge in the ventari's palm, the light of the energy vividly illustrated in the painting. Elle walked up alongside Nazere, looking at the magnificent strokes of oil-based paint used to describe the altercation between this ventari and the three-headed dragon. Elle stared at the picture, her face growing curious as to the artist of the illustration. And at the very moment she began to stare, Nazere grabbed his head as a thousand screams suddenly penetrated his skull like a storm.

"What's wrong Nazere?" Elle asked, holding his shoulder with a deeply concerned look on her face.

The screams continued to penetrate Nazere's mind, and he held to his head and dropped to his knees as the loud outcries overtook his entire being. He felt as if he was dying, the pain of the repeated high-pitched cries throwing his very core out of sync with reality.

Flash. Suddenly, Nazere stood in a black void, his body hovering in a darkness that completely surrounded him. A great mist came out and encircled him as it had in his prior dream. But this time, only one figure stood before him. As the mist surrounding him burst into flame, Nazere focused his eyes straight ahead. Before him was the dark outline of a man sitting in a chair with his fingers linked in front of his face. Suddenly, the earth and the stars beyond it appeared before Nazere like the snap of a finger. The stars beyond the earth's atmosphere served as a backdrop for the man who sat before him, the earth appearing as small as a baseball to the man‘s left; it was even tinnier than the globe-sized world the first rider Nazere had seen fired an arrow at. The man unfolded his hands as Nazere stood before him, taking a step out of the shadows. He walked in the center of space as if it had a solid surface. As he did, the image of a towering three-headed dragon came into view. There was little time to react to the dragon's emergence as the creature's reflexes were as dynamic as a jet flying at mach two. The dragon cocked back its central head like a whip, and diving all three heads forward it unleashed a great breath of green flame. Flash.

"Are you alright Nazere?" Elle said as Nazere returned to his senses, descending from his place at his castle in the air. He was still gripping his head with his fingers, but the screams had dissipated. He dropped his hands to his side as he took a stand.

"I'm fine," Nazere replied calmly. He then walked up to the painting and put his hand on the surface of it. All of the events that had been transpiring were a cipher, all too strange for him to decrypt. He couldn't understand why these miraculous events were playing out like an in-depth script.

"Come here, my boy," Hayden instructed as he veered his eyes over toward Nazere. Nazere removed his hand from the painting and turned his attention to the origin of Hayden‘s voice. Hayden was standing in front of the large iron chest in the center of the room. Reaching into his robes with his left hand, Hayden withdrew a silver key with angel-like wings extending out of the top of it. "I have something to show you." Nazere and Elle walked over to where Hayden was standing, watching his every movement. Crouching down in front of the iron lockbox, Hayden inserted the reflective silver key into the chest's antiqued face. He then turned the key gently, the old container slowly creaking open.

Within the box, what appeared to be a long golden handle sat covered in layers of thick dust. Hayden lifted the handle out the box, placing the handle in front of his mouth and blowing the accumulated dust off of its surface. He then picked himself up, holding to his staff as he came to his feet.

"A handle?" Nazere asked, curious as to the relevance of the item in Hayden's hands.

"Indeed," Hayden replied. "But this is no ordinary handle. It is the priest's handle to the Ark of the Covenant."

"You're telling me that you have a piece of the Ark of the Covenant?" Nazere asked. "I heard it was destroyed during the ancient times of Nebuchadnezzar. There has been much history written on it."

"Look at the marks on its side," Hayden said as he pointed to the surface of the golden rod. Nazere's display immediately focused in on vividly detailed inscriptions on the side of the rod. They looked as if they had not aged a day.

"Ancient Hebrew," Nazere's digital display indicated as his internal crosshairs focused In on the text. Nazere wondered to himself what the text might read, but just as he did a new display appeared before him. The ventari suit was well in-tuned to Nazere's every single thought. The display read, "The handle of Malachi, High Priest of Israel. He who carries this in times of peace or war bears the blessing of the Everlasting One." Nazere read the text out loud, and Hayden laughed in reply to his words.

"So where is the remainder of the ark?" Nazere asked.

"Shattered," Hayden replied, his face becoming straight. "Into a hundred pieces. The handle is necessary to capacitate the Head of the Churbim. The head holds the power to kill anything it touches."

"The head is deadly?" Nazere asked, as curious as ever.

"Of course," Hayden replied. "It was crafted by the Master's hand. The wood of the ark was once deadly as well, but its fragments were warped in the waters of the earth. The Head of the Churbim is a very well guarded relic. Held deep within the Bastion of Lights' End, it is essential to forging a sword capable of delivering death to any who challenge it. Many have made attempts at infiltrating the head held within the bastion, but all who have tried have failed."

"So let me guess…" Nazere started.

"Yes," Elle interjected. "The Blade of the Unbroken will be forged using the handle and the head fragment. I have foreseen it. Am I correct in my words, Hayden?"

"You are," Hayden replied. "Your visions have served you well. But there is a requirement for the blade to be fully completed. The sword must be double-edged, and the first fragment will only serve for the first edge. When it becomes twin-edged, the sword shall henceforth be known as the Blessed Blade of the White Rider. It is then that it shall truly be completed, and the wielder will be made perfectly unbreakable."

"So where is the second fragment? And how did the ark become shattered?" Nazere asked Hayden.

"The second fragment is in the hand of the enemy," Hayden began as his face became serious. He squinted into Nazere's eyes as he spoke with the utmost sincerity. "It is Vice Lord Xar's most precious possession, and he will not give it up without a fight. As for the ark, it was found and broken into pieces by King Nebuchadnezzar of Babylon as you said; his armies found it in a cave under a tall mountain, and it was tossed within the Sea of Galilee long ago. It was only within the last fifty years that the ark was discovered. One by one, prophets dove into the sea and used the handles of the ark to lift its shattered fragments to the surface of the water. The pieces went into hiding, until after some time Vice Lord Xar rose to power. By means of his corruptive position of political power, he secretly sent out assassins to retrieve the pieces of the ark. It wasn't long until one of the pieces was found, and those who hid the pieces were murdered. Xar hid his despicable actions from public knowledge. Alongside High Lord Alune, Vice Lord Xar now reigns over the free world. He has allowed for all matter of evil to be set loose; for in this modern state of advancement, the consequences of a man's actions can be easily remedied. Men live unnatural long lives, seek genetic alteration, and feed off of one another's darkest desires. In so much as that is true, mankind has fallen from all grace. Now the wars have begun, and the word of the wars will be spread throughout the world. You are the harbinger of the coming wars, Nazere." Hayden extended his arm and handed the handle of the ark to Nazere. "It is your duty to deliver this to the head blacksmith of the white rook. He will see to it that the Blade of the Unbroken is forged when the time is right."

After speaking, Hayden walked alongside his staff to a point in the center of the left wall. He then took his staff and struck the side of the wall, a small cavity opening at the bottom of the wall below where he hit it. The cavity was a petite, two by two foot black space. Crouching down again, Hayden held to his staff as he reached underneath the dark opening in the wall. "I know it's in here somewhere," Hayden said as he maneuvered his hand around in the small black space. "Ah," Hayden began as he reached something. He withdrew a thin silver necklace from the hole. "Here it is!"

Hayden picked himself up to his feet and walked over to Elle. He then placed the chain-linked silver necklace around Elle's neck, smiling as he took a step back to take a good look at her. "Magnificent!" Hayden exclaimed as he looked upon her. "I hereby grant you, Elle Winstrom, the Amulet of the Lifeseeker. May it forever keep you well in trying times."

Elle looked down upon her shining chain necklace, its center in the shape of a feather with emeralds adorning the finely crafted metal on three sides. The jewelry completely captured her eyes' focus, her eyes lighting up like a lamp at the sight of the green gemstones that formed a triangle on the feather's silver surface.

"I will always keep it close to my heart," Elle said as she embraced the amulet with her left hand. "And I will use it well." Hayden walked to the entrance to the Hallowed Adytum.

"That is all there is to be accomplished here," Hayden began. "You may now go about your business. We depart for the Bastion of Lights' End shortly, so I advise that the both of you go and prepare yourselves."

Hayden walked out of the room and began descending the winding staircase. Nazere reached out his hand and took of Elle's. The two then walked behind him, stepping side by side down each individual stair.

"What is the purpose of your necklace?" Nazere asked with the utmost interest as he looked down into Elle's hazel eyes. Elle smiled.

"It is blessed," Elle replied, still holding to her amulet. She looked up into his eyes in return, her sincere gaze intriguing Nazere as to what she might be holding back. He knew there was something, but he kept his inquiries locked away. "In time, you will see."

Continuing to walk down the staircase, Elle took a right into her room and closed the door behind her. Nazere walked to his room, opening the door and sprawling himself across his bed once he was inside. As he lay in his bed, thoughts of the homeless life he left behind abruptly overtook his entire essence. The truth was that he never thought he would surmount his crippled state of depravity; days without the opportunity to taste food; hide beneath the bulwark of shelter; hold to the possibility of hope. He could see the faces of those he used to share the streets with floating around in his mind like the seeds of a dandelion that had been blown into the wind. They had all been killed or moved to stasis by now, and were but distant memories. For a split second, the pain of the isolation of being alone returned to him like a jagged edge being forcefully driven into his chest. And in that moment, the sympathy for those he had come to know on the streets cut him to his true core. As the feeling subsided, he turned his head to the right. Keldrid still held his place in the corner of the room, silently standing in the exact position he was in before Nazere departed from his room earlier in the morning. Verus was awake, walking around the room and whimpering. How things had changed.

"Do you need to go outside, boy?" Nazere asked, leaning up from his bed. The answer was obvious. "Come on. I'll take you out." Nazere walked to his door and Verus followed close behind him. He walked Verus to the main entrance to the Undrum cabin, opening the large, creaky door and stepping foot into the great outdoors. Precipitation in the form of perfectly different crystal flakes was falling heavily from the gray sky. Verus circled around and leaned over to relieve himself in the thick snow. As Verus finished his most necessary activity, David walked around the left corner of the cabin from the spot where the Redeemer was positioned in waiting. Nazere turned his head in David's direction.

"She's all ready," David said as he approached Nazere. "Let's go in and get the others. They should be ready to fly." Nazere nodded.

"Come on, you fluff-ball," Nazere said as he glanced down at Verus. Verus ran to Nazere's feet, and Nazere pet him as the man and his companion walked to the entrance of the cabin together. The Gathering of the White Knight stood fully accounted for when David opened the noisy, old door. Nazere stood in shock.

"I wonder where Keldrid is," Nazere said out loud.

"Keldrid?" Ryan asked with a confused look on his face.

"Never mind," Nazere replied, trying to negate the subject. I'm sure he'll show up.

"I told you they'd be ready!" David exclaimed as he turned around to Nazere and smiled. "Let's get over to the Redeemer, shall we?"

Together, the gathering tread through the fluffy, white snow to where the Redeemer perched with its many feathers untouched by it. The snow began to cover the gathering's bodies, but as the many snow flakes in the sky landed on Nazere's ventari suit they immediately transitioned into drops of scalding hot water. His suit's internal circuitry was capable of adapting to the environment around it to ensure that a level of comfort and stability was maintained. David walked directly in front of the Redeemer.

"Deactivate your ion shield, my dear," David spoke in the direction of the Redeemer. The massive shield around the Redeemer came down in a series of yellow flickers, and the bird shook its head as snow began to accumulate on its metallic surface. "Wings up!" The Redeemer's impressively large wings came flying open, and David drew out his trentorod. He then inserted it into the door, prompting it to pop back and roll open. "Everybody in," David instructed as he waved his arm for all to enter.

Everyone standing outside of the Redeemer quickly entered in, each individual walking to their respective seats. Verus panted as he climbed aboard and jumped atop a seat next to Ryan. Hayden was the last to climb in, his staff by his side as he took a seat next to Nazere. David pulled up his two control panels with the push of the manual red button to his right side, configuring the suspended images in front of him as they prepared for lift off. Ryan put in his earpiece and grinned as he looked at David. David pushed a small holographic button on the control panel in front of him, going to work in swinging and maneuvering touch-activated sub-panels as he always did in preparation for flight. The ribbon belts came out from behind the seats, flying in the air as lively as ever in securing all on board.

"Oh, I do enjoy a good flight in the Redeemer," Hayden said as leaned over in Nazere's direction, smiling.

"Yes," Nazere snickered, flashing back to the last flight he had in the Redeemer. "A smooth flight would be nice today."

"Here we go," David said as the Redeemer began to flap its wings. The countdown timer had started. And as the timer hit three, the eagle began to move its talons forward, running at an impressive rate of speed in a clearing near the frozen lake before it took to the skies. The Redeemer let out a mighty call as it climbed to a much higher altitude. "How are you doing today, my beautiful girl?" David asked, smiling as leaned back in his oh-so-comfortable captain's chair.

"Satisfactory after the repairs, David," the Redeemer replied.

"Hey, Redeemer," David began. "I'm feeling like I need a coffee today. Can you help me out, gorgeous?"

"Certainly, captain" the Redeemer replied. To David's side, a coffee popped up out of a circular hole in his armrest.

"You gotta love her," David said as he turned to Ryan.

"You need a girlfriend very badly," Elle interjected as she rolled her eyes at David's remarks.

"What is the current destination?" the Redeemer asked. David began to twirl the configurations in front of him, shifting panels into position and marking the landing zone.

"Set a course for the Black Forest, Germany," David said as he continued to manipulate the program in front of him. "We are going to the Bastion of Lights' End. Take it nice and steady." David leaned back in his chair a bit more and put his hands behind his head with a relaxed look on his appeased face. He then reached to the coffee to his right and took a sip.

"Increasing speed to four-hundred and one miles per hour," the Redeemer reported.

"Take us all the way up, babe," David instructed. "And reengage your ion shielding."

"Affirmative," the Redeemer replied as it raised its head to the clouds above. "Increasing speed to six hundred and eighteen miles per hour." Rising above the mesosphere, the Redeemer threw its wings forward as it burned through the thermosphere beyond it. Nazere looked at the display as Earth came into plain view, the lights below blazing like a thousand candles all spread out. The Redeemer spread its wings as it hit the blackness of space, flying freely amidst satellites and space stations to its left and right. On Nazere's internal display, his crosshairs began to identify the various constellations within sight.

"Look there," Nazere whispered as he leaned over in Elle's direction. "There's your favorite star." Elle turned to Nazere and smiled, blushing as a glow overcame her face. Hayden stared at the display before him, looking on the earth with a melancholy twinkle in his saddened eyes.

"Descending on the indicated target," the Redeemer began. The Redeemer then came full circle, moving back in the direction of the earth as it swang around. "Beginning descent now." Letting out a wild cry, the Redeemer threw its wings forward and flew full force into the earth's atmosphere. The ground came into view rapidly as the great eagle reached the clouds. Dense forest covered the whole of the visible terrain, one of the few remaining locations where lush, green plantlife had a chance to flourish. Evergreen trees branched out by the hundreds on the ground below, and beyond them the small image of a castle on the horizon appeared on the left display.

"Now approaching the Bastion of Lights' End," the Redeemer reported as it threw its wings out and began to flap them. "Reducing speed to two-hundred and twelve miles per hour."

"It's been a long time since I've been here," Ryan said as he took the headphone out of his right ear and looked at David. "I wonder if she's waiting for me right now."

"Who's that?" Nazere asked as he turned to Ryan.

"You'll find out when you get there," David said laughing, again beginning to modify the control scheme in front of him.

The Redeemer flew low to the trees underneath it as it closed in on the once small image of a castle in the distance, its wings stationary as it continued to reduce its speed. When Nazere redirected his attention to the display, he noticed the castle was no longer as miniature as it had appeared only moments earlier. As the Redeemer flew closer yet, flapping its wings steadily as it made its final approach, the magnificent Bastion of Lights' End came into full view. The immense, sandstone white castle had three separated walls, with a perimeter of four turrets guarding the entrance to the city. A tower with a violet-coned top and eight great, circular platforms surrounding it marked the center to the construct. There were two smaller, equally spaced out, violet-cone roofed towers slightly below the central one. The walls of the castle were incredibly long and had flat, smooth surfaces. There were four mechanized dragons with long, pointed noses atop each turret that stood about eighty feet above the front wall. Unlike the vizedrones, these machines had a more slender frame, with a wingspan slightly longer than their round-faced draconian opposition. They had a light-blue color about their many scales, and their eyes were a piercingly bright green. The horns and spines on the dragons were silver, and they protruded from their wings. There were eight horns on each wing, and one sharp spine accompanied the horns at the ends of the wings.

Within the first wall of the city were cottages and medieval-fashioned homes, with hundreds of people walking in the middle of the streets in both directions. Every man, woman and child walking the streets were as busy as a hive of worker bees. They moved in and out of the violet, red, and brown brick roofed cottages and homes of the city here and there. They were quick in their steps amidst the traffic of the heavily populated street. Planted Californian redwood trees connected rows of homes every five buildings or so. They were planted in rich, brown mulch and adorned with purple electronic lights that added a bit of character to the city from afar. The second wall towered over the first, serving as the second tier and as a separator from the city below it. Beyond the second wall was a great green field of lush bluegrass. A great stone circle with orange, blinking lights in two arched segments was positioned in the very middle of the long, wide, green field. Flowers in a wide array of colors and breeds grew along the base of the entire perimeter of the second wall. In the lively grass, a group of four people stood off to the right side of the stone circle with the blinking orange lights. The field of grass and flora was about three miles in perimeter. The third sandstone wall at the backside of the second wall was about a half of a mile tall, and only dimly-lit windows at the top of it were visible from the ground below.

Amongst the four people to the right of the stone circle was an enormous machine, its body extending well above the second wall's perimeter. The machine had a broad chest, with enormous arms and legs that put the trunks of Sequoia trees to shame. The machine had a huge head with a face like a man. It had eyes with pupils and irises, a nose with nostrils and a closed mouth with plump, detailed lips. Its entire exterior had the appearance of dark gray gunmetal, and the behemoth's eyes had an amber glow about them. The machine stood motionless with its hands at its side as the Redeemer hovered over top of it. Next to the mighty machine stood the Deliverer, its red eyes looking up as the Redeemer kept its place in the sky.

The Deliverer let out a loud roar as the Redeemer began to lower itself. The Redeemer held its wings stationary as it slowly dove down onto the stone platform in the center of the grass. Spreading its wings and feathers into the air into a perfectly pristine vertical position as its talons touched the stone circle, the Redeemer suddenly became completely idle as it finalized its landing process. And as the door to the Redeemer came rolling open, Hayden stepped out of the bird with his staff in his hand. Behind Hayden, the remainder of the ship's occupants climbed out of the eagle. All of them, of course, except for the captain.

"David has always got to pay his final respects," Ryan said to

Nazere in a whisper. "Get used to him falling behind us a bit. He loves his bird. And that's an understatement." Nazere looked across the field where four unknown people stood across from him.

"James, my good friend," Hayden said as he walked over to a man who stood in the center of the four. Hayden immediately wrapped his arms around the muscular man. James was tall, with long, dirty-blonde hair and a tall spear in his right hand. His face was rugged, and he wore a black leather vest with black leather bracers, leather leggings and high, steel-toed boots. His spear was ten feet long, with a silver body and a razor-sharp, gunmetal head. The center of the thin spear's head bore the shape of a stretched kite, glowing with a brilliant white fluorescence. Next to James stood two other men and a young woman.

"So good to see you, High Prophet," James began as he held on to Hayden's shoulders. "These are trying times, and the executions in Ordren have begun as you well know." James looked around him. "I have awaited your arrivals. I am deeply concerned about the safety of our teacher."

"We are in good company now," Hayden began, pointing to Nazere. "The prophecy has begun to take its course." James set his gaze upon Nazere and smiled as he approached him.

"A ventari," James said as he scanned Nazere up and down with a startled look on his face. "It is my pleasure to finally meet you, my friend." James looked behind him and shifted his left arm backward in the introduction of those Nazere did not know. "These are my comrades and brothers. To the left you'll see our head blacksmith, Felix Amaldores." Felix nodded his head and smiled in the acknowledgment of James' introduction.

"Pleasure to meet you, Nazere," Felix said. Felix was tan skinned, with unkempt black hair, a well shaven face and brown eyes. His clothes were comprised of a maroon long-sleeve t-shirt, boot cut jeans and steel-toed, black boots. He was of a medium build, and stood with his arms crossed as his active eyes watched James present the rest of the small group outside of the bastion.

"Next to Felix stand my very closest companions," James began, looking to Nazere and then twisting his hip and veering his eyes toward the others behind him. "Allow me to introduce you to Lily Anderson and Aaron Tidekeeper." Nazere walked up to the three standing beyond James, and the remainder of the Gathering of the White Knight followed behind him. Nazere set his attention on Lily first as she was closest to him.

"Pleased to make your acquaintance, miss Lily," Nazere said as took her hand. Lily was about the same height as Elle, with a thin build and breathtaking blue eyes. Her hair was blonde, and she wore a blouse with the picture of a violet flower on it with blue jeans and white leather boots.

"The honor is all mine," Lily said as she smiled and briefly glanced behind Nazere. Moving to Lily's side, Nazere stood in front of Aaron and reached out his hand. Aaron skipped out on the handshake, immediately reaching his arms out and wrapping them around Nazere. Nazere laughed as Aaron's body firmly collided with his. Aaron stood about the height of Nazere, had white skin, long brown hair, brown eyes and a thin build. He wore a brown jacket with a t-shirt underneath, jeans and a pair of beat-up tennis shoes. Aaron looked younger, perhaps in the same age range as Nazere.

"It is so good to see you, bro," Aaron said as he drew back from Nazere with his arms still on his shoulders, giving him a thorough look in the face. "You don't know how we've all looked forward to your arrival." Moving beyond Nazere, Lily approached Ryan slowly with an excited gleam in her eyes, running her hand through his smooth, black hair as she reached the place where he stood. She walked her body within inches of his.

"Ryan Galeheart," Lily began slowly as she looked deeply into Ryan's eyes, now holding her hand to the side of his face. "How I've missed you."

"And I you," Ryan whispered as he drew even closer to Lily. Wrapping her arms around Ryan's body, Lily softly kissed Ryan's neck.

The wind began to blow as the Deliverer let out a mighty roar, a circular lift dropping from the center of the great machine. Verus barked at the Deliverer as it began to move, the dog excited at the very slightest movement of the lion. The lift hovered about three feet above the ground when it reached its lowest point. Nazere looked over and smiled as his eyes caught a glimpse of a few friends.

"High heels are no good for anything!" Sara Maple exclaimed with a disgusted look on her face as she took Drake's hand and stepped off of the lift's platform.

"Be careful, Sara," Drake said. "I wouldn't want you to break a nail."

"Ha. Ha," Sara said slowly and sarcastically as she stepped off of the lift. "You try wearing high heels and get back to me on how easy it is to get around."

"Yea, you do that Drake," Adrax said laughing as he hopped off the lift alongside him. "I can see it now," Adrax began, forming two corners of a picture frame with his hands. "Drake struttin' it on the runway. I think you'd look good, brother." Drake shook his head as he stared at Adrax with a discontented look on his face. Owen Candlefire aided Arthur Nedrem in taking careful steps off the lift. Once on the ground, they stood alongside Sara, Adrax and Drake in a tightly-knit group on the grass below.

"Where is Endarius?" Hayden asked Arthur as he approached him.

"He is piloting the Deliverer," Arthur replied. "I'm sure he'll be down in a few moments." Hayden nodded. Setting his sights on Hayden, Arthur reached his arms out and embraced Hayden.

"The unseen one," Sara began as she addressed the high prophet of the Gathering of the White Knight. Sara curtseyed before Hayden as she walked before him. "Good to see you here, High Prophet Hayden. It seems like ages since the last time I've set eyes on you."

"I've been quite busy," High Prophet Hayden replied. "But, I am glad to see that you are in good health, Sara. I do think of all of you at the Gathering of the White Lion all of the time. I've missed so many of you." In the mean time, Adrax walked up to Nazere with a wide smile upon his face.

"I love the new look!" Adrax exclaimed as he put his hands to his side. "So you were successful after all? I never had a doubt." Nazere nodded.

"With the help of Ryan and Verus," Nazere began, not mentioning Keldrid's name. "They stood by me the whole way." Elle knelt down and moved her hand through Verus' fur, smiling as she did.

"I miss having a kitten," Elle said as her eyes met Nazere's. "I love all animals equally, but I love cats especially."

"I love them, too," Nazere replied to Elle with a smile on his face. Nazere flashed back to the abandoned cats he had seen on the streets of Baltimore. He adopted a black and white stray cat that was unbelievably thin; he didn't think it would survive. His cat was named Bobo, and he would feed the cat day in and day out; he would save what little money he had to buy the cat food necessary to keep the animal fed and healthy. He empathized with its suffering, the pain of being hungry, stranded and alone. The cat gained weight after having been fed over a period of time, and Nazere would always look forward to seeing his fluffy little buddy find his way back to him on the streets at sunrise. He remembered seeing so many suffering animals in the streets, and the look in their eyes when they would approach him; but he knew he could never save them all. Deeply, he missed that cat with every ounce of his heart. His furry little friend had passed away right before he was taken into custody by the ventari peacekeepers. He snapped out of his cataleptic state of staring into nothing when Adrax replied to him.

"Don't forget the Master," Adrax said. "I know that He had his arms around you the whole time." Nazere nodded.

"Let's get inside," Hayden said as he addressed everyone standing around him. "We need to get settled in at once. We are allowed only a few days to prepare for the battle front. I know the day of Baun's scheduled execution. I know the exact minute he will be sent to be killed."

"Inside we go then," James said, his eyebrows raised as he turned around completely and led the way inside of the castle. The group outside of the bastion began moving toward a great stone wall behind James. On the surface of the stone wall was the iron imprint of a spread-out hand. James took his hand and placed it into the imprint, his hand the exact size and shape of the imprint. As soon as he did, the wall began to move. The wall gradually fell backward, becoming a bridge to the interior of the building. James directed the group forward by waving his right hand forward. Snapping his fingers, James caused orange flames on both sides of the bridge to come to life. The flames came from torches that hovered in midair on the right and left side of the bridge. There were exactly seven of them spaced out evenly on each side, and they dimly illuminated the sandstone path ahead of the group. Across the bridge, a large door with the painted, white insignia of a rook upon it marked James‘ destination. Nazere looked at the enormous man-like machine that began to move alongside the Deliverer into the confines of the bastion behind the gatherings. He then turned to Elle as he walked.

"What is that thing?" Nazere whispered, leaning his head close to Elle‘s.

"That is the Colossus," Elle replied back in a whisper, smiling. "It is quite an impressive machine when set into full motion. And it is capable of operating itself. It can be totally unmanned and move on its own."

"Is that right?" Nazere whispered back in question. "That's intriguing. He's huge. I wonder what sort of weapon systems he's equipped with. My display can't diagnose his capabilities." Elle gently pat Nazere's back.

"I think that suit is taking over a little much," she snickered in a whisper. "The dork in you is coming out." Elle began giggling at the prospect in her mind.

"What is that supposed to mean?" Nazere asked out loud with a frustrated look on his face.

"I like dorks," Elle whispered to Nazere, her giggles leading her into a snort. "It's no insult, I assure you."

"Well, I happen to like girls that snort when they giggle," Nazere whispered to Elle, wisely taking advantage of his ability to jest back. "It's no insult." Continuing to giggle uncontrollably, Elle snorted again.

"Shhh," Sara Maple whispered to Nazere as she nudged him. "We have to get focused now. Serious business beyond this wall, you know." Verus took a seat as the group came to a stop before the large door.

"Password: Unshaken," James spoke into the door. The perimeter of the entrance beamed rays of violet light from it as the large iron door slowly came creaking open. James put his hand in front of him as a kind gesture for all those surrounding him to pass him by. "Welcome to the Bastion of Lights' End," he said slowly, smiling as he held his right arm in place, now holding his spear with his left. Immediately, everyone began to step into the chambers beyond the door.

The view from the entrance to the bastion was astonishing. A staircase in each corner of the room led up to a higher floor. On the floor the stairs led to, elucidated corridors led to unknown destinations. Each of the four staircases were crafted of fine redwood, and the banisters and railings reflected light from above as they had a high-gloss redwood finish. The floor was also made of fine redwood, creating a uniform atmosphere for the entire room. The staircases were adorned with rolled-out, velvet, violet carpets that led to a large, finely tailored violet carpet in the center of the room. The thread in the center of the carpet in the middle of the room was gold and pictured an illustration of the Bastion of Lights' End in fine detail. The room was about five times the size of the interior to the Undrum cabin. It had two tables with about two-hundred total chairs around them to the left and right of the room. The chairs were completely empty. In the center of the room, above the golden illustration of the castle, was a great triangular stone table. A raiditor hovered directly above it. The stone table had the imprint of a rook in its center, and there were ten redwood chairs on each of the three sides of the table. Larger, red, leather-backed chairs sat in place on each of the triangular table's three edges.

A single candle stood unlit in the center of the stone table. The light from the room came partly from a series of about thirty lamps in the shape of turrets hovering high above the tables below. They were constructed of pine and colored with the same red, high-gloss finish as the rest of the room. Above the lamps was a massive dome, the light pouring into the room through a Tiffany ceiling. The glass was colored white, silver and violet, and was artistically crafted in the image of angel with its wings outspread and its sword held in its center. The edge of the angel's sword was at its feet. A door in the back of the room marked with yet another insignia of a rook led to an unknown destination.

The first men to enter the chambers were Hayden and Arthur. Hayden walked into the room with his staff by his side, and Arthur walked in with his cane by his. Everyone stood awaiting the two high prophets to take their seats. Hayden took a seat in one of the large, leathered chairs on the right side of the triangular stone table. Arthur took a seat in a leathered chair on the left edge of the table. Adrax, James and Ryan entered next. Taking his seat by Hayden's right side, Ryan put his hands up on the table and folded them in front of him. He glanced over to Lily, winking right at her. She smiled back, a glow that spelled happiness painting her cheeks in pink. Adrax sat next to Arthur, also placing his hands on the table and folding them in front of him. Finally, James took his seat next to the empty red-leather backed chair. He put his right hand on the corner of the chair, staring into space as he held his spear in his left.

"Wait here," Elle whispered to Nazere as he was about to take a step forward. "They have a proper order to their seating when a meeting is being conducted."

The next to enter the room were Drake, Aaron and David. David took his seat next to Ryan, Drake next to Adrax, and Aaron beside James. Finally, the girls entered into the room. And in the same fashion as the others, Elle sat next to David, Sara sat next to Drake, and Lily sat next to Aaron. Nazere set his eyes on Elle as she was a guide for him when he had no clue what was going on.

"Where shall I sit?" Nazere asked. Hayden smiled, turning his head in Arthur's direction.

"With the absence of High Prophet Baun under consideration," Hayden began, veering his eyes about the triangular table. "I hereby motion for our new brother, Nazere, to join in the Gathering of the White Knight." Hayden then glanced up at Nazere and winked. "All in favor of this motion?" Everyone at the table raised their hands in the air in unison.

"Then there we have it," Arthur began, placing his pipe in his mouth and lighting it with an electronic lighter he always stored in his jacket pocket. "Nazere is henceforth a member of the Gathering of the White Knight." All at the table stood and clapped, Elle gleaming in elation as she looked on Nazere with pride.

"Ooo! Ooo! Ooo!" Adrax cheered as he raised his hands in the air. "We have a new brother in our midst! And he's a ventari!" Nazere stood in place for a moment, startled at the applause he was receiving. He had never had anyone clap for him before.

"You can come in now," Elle said softly as she waved Nazere in her direction, a smile still plastered to her face. Nazere slowly walked in and took his seat next to Elle, and the group continued to stand and clap as he sat amidst his gathering. Elle sat down and slipped her anxious hand under the table and took hold of Nazere's with the utmost gentility. Nazere's heart never failed to jump in his chest at the simple touch of Elle's hand to his; he thought her hands were perfect. Following behind Nazere, Verus climbed under the table and in between his knees. The Collosus and the Deliverer remained at the end of the bridge where they stood stationary.

"Welcome to the gathering, my boy," Hayden said to Nazere as he smiled.

"Welcome, brother," Ryan said as he reached across the table and nudged Nazere's shoulder.

"Yes, a second welcome is in order," David said as he patted Nazere's back.

"I don't know what to say," Nazere said as he sat in the midst of the applause.

"Then don't say anything at all," Drake said as he winked across the table. "You were family before, and now you're family all over again. We love you, my friend."

Swiftly, Hayden stomped his staff on the ground before him. "Let us all take to our seats." Everyone that remained standing sat down in their assigned seats and came to silence. Elle gently rubbed Nazere's hand with her thumb, her eyes fixated on the center of the table. "Firstly," Hayden began. "I am proud to announce that Operation Maelstrom's first task has been accomplished, as all of us can plainly see." Hayden waved his arm in the direction of Nazere. "We have successfully infiltrated a ventari suit for the chosen vessel, and must now begin a far more daunting task."

"Baun, as most of you know," Arthur slowly began in the continuance of Hayden's introduction. "has been captured and confined in stasis in the province of Ordren. As has been revealed to me, he has been removed from stasis and is now within the prison of Ordren where he awaits execution. We have come together to determine the appropriate course of action in seeing to his release, as his release has been foreseen. We can see the destination; now we must determine how we're going to get there."

"As I mentioned earlier, we have a considerable number of days before Baun is to be executed," Hayden said. "However, it is imperative that we make the necessary plans to see to his deliverance."

"And planning will be essential for this," James interjected. "Ryan. Adrax. We need to meet immediately following this counsel to discuss our operations."

"The most important element I must stress upon is work," Arthur said as he spoke to those at the table. "Faith without it is nothing. Everyone should spend their time doing what they do best, and honing their individual abilities. Nazere, I suggest you spend some time upstairs with James, Adrax and Ryan."

"I agree," Hayden said as he nodded. "The chief battle prophets will see that you are properly prepared to encounter what awaits you in Ordren."

"The ventari there are impressive in number," Drake said, an undercurrent of business in his voice. "We will have to hold them off in order to ensure security on the ground in Ordren." Ryan leaned back, extended his arm, and held Nazere's shoulder.

"I've worked with Nazere before," Ryan began. "He's my friend, and I have the utmost faith that he will lead our gatherings to victory. A little educational fine-tuning and he'll be just fine."

"Now, we have one final matter to discuss before we adjourn," Hayden said. "The time has come for the forging of the Blade of the Unbroken." Gasps echoed around the table at the very mention of the sacred blade. Heads turned and eyebrows were raised as those who sat at the table considered the gravity of shaping such a power.

"Who will forge the blade?" Adrax asked Hayden as he leaned forward.

"Even my skills are insufficient to bind the gold without risking death," Owen said as he too leaned forward. Felix glanced at James for a second. He then looked at Hayden.

"I will do it," Felix said. "With Owen's assistance, we should be able to forge the blade. Our combined efforts will suffice. However, we will require the hilt."

"And he who will wield the blade is in possession of it," Hayden said as he turned to Felix. "It is not my choosing, but the Master's. Nazere has been given the handle of the Ark of the Covenant from the Hallowed Adytum, and shall wield the legendary blade when it is prepared."

"It is settled then," Arthur said. "The blade shall be made in the Forge of Elders deep within the Bastion of Lights' End. Owen and Felix will see to its crafting. And Nazere shall be the carrier of the sword." Hayden nodded.

"Let us all begin now, then," Owen started. "We have much work to do to prepare for the salvation of Baun from his captivity. And the sword will take time to refine."

"This meeting is adjourned, then," Hayden said. "We shall meet again on the morrow in continued preparation for battle."

Hayden rose from his seat and walked over to where Arthur was sitting, taking a seat next to him. Everyone else rose from the table at once, moving in separate directions. Adrax, James, Ryan and Lily walked up the staircase in the upper right corner of the room. Owen, Felix, David and Drake walked up the staircase on the upper left. As Nazere stood up, he noticed everyone had begun walking down the dimly lit hallways on the second floor of the meeting room. Approaching Nazere with a smile, Aaron reached his hand out and grabbed hold of Nazere's. He shook it while keeping his eyes on Nazere, all smiles and fascination. Verus followed by Nazere's side, sitting as he arrived to the place of his master.

"Again," Aaron began with a hint of excitement to his voice. "I just wanted to say how great it is to finally meet you, bro. You don't know how long we've been waiting for you."

"How long has it been, exactly?" Nazere asked.

"About four years," Aaron replied. "But who's counting? You're here, bro, and that's all that matters. Come on." Aaron waved his right arm at Nazere. "Follow me this way, bro." Elle began to walk beside Nazere.

"Mind if I come along?" Elle asked.

"Not at all," Nazere replied. "Take my hand, Elle. We will walk together."

"Alright," Elle said smiling as Nazere outstretched his arm. Aaron glanced back at Elle and Nazere, who walked hand-in-hand beside one another.

"You two are cute," Aaron said as he turned and smiled. "I've never seen a girl holding hands with a ventari. But you're still human upstairs, Nazere. So it's all good." Elle glanced up at Nazere without his noticing. Nazere's eyes were set straight forward as he walked. When her eyes watched his, she looked to be the most excited woman in the entire world. Her heart would beat just a little stronger whenever he was around, her spirit rising off of the ground every time her skin met his. Walking up the lower left staircase, Aaron hung a right and then another left down a narrow hallway. The hallway was completely carpeted in violet. Down the hallway were equally spaced out redwood doors, and each had a wreath of lilies adorning it.

"Those are beautiful flowers," Elle commented as she looked at the wreaths.

"Well, you know Lily," Aaron began. "She likes to decorate."

Walking down to the end of hallway, Aaron stopped next to the last door on the left. Beside it, a window displayed the hustle and bustle of the city outside. Nazere briefly peered outside, getting a closer glimpse of the beautiful city. Houses were painted in a variety of colors, and each was constructed of wood, sandstone or brick. People were walking about with bags in their hands, carrying fresh produce and goods from the many stores in the city. Wooden signs hung from iron poles that jutted out above the entrance to almost every building in sight. Each was ornately painted and carved with varying emblems and words. One sign in view read "Bradford's Old-Tyme Bakery," while another read "The Shieldmaiden's Salon."

"This is your room," Aaron started as he pointed to the door directly in front of him. "It's pretty self-explanatory. You open the door and you close the door." Aaron quickly illustrated this simple procedure for Nazere as if he needed the demonstration. Verus took the opportunity to run into the room as soon as Nazere's door was opened. "You don't need a key or anything, so no worries there, bro." Aaron then patted Nazere on the back. "That's all I've got for you, bud. Take care now. I'm off to talk with David about some electronic issues I've been having with the Colossus. It's a little complicated. But you two have fun. Take a walk around town. Elle has been here before. She can show you all the sights, Nazere." Elle nodded, eagerly leaning back and forth on her tip-toes and smiling in anticipation. "Anyways, I'll see you both a little later. Have a great day you two." Aaron turned around and quickly walked down the hall, proceeding to hang a left at the end of the corridor where he moved out of sight. Nazere looked down at Elle.

"So where's your room?" Nazere asked.

"I'm down the northern corridor," Elle replied. "This is the south-western corridor."

"Well," Nazere began, his eyes pressed upon Elle's. "Would you like to walk around in the city outside with me? It looks like there's quite a few new sights to be seen."

"I'd love to," Elle replied, still holding Nazere's hand. "I want to take you to Parrion's. We could have lunch there together if you'd like."

"It's a date then," Nazere said, still looking into Elle's breathtaking eyes.

"A date, huh?" Elle asked, glowing. "Well in that case, let's get going. I want to take every advantage of the time we have to share together."

Together, Nazere and Elle walked down the corridor and back down the meeting room's steps to the great door at the back of the room. Pushing the door open to new surroundings, Elle escorted Nazere through the door marked by the rook's emblem. Before them was a twelve foot, circular platform in the middle of an iron, spiraling staircase that led both upward and downward. In the back of the platform was a door marked by the painting of a white house with a chimney. Elle pushed this door open and led Nazere through it. A long flight of sandstone stairs descended to the streets of the city below. Elle and Nazere walked slowly down the stairs, the two cherishing the simple opportunity they had to spend quality time with one another. The savory scents of freshly prepared food, a breath-taking view of the old-fashioned landscape, and the soft breeze of the cool air captivated the whole of their senses.

Outside, the trees pinched in between quaint little clusters of houses lining the right and left sides of the cobblestone road accented the lovely city of the Bastion of Lights' End. The sky was a gorgeous shade of light blue, with white, fluffy clouds encompassing the whole of it. The rooftops of nearby houses were tiled with red and brown brick, painted signs hanging from each and every residence in sight marking points of interest. The soft drift of wind blew through the air as the couple stepped out onto the streets, arousing Nazere's artolium skin. The air smelled primarily of pressed grapes, just out-of-the-oven bread and the spices of cinnamon, nutmeg and clove. The two stood facing a purple painted building, labeled "Simple Spice and Everything Nice" by the sign that hung above it.

"It smells like pumpkin pie and wine out here," Nazere whispered to Elle as he leaned toward her.

"The scents change as you walk, my dear," Elle whispered in reply. "There's a brewery, a coffee house and a number of produce stands right down there." Elle pointed to her right.

A sign with one of the long-nosed dragons Nazere had seen on the turrets surrounding the castle caught his alert eye to the right of the spice shop. The words below the sign read "Tapperton's Parts and Repair." As Nazere walked out into the open with Elle at his side, people who had been meandering about all began to slowly gather around them. Soon, the conjunction of traffic in the streets became a heavily congregated circle of citizens. Their faces spoke a thousand volumes, mouths gaping open and eyebrows raised in amazement. Nazere could hear the people speak out of sheer shock at the sight of him.

"Is that him?" one person asked.

"I think he's finally here," another said.

"Look, mom!" a young child with long, blond hair said excitedly as she jumped up and down. "A ventari!"

"Don't mind them," Elle whispered to Nazere. "Just keep walking. We're heading right. Just follow my step."

"Okay," Nazere replied, feeling like a freak at a sideshow in the midst of the commotion.

Stepping forward, Elle gripped Nazere's hand firmly as she guided him through the crowd that encircled them. Elle lead the way, moving through people that stood in the way of the couple. Step by step, the two of them walked through the streets. The crowd dissipated as soon as Elle had fully walked through the large grouping, but people would still stop what they were doing to stare at Nazere. One man dropped a crate full of fresh fruit all over the ground, contingously hypnotised by Nazere's startling sight. He remained motionless like an animal in fear of a predator until Nazere had well passed him by.

"Just keep moving," Elle said as she led the way. "Parrion's is just up here. It is my absolute favorite place to eat!"

"I'm sure we'll have a wonderful time," Nazere replied, his words smooth and collected. "A chance to spend time with you is wonderful enough in and of itself."

Soon, their destination was within sight. Passing an abode with a sign bearing the white painted words, "Hendrel's Chapel," Nazere could make out the sign that read "Parrion's Café" only yards away. Nazere walked up to the door of the café and opened its green, oak entrance.

"After you, my lady," Nazere said as he held the door for Elle and bowed slightly in a gentlemanly fashion.

"You are much too kind, good sir," Elle replied with a smile as she took a step inside. The interior to Parrion's was busy with customers, each of them seated at circular glass tables. Fancy green napkins and dinnerware accompanied each table, the entirety of the bottom level of the house filled. Every glass chair in sight was occupied. A small wooden staircase led to the upper level of the restaurant. Spices of all kinds, olive oil, seafood, and the fragrant scent of fresh vegetables captivated the air in notes of a delicious melody. Elle approached the hostess of the establishment, who stood behind a podium with a white rook painted on its blackwood face.

"Good afternoon," the hostess said as her surprised eyes veered over at Nazere. She had brown hair and brown eyes with tan skin, a beautiful young woman to say the least. "Seating for two?"

"Yes," Nazere replied as he quickly examined the establishment's composition. "It looks like you're all booked up today."

"There's seating upstairs," Elle said. She then redirected her attention to the hostess. "Can we have a table for two upstairs, please?"

"Of course," the hostess replied. "Can I have the name of the party?" Nazere leaned over next to Elle.

"She isn't a prophetess?" he asked in a whisper, a subtle paranoia taking control as he was gambling on whether or not the hostess could hear his hushed words.

"No," she whispered back. "Not all in the city here are... only those who are chosen to be by the Big Guy upstairs."

"The name of the party is Roivas," Nazere informed the hostess. The hostess nodded and smiled.

"Follow me right this way," she replied. Elle kept a tight hold of Nazere's hand and smiled up at him as the hostess began to usher the two upstairs to their table, enthusiasm immersing her in an undulation like the soft current of the mid-summer, sun-touched ocean. "I've heard a lot about you, ventari. The prophets around here say that your name is Nazere. Is that correct?"

"That it is," Nazere replied. When they reached the upper deck,

Nazere let go of Elle's hand and pulled out a glass chair at their designated table. "After you, my lady," Nazere said. Elle wasn't used to a gentleman's gesture, but she adored every moment of it—especially because it was with him. The hostess stood before the round glass table waiting for the two to get situated.

"Thank you, gentle sir," Elle said as she took her seat. As Nazere sat down, the couple shared the exhilarating feeling that they were in heaven; they were both filled with the precious joy of simply being together, inhaling and exhaling breaths of sheer euphoria.

"Here are your menus," the hostess said as she placed two menus down on the table in front of Nazere and Elle. "Take a good look over them and I'll be back in just a few. My name is Ashley, and I'll be your server for this evening."

"Thank you, Ashley," Nazere said with a wide smile on his face as she walked away. Elle picked her menu up and immediately opened it, scanning its contents up and down as if her life depended on making this decision. Nazere peered out the glinting glass roof of the café, its reflective surface picking up heavy light from the marvelous, afternoon sun. He then glanced down into Elle's preoccupied eyes. Her hazel eyes surpassed the beauty of anything he had ever seen. Being with her made him feel a way he never had before. He had so much he wanted to tell her, but he was patient in waiting for the right time.

"I'm terrible at deciding on what to eat," Elle began as she continued to evaluate her options. "But, you know what? I'm going to go with the Shrimp Scampi. It is so, so very good here." Nazere picked up his menu. His internal electronic crosshairs instantly began to scan the surface of the menu. On his display, a myriad of data was indicated before him. The data included everything from caloric content to the source of the material used to cook the dish.

"You know," Nazere began. "I'm going to have what you're having. It sounds really good, and I know that you have impeccable taste."

"Nope," Elle replied with a smile. "You can't choose the same entrée as me. Try something different and we can share. Sound good?"

"Ok," Nazere said as he again began to scan the menu in front of him. "I think I'll go for the Chicken Chesapeake then. It's ironic they have my local dish out here."

"You might want to order a double or a triple," Elle began. "You need to keep that energy up."

"How about a quadruple?" Nazere asked jokingly. "You think I could handle that?"

"You're a big guy," Elle replied. "Knock it out!" As Elle finished speaking, Ashley returned to the table, a notepad in her hand.

"So, what will we be having this afternoon?"

"I'll be having the Shrimp Scampi with asparagus as the side," Elle said.

"And what to drink with that?"

"I'll just take a water," Elle replied, a honey-sweet tone to her voice.

"And for you, sir?"

"Yes. Give me four orders of your Chicken Chesapeake. And I want four orders of asparagus for the side."

"And what to drink?"

"I can't drink," Nazere replied. "That's one of the downsides of being a ventari. I do miss a good cup of coffee. The funny thing is that I can still taste it in my mouth whenever I think of it."

"Alright. Well I'll be back in a few minutes with your food. Enjoy your stay here at Parrion's. If you need me, I'll be just a hop away."

"Thank you, Miss Ashley," Nazere said as the hostess walked away.

"You cheated," Elle said as she gave Nazere a stern look.

"What'd I do?" he asked with a confused look on his face.

"You ordered my side dish! That's a big no-no sir."

"Listen here, little miss clever… you didn't say anything about side dishes."

"And you're missing a little something aren't you?" Another look of confusion overwhelmed Nazere's face, quite certain that he hadn't misplaced anything. Although, that was a common issue he was often faced with; he would leave an area without completing a checklist of everything he had on his person before departing.

"I don't think so," Nazere replied. Elle reached into her pocket with a straight face and pulled out his tesporð, smiling as she placed the wand-like device on the table in front of him. "Oh. That."

"Yea," Elle began with a smug look on her face. "That. Where would you be without me?" Elle asked as he she shook her head and crossed her arms in the fashion of a disciplinarian.

"Utterly lost and hopeless," Nazere replied. Elle snickered and snorted uncontrollably, the two breaking out in laughter as they looked each other in the eyes. As the two returned to a straight face, a silence permeated the table.

"So," Nazere began as he moved his fingers on the glass table in a little tap-dance.

"So," Elle returned. She leaned forward toward Nazere. "Tell me, Nazere. What do you want out of life?" He calmy paused as a few thoughts entered his head.

"Stability. A home. A family. I guess I've always dreamt of those things."

"Well, you have a home now," Elle began slowly, also wanting to say so much. "And I want you to know that there are people that really care about you. I think you know that I care about you. I want to know more about your life, and about you. I want you to talk to me, and know that you can confide in me any time." Nazere stared into space for a moment. He was so very comfortable around Elle. That was unusual for him. He had held much back in his past, but he knew didn't have to do that with her. She accepted him, and he felt that he could tell her anything.

"I lived on the streets of Baltimore for quite a while. Being cut off from everything was very difficult for me. After losing so much, gaining all that I have is like an irreplaceable treasure that landed in my lap. It is complex in a way, and as difficult as it may be for you to understand, I want you to know that I don't want the life I lived on the streets anymore." Nazere's kept eye contact with Elle with every word he spoke, wanting to share his sacred truth with her. And as he did, Elle listened intently, her entire focus on him. "I slept under the stars on park benches, Elle. I was a vagrant, and I'm most certainly not proud of that. A lot of the memories from that time period return to me at random times. I can remember faces and the expressions of the hungry and depraved as if it were engraved in my head. What hurts the most is knowing that they're gone now. I lost a lot of people I had once called friends. I know you love cats, and I miss the cat I left behind on the streets with all of my heart. He was the only little person I could depend on being there for me every morning. Until the day he died, he was the only friend I knew I could totally rely on. I don't talk about it a lot, but I really feel like I can talk to you about every facet of my life; and I know it doesn't bother you… because you are a lot like me in so many ways that I see. I guess you take my fear away. I never had a father, and my mother was killed when I was young. I still remember her face, and I think of her every time I fall asleep at night." Nazere turned his eyes up at the sun for a moment, thinking of his mother's smile while trying to remain in the here and now. He then returned his focus to Elle, looking into her gorgeous and attentive eyes. "I'm glad I have you to talk to, Elle. I'm grateful that everyone that came into my life these past few days did. But now I will ask you, what is it that you want out of life?"

"I want a real family one day," Elle replied. "My mother and father died when I was eleven; all I know is that they were taken away and used as test subjects by the Scientific Magisterium. I remember their faces every now and then, especially my dad's. Hayden took me in; he took us all in. Ryan, David and I grew up together, the closest to a family I've known. And ever since then, I've dreamt of a family of my own. A house. A few children. I love having something to smile about. But you know what? Ever since you first came around, I've been smiling like I've never smiled before. You have a great heart, Nazere. I can see the 'me' in you all the time." Nazere nodded, empathizing completely.

"I was lonely for a long time, Elle," Nazere began, embracing the honest connection of the heart he held with Elle. "I've made a lot of mistakes in my life. But I have to say, for all its worth, you bring a smile to my face every time I look into your beautiful eyes. And here and now, it's nice to have you with me."

Elle reached her hand across the table and took hold of Nazere's.

"I just wonder, Elle," Nazere began. "What you must think of me now that I've become this… machine."

"You have a wondrous spirit," Elle said as she looked into Nazere's eyes. "That's all that really matters to me. In my eyes, you are the most beautiful thing I see. I don't pass judgments on your past, or on what you are now. Who you are is what holds the greatest meaning to me. And your heart is so much like mine. I laugh every time I think about it. I am thankful that you came into my life, Nazere. Spending time together is more than precious to me. It's a timeless memory."

The hostess returned to the table, a long, steel rack filled with aromatic dishes on porcelain, green plates before her.

"Alrighty! I have your Shrimp Scampi," Ashley began as she carefully placed Elle's meal in front of her. "And for you, Mister Roivas, I have your four orders of Chicken Chesapeake." Ashley placed all four plates of cuisine in front of Nazere one by one.

"Thank you, Ashley," Nazere said courteously.

"Not a problem," she replied. "Just holler if you need anything. I'll be downstairs." Ashley waved and then returned to her duties on the first level of the establishment.

"Hey Nazere," Elle began after she took her first bite, concocting a genius little plan in her head. "Do you want to go to the Regis Bell Tower after this?"

"Just show me the way," Nazere replied with a smile, beginning to move his tespord over his first plate.

"So what was it like on the streets?" Elle asked as she paused for a moment, lightly moving her fork around in her pasta dish.

"There are rules to the streets," Nazere began as his tespord completely consumed his first plate. His stomach began to take on a lighter blue shade as it was refreshed with nutrient-rich energy. "It is every man for himself, but survival is the principle you learn to live by first of all."

"I would have looked out for you," Elle began. "But go on. Tell me everything you know. I'm listening."

Together, Elle and Nazere sat together and ate for the remainder of the afternoon. They talked about every stroke that painted the portrait of their vivid pasts. Nazere talked of learning to sleep on the streets while avoiding bloodguards, and Elle spoke of her love of everything artistic — sculptures, paintings, pottery, and cooking. The two talked of the animals they both adored so dearly, and every, little, fine hair and detail of the pets they took care of. They discussed world events, and discoursed their shared love of everything music and literature. The two grew closer and closer the more they talked, and as their meals drew to a close, Elle began to escort Nazere out of Parrion's. There was the slightest twinkle in her eyes after having spent hours talking with Nazere.

"Don't we have to pay?" Nazere asked at the entrance to the café as Elle led the way.

"Everything in the bastion is free," Elle replied. "Everyone works as a service to the Master. Just keep following me. You're doing fine."

Elle took Nazere back through the door they originally exited to enter the streets. At the spiraling staircase, Elle pulled Nazere upward. And together they walked all the way to the very top of the staircase, passing a number of doors on the way there. At the top of the flight of stairs there was a redwood door marked by the iron imprint of a bell. Nazere attempted to push it open, but it was locked.

"There are perks to being a prophetess," she began, maintaining the spark in her eyes as she glanced at Nazere. "Password: Healing Grace." The door came swinging open, and as it did and Nazere took a step onto a sandstone floor. Above him was a domed stone ceiling painted violet. A thick steel chain linked to a giant bell made of iron stood directly in front of Nazere, the twisted strands of a rope hanging below it. As he looked down, he realized they were high atop one of the two towers very close to the central tower of the bastion. They were about a mile under the high tower, its violet-coned top out of sight from Nazere's vantage point. Below, all the homes and shops looked like tiny little dots- smoke rising from each chimney in sight creating a fog over the city.

"An old-fashioned bell tower," Nazere said, an intrigued look in his eyes as he rang the bell by tugging on the rope hanging from its center. The bell's ring resounded for miles, birds scattering through the air at the sound. "There's a gorgeous view from up here." Elle got a little closer to Nazere, facing him and placing her gentle hands on his broad chest.

"It's beautiful, isn't it?" Elle remarked. Nazere lifted Elle's chin and looked into her eyes.

"It is." Nazere whispered as he inched his head closer to Elle's. "But nothing I've ever seen compares to the beauty I see in you." Nazere reached his neck down, and Elle lifted herself up on her toes and turned her head slightly. And as the two kissed, Elle reached out her hand and pulled on the rope to the iron bell. The sound was a mirror image of what the two felt when their lips finally met.

"Perfect," Nazere said as he withdrew his head slowly.

"Perfect," Elle replied, still on her toes. As Nazere backed down, he began to think about the others in the bastion.

"Elle," Nazere whispered. "I really should be going now. Ryan, Adrax and James are probably waiting on me."

"Okay," Elle whispered back as her feet dropped to the ground, her heart still flying throughout the air. "I have to go do a little practicing of my own."

"Do you want to see each other tomorrow?" Nazere asked.

"More than anything," Elle replied excitedly. "We'll schedule date number two for tomorrow, then."

"A date it is. Goodbye for now, my beautiful girl," Nazere said. He then opened the door and shut it behind him. Exhaling a great breath and looking into the distance, Elle stayed atop the bell tower where she first kissed Nazere. She remained there for over an hour, her heart fluttering in her chest as chills ran through her body. She laughed to herself as she thought of his face, elated that she finally had the opportunity to do what she had so hoped for.

Nazere began walking down the winding stone staircase when he noticed Ryan and Lily pressed against each other, kissing one another on a part of the staircase under the platform that led to the meeting room. He slowly descended the stairs, smiling as he watched Ryan and Lily intimately engaged with one another.

"So," Nazere began. Ryan turned around with a startled look on his face.

"Nazere!" he exclaimed as he laughed to himself. "I didn't expect you to be down here until a bit later." Ryan pulled away from Lily's embrace, giving her a kiss on the cheek. "We've got to get to training, sweetheart," he told Lily. "I'll see you later tonight, okay?"

"Go ahead, honey," Lily said as she slipped her hands off of Ryan. "I know you both have work to do. I'll go spend time with Tygrys for a bit."

"Who is Tygrys?" Nazere asked.

"That's her pet kitty," Ryan replied as he began to take a step downward.

"She's got a little fluff-munchkin, huh?"

"Yea," Ryan replied. "I'm pretty fond of Tygrys myself."

"So where do we go from here?" Nazere asked, seeing an outline of the castle on his internal display but not having the faintest clue as to where any of the passages led to.

"Down the stairs to the lightgate. We're heading to Adrax's training ground."

"Lead the way, my friend," Nazere said as he laughed and patted Ryan on the back. In his mind, Nazere was happy to see his friend as romantically engaged as he had been. The feeling was immeasurably fantastic, a coil of pure happiness that lingered long after the romance was halted.

"Be careful, honey!" Lily yelled as Ryan began to walk down the stairs with Nazere.

"I will, my love!" Ryan replied.

"So she's your girlfriend I assume?" Nazere asked.

"Yes," Ryan replied as he descended the steps alongside Nazere. "Good guess, Nazere," he smirked. "Lily and I have a long history. She's the love of my life, and I'm going to marry that girl someday. She's just like me in the right ways, but completes me where I fall short."

"Sounds good," Nazere said as he put his arm on Ryan's shoulder. "I'm happy for you, buddy."

Nazere wanted to discuss his affair with Elle on the bell tower, but he decided that he'd keep it to himself for now. Instead of talking, he simply followed behind Ryan. Once they had reached the bottom of the staircase, three separate doors arched across the circular, stone surface of the staircase confronted Ryan and Nazere. Each was made of iron and they were equally divided, about six feet in between each door.

"We want the right one," Ryan said as he approached the door on the right. "Password: Farseer." The right door came creaking open, and within its confines was a dark room illuminated by a tall light much like the one in the House of Arthur. "Walk in right behind me." Following Ryan, Nazere fearlessly entered the blinding light on his own and was immediately transported to the forest, where the three tall turrets that were erected there seemed to touch the clouds. Nazere's heart still danced around in his chest as he daydreamed of Elle, the light scent of her perfume still with him. He was sure Ryan's thoughts were with Lily as well.

"Are we going into the first one?" Nazere asked as he turned to Ryan.

"Negative, my friend," Ryan replied. "We want the center turret. James and Adrax are already within. I can feel their powerful presence."

Together, Ryan and Nazere entered into the center turret. Inside, students of the battle prophets wearing red and violet armor with black goggles were firing photon cannons at the holographic images of phantoms that flew throughout the air in a flock-like pattern; their evasive maneuvers emulated the swiftness of the falcon, the predatory hunger of the raven, and the formation accuracy of a flight of geese. The noise of explosions within the turret was deafeningly loud, an ear-shredding sinfonia of constant fire. There were swarms of images throughout the turret, the bodies and tentacles of phantoms moving through the top of the building like squid through the sea. The goggles the violet soldiers wore had purple laser-sights attached to the right side of them, a plethora of lasers and released photon energy filling the upper portion of the turret where the phantoms flew. The red armored soldiers stood on the stone ground with their swords drawn, practicing their abilities to counter the tentacles of attacking phantoms in malicious melee.

Adrax and James stood in the midst of the soldiers, both attempting to tackle the projected image of a vizedrone. On top of the massive image of the vizedrone, Adrax was attempting to keep the dragon's great jaws open with his gift of matter control; he looked like a man riding a vastly oversized mechanical bull. His hands were positioned in front of him as if he were holding an invisible ball, and James was attempting to drive his spear down the monster's throat. The center turret was fashioned in the same way as the first turret, except for the fact that there was a single, violet flag of a rook hanging on the wall in the back of the space.

"Drive it in faster!" Adrax yelled to James. "I can't hold this thing forever."

"I'm trying!" James yelled. "Hold it right there!" And as Adrax held the image of the vizedrone's mouth wide open, James hurled his spear into the mouth of the gargantuan dragon. The dragon began to flare its ethalon blast up, and just as it did Adrax clapped his hands together, bringing the dragon's mouth to a close. The dragon's head then exploded as the spear clogged the cannon's fire, and the image faded away as if it was a trick of a master illusionist. James' spear fell to the floor to the sound of a cling after the projected enemy had dissipated. Adrax dropped to the floor underneath him, landing on his feet. He then set his sights on Nazere and Ryan at the entrance of the turret. Adrax walked up to James, breathing heavily. He shook his hand and gave him a nod.

"Good effort, brother," Adrax said to James, leaning his arms on his knees.

"A little more practice," James began slowly, also breathing heavily. "And we'll have them well contained in times of dire straights." Once Adrax's racing breaths had caught up with him, he refocused his riotous battle tactics into simple thought.

"Welcome back to training, brothers!" Adrax yelled to Ryan and Nazere as his eyes returned to them. "Tonight, we place all of our focus on controlling phantoms and vizedrones!" The room was overwhelmed with the sound of photon cannons being fired in all directions. It was difficult to make out any speech that wasn't shouted out at a high volume. "Alright, students!" Adrax began. "I'm going to need you to clear out of here! We have some special practice to attend to!"

All of the students in the room discontinued their fire and began to deactivate their photon cannons, as well as their red and purple laser sights. Once everyone was cleared out of the room, Adrax and James walked up to within two feet of where Ryan and Nazere were patiently awaiting instruction.

"Where we are going, there will be phantoms numbered in the thousands," James said as he looked at Ryan. Ryan turned to Nazere.

"The three of us have discussed it before I met with Lily," Ryan began as he addressed him. "You must be able to eliminate phantoms with your genora blades. They are the swords that extend from your forearms. Just think it, and they will instantly protract."

"Think the word 'obliteration,'" James said to Nazere. "That may help a bit. There needs to be a desire to withdraw the blades, as normal ventari are programmed to draw them only when certain conditions present themselves." Adrax looked around the large room.

"Let's give it a quick test run," Adrax began, his eyes becoming slits as he imagined the first round of training. "Now that we have a ventari, we should be able to tackle one-hundred phantoms in little time."

"I have worked alongside Nazere," Ryan began. "And I know what he is capable of. I suggest that you summon two hundred phantoms."

"Two hundred?" James questioned with one eyebrow lifted.

"Let's do it," Adrax said, a touch of intrigue in his voice. "I have faith in our ability to down them like the bottom feeders they are." James nodded his head, a serious look on his rugged face.

"Very well," James agreed. "Two hundred phantoms it will be."

"Withdraw your blades," Ryan instructed Nazere. "You will need to have your best wits about you." Nazere nodded.

"Obliteration," Nazere spoke out loud, envisioning the trial that awaited him. Per his command, two thick, double-edged knives came flying out from the middle of his forearms. They appeared to come out of nowhere, with no linkage to his internal cannons and no wiring attached to them; no physical pain resulted from their forthcoming. Adrax drew his stout saber, and it began to glow red as it ordinarily did whenever he took hold of it. Ryan drew his sword next, a green glisten embodying the gunblade.

"Here we go," James began with his spear at his side. "Generate a phantom times two hundred!" And all of a sudden, the roof of the turret became overwhelmed with the projected holographic images of two-hundred swarming phantoms. The phantoms moved around in the air for a few moments, and then began extending their blue-ringed tentacles as they ascertained their targets. The first two tentacles twirled as they hit the ground, sending white sparks flying everywhere on the stone floor.

"Dodge everything that comes at you, Nazere," Ryan said. "You must move quickly in here. These machines are extremely intelligent and precise in their strikes. Never underestimate them." As the second and third phantom sent their six tentacles to the ground, Adrax and James jumped up to a miraculous height and cut the tentacles down from the mid-section. They landed like two astoundingly agile cats, stable on their feet as they met the ground.

"And whatever you do," Adrax said as he cut down yet another phantom's attacking tentacle. "Keep the faith close to your heart. Nothing can break you when you carry adequate faith and act upon it."

Nazere picked himself up in the air and flew directly into the black field of phantoms overhead. Eighty tentacles came flying from every direction in an attempt to take hold of Nazere, but his reflexes were peaked as he slipped around them like a running back miraculously evading tackles in a game of football. One by one, Nazere drove his genora blades into the heads of every phantom he could see. His internal targeting system was going crazy, his crosshairs moving from phantom to phantom as uncontrallably as a torrential downpour. From behind, a phantom prepared to fire a shot of ethalon from within its crab-like face. Nazere was fully aware of everything around him, and he could hear the subtle whisper of the ethalon charge over the wind-breaking thrusts of the tentacles trying to tear him down. Cutting the ethalon-charging phantom's face in two, Nazere dropped the projected machine without the slightest inkling of a struggle.

"I told you," Ryan said as he watched the action from below. "He has the gift."

"I can see," James said as he stood unmoved, amazed at the fluency Nazere was demonstrating.

Within Nazere's internal targeting system, the total count of phantoms indicated was falling faster than the seconds as he moved like a dynamo throughout the air. Over and over, the phantoms fell to the ground and flickered out of existence.

"Eighty-one to go," Nazere said as he drove both of his blades through two phantoms on his left and right simultaneously.

"Keep going, Nazere," Ryan said. "I have faith in you."

As tentacles dropped to the floor in an attempt to attack, Ryan, James and Adrax would cut them down. But for the most part, there was not much intervention required of the prophets on the ground. As Nazere flew through a mass of images, he spun and dove in a whirlwind of shining artolium, driving many phantoms to the floor at once.

"Thirty-five to go," Nazere said as he drove his genora blades through two additional phantoms. And within two minutes, Nazere descended to the floor. He hovered above James with his arms at his side, the tower cleared of all phantom projections.

"Well done," James said. "About six more waves, and we'll call it a night." Adrax nodded.

"Six more waves?" Nazere asked, beginning to feel the first spurt of fatigue hit his core.

"Generate a phantom times three hundred!" Adrax exclaimed, smiling in confidence with his saber sheathed behind his back and his arms folded.

"Go get them, Nazere!" Ryan cheered. Nazere charged up into the air, and began engaging in combat once again by driving his right genora blade upward toward the first image his internal display registered.

For the remainder of the evening, Nazere battled against flight after flight of mustered phantoms. As night began to fall, Hayden sat in the meeting room across from Arthur. The two of them were engaged in a game of chess at the stone table, each of them moving pieces without the use of their hands. Hayden looked across the table at Arthur, his eyes noticeably light.

"Checkmate," Hayden announced.

"Well played, my friend," Arthur said, a pipe hanging from his mouth. From the bridge in the back of the room, Endarius hastily entered the meeting chambers.

"Good evening, Endarius," Arthur spoke in greetings.

"I do not mean to bother you, but there are some matters of concern I mean to address before the both of you." Endarius' voice was as cold as ice.

"Take a seat, my friend," Hayden said as he pulled out a chair. Endarius had a grim look upon his face as he sat in the chair next to Hayden.

"I have had a troubling vision," Endarius reported. "I mean to discuss it with you." Hayden and Arthur had a puzzled expression on their faces as they looked upon each other.

"Please," Arthur began as he took a puff from his pipe and set his eyes upon Endarius' very pupils. "Elaborate."

Back at Adrax's battlegrounds, Nazere dropped to the floor. Three vizedrones fell to the ground and glinted away behind him. His position was crouched on the ground as he looked up at his three standing comrades.

"You have done well today," Adrax said. "I feel we have accomplished a good day's training. Go now and rest, Nazere."

"Yes, Nazere," Ryan said as he sheathed his sword. "You have worked astonishingly hard today. I feel we are well prepared for what is to come. Go get some rest, my friend. There will be a new meeting in the morning." James formed a golden grin across the rugged terrain of his face.

"We are ready for them," he said, his voice as solid as steel. "The question is a matter of what we will be confronted with when we reach Ordren." Nazere nodded as he took a stand.

"Some things remain to be seen," Adrax interjected. "Farewell for now, my brothers."

"Through the gate we go, then," Ryan said, stepping toward the door of the turret and motioning with his hands for Nazere to move in his direction. "Come along with me, Nazere. Your sleep is as essential as your practice. You should sleep well tonight." Nazere followed Ryan through the lightgate and up the winding, iron stairs. When they stepped foot into the meeting room, Hayden, Arthur and Endarius were gone.

"I suppose this is where we part ways for the night," Nazere said.

"Congratulations on a job well done today," Ryan said to Nazere. "I'm off to see Lily for a bit, but I am quite sure that I will see you in the morning."

"Goodnight, Ryan. Keep me in your prayers."

"I will. Always."

Walking to his room down the southwestern corridor, Nazere retracted his thick, reflective genora blades. Opening his door, he was met with the humerous portrait of Verus snoring with his body all spread out and his nose upright on the floor. And as always, Keldrid stood in the left corner of his room; his feet were firmly positioned at the exact angles Nazere last saw them as if they were welded into place.

"Well done today, human," Keldrid said, his tone the darkest shade of black. "Your skills grow with every passing second, it seems." Nazere pulled his comforter up and snuggled himself into position under the white blanket.

"How did you know how well I performed? I didn't see you anywhere."

Can he hear my thoughts from afar? Nazere thought. I wonder.

"I have ways of knowing without seeing," Keldrid replied. "That does seem to be the primary struggle of humanity, doesn't it?"

"It does," Nazere replied nonchalantly. "Goodnight, Keldrid,"

Nazere said as he turned to his side. “I will see you in the morning.”

“In the morning, indeed.”

Several hours passed, and Nazere slowly drifted off to sleep. As Nazere slept, deep within the Bastion of Lights’ End at the Forge of the Elders, Owen withdrew a sword from a pool of molten gold that was set in the center of a large steel room parallel to an anvil. Stone statues of kings stood erect in the four corners of an otherwise empty chamber. The blade was red hot when it was withdrawn, and it was with the utmost care that Owen set the single-edged sword on the black anvil next to the melting pot. Felix, standing off to the side of the anvil, pulled a welding shield down over his face as he held a wireless purple rod in his hands. He then took the rod and pressed a manual button on its side, firing the torch up. The ends of it began to spark as he welded the edges of the blade into form.

The next thirty days were spent in repetition. At the start of every morning, there was a gathering in the meeting hall. But plans were not yet drawn out, so the prophets were directed by Hayden and Arthur to continue training. During those three days, Nazere noticed that he hadn‘t been confronted with any strange dreams. Days were spent taking long walks with Elle in the city, kissing in the bell tower and talking for hours on end. The two would discuss just about everything that came to their minds. All the little things Nazere would say meant the world to Elle. And every time Nazere kissed Elle, he felt as if nothing could bring his spirits down. When Nazere departed from Elle, his heart would drop in his chest. And atop the bell tower, Elle would spend some alone time dreaming of a life with Nazere by her side. He made sure to spend time each day walking through the city with Elle before he went off to hone his skills.

And every day, the training was vigorous. Adrax, Ryan and James pushed Nazere to his very limits. They called on phantoms and vizedrones again and again to properly prepare Nazere for battle. On the thirtieth day, a knock came at Nazere’s door at it had for many days prior. This time, however, Verus was barking at the door. Walking up to the door and opening it, Nazere was met by Hayden. A serious look on his face, Hayden stepped foot into Nazere’s room. Nazere looked down at Verus and withdrew the summtorant that was held in his dresser drawer.

"Inside, Verus!" Nazere commanded. Disappearing in a ball of smoke, Verus returned to his summtorant.

"The day has come, my child," Hayden began. "Today is the day that Operation Maelstrom comes to its close. We shall gather in the meeting hall at noon. Prepare yourself for the day to come, for it will be far more trying than I had first anticipated."

"How so?" Nazere questioned.

"Patience, my child. Just be at the meeting hall at noon. There, all you need to know will be explained to you."

After Hayden departed from Nazere's room, Nazere set his summtorant down and sprawled himself out across his white bed to give himself a much needed break to mentally prepare for the unknown. After a few minutes, he decided to get up and make his way out of his door. He walked down his hallway and into the empty meeting room. He stepped to the bridge and walked across it as it was still down. He veered his eyes toward the Redeemer as he walked across the bridge, the eagle still perched on the circular landing pad in the field. The sun was shining outside, and the scents of green grass accompanied by a blend of sweet flora filled the air as if it were the first day of Spring. Lily was amidst the grass, crouched on the ground. As she ran her hand through the grass, flowers would sprout from the soil in all shades and colors. A fluffy, white Persian cat walked in the fields beneath her. The cat would sniff the fragrant flowers as soon as they blossomed, walking eagerly from plant to plant. As Nazere approached Lily, she turned around.

"Good morning, Nazere," she said as she remained crouched down, her eyes focused on the flora before her. "I do hope your rest was well."

"It was," Nazere replied. "What beautiful flowers you manifest. I suppose that is your gift?"

"Amongst other things," Lily replied. "Sara, Elle and I have been training ourselves. Hasn't she told you?"

"Told me what?" Nazere asked. A thousand questions entered

Nazere's mind all at once. What could she be hiding? he thought. She wouldn't hide anything from me. Lily laughed.

"You will know in time. Today, I pray for the safety of our gatherings. We go alone into the province of Ordren, and many enemies lie in waiting for us. There is no guarantee for our lives."

"You seem overly concerned. What is the problem? What do you fear, Lily?" Lily took a stand and looked Nazere in the eyes as the morning sun reflected off of her golden blond hair.

"I fear that which is unseen, Nazere. I fear that which you do not know."

CHAPTER FIVE

The Battle of Ordren

In his dimly lit chambers, Commander Entril sat upon his chair within his towering lair in the city of New York. His hands were clasped together in front of his face as he looked upon three holographic images in front of him. Each holographic image was about twenty-four inches long and displayed the province of Ordren from three separate vantage points. Through the entrance to his room, Lieutenant Galen walked in with his head lowered. He slowly advanced up to the chair the commander was sitting in and knelt before him, fortunate to be alive after his failure to intercept Nazere. The commander paused as the lieutenant sat on one knee before his feet. As the lieutenant held his position, Commander Entril unclasped his hands and took a stand. He then pointed to the holographic image before him.

"You have utterly failed me, Galen," Commander Entril began in a calm voice.

"The ventari was unstoppable," Lieutenant Galen replied with his head still lowered. "He was moving at speeds that only other ventari move at. It was a comission that was…"

"Unlike you," the commander interrupted, a fiery spark to every word he spoke. "I seek solutions to such problems. You, on the other hand, have but one choice before you. My intelligence agents have reported that these little sects of prophets are heading for the site of Ordren. They wish to free one of their high prophets, as his execution has been scheduled for today. Apparently, their technology is overcoming your abilities to perform your duties."

"By no means, commander," Lieutenant Galen replied as he slowly lifted his head, sweat dripping from it. "What is it that you wish for me to do?"

"I am sending you to the province of Ordren, and I am allotting you an entire fleet of dreadnaughts, vizedrones, and phantoms. I want every last one of these pests exterminated." The commander changed his tone from calm to vehement. "Is that understood?!"

"Yes, Commander Entril."

"Excellent," Commander Entril replied as his voice plummeted from the heights to a frozen stand-still, returning to his seat and clasping his hands in front of his face. "I am sending you in on your own personal dreadnaught. This time, you will fight to your last breath. Fail, and you shall simply embrace death."

In the fields outside of the Bastion of Lights' End, Nazere stood before Lily. And from behind him, a man came walking up and placed his hand on his shoulder. It was Arthur, and as soon as he laid his hand on Nazere, everything in the ventari's field of vision faded to black. His body suspended in the void, another thick mist coiled itself around Nazere in a full circle. And out of the mist came a thousand bright, dancing swords, the edge of each glowing blade encircling his figure above the mist at a wild speed. In the center of the chaos, a burst of flame ignited out from the nothingness only several feet away from Nazere. The flame began to take shape, forming itself into the detailed image of a horse. And on the horse was a blue ventari with a sheath at his hip, gripping the burning reins of the steed with all its strength. The horse had a long fiery tail, and its eyes burned with molten fury as if they were made of metal. The rider reached to the sheath at his side and withdrew a golden sword. And in one swift motion, the rider drove the sword into the darkness. The darkness became a wall of stone, and the wall began to crumble and quake under the rider's terrible blade. And as the wall fell, the rider pulled up on its horse's reins and turned its back on Nazere. Running at full speed, the horse dashed into the distance, the rider's sword high in the air. The horse's treads left a fiery path, and as the horse rode out of sight, the thousand swords flying around Nazere like a windstorm united and became one blinding, white sword.

"Nazere, my boy," Arthur began as Nazere came to, returning from his reverie and greeting him in an upbeat tone as if nothing had just occured. Nazere turned to Arthur and looked him in the face, showing no visible signs of alarm. "The preparations have been made. I am to escort you to the Forge of Elders beneath the base of the bastion. There, you will be presented with the gift of ancient kings. Come, and follow me." Arthur turned around toward the bridge and Nazere promptly followed behind him. The two of them walked through the empty meeting hall to the rook-marked door straight beyond it. Arthur placed his hands against the painted door, and it immediately came flying open as if someone had shoved it with all of their might. Continuing to lead Nazere, Arthur began to descend the winding iron staircase beyond the signed door. Walking all the way down, Nazere and Arthur stood before the three doors on the very bottom of the staircase.

Arthur walked up to the left door and extended his cane out in front of him so that it made subtle contact with it. The door miraculously threw itself open as if someone had rammed the door with their shoulder, and Arthur and Nazere walked into the next area. Beyond the door was a small circular room with a round, violet carpet in the center marked by the emblem of two crossed swords in black threading. Hovering above the carpet was a violet, holographic display shaped in a square with the projected images of an anvil and a line of text next to it. The line of text read, "Indicate Password To Proceed," in scarlet lettering. Arthur opened a prompt on the holographic display, allowing him to input characters into it. Typing a few letters, Arthur stepped back from the display. And as he did, the circular room began to shake as if it were unwell with a serious case of essential tremor. Within moments, the room began dropping downwards in a gravity-defying free fall.

It fell for a total of fifteen seconds before it came to a tranquil stop. As soon as it discontinued falling, the holographic display read, "Destination Reached." A door was positioned on the exact same side as the door floors above. But this door was made of titanium and embossed with the image of an upright sword on the right and a hammer striking an anvil on the left. There was a crease down the center of the threshold, a line of separation between the sword and the hammer.

"Within we go," Arthur said, glancing at Nazere as he held his cane to the door. The steel-capped end of his polished, wooden cane became briefly consumed with an amber glow as it made soft contact with the threshold's titanium surface. As soon as it did, the door split apart from the crease in its center and slid into the wall. The Forge of Elders was unveiled beyond it, the sound of seething metal sizzling like an oil-coated frying pan. Entering the room, Nazere noticed a glimmering, golden blade hovering right-side up above the melting pot in the middle of the room. The blade illuminated the whole of the chambers with an astoundingly bright, yellow glow. To the left of the blade stood Owen Candlefire, and to its right stood Felix Amaldores. Both had sweat dripping down their foreheads, a combination of perspiration from the heat of the flames and the intense muscle they put into honing their craft. Felix held a long, solid gold item in his right hand with some sort of fabric attached to it. They both dropped to their knees in reverence as Arthur entered into the room. Arthur walked beside Nazere, and immediately motioned for the two men to rise as he stopped in his tracks.

"It is accomplished," Felix began as he returned to his feet. "For three days we have toiled and refined the sword in the Fires of Purity."

"Behold," Owen said as he reached out with his left hand and grabbed the sword from the hilt. As soon as he had taken hold of the sword's hilt with his fingers, a bright, golden glow consumed the entirety of his body. His skin beamed radiantly like the relentless rays of the midsummer sun as he moved the sword to the center of his figure. "The first of the Master's precious, covenant alloys have been sealed together." Owen set his sights upon Nazere, his somber eyes displaying the veneration he had for this special sword. Despite his clear exhaustion, his voice was as gentle as pure cotton as his lips formed words a small step above a whisper. "I proudly present you, chosen wielder, with the Blade of the Unbroken."

"Before you take it," Felix started with a concerned expression on his face and a precautious tone to his voice. "I warn that you dare not touch the sword's surface at any time. This blade brings forth destruction, and whosoever lays a single hand on it shall be stricken dead immediately."

"Even the ventari cannot touch the blade," Owen added. "By the hilt you shall carry this blade into battle. You must know the true nature of the blade before you take hold of it. It is, in every sense of the word, unstoppable. When you hold it, you hold the treasure of ancient kings and the very hand of the Master." Nazere nodded in acknowledgement of the blacksmiths' forewarnings. He outstretched his arm and opened the fingers of his right hand, ready to receive the exalted brand.

"I will carry it with the utmost care," Nazere assured as Owen held the hilt of the sword out to Nazere with his left hand. His outward appearance in the moment he gave the sword away would make you think he was losing a loved one. Passing the brand from hand to hand, Nazere took on the hilt of the Blade of the Unbroken. The hilt was designed with a lion's head at one side of the golden hilt and a horse's head at the other side. And as immediately as Nazere grasped the hilt, his very core began to erupt with blazing, golden fury. His whole body took on a glimmering, golden shine, his eyes veering around in infinite interest as little, white sparks waltzed on the surface of his artolium skin. Every artificial muscle and wire within him took on the appearance of solid gold, synthetic adrenaline flushing through his nervous system like the Nile River. His ethalon core seemed to expand as it took on the shimmering, yellow glow; small flares of golden light gravitated around the charge and enlarged its appearance.

"You will not carry the sword at all times," Felix said. "So we constructed a sheath from the blessed gold from the handle of the Ark of the Covenant. It will shield the sword from its own uncanny force." Felix reached out and handed Nazere the sheath he was holding, a purple strap attached to it representing the royalty of the wielder. Nazere took the sheath and threw the strap around his back, honored by his gifts. He then carefully reached the sword behind his back and slipped the Blade of the Unbroken into its sheath. At once, Nazere's body returned to its normal state; his heightened nerves to homeostasis. His core and the wiring throughout his body returned to their typical blue condition, the incredible rush of power he felt surge through his being instantly subsiding.

"I thank you both for your labor," Nazere said slowly and sincerely as he turned his eyes from Owen to Felix. "You are my brothers, and I will adhere to the words you have spoken. I will honor the sword." Arthur put his hand on Nazere's shoulder and closed his eyes.

"May the Master bless the wielder of this sacred blade," Arthur began. "May it shield him from all the forces of darkness that await him beyond this place." Nazere looked around at the statues standing in the four corners of the room as Arthur withdrew his hand, a spark of interest in his eyes.

"Arthur," Nazere began. "What are the significances of the statues within this forge?" Arthur opened his eyes.

"Come," Arthur instructed. "Follow me to this side of the room." Arthur walked to the bottom left corner of the room to the statue of a shepherd boy with a crown upon his head. "This," Arthur began as he pointed. "Is the statue of David, High King of Judah." Arthur then began to walk to the upper left hand corner of the room, and Nazere followed closely in his tracks. The statue that stood there was of a bearded king, with long hair and a crown with many sculpted jewels of stone upon his head. "This is Solomon, the wisest man that ever lived and one of the greatest kings of all time. One of the sons of David, his temple was the greatest mankind ever constructed." Next, Arthur walked to the lower left hand corner of the room. Nazere walked behind him, remaining as silent as a shadow as he yearned to know more of these ancient kings. Before them stood a statue of a bearded man with a winged angel at his side, the man dressed in torn clothing. "The next sculpture is that of Jacob, son of Isaac, and the father of Israel. He was known to have wrestled with an angel."

Arthur laughed, humored as he scanned the statue intently up and down. "Of course, the angel won."

"I've heard of all of these men," Nazere said. "I've been reading up on them, and I remember bits and pieces of their stories vaguely." Finally, Arthur walked to the upper right hand corner of the room. The sculpture was crowned, but a tear was falling from the sculpture's eye. "This sculpture is that of the Prince of Egypt, who led his people out of great captivity. You should know him better as Moses."

"Why the tear?" Nazere asked curiously.

"He was never able to see the promised land," Arthur replied. "A mighty ruler he was, though. As well as a great testament to the power of faith in overcoming otherwise impossible circumstances."

"So these are all of the sculptures within the bastion, then?" Nazere asked.

"No," Owen interjected as his eyes veered toward Nazere. "There are two others. They are high atop the bastion in the Sanctuary of Revelations."

"Well, let's go there now," Nazere said to Arthur, determined to see the final sculptures.

"Unfortunately, it is now fifteen minutes until noon," Arthur said. "Everyone should make their way upstairs. The time has finally come to begin our official battle plans for the assault on Ordren." Owen and Felix nodded.

"Lead the way, High Prophet Arthur," Owen began. "We will follow you."

Together, the four in the Forge of Elders made their way onto the circular lift and returned to the iron staircase above. In the mean time, Ryan was outside in the field where Lily still sat amidst her flowers. Tygrys ran around in the field, which was now covered primarily with roses of every shade and style. As she began to grow a bloom of lilacs across the stone wall to the left of the bridge, Ryan quietly approached her.

"A beautiful array of flowers coming from the most beautiful woman in the world," Ryan said slowly as he stopped several yards behind Lily. Turning around with a startled look on her face, Lily seemed to freeze in place. She then smiled and ran to Ryan, throwing her arms around his neck and meeting his lips with a passionate kiss. Lily then drew her face back ever so slightly, looking into Ryan's eyes.

"I've missed you," Lily said slowly, her head close to Ryan's face and her body still enveloped in his strong arms. Ryan looked back at her, his eyes set firmly in place as they looked into Lily's. His heart never failed to twirl every time he looked into her bottomless, bright-blue eyes.

"As I have you, my love," Ryan replied, kissing Lily's forehead softly, lovingly.

"I wish that you didn't have to go today," Lily said. "I can't see what is going to happen."

"Nor can I," Ryan replied, his unshaken tone a hearty resting place for Lily's concern. "But I am going forward believing that the prophecy is true. We have come this far. We have to complete what we set out to do."

"I know," Lily said as she sighed and leaned her head on Ryan's shoulder. "I just feel uneasy." She then backed off of Ryan for a moment. "I'm afraid, my love," she said with a look of worry in her eyes. "I fear what is about to happen."

"Don't be overtaken by fear," Ryan whispered as he lifted Lily's chin. "Remember what I always tell you. You can't control what you don't know. There's no effort in trying. So rest easy. And know that I love you." Lily drew close to Ryan and wrapped her arms around him again, resting her head on his chest. "I always will."

Deep in the confines of the jails of Ordren, an old man with long brown hair, a gray jail uniform, and a well shaven face sat on an artolium floor in a jail cell kept closed by means of a wall-sized ion shield. He was laughing to himself hysterically as his wide eyes stared at the floor. The ion shield flickered an aquamarine color, and outside of the shield a man with a pistol-shaped photon cannon in a holster at his side sat in a steel chair that was welded to the floor. The man was dressed in an all black uniform, tidy and neat, with a high-and-tight haircut and a barcode tattooed on his neck; he was clearly the guard to the cell. There was a door on the left and right side of the room, each marked by a circle of iron that was painted and embossed to depict the head of a red dragon breathing flame.

"Stop laughing, old fool!" the guard yelled as he rose from his steel chair, belligerent as he took a step toward the ion shield. The old man kept laughing despite the guard's demands, looking straight into the eyes of the guard as if he hadn't a care in the world.

"Peace be with you," the man on the floor said as he laughed between his words. "I am not mocking you. I merely find myself amused with the current situation."

"The current situation?!" the guard screamed at the old man. "And what exactly is that, you useless lunatic?!"

"Salvation comes with a swiftness," the old man said, heaving hysterical laughs at an invisible anecdote. "Tell me, what do you believe in?"

"I believe in the order and society of science and government established by High Lord Alune!" the guard yelled, his face growing red with anger. "There is nothing else!"

"Unfortunate," the old man said, his speech a cool vibration, still laughing. "Those who come for me cannot be stopped. I will be delivered from this place on this very day."

"So you keep saying," the guard said as he calmed down and returned to sitting in his steel chair. "Little do you know, all your plans are already known." The man reached his neck forward, his eyes widening as he longed to pierce the man's spirit. "There is much you don't know, old man. Today, you will die. And anyone who rises up to save you is doomed. There is no chance. Do you hear me? No chance." The old man kept looking at the guard, smiling as he sat on the floor of his cell.

Ascending the winding staircase, Arthur, Owen, Felix and Nazere came to the rook-marked door leading to the meeting room. Owen pushed the door open, and the group stood at the entrance as their eyes became captivated by the view before them. All of the room was as quiet as a library, not a whisper to be heard in the muted meeting room. Inside, the tables on both sides of the triangular stone table were at full capacity; almost all members of the three gatherings were present. On the table at the right side of the room, men and women in purple armor and goggles sat with photon cannons strapped to their backs. On the left, battle ready patrons in red armor sat with swords sheathed at their sides. The raiditor was gone from the top of the stone table, and in its place was a small, white feather. It sat lightly atop the table, but nothing moved it from its stable position. Hayden sat in his red, leather chair at the corner of the stone table, looking over to Arthur as he entered the room. Moving swiftly off to the right with his cane advancing alongside him, Arthur hastily moved to the red, leather seat at his corner of the triangular table.

"Remain here for a moment," Owen whispered to Nazere. Nodding in acknowledgement, Nazere looked out into the room and made eye contact with Elle.

Owen and Felix then walked into the room together and took their designated seats around the stone table. Walking in from the bridge at the opposite side of the room, Ryan and Lily entered into the meeting room side by side and took their proper seats. As soon as they had taken their places, Elle widened her eyes at Nazere and waved for him to head down to his spot. With a look of astonishment on his face and all eyes upon him, Nazere slowly walked to his chair next to Elle, pulled it out, and sat down. As soon as all members were in place, there was much commotion stirred up, people at both sides of the room chatting amongst themselves. Hayden was bearing a staff of a different shade than the pale oak one he ordinarily did. He took his black wooden staff and drove it into the floor like a spear. As a crash like thunder resounded throughout the room, everyone became silent. Hayden then gripped his staff and rose to his feet, his eyebrows as stern as the heat of battle.

"Silence, one and all!" Hayden yelled, his voice a striking blow. "We have gathered together here on this day to complete the mission set forth before us. I need every one of you to pay careful attention to every detail of information that is spoken to you. For on this day, High Prophet Baun shall be returned to the bastion and take his proper seat at this table." Hayden reached down to the feather on the table and picked it up with his right arm. Holding the quill of the feather, he moved his right arm in a large, circular fashion. The horns of the feather generated a wide, circular, visual display in the middle of the table. The display could be seen from all angles, the circle in plain view of one and all that sat in the room. Within the circle was a live vision of the Ordren province from an aerial vantage point. Hayden placed the feather in the center of the visual exhibit, using the feather's horned end to zoom in slightly. Once he had done so, a general view of the Ordren prison and several structures that surrounded it became distinguished.

"This is the final task of Operation Maelstrom, and a trying battle is indeed ahead of us!" Hayden exclaimed for all to hear. "There may be loss, and there may be sacrifice. But with a little hope, and the tiniest seed of faith, we will succeed. As you can see, before you is a vision of the Ordren prison." Hayden turned the feather around, utilizing the quill of the feather to mark a spot on the large, circular image that floated in the space above the stone table. The vision rippled like a droplet of water falling into a pool as he made his inscription.

A white "X" marked a wide clearing in the midst of towering metal and glass structures to the left and to the right. The roadless opening was directly next to the province's stasis chambers. All who were looking on the image could see that the stasis chambers were now completely emptied, its former occupants awaiting extermination.

"We will land our forces here," Hayden began, pointing at the mark on the live image. "There, we will stand our ground directly outside of the Ordren prison. Please note that proper organization is key." Turning the feather around in his hand, Hayden used the soft side to zoom in closer to a series of large, artolium doors outside of the prison. Everyone in the room had their eyes glued to the adhesive vision in the center of the stone table. As they did, a still silence permeated the entire space like the ambiance of the looming lamps that hovered overhead.

"These are the artolium doors to the prison's entrance," Hayden spoke loudly for all to hear. "There is only one entrance to the prison that can be penetrated." Turning the feather in his hand around once again, Hayden marked a white circle around the door on the far left of the prison. "There is a digital control panel on the right side of this door, and with a bit of providence we will enter it. Please make your presence known, Aaron." Standing from his chair, Aaron held a strange white device out in his right hand for all in the room to see. The device was shaped in the form of a thin box, and a small, white stem resembling a trentorod protruded from its top. The device was only a half a foot long, and had a small liquid crystal display.

"Hey everyone," Aaron said in greetings as he stood and glanced around the meeting room. "What I have here is a little invention of mine, which I call a hakrolend. Its primary purpose is basically to hack the digital code embedded into the door High Prophet Hayden marked. It can hack other things, as it immediately writes consecutive, malicious programs using an artificial intelligence protocol to undermine and conquer even the most advanced hardware. The device uses a five-hundred terracore bioprocessor with wireless neuro-transmission memory, temporary access memory, and hard-drive space. My goal is to use this device to get through the door outside of the jail first. Afterward, the device can be used to open secondary doors inside of the Ordren prison. My comrade and brother has offered to break in with me." Lily looked over with a concerned look in her eyes as Ryan promptly took a stand. "As long as the outside is under control, we should be able to get High Prophet Baun out of the prison's confines without any loss."

"I will keep Aaron safeguarded," Ryan said. "My sword will be by his side the entire way." Arthur took a stand as he prepared to speak.

"Hayden and myself will be amongst the forces outside," Arthur began, his tone a mellow breeze. "We shall provide as much assistance as possible to those engaged in combat." Adrax and James then took a stand simultaneously, thinking on the same wavelength.

"We've talked it out," Adrax began as he placed both of his muscular arms on the table and leaned on them. "And James and myself will command the defensive front. We will remain on the ground level amidst our students and provide guidance."

"Everyone has been properly instructed to obey the orders given them!" James shouted, a commanding authority in his voice to shepherd his flock. "No one is to engage the enemy until it has been deemed necessary to do so! Safety is the number one priority! I shall make the call to battle!" Taking a stand from their chairs, David and Drake walked out into the open next to one another behind the stone table.

"The Redeemer is prepared for flight," David began. "I will be piloting her, and Drake will be piloting the Deliverer."

"The Deliverer has all its cores active and is ready for action," Drake said, an underlying passion in his words. "David and myself will maintain communications between the ground forces, the Colossus, and one another." Elle and Lily looked at each other. Lily took a stand first, and Elle behind her.

"Elle and myself will be doing what we do best," Lily said. "We will accompany the first to enter the battle."

The first to enter the battle? Nazere thought to himself, his heart calling out to Elle.

"I will do my best to carry you all through," Elle said, her voice a sweet nectar. "I pray we are all carried through this in one piece." Nazere stared at Elle as she addressed the gatherings. His core fluttered like the wings of a hummingbird when she took a stand. He was determined to keep her from all harm, no matter the cost.

"Rest assured, you will all be in good company," Endarius said in a twisted voice as he remained in his seat. "Death is not a thing to fear. But I will do what I can to see that the enemy is driven back so that we reduce such incidences occuring on our side. And I have quite a few tricks up my sleeve to see to it that we are safeguarded."

"What of the ventari?" a voice called out from the left side of the room. Hayden smiled as he turned to Nazere. Standing up, Nazere drew the Blade of the Unbroken for all to see.

"You know," Nazere began in a solemn tone, glistening like the sun. The room broke out in chatter at the very sight of the sword's resplendence. "I never dreamt I would be carried out of Ordren. For years, I lived in the lowest places any one of you could imagine. But from the ashes, my brothers have picked me up. I make no promises to anyone. I can only give back all that has been given to me. Things have changed in my life in ways I never could have expected. Against what I foresaw my future holding, I have been given a second chance at life. Alongside my friends, I trust that we will return victoriously. I will give this effort every little thing that I have to offer." Hayden nodded.

"And so it begins," Hayden said as the vision above the stone table disappeared into thin air. Hayden placed the feather back on the table, and it swiftly flew away weightlessly as it returned to its conventional state. Its use was complete. "Everyone make your way to your stations now! We must make haste to make it to Ordren in time."

"Rise, Alpha Call!" Adrax yelled. And upon his command, the left table stood simultaneously, beginning to make their way onto the bridge and out of the room. Once every one of them was on their feet, James raised his spear high above his head.

"Omega Call! To your feet!" James commanded. The right table mirrored the left, rising to their feet all at once and starting to walk out of the room in a single file.

"We're off to the Deliverer, then," Arthur said as he turned to Hayden.

"We will meet you on the other side," Hayden replied. "Godspeed, my dear friends."

"As with you," Arthur returned, veering his eyes toward his gathering. "Come, my brothers."

"And sister," Sara interjected with a smile.

"Heavens," Arthur said, laughing as he began to walk. "How could I forget you?" Together, the Gathering of the White Lion made their way out of the meeting room and toward the field.

"We're off as well," James said to Hayden, cool and collected. "The Colossus awaits us outside."

"We'll be right behind you," David said, ready to do what he did best. "Are you ready, Hayden?"

"There could be no greater time," Hayden said. "To the field."

Together, the remainder of the gatherings of the white rook and the white knight made their way to the bridge. Nazere walked alongside

Elle, and she smiled up at him as he looked over to her.

"Everything's going to be just fine, today," Elle said sweetly, with twinkling diamonds of hope in her eyes as she glanced at Nazere. "I'm glad to have you by my side. Just don't lose sight of your faith. I know in the end, you'll have proved to be the strong man I know you are."

"I'll look out for you, Elle," Nazere said as he glanced back. "With all that I have and all that I am, I'll watch over you."

As the group met the end of the bridge and the beginning of the grassy, flora-filled fields beyond, they were met with quite the ensemble. Eight of the long-nosed dragons Nazere had seen on the turrets in the front of the bastion were positioned in the back of the field. They were set up in two parallel ranks, armored warriors adorned in red and purple being lifted into their bellies via a hovering, circular lift. Nazere leaned over to Elle.

"What are those things exactly?" Nazere asked in whisper, pointing to the organized dragons.

"They are called leviathans," Elle replied back in a whisper. "Their purpose is twofold. They serve as transports for the troops and are quite agile fighters in the sky."

"Gotcha," Nazere whispered as he looked around. To his immediate right, Nazere looked on as the Colossus' stomach slid to the side. As it did, a steel staircase rolled out from within like a scroll being quickly unraveled. The staircase reached the surface of the grass, where it awaited its patrons. James, Felix, Lily and Aaron began ascending the stairs to the man-like machine as soon as it touched the ground. Next to the Colossus, the Deliverer dropped its lift from its midsection where it hovered in the air. Adrax took Sara's hand as the wind blew fiercely, her legs struggling to get aboard the circular lift. Hopping up behind Adrax with the greatest of ease, Drake took Arthur's hand and assisted his aged body in climbing aboard next. The Redeemer sat on the round landing surface, the orange lights surrounding its surface flashing on and off. Adrax waved to the Gathering of the White Knight as the lift to the Deliverer slowly retracted into the lion's belly, carrying the occupants on its circular surface inside.

"Here we are, then," David began as he started walking toward the Redeemer. He withdrew his trentorod from his side as he moved. "Wings up, my beauty!" David yelled. The Redeemer let out a might cry as it flung its wings to the upright position. "All aboard who's going aboard!" David yelled. He walked up to the eagle's door and placed the trentorod in its key position. The door was propelled backward, and rolled to the side. "Ladies first," David said as he turned to Elle and waved for her to enter with the slightest motion of his right arm. Elle turned to Nazere, lifted her feet, gently took hold of his face, and kissed him passionately. Nazere wrapped his arms around Elle as the couple became fully interlocked for several seconds. As Nazere slowly withdrew his arms, Elle turned back to David.

"Well then," David said with a surprised look on his face, scratching his blond hair. "Didn't see that coming."

"Thank you, kind sir," Elle said to David as she walked aboard the Redeemer.

"Need any help up, Hayden?" David asked.

"I think I'll manage just fine," Hayden replied with a smile. "But thank you for your kind offer."

"Not a problem, high prophet," David said. Hayden promptly pulled himself inside of the circular opening of the Redeemer, holding to his black staff as he entered. As Ryan was about to climb aboard, David grabbed his arm firmly. Ryan stopped, turned and looked at him. "Be careful out there, Ryan," David said as he focused on Ryan's face. "You're the first brother I knew."

"No worries," Ryan said as he smiled at David. "The Master will be with me." David nodded as he released his hand, leaving Ryan to enter the Redeemer. Nazere entered next, and David followed directly behind him. Everyone sat in their proper seats, and the ribbons behind the chairs strapped everyone in as the captain pushed a red button to his right. David immediately began pressing buttons on the suspended control panel in front of him as was the norm.

"Are we ready to take flight, my beauty?" David asked the Redeemer, his spirit in flight already.

"That would be an affirmative, captain," the Redeemer replied.

"Do me a big favor and fire up all communications lines, Redeemer," David commanded. A few buttons flashed on the holographic image to his right.

"Initializing open communication lines," the Redeemer replied.

"This is David, confirming communication connections with all networked vessels."

"This is the Deliverer," Drake replied, an image of his face appearing on the lower right-hand corner of the left display. "We're standing by for lift off, my friend."

"Nice to hear your voice, Drake," David said smiling, pressing and twirling controls rapidly.

"This is the Colossus," the Colossus said in a booming voice. "All cores engaged for take off. We are ready for launch."

"Leviathan one confirming a good connection. We're ready to fly."

"Leviathan two announcing all soldiers onboard."

"Leviathan three has all cores up and running."

"Leviathan four reporting in. Setting coordinates now."

"Leviathan five is all set to fly. We're ready for anything."

"Leviathan six just getting everyone in. Preparing for lift off."

"Leviathan seven is networked. On your mark."

"Leviathan eight has all shields engaged. Let's take it to them."

"Copy that," David replied to all ships. "Redeemer, set your destination to the Ordren Province." David paused for a moment as he pressed a few final control keys. "This is a call to all networked ships. We're heading all the way up. And that means to space, Drake."

"I have absolutely no clue what you meant," Drake snickered. "Orders confirmed, my friend. Awaiting your mark."

"Everyone brace yourselves," David began, the countdown timer in motion. "Engaging flight in three...," The Redeemer began to move its talons on the surface of the ground, and Nazere looked at the display as the leviathans also began to pick up momentum. The Colossus began to levitate off of the ground, and the Deliverer crouched down in the pounce position.

"Two...," David continued. Picking up speed, the Redeemer transitioned into a run. "One. All ships, take it up!" The Deliverer immediately released its position, zooming upward and out of sight.

"Woo-hoo!" Drake exclaimed over the intercom. "You have to love micro-gravity!" The Redeemer let out a loud shriek, flapped its wings, and pointed its head upward. It flew straight up, rapidly moving toward the clouds. The rising Colossus and the leviathans beating their wings flew close behind, catching up to the Redeemer in little time as they increased their velocity. Nazere looked at the display and noticed a ball of flame as the Redeemer flew above the clouds. The Deliverer had already hit the outermost part of the atmosphere, and its ion shield was burning as it continued to ascend. Seconds later, the Redeemer threw its wings forward, the Colossus flying right next to it. The Colossus turned its head to the Redeemer as it reached its altitude; the mighty machine had a mind of its own.

"Increasing speed to six-hundred and ninety miles per hour," the Redeemer reported.

"Sounds good," David replied. "Keep it steady, flight. We're doing great." The Redeemer, the Colossus and the leviathans hit outer space together, slowing down once they had reached a set altitude. The Deliverer slowly span around in a curled-up ball; Drake seemed to be taunting the Redeemer as he slickly maneuvered his pristine lion. It purred as the rest of the flight reached its location. The eagle and the gunmetal man gently glided around the Deliverer in a perfect circle. "All networked ships, follow my lead. Set your coordinates accordingly if you haven't already done so."

"That's a big roger," Drake affirmed over the intercom.

"Coordinates downloaded and duplicated," the Colossus said. "I have your target, leader."

"Alright, baby," David began as he addressed his beloved Redeemer. "Don't fail me now. Begin your ascent to the destination of the Ordren Province. Let's get this party started." The Redeemer threw its wings out into space, a final float before the drop.

"Beginning descent now," the Redeemer replied. Elle turned to Nazere.

"Nazere," she began.

"Yes, Elle?" Nazere asked, looking at her in return.

"There's something I want to tell you before we land. I..." Suddenly, the Redeemer let out a shriek and pointed its wings forward as it dropped down into the earth's atmosphere like a piano off a ten-story building.

"What is it?" Nazere asked as microgravity took over.

"Nevermind," Elle said, struggling to talk. "It isn't important right now."

Everyone on board the Redeemer held tightly to their seats as the bird began its rapid fall toward the earth's surface. A twirling ball went flying by the Redeemer at an unbelievable speed, faster than a heat-seeking missile in striving to reach its target.

"We're on the ground," Drake said over the intercom only seconds later. "I have my cloak engaged. Keep up, David!"

"Yea, yea," David smirked. "We'll be at the site in a few moments. Redeemer, engage your cloak."

"Cloak engaged," the Redeemer replied. The Colossus and the leviathans behind him followed, becoming invisible in the light-blue sky as they continued their descent through the clouds. Within several seconds, a familiar sight came into Nazere's field of vision. As the Redeemer pushed through the remainder of the clouds with the rest of the flight following behind, Nazere made out the outline of the Ordren stasis chambers on the display to David's left.

"We're taking her down," David announced over the intercom. "Everyone initiate your landing sequences."

"Affirmative," the Colossus replied. "The landing zone is now within range."

"Now reducing velocity to landing speed," the Redeemer said. The great eagle flapped its wings out as it hovered over the city, Nazere's artificial adrenaline pumping heavily in full acknowledgement of where he was. He could only imagine what the others must be feeling, a slight twitch catching the tap-shoes that were his fingers.

"Get ready for anything," Ryan said. "This province is jam-packed with ventari." The Redeemer circled around slowly, dropping its talons on the dusty, brown, dirt-covered ground. The Colossus landed next, with the flight of leviathans dropping their claws on the ground behind it.

"I'm not seeing anything on my radar," Drake said slowly over the intercom, a hint of doubt in his voice.

"Me neither," David replied as he looked in all directions on his left display. "It appears the city is ill-defended. There's nothing in sight."

"Not a thing," Ryan confirmed, taking a quick glance at the right display to retrace David's steps. "The radar is completely blank."

"I'm disengaging my cloak," Drake said. "James is going to rally the troops on the ground below. All forces meet at the flag of the white rook."

"You heard the man," David said. "All forces drop to the ground and rally at James' position. Drake and myself will remain onboard our vessels."

"Disengaging cloak," the Colossus said. "I'm deploying my staircase now."

The ribbons behind everyone onboard the Redeemer's chair flew off animatedly, and all aboard except David rose from their seats.

"Good luck out there," David said, his face preoccupied with the controls to his eagle. Ryan put his hand on David's shoulder in passing.

"Luck has nothing to do with it, my friend," he said with a smile.

"Off we go, then," Hayden started as he advanced toward the door of the Redeemer, staff in hand. "We need to get to our proper places in the clearing immediately."

"Wings up, Redeemer!" David exclaimed. The Redeemer let out a resounding call as it lifted its wings. The door then pushed toward those aboard the Redeemer and rolled to the side. Looking outside as he climbed out of the ship first, Nazere saw forces joining together in ranks and files besides James. Red armored soldiers stood in organized ranks off to the left of James in files of ten. Ranks of purple armored soldiers stood on the right, also in files of ten. The soldiers kept their weapons out of their hands as they stood at an erect position of attention, faces forward, outstretched fingers at the middle of their thighs. James carried a long, brass pole with a pennant flag at its top in one hand and his spear in the other. The pennant flag was violet, and bore the insignia of the rook in white. The flag he held flapped in the air as the wind blew it every which way, but he held the pole upright, firmly in place. Aaron, Felix, Endarius and Lily stood in a small line directly in front of James. Sara stood by James' side on the right, standing in a still pose as she awaited others to join them at the rally point. Adrax stood on the left of the red ranks of soldiers, his sword sheathed behind him, his eyes watchful. He too carried a pennant flag on a brass pole, but his was red with the black imprint of a lion on its fabric surface. Ryan, Hayden and Elle made their way out of the Redeemer and alighted themselves on the dusty, light-brown ground below. Together with Nazere, they joined the others who were organized in the area in front of James' flag.

The door on the Redeemer closed, and the lifts to the Deliverer and the leviathans on the ground floated back up to the stomachs of the machines. The Colossus retracted its staircase, the metal on its chest coming to a sliding close once the roll of stairs was inside. Not a word was spoken on the ground, every soul awaiting instruction like a still pause in an awkward conversation. Nazere turned to Elle, who was already looking back at him, the two exchanging understanding of the heart through a tacit stare.

"Confirming communications with allied vessels," James said, speaking out into the open.

"I hear you loud and clear," David said. "I think we're free to go forward."

"All is silent," Hayden said as slowly as tortoise, his eyes becoming slits as he peered around at the area surrounding him.

Too silent, Nazere thought to himself, his eyes turning straight ahead to the doors of Ordren. He knew the rules of engagement on the streets of his home city of Baltimore all too well; the conventional principles of battle and survival. And he knew Ordren, and how very well guarded its institutions were. The escape he made with Keldrid was barely possible because of its well-structured, highly-manned, vigilant defenses- its blue flames close to catching that which is divine. How could this be any different?

"I think we're ready for the go-ahead," James said, his voice a sedated tune. He turned to Ryan and Aaron, who stood next to each other. "Are you ready, Ryan?" James asked.

"I am," Ryan replied, his heart beating at a steady pace like the pounding of a war-drum.

"And you, Aaron?" James asked again, calm and assured.

"I've got my hakrolend in hand," Aaron said, surefooted before he had taken a step. "I know what I have to do." He turned to Ryan with a straight look upon his face. "You ready to head in, bro?"

"Let's do it," Ryan replied, his heart beginning to pick up speed as adrenaline rushed throughout his body like a racing river.

High above the gatherings in the partly-cloudy sky, Lieutenant Galen leaned over to look at the display before him. He was fully armored in white, a black cape bearing the emblem of a red dragon on his back. All that was exposed was his shaven head and the mark of the beast on his neck. His eyes gleamed as his targeting systems locked onto the group below, the fate of his blinded prey under his control; he could feel it. The crosshairs of his vessel had a dead aim at the unknowing assemblage below him, eager to bring forth destruction. The blood that rushed through Galen's veins presented him with a natural euphoria of unequalled delight as he simply stared at his holographic display. The cabin of his ship was extravagant, with sixty men in all-black military uniforms manning multiple, smaller, control panels in steel chairs welded to studded, steel floors on both sides of the lieutenant.

"What a delicate treat," Galen began, almost to the point of laughter. "They are all within my very hand's grasp!" The lieutenant glanced to his left. "Petty Officer Louis!"

"Yes, lieutenant?" the petty officer asked.

"Our little assembly below us has a ventari in their midst. I am ordering you to deploy the test wave. I want to see what this little runt has to offer."

"Yes sir, Lieutenant Galen," the petty officer replied.

"And Petty Officer Louis," Galen said before the petty officer turned to walk away, his voice wickedly sharp and drawn out. "Fire a few low end charges at the group. I don't want to see them die. I want to see them bleed out." The petty officer acknowledged the lieutenant's commands, nodding and turning around to see to the fulfillment of his orders.

The Deliverer looked from side to side, its red eyes scanning the ground in front of the massive artolium doors of the Ordren jail. The Redeemer veered its eyes in all directions, completing a second radar scan to ensure that there were no enemies within the group's vicinity. "Still nothing," David said over the intercom. "Send Ryan and Aaron in now!"

As suddenly as David spoke, a green ethalon flare descended from the clouds to where the gatherings were assembled like the forthcoming of disaster. Sara dropped to her knees immediately and threw her arms out behind her, agile, alert, and fluid in her practiced movement. A massive, prismatic shield surrounded the group in a wide circle, the orblike shell instantly prepared for the coming tide. The shield glistened like white sand reflecting light from the sun on a midsummer's day, and stretched out well beyond the group to provide additional protection. The shield was about three hundred feet tall, serving as a supernatural defensive mechanism for both men and vessels alike. The rounded shell rippled in a multitudinous blend of all colors as the bombardment of green ethalon hit the surface of it with tremendous force.

"Where did that blast come from?" James asked, remaining still in place but glancing behind him into the great blue yonder. Deep inside, he was cognizant of what was coming.

"I'm scanning again now," David replied, a rushed tone to his voice. A few seconds passed as he manipulated his controls and initiated another radar scan on his right holographic display. As he did, a second green ethalon blast came flying like a comet from the same direction- hitting the emblazoned shield around the gatherings once again. The Colossus looked to the sky, and as he scanned the air he immediately engaged his weapons' systems. On his shoulders, six, round sockets popped up and bolted open; there were three sockets on the left shoulder and three on the right. From within, ethalon cannons fully extended to the battle-ready position- each long, black cylinder protracting in three clicks like a scope. The cylinders were connected to a black, rotating, ball joint, allowing each individual cannon to be aimed in a specific direction.

"Radar!" Drake yelled at the top of his lungs. "Radar!" David looked down at his display within the Redeemer and sat motionless in his chair, frozen in place by the view that was revealed to him; his radar was painted red. High above in the clouds, a sky-reigning ship had uncloaked itself. Swarms of phantoms encircled it in two directions like electrons being driven around the center of an atom, their appendages zooming around in a vortex of heavy metal. From the ground, Endarius looked up and squinted his dark-brown eyes in an attempt to catch a glimpse of the dark parade underway. He could barely make out the blue-ringed tentacles of the phantoms as they moved at such an astoundingly high rate of speed. But he did make out something else, and they were all looking straight down at him. Amongst the phantoms, and clinging to the side of the overwhelmingly gargantuan ship, were over one-hundred vizedrones.

The ship was larger than the whole of the city, its sheer size casting a massive shadow on the earth below. Shaped like an octopus, its bronze-colored shell gleamed brightly- the vessel comprised primarily of artolium. There were six, neon-green windows shaped in an octagon surrounding its forward frame. Attached to its rear were sixteen green tentacles that swirled around in the sky as if treading through the sea. They were anatomically correct, the tentacles mirror images of their nautical neighbors. United with its choir of fighter ships, the dreadnaught had initiated the resounding symphony of battle.

"Dreadnaught!" David yelled out as loudly as he possibly could, realizing the presence of the heavy battleship.

"God help us!" Drake exclaimed as he stared at his display in a stupor. "They've sent an entire fleet! My radar is completely overwhelmed!"

"Hold your fire!" James yelled as he commanded the troops on the ground. They remained pacific, silent, unmoved. "Stand your ground!

I am sensing something else here."

Out of the shadows, approaching slowly from the left and right sides of Sara's shield as if queued to do so, hundreds of dreadhunters came out their cloak and moved to the front of the group. One dreadhunter growled and swiped at the prismatic shield Sara was holding in place, hungry to enter in and devour the steadfast saints. From above, stormdivers who had just uncloaked hovered over the dreadhunters. As they were also numbered in the hundreds, electricity arced across the air in every which direction. Bolts of electricity hit the shield held by Sara, but Sara was unshaken in her stance. She held her position without so much as a hint of movement.

"Prepare!" Adrax screamed, each of his facial muscles tightened as he pulled a summtorant from his pants' pocket. "Borexis! To my side!" As Adrax called out, a great, gray husky appeared in a cloud of white smoke by Adrax's side. The dog looked up to his master with his happy, light-blue eyes, and Adrax glanced down at Borexis. The husky knew his master's eyes, and immediately sensed that something was amiss. It was then that he turned and began to snarl viciously at the dreadhunters beyond the brilliant shield, his nostrils opening widely as they collected the scent of the impatient panthers. Arthur pulled his summtorant from his breast pocket, and Hayden followed directly behind him by reaching into his robes.

"Cadra! Come to me!" Arthur yelled. Out of a stormy, black cloud, a black horse with red eyes and a fiery, red tail trotted to Arthur's side. A harmless, burning staircase allowed the high prophet to hop on the horse's back with his cane still in hand.

"Come Elothis!" Hayden called out with his summtorant in hand. And a out of yet another black, stormy cloud came a white horse with four eyes and four tails. Climbing atop the horse, Hayden raised his staff in the air and held his poise.

"Judgmane!" James yelled as he pulled out his summtorant. "Come forth at once!" And to the side of James in a ball of flame came a black lion with black eyes and a thick, black mane. The lion roared and growled viciously at the beasts that awaited him beyond the shield, increasing his size by twelve as he eagerly awaited the engagement to come.

"You are unleashed, Bloodfang," Endarius said in a tone like black ice, smiling. "Bring death to them." To his side, a ball of smoke took the form of a wolf with an unusually large set of jaws. Bloodfang ran toward the edge of the barrier for a moment, displaying his boastful collection of teeth to the dreadhunters beyond; his incisive fangs put the sharpest of razorblades to shame.

"Come my precious," Lily said, cool and collected as she pulled out her summtorant. Out of a little puff of smoke came the itty-bitty Tygrys, meowing as she glanced her little eyes up at Lily. Elle looked at Nazere and shook her head, throwing him the summtorant he realized he had left on his bed.

"Good looking, honey," Nazere said as he caught the device.

"Not a problem, babe," she replied. Veering his eyes to his side and holding his summtorant, Nazere looked upon the miniscule Persian cat with a questioning expression on his face; he had to wonder how well Tygrys would fair against a dreadhunter.

"Rise, Tygrys!" Lily commanded. And as Lily instructed, Tygrys took the form of a white mountain lion with irregularly large paws. As Lily hopped on top of the majestic animal, Tygrys instantly increased her size tenfold.

"Come on, boy," Nazere said as he held his summtorant out. Rolling out of the smoke, Verus stood by Nazere's side. Nazere kneeled down and hugged his friend, an embrace he didn't have the guarantee to have again. "Be careful out there, boy," he said as he slowly withdrew his arms. Verus barked repeatedly as his eyes met the dreadhunters and stormdivers, the German shepherd showing no signs of fear. His teeth became fully exposed as he turned his body fully towards them and crouched in anticipation, increasing his size twelve-fold.

"One last call," Elle began in a voice like velvet as she calmly pulled a summtorant from her pocket. Her eyes briefly glanced up at Nazere, knowing what he was thinking. A selfless person, Elle was completely afraid for Nazere; her heart dropped in her chest as she continued to think of him in combat. But as she focused on the cube in her hand, she let all of her fears go. "Umerald, you are needed my dear." Nazere looked on in shock as an emerald green tiger was summoned to Elle's side. Elle hopped on top of the tiger, and the tiger increased its size by ten.

"You never told me you had a summtorant!" Nazere exclaimed, his facial expression a mix of fear and concern.

"Well," Elle began, trying to hold back her sense of fear for him. "Now you know."

"Everyone hold their ground!" James exclaimed as he held his illuminated spear in the air. The summoned animals all aligned themselves in a row in front of the rest of the group, looking at their opposition outside of the shield. The high prophets remained back from the rank of animals with Nazere and the others, but Lily and Elle were with the aligned summoned. The animals were hungry for combat, growling, snarling, barking and ready to snap. Each was loyal to its master, and the animals' display of vigilant angst against an overpowering army demonstrated their love quite clearly.

A thousand thoughts became terpsichorean in Nazere's mind, fluidly moving about like a dancer in the middle of a rambunctious nightclub. He watched Elle stand in the middle of a line of enraged animals, praying that she would not be hurt. He wondered what Ryan must be thinking about Lily at the same time. Then came the idea of his own confrontation, which he hated with all of his essence. He had established an inner turmoil of pain and frustration over a series of years of being worn down on the streets; he was conditioned to lose. On its most basic level, the sequence of negative events he experienced would bottle down to whether or not he was capable of looking beyond all the memories of defeat that haunted him.

"Elle!" Nazere yelled. Elle glanced back at Nazere, holding to the sides of her emerald cat. "Please be careful out there." Elle smiled, still knowing that Nazere was fundamentally thinking the same thing that she was. She knew that he cared for her with all of his heart.

In the sky, a black vizedrone looked down acutely at the ships below, targeting them with its internal sensors. Lifting off from the dreadnaught by shoving its massive claws against the artolium ship's hull, this unusually oversized vizedrone opened its immensely broad wings in the air. The thrust of these black wings sent a shockwave throughout the sky, a taunting challenge to any that should oppose the prowess of the dragon.

"Engage the first wave now!" Petty Officer Louis yelled out, cleverly timing the establishment of his orders. The fleet responded in immediate execution. Ten vizedrones forcefully drove their bodies off the side of the dreadnaught and joined the black dragon in the sky, spreading their incredible wings next to the leader. Exactly one-hundred phantoms contiguously discontinued their flight pattern and began to descend from the dreadnaught, propelling their tentacles out in the air in a lineal dive downward. A number of compartments opened up underneath the dreadnaught directly thereafter, artolium panels sliding backward to reveal dark, open spaces. From these square holes came fulgent flashes of blue light, trails of blue energy moving in the same direction creating a zephyr that flushed over the gatherings' shell. The lights merged and became more vivid as ten blue flames began assuming a formation in the sky. As the flames came to a stop in the air, earthshaking shockwaves tried the integrity of the undulating, glimmering shield far below. These were the ventari peacekeepers, the enders of all known resistance, and the mightiest manifestation of the supreme society of science. Holding her body as firm as an unassailable fortress, Sara kept the shield wall surrounding the group in solid place.

"We need to do something!" Sara exclaimed, her eyes set on the dreadhunters outside of the prismatic shield. His targeting systems were in full cognition of the bringers of the blue flame, realizing that the day of reckoning with the ventari had arrived. He reached his arm to the sheath behind his back, slowly inching his fingers around the hilt to the sword that it held as he kept his eyes straight forward. And with the strength of a charging bull, Nazere drew forth the Blade of the Unbroken. His whole body became like irradiated gold with the embrace of the covenant weapon, his artolium skin as brilliant as the surface of the sun. He veered his eyes up at the teasing flames standing motionless in the skies above him. The ventari in the sky stared down intently in return, unimpressed by the golden energy source in the center of the supernatural shield.

"I will deal with me," Nazere said slowly, continuing to look up at the ventari gazing back at him. Nazere turned to Elle and looked her in the eyes.

"If only you didn't have to go," Elle said, unable to hold back any longer, a melancholy look in her eyes. "I am scared for you, Nazere!"

"Do not be afraid, Elle," Nazere replied, as calm as he could possibly be in his words to soothe her spirit. "I will return to protect you." And in a flash, Nazere dashed up into the midst of the enemy ventari in a glittering, golden flame. Bypassing Nazere, the swarm of one-hundred phantoms continued advancing further toward the shield. Their tentacles' blue rings increased the amplitude of light they projected the closer they drew within range of the group below. As soon as the group of one-hundred phantoms were within able proximity of the group, they began attempting to leech their tentacles into the circular shield. The phantoms withdrew drills and ten, finger-like appendages on the ends of their tentacles in determination to penetrate Sara's shell.

"We can wait no longer!" Sara shouted as hundreds of drills began to go to work above the group, sparks hurling themselves around like fireflies in their aftermath. "Send them in!" James raised his illuminated spear high in the air, a beckoning beacon for the Battle of Ordren.

"We are hopelessly outnumbered!" James cried to his companions. "Let us show them our greatest efforts! Let us show them who we are! Send in the summoned!"

"Forward, Tygrys," Lily commanded, as calm as ever. And together as one, Elle, Lily and the aligned animals charged forward at full speed into the aggregation of blackness that awaited them. Hayden and Arthur remained in position side by side, looking out at the combat that had just begun beyond the shining shield. Colliding with the amassed dreadhunters on the other side, the animals went rolling in all directions in spheres of teeth and claws. But Elle and Lily stood tall above their resilient cats, keeping a watchful eye on the allies around them. Spinning around with two dreadhunters at once,

Verus tackled one to the floor and sank his teeth into its neck. With eight panthers crawling on his back and many more surrounding him, Judgmane roared and violently threw a dreadhunter to the floor with his agile, right paw. Bolts of lightning from the stormdivers above hit Bloodfang as he charged, and dreadhunters from all directions crawled onto his back. Tygrys swiped at dreadhunters in front of her, keeping her master secured while fending off oncoming stalkers. On his feet after quickly ending his first panther, Borexis snarled at a group of twenty dreadhunters that growled ferociously back at him only a few yards away.

In the sky high above, the black leader began to make his descent with the ten active vizedrones following closely behind. Their tails whirled and swerved behind them, slippery in the air as they flew in formation. They then stopped in unison once they had reached the desired altitude, flapping their wings in mid air as shockwaves generated by the expanse of their wings brought them to a tremendous halt; the dragons were all perfectly parallel to one another. "Keep my target," the black leader commanded with a vile snarl. "Negate them all." In concurrence, the vizedrones all opened their jaws to their widest point. In conjunction, they began to charge orange ethalon blasts in their mouths. Inside of the Colossus, the gunmetal man's crosshairs moved from target to target; it was marking six total vizedrones.

"They're beginning to fire!" David yelled, compulsive as he looked at his display. "Take us up Redeemer! All leviathans, engage the enemy! Await my signal to fight!"

The Redeemer spread its wings with all its strength and launched itself high in the sky, unleashing a deafening battle-cry as it ascended. The eight leviathans lifted off of the ground with a strong push that left the dirt on the ground shooting upward, quickly catching up to and flying alongside the Redeemer. They flung out their green, threatening wings in preparation to attack as they flew, seven of the leviathans targeting seven opposing vizedrones. All of the leviathans protracted their foremost artolium claws, the polished metal of the thick, sharp claws shining brilliantly. The Redeemer stopped directly across from the vizedrones charging their fire, where the eight leviathians aligned themselves in parallel with it. The long-nosed dragons awaited fire from the eagle and the gunmetal man before pursuing the enemy, calculating their route of attack as their squinted eyes stared at the orange orbs of ethalon in each vizedrone's jaws. The Redeemer locked its crosshairs onto the seventh vizedrone in line, as the Colossus had targeted the six before it; the internal computers of all allied vessels were in sync with one another. The eagle then opened its beak widely and began to charge its white ethalon cannon, face-to-face with fully readied vizedrones. "Colossus, I have your targets. I'm taking my own. Begin firing now!"

"Let it begin!" the Colossus replied in a booming shout. And out of the six ethalon cannons on the Colossus' shoulders came instantaneous amber charges, flying upward at the six locked targets.

"Fire now, Redeemer!" David yelled, leaning toward his holographic display in eager anticipation. Spreading its wings to their fullest length, the Redeemer fired a clever, preemptive blast at the seventh target. The seven targeted vizedrones went flying backwards as if they were forcefully shoved, their external ion shields fazed by blasts from the Collosus and the Redeemer- the ethalon flares hitting their objectives simultaneously.

"Their ion shields are down!" David announced, his eyes fixated on his display as he manipulated his controls like a surgeon at work. "Hit them now!"

Immediately flying in pursuit, seven leviathans knocked the seven dragons they had targeted toward the ground below. They dove their wings forward like pikes, two sharp spines on the ends of their wings piercing each exposed vizedrone's scales. The dragons began clawing and biting one another like rabid dogs as they hit the ground of the clearing, about a quarter mile from the edge of Sara's shield. Four remained in the sky, including the black leader, attempting to regain their bearing from the aftershock of the nearby blasts. As the four that remained still had their fully-prepared ethalon charges aimed at the ground, the remaining leviathan charged ahead into the congregation of dragons. The leviathan charged the razor sharp spines on both wings with a purple proteon charge to ensure maximum impact, four outspread daggers aimed to down each vizedrone. Charging ahead with its wings properly adjusted, the leviathan hit its four targets as accurately as an arrow being shot through an apple from afar. Falling into buildings below, the four vizedrones tumbled backward like kicked sand-castles after being stung by the proteon spines. Three went cascading down the side of a large glass structure, the glass shattering into countless, little, reflective pieces. Their bodies hit each other as they fell, compounding with the devastating proteon damage already sustained, ripping their outer hulls to shreds. The last was knocked face-first into a nearby building, the steel structure of the building collapsing under the pressure of the vizedrone's heavy weight. This was the leader. The black vizedrone lifted his head, squinted its eyes, and set its sights on the Redeemer immediately after it fell. It was as if it was completely resilient to the crushing blow dealt to it.

"I have you now, meager bird,“ the black vizedrone snarled, enraged. The seven leviathans that were on the ground were now flipping in all directions, disoriented after their collision with the silenced vizedrones. They flapped their wings in an attempt to regain stability as their opposition fought to gain a modicum of control underneath of them. The Deliverer opened up its mouth in the face of the dreadhunters and stormdivers, a red light beginning to grow from within.

"Hold your fire!" James yelled, maintaining order on the ground as choas ensued outside the shield. The soldiers to his left and right were still and quiet, serene as they seemed to be unaffected by the phantoms still campaigning against the chameleonic sphere.

Directly below the dreadnaught, Nazere stood in the midst of ten mirror images of himself. The ten venari stood about ten yards away from Nazere, glaring at each other with blank expressions after first looking upon him. Their circle had opened up to an arched semi-circle, and they seemed to be beyond the point of fear. This would be the first time Nazere would engage the ventari in combat, and although he was afraid, he didn't want to miss a single opportunity to eliminate his endessly intelligent foes; this was a do or die situation, and he could not afford a second for hesitation. Spinning his blade like a pinwheel, moving his sword forward with unpredictable speed, Nazere blasted into the grouping of ventari. The sword penetrated the first ventari's core spot on, just as it was about to raise its arm, before it was able to react. A crash of thunder penetrated the airwaves around Nazere — a sign of the Blade of the Unbroken's sheer power. Losing the light of its core, the stricken ventari fell motionless- completely colorless- to the ground a half a mile below as Nazere withdrew the golden blade. Floating around Nazere to gain some seperation, the remainder of the ventari protracted their genora blades simultaneously; their eyes were calculators, their muscles pumping particles of angst. They all set their internal crosshairs on Nazere, charging toward him at an astounding speed. Dancing around them, Nazere tightened his biceps and twirled the Blade of the Unbroken in a whirlwind. The sound of air-shredding thunder again reverberated throughout the sky. Six ventari fell to the ground below, their cores fading to gray as they descended. Their bodies had been sliced in two, accurately cut from the chest.

One of the remaining ventari flew to the front of Nazere and retracted his genora blades. The other two blinked behind him, grabbing hold of Nazere's arms in a firm grip. The ventari facing Nazere looked him in the eyes, extended its left arm, and opened the eye of its palm. Nazere struggled to move, tugging repeatedly to free himself, but was restrained by the arms of the two ventari holding him in place. There was only one option. As the eye of the ventari's palm began to glow with a white light, Nazere took his sword and rapidly drove the Blade of the Unbroken through the legs of the two ventari grasping his body on his left and right; he swiftly pierced the blade into one ventari's leg, and then immediately switched to the other. The ordeal was over in two seconds. The two ventari fell back with barren cores, their legs sparking as they were left with gaping holes in the both of them. Before the ventari in front of Nazere released his sterai beam, Nazere blinked behind him. The Blade of the Unbroken marched through the ventari's core like an unstoppable army, the slice producing a roaring crash that sealed its fate. As the ventari looked down in its final moments of consciousness, it noticed that it had lost all of its precious, blue radiance. Nazere withdrew his blade, and the ventari was cast to the sediment below in two separate pieces.

On the ground level, in front of the prismatic shield Sara was still holding in place, the animals fought valiantly against one another. Each summoned animal made every attempt to gain the upper hand over the dominant presence of the panthers and stormdivers. But the summoned were being torn to pieces. Bloodied after being bitten in the chest by several dreadhunters, Verus limped and whimpered as yet another three dreadhunters surrounding him pounced on his back and took him to the floor. Judgmane roared as he pinned his eighteenth dreadhunter to the bloodied dirt, dead panthers all around him, bolts of lightning striking him in the back like a whip. Withdrawing a reflective, silver claw from his enormous right paw, Judgmane pulled his paw upward and drove his tool of death through the heart of the dreadhunter beneath him. Looking up with pain in his saddened, black eyes, Judgmane also limped. Shred marks and burned hairs revealed the raw flesh underneath his black fur and thick mane. To the left of Judgmane, Blackfang was completely overwhelmed by a group of twelve dreadhunters biting at his tormented body. Borexis lay on his side, next to the bodies of ten slain dreadhunters. He whimpered helplessly on the dirt in a pool of his own blood as his eyes began to shut.

"Now is the time!" Elle exclaimed as Umerald held her ground, dreadhunters attempting to jump up and claw the tiger down. The amulet that hung around Elle's neck began to glow brightly as she set her eyes on Borexis' torn body. "Hands on Borexis!" she cried out. And as she reared Umerald near Borexis' body, the wounds on all sides of him began to seal instantly. Within a second, Borexis rolled to his feet and returned to his fully animated state. He immediately growled at the remaining opposition, his eyes wide with fury. Elle's amulet allowed her to heal the wounded without physically touching them. This was her gift: to restore and replenish the injured.

"Hands on Judgmane!" Lily yelled out. And as she reached down and touched Judgmane, his wounds immediately healed. Lily had the same capabilities as Elle did, but without the amulet it was required that she make physical contact with the wounded. Jumping back into action in fresh form, Judgmane continued to tackle nearby dreadhunters. He roared in the announcement of his dominance over his enemies, unshaken by pain.

"Verus, Blackfang, Umerald!" Elle yelled, noticing her own cat had quite a few claw marks down her sides. "Hands on you!" Kicking the mass of dreadhunters on top of him upward, Blackfang jumped to his feet. His mouth exposing his bringers of death, Blackfang jumped face first into one of the disrupted dreadhunters that had driven him down. Looking to the skies for but a moment, Verus barked up at his golden master.

Zooming his internal display in from afar, Nazere looked on as Elle healed animal after animal. And one by one, they regained their bearing and returned to the fray as if nothing had ever fazed them. Nazere's eyes probed the ground, taking notice of the vizedrones that were now immobilized on the ground; they appeared to be struggling to get up, but were unable to do so. His attention was peaked when his eyes captured the sight of the odd, black vizedrone.

"All networked agents begin firing on the incapacitated!" David charged. The flight of leviathans had destroyed their enemies' wings, cutting repeated holes in them with their slivering spines. They rallied with the Redeemer and angled themselves hundreds of feet above the ten vizedrones, the crippled dragons bellowing in the dirt. In one parallel line and in unison, the Redeemer and all eight leviathans threw out their wings and began charging the ethalon cannons in their mouths. The Colossus began to take flight, propelling itself into the air like a shuttle with its hands at its sides. As it flew next to the Redeemer, it turned its head briefly and smiled. It then turned its face forward, targeting the vizedrones beneath it. The Colossus' metal mask retracted back, unveiling an unusually large cannon. The Colossus promptly began to charge it, a great white ball of ethalon at the cannon's end expanding like a balloon at a rapid pace.

"Let them have it!" David commanded. All at once, the allied vessels fired, annihilating all of the targets on the ground in a series of consecutive explosions that appeared as semicircles of blinding light. Of the first eleven, there was only one vizedrone that still remained.

"I have seen far enough!" Lieutenant Galen yelled from within his dreadnaught, fuming with disgust. "Deploy the second wave! We will end this now!" And upon his command, nine additional vizedrones lifted off of the dreadnaught and aligned themselves across from the allied vessels.

"Everyone prepare to fire!" David yelled over the intercom. Face to face with the enemy, the leviathians, the Colossus and the Redeemer all began to prepare their next wave of heated shots. The vizedrones aligned across from the flight of the gatherings were also charging their fire, the black leader flying to their right side and spreading his wings. The black leader kept his eyes set on the Redeemer, completely focused its desired prey. Timed a split second apart, the ethalon charges of the vizedrones, the Redeemer, the leviathans and the Colossus collided. Magnified orbs of ethalon exploded between one group and the other, the vizedrones beginning to charge a second round in retribution. The vizedrones were charging their particles faster, and the split second differential of the prior explosion gave them the advantage for the next attack. Their charges grew to their full capacity, the allied vessels unable to evade or preemptively fire to defend themselves in time. But Nazere knew that, descending from a higher altitude like a golden fireball.

He flew through three vizedrones with one swift swipe of his sword, slicing through the neck of each dragon with his impenetrable sword. And as the sound of three sequential crashes of thunder subsided, the motionless dragons plummeted to the dusty earth below. As fluid as mercury in his movements, Nazere quickly drove his sword through a fourth vizedrone's heart and withdrew the sword with haste. The dragon screamed as its artolium hull became molten, the vizedrone wasting away into a stream of liquified metal that poured onto the side of a tall building below it. Twirling his blade in his right hand, and knowing the allied vessels now stood a chance to overcome the oncoming blasts, Nazere set his eyes on the black leader with his sword at the ready. The leader redirected its attention to Nazere, discontinuing its fire as its right eye widened at the sight of the empowered ventari. Out of absolute fear at the very sight of Nazere, the dragon flapped its wings and began to retreat. As its tail went swooping near the side of the dreadnaught, the black leader cloaked itself out of sight.

"Altogether now!" David yelled. "Knock out the last of them!" The Redeemer, the Colossus and the leviathans charged up their cannons as the remaining vizedrones shut their jaws. Knowing they were outmatched, and trying to evade the coming bombardment, the vizedrones flew in desperate, alternating patterns. But their attempts were in vain. Vizedrones are not especially fast creatures — certainly not fast enough to outrun ethalon fire — and the charges sought them out like lightning-fast, heat-seeking missles. With the sheer number of shots fired, their ion shields were insufficient to protect them from disintegration. Hit again and again in succession, all five vizedrones that struggled to escape combusted in a blazing inferno of detonations. The ethalon flares completely consumed them. "Direct hits!" David exclaimed, nearly jumping out of his seat in excitement. "Keep a steady look out, flight. We're not out of the woods yet."

Within the dreadnaught, Lieutenant Galen laughed as he leaned back in his chair. "Petty Officer Louis!" he yelled out.

"Yes sir?" the petty officer inquired as he approached Galen's chair.

"Get me a beer. And send the rest of the fleet. This ventari has amused me, but it's time to shut him up."

On the ground, the one-hundred phantoms began moving toward the dreadhunters and stormdivers. Picking Blackfang up with its fingers, a phantom opened its head, engaged its firestorm cannon, and fired a single bolt of blue ethalon at the wolf. The phantom then tossed the motionless creature to the dirt and set its menacing sights on Lily. Another phantom threw out two tentacles in the direction of Elle, but retracted them when they hit the ground hard, missing completely. Adrax drove his flag into the ground and drew his saber, the red glow of the curved weapon giving it life. At the same time, another green charge came from the dreadnaught above. This one was far more potent than the previous charges, shaking the ground and rippling the shield above the soldiers who still stood at attention.

"I can't take any more!" Sara exclaimed, an undercurrent of

desperation in her voice. "We've got to go now!"

"Alpha Call!" Adrax yelled, increasing the size of his saber tenfold. "Engage your ion shields and draw your weapons!" Fluent in their militaristic movements, those adorned in red armor in files and ranks on the right of Adrax drew their swords and activated their refractive shields. "I am with you, my people! Hold to the faith! We're going straight ahead!"

"Take aim, Omega Call!" James yelled as he too drove his flag into the ground. "Prepare for what is to come! Set your sights on the phantoms!" Each of those armed in purple withdrew their cannons, triggered the laser sights on their heads, and activated their ion shields. They then did an about-face, aiming their guns toward the many phantoms still trying to break through the shield.

Atop their horses, Arthur and Hayden turned their faces toward each other. With an underlying understanding in their eyes, the two nodded in agreement. Hayden reached out his hand, and Arthur took hold of it. He gripped it tightly as both of the high prophets slowly dropped their heads and closed their eyes. "Where two or more are gathered," Hayden murmured. And as soon as the words came from his mouth, two tremendous bolts of lightning struck both sides of the dreadnaught from the partly cloudy, blue skies above it.

"Weapon systems and communication lines are down!" a petty officer off to the left corner of Galen turned and reported, a startled look on her face.

"What?!" Galen exclaimed, infuriated. "That is impossible! Start getting the communications systems back online now! And you had better be quick! We need to get the rest of the fleet to the ground!" Turning toward the display with a revolted look on his face, Galen stomped his fist on the armrest to his right.

Still knelt under the prismatic shield, Sara Maple had a complacent look upon her face. "The Master be with us," she said slowly as she closed her eyes for but a moment and exhaled a nervous breath. "I'm dropping the shields." There was a break in the stillness within the shield as Adrax glanced at her and nodded. Sara stood up and lowered her hands to her side, turning around to face the opposition slowly.

As soon as the shield disappeared, the phantoms immediately began to project their tentacles toward the soldiers on the dusty surface of the ground. Sara opened her palm and began to fire bolts of light-red energy from it at the phantoms above, her movements velvety smooth. The first bolt hit a phantom in the face, searing it and sending it rocketing backward like it had been smacked.

"Open fire now!" James yelled as he gripped his spear and threw it into the head of the closest phantom. It had all come down to this; all the training and all the work over the course of a month and beyond it bottled down to finishing what was started. A barrage of photon fire enveloped the sky as the Gathering of the White Rook's troops unleashed the light on the phantoms above, Felix Amaldores firing his weapon to the left of the gunners. The machines were driven back by the repetitious fire, although they pushed forward with their deadly appendages with all of their might.

"My brothers and sisters!" Adrax cried, pointing his saber toward the dreadhunters with his muscular right arm. "On my mark, we show them what we're made of!" The red-armored troops to the right of Adrax drew their swords together, the sound of sharpened metal enveloping the air. Endarius reached to his side, and his sword became as black as death as soon as he drew it from its leather sheath. Owen Candlefire stood at the ready with Jentaru in hand. He turned and winked at Adrax.

"We are with them," Owen said, calm in his collected tone. "Endarius and myself will distribute ample judgment on the beast's manifestations."

"Now!" Adrax yelled at the top of his lungs.

The Gathering of the White Lion then charged into the conglomeration of dreadhunters and began to drive their swords through the chest of every exposed panther in sight. Running alongside of them, Adrax picked up five nearby dreadhunters using his gift to control and manipulate matter. In the air, the panthers lashed out and struggled to move. Still holding the dreadhunters, Adrax then separated his saber. The one curved blade became five, reproducing in fission like a bacterial cell, and the sabers danced around him like ballerinas. Withstanding several arcs of electricity to his side, Adrax raised his right arm slowly and tightened his fist. The five sabers aligned themselves properly, promptly propelled into the chests of the struggling dreadhunters above as Adrax released his fixed grip. The dancing sabers then went to work on the rest of the dreadhunters, awake and alive with Adrax's powerful spirit.

At the same time, Owen Candlefire used Jentaru with the utmost precision in cutting down stormdivers that were within his reach. Endarius' tactics were quite different altogether; he called forth a being made out of blood that had accumulated on the ground using ancient Hebrew words. The being was twelve feet tall, and appeared as a crimson man with exceptionally large hands. The hands reached out to two dreadhunters clawing at Verus, picking them up and holding them in place until they gradually drowned in the very blood they spilled.

"What incredible craftsmanship death truly is," Endarius said with a smile on his face, standing back to back with Owen Candlefire.

"Your plague will only last so long," Owen said to Endarius while maneuvering his blade, swiping down at an attacking dreadhunter. "We can only hope that it stays for a while longer."

"Go now!" James yelled, glancing back in the direction of Ryan and Aaron after having thrown his spear through the head of another phantom. The two nodded, sprinting for the door on the far left of the prison complex without so much as a word in reply. Holding his arm in the air, James' spear gravitated back to his hand as if it were a magnet. The phantom with its sights set on Lily launched three tentacles in her direction. Noticing this with his keen right eye, James levitated off of the ground for but a moment. In the next second, his arms at his sides, he launched face-first into flight. He dashed through the air at an inhuman speed, cutting off all three tentacles with his shining spear just as they were about to reach Lily's location. He then became a quick wave, his chest parallel to the ground, flying to the side of yet another phantom and driving his spear through its head. The phantom's six eyes became dark and its body came tumbling to the side like a tree that had just been axed down. James withdrew his spear instantaneously and ascertained his next target, his eyes appalled as they glanced above him.

The sky was black with the heads of fully erected phantoms, their blue and silver tentacles picking up soldiers everywhere, firing deadly ethalon flares at their bodies, and tossing them to the side remorselessly. One phantom picked up three red-armored soldiers at once, tearing one of the soldiers apart- blood spewing forth from his insides. As the phantom threw the first soldier at the ground in two pieces, it sequentially ripped the other two asunder and flung them to the dirt. Storming over to their location, Lily and Tygrys stood in the midst of the separated bodies. In pounce position, the Deliverer began to charge a furious red beam in within its mouth- the lion's light growing with every passing second.

"Hands on the fallen!" Lily yelled out, her eyes horrified, reaching down and touching each bloodied, torn body. The separated torsos on the ground dragged across the dusty ground and reconnected, gripping their blades and guns once all of their wounds had completely sealed; the healed soldiers returned to the battle as if nothing had happened. As phantoms continued to attack the front lines, Lily had her hands full with the injured gunners of the Gathering of the White Rook.

"What say you, Arthur?" Hayden asked, smiling in confidence.

"It has been quite some time," Arthur replied nonchalantly, his eyes lighting up in anticipation. "Let's have at them." Hayden raised his staff up, gripping it tightly and pointing it in hot defiance of the stormdivers in the air. Taking hold of his cane with his right hand, Arthur aimed at a phantom to his left- the cap at the end of the cane beginning to glow blue.

"To the abyss with you, possessed creatures!" Hayden yelled. And as he shouted, his staff's end became animated with fire, the stormdivers above the dreadhunters gravitating together as a cluster in a vacuum of supernatural wrath. From the end of his burning staff, a great fireball followed by a trail was bombarded into the dead center of the stormdivers gathered in a restrained and resisting group. The majority of the bats burst into flame, falling to the ground below in shredded, burning flesh as they met their demise. The flame on their corpses then took the form of a seventy-seven-foot cobra, the slithering apparition showing its two fangs as the breath of life came upon it. The sentient cobra coiled around three dreadhunters, incinerating their bodies on contact. The remaining stormdivers in the air attempted to evade the cobra, separating in all different directions in despair. The cobra flung thirty fireballs into the air in less than thirty seconds, reducing the bats to ashes, consuming what remained of the stormdivers in venomous conflagration.

In the mean time, the remainder of Arthur's cane ignited with blue fury as it locked ten phantoms in place by means of hoarfrost. Photon fire from below hit the icy-white phantoms, shattering them into hundreds of frozen fragments. As a nearby mobile phantom grasped four soldiers in its tentacles, Arthur lifted his left hand up and softly waved it in a circle. The appendages of the phantom became paralyzed, and the purple and red armored soldiers returned to their proper places when they fell to the floor — freed. Pointing at the phantom, Arthur's cane froze another series of ten phantoms in place. Once again, fire from the ground shattered the phantoms and sent them flying apart in countless shards of ice.

"Keep your fire up, Omega Call!" James yelled as he flew throughout the air. He then dove onto the facial, side-surface of a phantom that stood parallel to another and ran his spear through both of them. From behind, a phantom took hold of James with its mechanical tentacle, drawing the body of the battle prophet close to his black face. Coiled in the phantom's lengthy tentacle, James looked to the ground in faith. A great red blast hit the face of the phantom, completely annihilating the head of the phantom while avoiding James. The Deliverer pounced out in the direction of James, opening its jaws and obliterating the remainder of the phantoms that had landed on the ground by moving its tempestuous ethalon beam from left to right. One by one, the phantoms fell like one domino hitting another.

In the sky, Nazere stood in front of the Redeemer, the Colossus and the leviathans. He looked at the side of the dreadnaught, patiently awaiting the black vizedrone to disengage its cloak. Suddenly, out of the compartments that remained open underneath the dreadnaught came an unending trail of blue flames. Nazere couldn't count the number of flames that flew throughout the sky, his pulsating chest quivering, overwhelmed with fear as he watched the congregation of the damned machines irrupt the airways. In total there were exactly one thousand of them, and their motivated masses were headed directly toward Nazere's location. In a black and smoking wall of shadow, a familiar guise made an appearance by Nazere's side.

"To a higher altitude, my friend," Keldrid said in his deep, ghastly tone as he turned to Nazere and unsheathed Entryu. "We must move above the dreadnaught." Nazere nodded. In a spiral of gold flame and shadow and smoke, Keldrid and Nazere ascended high above the dreadnaught and beyond the clouds behind it.

"What of the others?" Nazere asked Keldrid nervously as he turned to him.

"The ventari aren't after the others," Keldrid said, his voice grim. "They are coming for you."

In a flash of blue light, with eyes bent on annihilation, a thousand ventari encircled Nazere in a twenty yard radius. They all lifted their hands in chorus, exposing the eyes of their palms and beginning to charge irrevocable streams of doom.

"Sheath your sword and raise your hand," Keldrid ordered sharply.

"Are you insane?!" Nazere asked in a panic.

"I am," Keldrid began slowly. "But you have trusted me thus far. Never lose hope." Sheathing his sword in obedience and returning to his blue state, Nazere raised his right arm in the air. The eye of his palm began to flare up as he looked straight at his impossible opposition. Keldrid cupped his hands, and out of it crawled a small, furry caterpillar. In two seconds' time, all of the ventari behind Nazere were instantly transported in front of him. Keldrid cackled. All of the ventari fired, lighting up the atmosphere in blinding white, and Nazere released his blast in uncertain resistance. As the blasts hit each other, a blinding white orb was placed ten yards between Nazere and the thousand ventari that stood in front of him. The sterai orb began to move in the direction of Nazere, gaining size as it slowly moved in his direction. The rain of sterai beams coming from the ventari in front of Nazere seemed to spell out his destiny in so few letters. This is madness, Nazere thought to himself, sweating bricks in his mind. I am up against a thousand of myself. There is no way I can handle this alone! Keldrid held his hand out next to Nazere's slowly, meticulously. And as soon as he did, the orb immediately decreased momentum.

Fifty yards above Nazere and Keldrid, yet another wall of shadow and smoke took a hideous form. The figure had large, green, nocturnal eyes, the nose of a snake, and six midnight-black arms. Its head had eight, white bone spikes protruding from it in the fashion of a Mohawk, and the figure's body was as thin as a skeleton; its ribcage protruded from its chest. Behind his back were six black, leather sheaths with six, shining, silver hilts sticking out of them. Beyond the six sheaths, a pair of black feathered wings equal in length to Keldrid's white ones presented themselves in all of their malefic glory. Across its chest was a long slash of a scar, as if the being had been cut open by a large sword. The figure opened its mouth to expose a mouth full of razor sharp teeth.

"Keldrid!" the figure yelled down, hissing in a voice like death. "Come and take me, pitiful wretch! It has been far too long since I have tasted your essence, my eternal adversary!"

Disrupted in his focus and dropping his hand, Keldrid looked up to the sky and cast out his enormous wings. "Apollyon!" he exclaimed, his voice a dark plosion of rising tension. "You interrupt my business, demon! And I take no joy in interruptions!" Keldrid turned to Nazere and Nazere glanced back at him. "Fear not," Keldrid said reassuringly. "With heart, you will overcome." The circle of energy began to move toward Nazere faster as he no longer had support, and he stuck out his second hand in a desperated effort to reverse the coming tide.

With heart?! Nazere thought in fear and frustration. There is no chance!

Keldrid flew to Apollyon in a stream of black shadow and smoke. As Keldrid reached the demon's location, he gripped Entryu with both of his hands. He hovered in waiting ten yards away from his ancient opponent, staring him down with his blade at the ready in front of him. Apollyon drew forth his six swords as he hissed, each of the blades fashioned akin to a samurai's sword.

"Entryu, I see," Apollyon said as he smiled. "I have thirsted to feed from your essence for an eternity, Keldrid. Come to me now. Come and taste the Blades of the Abyss!" Charging toward Apollyon with dynamic speed, Keldrid drove Entryu forward. Blocking with his six blades, Apollyon laughed to himself morosely in the face of the angel.

At the entrance to the prison, Aaron placed his hakrolend up to the holographic image of an electronic circuit. Within seconds, the artolium door was raised and fixated into place.

"Not too shabby," Ryan said as he smiled at Aaron.

"It's not bad," Aaron replied as he held the hakrolend out in front of him. "I didn't want it to take more than a few seconds to hack, bro. Took me a while to make this thing." Ryan nudged his head in the direction of the door.

"Come on, buddy," Ryan began, patting Aaron's shoulder. "Let's go save the high prophet."

Yards away from the door, Elle reached down and laid her hand on Adrax. His body knelt down in bitter pain, cuts on all sides of his muscular body healed upon Elle's touch. Looking around him, Adrax noticed that the remainder of the dreadhunters had been slain. Their bodies littered the area where they had first gathered outside of Sara's prismatic shield, along with what remained of the burning bodies of stormdivers. Riding to Adrax's position, Lily reared Tygrys. As she did, the apparition of blood brought forth by Endarius splattered into a pool on the ground.

"What a shame," Endarius began, looking at the puddle of blood on the floor and shaking his head. "If only it could stay for a bit longer."

"All of our brothers and sisters are healed!" Lily announced in exclamation. "The fields are clear, and we have all members intact."

"Behind us!" James yelled in a fright as he flew to the ground, his eyes at a heightened state of alert. "It is far from over! They are coming in grave numbers!" Behind James, twenty round artolium pods dropped to the ground below from the dreadnaught above. When the pods opened, a great deal of mist and gases escaped from them. Out of the pods marched bloodguards and dreadhunters, walking down steel platforms that extended from each pod. Numbered in the thousands. they all gathered together in one mass and began to move toward the gatherings. As Adrax's eyes captured the sight of the oncoming enemies, his demeanor changed completely. Weighed down like a paper boat with an iron anchor, his tired face wore the heart that beat out of rhythm in his chest. The Deliverer prepared another red charge from within its opened mouth as the enemies began to sprint toward the gatherings.

"There are far too many for us to handle," Lily said, a tone of fear in her voice. Hayden and Arthur reversed the position of their mighty steeds and faced the oncoming enemies.

"Keep the faith," Hayden said, an unexpected smile rounding his face. "Deliverance will come."

The deck of the dreadnaught was booming with commotion, every petty officer on board manning their controls diligently in repairing all of the battleship's systems and getting them back online.

"All networks are back online, sir!" a petty officer to the left of Lieutenant Galen exclaimed. "We have communication with the rest of the fleet!"

"Have all linked phantoms and vizedrones sent into combat immediately!" Galen screamed in demand. "I will not so much as falter before these lunatics! Take out their ships first! The ventari is being properly dealt with!"

On the side of the dreadnaught, after being signaled to do so, the rest of the phantoms orbiting the dreadnaught began to descend through the skies below them. This time they were numbered in the thousands, and they were approaching the place of the allied flight at sound-breaking speed. Their sights were preset on the vessels, fully prepared to drill through them and tear them apart. At the same time, the black vizedrone came out of its cloak, a malevolent grin on the machine's face. The dragon launched itself from the side of the enemy's capital ship, along with over fifty vizedrones that comprised the remainder of the fleet; they flapped their wings off of the dreadnaught as they followed the leader.

"Acquiring targets," the Colossus said, a slight attenuation to its deep voice. "It does not appear we are going to surmount this obstacle."

David's radar lit up like a Christmas tree, red dots depicting figures rapidly approaching his location. Sitting back in his seat, David closed his eyes.

"Well, we have over fifty vizedrones up here. There appears to be over two thousand phantoms behind them," David announced over the intercom in a slow, serious tone. The shadow of death and defeat began to rear its ugly head, and it was rending and tearing at David's heart like a butcher's knife. But he was not one to give up so easily, thoroughly equipped with his weapon of the spirit: insurmountable faith. "Should we fall, it has been a pleasure working with you all. Until then, baby girl, let's give it all we've got! Come together, flight, and rise with me!" The Redeemer and the leviathans that surrounded it circled around as they awaited the vizedrones that were charging in their direction. The Redeemer let out a great cry that pierced the airways once it was aligned with the rest of the allied flight. And Nazere could hear it.

In the clouds, thunder cracked as Apollyon and Keldrid clashed blade with blade in the middle of a black storm cloud. Dancing in the sky and streaming from position to position, the two seemed equally matched. Keldrid would thrust Entryu forward, and Apollyon would block and swipe his six blades as Keldrid dodged. Suddenly, Apollyon stopped in front of Keldrid and cut into his right shoulder, a beaming light coming from the tear in Keldrid's robes; Apollyon began outperforming the angel. Keldrid held Entryu at the ready in front of him, holding his left hand over the wound on his shoulder and cupping the escaping light.

"Weak," Apollyon said to Keldrid, hissing. "You always were one pathetic waste of an angel! How does it feel to be consistently defeated? Does the pain please you?" Lightning cracked across the sky as Apollyon extended his neck toward the heavens, laughing as Keldrid stood motionless before him.

Not so far below, the ball of energy in front of Nazere had finally reached his hands. Becoming molten by the unstoppable orb, Nazere's artolium hands began to become unable to capacitate the amalgamated charge. Blink! he thought. Why can't I blink out of this? Unbeknownst to Nazere, once engaged in sterai combat, a ventari is unable to blink out of the energy's path. Pain flared throughout the artificial neurons of his body in series of searing, stinging, throbbing sensations. The low-intensity noise inside of his head called out to him in temptation; perhaps if he would surrender he would become free; the call beckoned him to give in to the collective ventari — to give up. Nazere turned his head to the skies in bold defiance of the inescapable urge. "Please!" he yelled out in anguish. "God help me now!'

Keldrid laughed as he increased Entryu's size tenfold, the rip in his shoulder sealing miraculously as he removed his hand and attained a greater grip on his sword. Driving the sword into Apollyon's ribcage, Keldrid looked down into the eyes of his opposition as he slowly faded to dust. Apollyon's face laughed in reply to the strike as the demon slowly disintegrated, his body blowing like loose sand into the wind. "Ashes to ashes," Keldrid began after Apollyon had faded away, standing over where Apollyon once was, twirling his sword in the air. "Dust to dust." Wasting no time, Keldrid blinked to Nazere's side in black and gray.

"All is well, human," Keldrid said as he looked at Nazere. Keldrid then maneuvered his right hand as if he were a master painter, once again aiding Nazere in pushing the orb backward with the flick of his wrist. Slowly, the orb lifted off of Nazere's hands, his fingers rapidly cooling and returning to their normal state. Pushing forward with both hands, Keldrid and Nazere continued to drive the ball of light back at the ventari in front of Nazere. "And now," Keldrid began, an undertone of a smile in his voice. "I want you to believe that all of those ventari before us are already destroyed." Nazere nodded. And as he pushed with all his might, bracing his facial muscles and clenching his teeth, the accumulated energy flew faster than light into the vast army of ventari. Unable to see through the blinding explosion, Nazere put his hands it front of his head to shield his face. And as he dropped them, his astonished eyes witnessed that all of the ventari were gone.

"All Targets Neutralized," Nazere's internal display indicated.

"Now go and finish this task on your own," Keldrid said. "I will always stand by your side. And do not ever lose heart. Believe that it will be and act upon it. When you carry that sense, human, you become that which is truly immortal." Nazere nodded, flying to the skies below him in a great blue and white flame. Keldrid watched his man storm away in a flash, standing amidst the clouds above the dreadnaught.

The Deliverer began firing its red ethalon flare as bloodguards and dreadhunters reached firing distance. The ground forces beside Adrax stood ready with their swords in their hands, standing in a row at attention and holding their swords at their sides. Firing as rapidly as possible, Omega Call attempted to hit as many of the incoming enemies as possible with their photon cannons. Breathing heavily, James looked up and watched as the Redeemer was driven into a steel and glass building by the black vizedrone. Survival seemed to dangle on the thinnest thread as overpowering forces charged toward the heavy-laden prophets.

"I can't take them all!" Drake exclaimed, manipulating the controls within the Deliverer and straining to hold to his constitution with every ounce of his faithful heart.

"All my shields are down!" David exclaimed. "I'm taking serious hull damage from the black leader!" Leviathans collided with vizedrones in the sky, rolling around and crashing into buildings on the left and right of the clearing as they attempted to reduce the number of enemies in flight.

"I wish I could help you, brother," Drake replied, a deep tone of concern in his voice for his beloved companion. "We've got a legion heading in our direction at full speed, and I'm not even able to target all of them. Hopefully the Master grants us leniency from the coming onslaught."

There was a dead silence on the ground. Imminent reality began to sink into the skulls of those who had fought with all they had as faces started to become heavy with the burden of accepting defeat. But when you have given all you have to give, there is only the innate drive to persevere that remains. The forces that were watching their dreams begin to shatter fought on in the province of Ordren, despite the innumerable eyes of advancing phantoms and foot soldiers that riddled them with doubt.

"We have lost," James said as he dropped his spear, his eyes beginning to tear up. "I suppose there are just some things that are not meant to be overcome." James shook his head as his widened eyes watched the advancing foes. "There are just too many."

Adrax grabbed James' shoulder with his right hand and smiled. "You fought well, my brother," he said as as looked James in the eyes. "In the end, it can be said that you've done all that you are able to."

Abruptly, a crash like thunder shook the gathering on the ground in a violent vibration as if the earth were trembling in fear. And as everyone attempted to hold to their footing, a golden sword came flying into the dirt ten yards from Hayden's location. It was the Blade of the Unbroken, and it shook the very air in a mighty gust of wind, an earthquake erupting under the weapon as most of the blade and the hilt of the sword protruded from the light-brown dirt. The ground was ripped apart, separating and cracking, torn by the very touch of the holy sword. As Hayden looked up, the great, blue stream of fire that was Nazere illuminated a darkened sky.

Landing tall next to Hayden, Nazere turned his head to Elle and winked. Elle smiled back at him, her toes lightly lifting off the floor in elation that he had survived. Nazere then set his eyes straight ahead and fully extended his right arm. Enemy forces were now within twenty yards of the group, racing toward the prophets at full speed, embodying the whole of the clearing in front of the assembly. A bolt of white light grew in Nazere's palm, and he took a step forward away from his comrades; all eyes were intently bound to him as he made his subtle advancement. "Target all of them!" he cried with a passion, his internal sensors instantly following his orders. He then pulled his right arm behind him and swept it outward in front of him like he was throwing a curveball, his biceps and triceps constricting as he hurled his hand with all of his physical strength. A great, white sterai wave was generated, blinding all that stood behind Nazere. As the light gradually subsided, Hayden's eyes slowly opened to slits. All that were charging toward the group- the phantoms, the bloodguards, and dreadhunters- were gone, and the artolium pods that stood behind the legion with them. Gliding over to its position in seconds, Nazere pulled the unscathed Blade of the Unbroken from the devastated ground. He then turned to Hayden and smiled widely as he took on a golden glow.

"Hold on," Nazere said to Hayden calmly. "I will return in a few moments."

He then rocketed into the air in a glittering, golden flame with his sword in his right hand, heading for the spot where the black vizedrone had the Redeemer on the ground. Holding the eagle's wings down with its overbearing claws, the orange ethalon charge in the black vizedrone's mouth had fully charged; the machine's eyes seemed to laugh in the face of the Redeemer as they widened in anticipation of the bird's death. Nazere stopped only five yards above the vizedrone after having flown in an arc, the dragon blinded to his presence, gripping his sword with two hands as he carried himself with equanimity. Dropping his body directly behind the vizedrone's domain of view, Nazere swept his blade down on the neck of the mighty machine. Its eyes dilating in a still moment of realization, a great crash of thunder spelled the dragon's end. Its head rolled off to its side in a pool of molten artolium, its ethalon charge disengaged. The Redeemer immediately regained its ankling and shook its wings off, taking to the air in a gentle glide. It hovered in position for a moment, gaping holes throughout its exterior, just flapping its wings and veering its eyes down at the golden ventari in amazement.

"Nazere!" David cheered. "Pretty close to right on time, my friend!"

"David?" Nazere asked with a surprised look on his face. "You can you hear me?"

"Yes," David replied. "Loud and clear, my brother. I linked you on my network."

"Take the Redeemer back to the prison's entrance, David. I will watch over the others that remain in the sky."

"You got it," David said in quick response. "Redeemer! Take us back to the entrance, beautiful!"

Inside of the Ordren prison, the old man in the ion shield still sat on the floor laughing. The guard outside of the ion shield stood up and deactivated the shield.

"The time has come, pest," the guard began, sneering. "I have to wonder to myself where exactly your supposed saviors went off to. Maybe they decided on a vacation to heaven." The guard reached over to the old man and grabbed his arm. From the right of the room, a loud noise startled the guard. A green sword was being driven through the door's control panel, and as it slowly inched its way around the square of circuitry, Aaron kicked the door open.

"Hand over the old man, bro," Aaron said, stepping into the room with his arms crossed.

"Hello, Aaron," the old man said as his laugh came to its close.

"Who the hell are you?" the guard asked, a stupified look in his arrogant eyes. Stepping through the door, Ryan placed his gleaming, green sword in the guard's face.

"We're friends if you want us to be," Ryan began. "But then again, that's all your choice." The guard released the old man's arm and stepped back into the corner of the room. The old man turned to the guard and shrugged his shoulders.

"I told you so," he said with a straight face.

"Let's go, High Prophet Baun," Aaron said. "I'm sure they'll want us to be quick getting out of here."

Outside of the Ordren prison, Nazere flew in midair above the pinned Colossus. His body shined in the golden glory of the sword he held in his right hand. He took his sword and sheathed it behind his back, returning his arms to his side as his blue vibrance returned. Three headless vizedrones slipped to the ground around the gunmetal man, all of them having struggled to finish the Colossus.

"That should be the last of them," Nazere said.

"One target remains," the Colossus replied as it climbed to its feet.

Claw marks covered the face, chest and legs of the Colossus, the right side of its body limping as it moved. As soon as the Colossus had taken a few steps forward, it pointed to the dreadnaught in the skies above. "That is all that remains."

From his seat, sweat dripped down Lieutenant Galen's face as his eyes scanned his radar. "Over a thousand ventari!" he exclaimed, laughing to himself in an intensified state of sheer lunacy in consideration of the events that had transpired. His face was red with rage as he leaned forward in his seat and became furious. "An entire fleet of phantoms and vizedrones!" he shouted. "Someone!" he yelled to the petty officers aboard his vessel. "Please explain why this mission was an absolute failure!"

"Maybe there is no explanation," one petty officer blurted out.

"There is an explanation for everything!" Galen screamed in rebuke. "No one speak unless I command you to! Just do as you're told! Are the weapons systems back up yet?!"

"They are at forty percent, sir," another petty officer replied.

Rallying together at the point they had arrived in on, the united gatherings eagerly awaited sign from the far left door of the installation. Everyone's weaponry was out of sight, returned to their original places in sheaths and behind backs. The Colossus, the Redeemer, the Deliverer and all eight leviathans awaited outside of the jail in a circle beside the prophets. Atrons had been deployed and were crawling all over the mauled machines, repairing heavy damage.

"I'm up to ninety percent repaired already," David announced.

"Seventy-seven percent, here," the Colossus reported. "I like that number."

"All our little animals are healed and in their proper summtorants," Elle said to Hayden, placing her summtorant in her pocket and standing next to Nazere.

"So that is what you've been hiding from me?" Nazere asked with a spark of amazement in his eyes; he was proud of Elle.

"I haven't been hiding it," Elle replied, stepping within inches of Nazere and looking up into his eyes. "Some things simply remain to be seen. And I guess it's just one of those things." Nazere reached out and wrapped his arms around Elle, holding her tightly like he never wanted to let go. She kissed his chest and rested her weary head upon it, relaxing in the break of battle. Happiness, Nazere thought. How lucky I have become.

"Look!" Sara exclaimed, looking up and pointing with her right hand. "There they are!"

Walking outside of the Ordren prison, Ryan, Aaron and High Prophet Baun emerged from the far left door. Ryan ran full speed at Lily and picked her up, kissing her on the cheek while he held her in the air. Aaron and High Prophet Baun kept a slower pace as Baun was exhausted from having remained awake for days on end.

"I missed you so much, my love," Lily said as her face was close to Ryan's.

"I told you," Ryan began, widening his eyes as he looked upon Lily's. "Everything that is meant to be will be." Lily hugged Ryan in a soft and secure embrace as a bright, triumphant grin rounded her face. Approaching the group, High Prophet Baun smiled at the gatherings before him.

"Well done today, Aaron," Adrax said as he wrapped his muscular arms around him. "You came through, and that deserves much honor."

"There were a few bloodguards," Aaron started. "But you know Ryan." Adrax nodded as his lips curled upward. "He wasted them, bro."

"High Prophet Baun!" Hayden exclaimed as he walked up to him and threw his arms around him. "How I have longed to see you again."

"The Master has seen us through," High Prophet Baun replied slowly, holding to High Prophet Hayden.

"Let's get moving people," David said, a bit hurried in his voice. "I'm not trying to wait around for this dreadnaught to start firing again."

"Everyone get to their ships!" Arthur yelled out. "We will discuss where we go from here once we get back to the Bastion of Lights' End."

"I'm on it, High Prophet Arthur," Sara said, moving toward the Deliverer. "Adrax!" she yelled. "Come help me up! High heels!"

"I'm coming, Sara," Adrax said, shaking his head and smiling.

"You ready to get out of here?" Elle asked Nazere, still resting on his body.

"I am," Nazere replied softly. "Seeing you after all of this is such sweet redemption. I am unspeakably happy to know that you are safe."

"Are you flying with us or on your own?" she inquired again, smiling as she lifted her head and looked into his eyes.

"I'm flying with you," Nazere said, leaning his neck down and kissing Elle on the forehead. "I enjoy my seat next to yours."

"Hayden," High Prophet Baun began, still standing in front of him. "if it would be alright with you, I would prefer to fly in the Redeemer on the ride back to the bastion."

"Of course that's alright," Hayden replied. "You are always a welcomed guest amongst the Gathering of the White Knight. We would be honored."

"Everyone get in!" David yelled, glancing at the portrait of Ryan and Lily in the middle of an intimately intense kiss. "I want to get back to the bastion post haste. This means you, Ryan and Lily."

"Yea, yea," Ryan said as he backed off of Lily. "I'm coming, David! Hold your girlfriend."

One by one, the Gathering of the White Knight climbed into the Redeemer. Accompanied by High Prophet Baun, everyone took their appropriate seats in the restored eagle. Baun sat next to Nazere, and Hayden on the other side of Baun. As the ribbons secured everyone in their seats, Baun looked over at Nazere's face and smiled.

"Alright my pretty baby," David began, the countdown timer on three. "I love ya. Let's take her up." With a loud shriek, the Redeemer took to the air and began flying low as it navigated around the dreadnaught. The leviathans and the Colossus followed close behind, while the Deliverer curled itself up in a ball and took to the outermost atmosphere long before the others.

"Woo-hoo! Micro-gravity again!" Drake yelled. "I'll see you all up here."

"Roger, roger," David said as he continued to fly the Redeemer under the dreadnaught above fearlessly.

In his chair, Lieutenant Galen glanced at the many holographic panels before him. Petty Officer Louis approached the officer's seat and stood at attention at the right side of his chair.

"The weapon systems are fully online, sir," Petty Officer Louis reported.

"Follow them!" Galen yelled. "I want every targeted ship taken out now! Fire all forward cannons!"

As the Redeemer pointed its nose up toward the clouds, the dreadnaught behind it began to tilt in rotation. Turning full circle, the dreadnaught fired a barrage of ethalon blasts toward the allied flight. Missing the Redeemer by a hair, the blasts exploded in the air all around the evading flight in a bunch of magnified green orbs.

"Little problem down here, Drake," David reported. "It appears that the dreadnaught has turned around. I just had twelve ethalon charges on me." Appearing slightly behind Nazere's side, Keldrid's black hood leaned over to Nazere's ear.

"He who steers the dreadnaught has a hardened heart," Keldrid whispered. "He will persue you in all of his anger. You must finish the machine." Nazere nodded in agreement.

"Keep the Redeemer flying upward, David," Nazere said confidently. "I'll be returning shortly."

Blinking outside of the Redeemer, Nazere made a levitating stand in between the dreadnaught and the allied flight. He then pulled out the Blade of the Unbroken, the golden potency of the blade consuming his being. He held the sword out in front his face with both of his hands, a thick cloud surrounding him like a blanket, making his presence known to the battleship before him.

Looking at his display, Lieutenant Galen laughed. "A sword?! He dare challenge a dreadnaught with a sword?! Fire everything we've got at the ventari!" As the dreadnaught continued to move, its multitudinous cannons extended in preparation to expell their highest-power charges. They then locked onto their target and fired repetitiously at Nazere in a sequence of simultaneous booms. There were eighteen shots in total, and Nazere moved in a golden flame-allowing the ethalon blasts to follow him.

"What is he doing?!" Galen yelled in frustration as Nazere disappeared from his display.

Blinking underneath the ship, the thick cloud surrounding Nazere remained with him, and every one of the eighteen ethalon blasts that sought out Nazere hit the ion shield surrounding the dreadnaught.

"Shields at zero percent, sir!" a petty officer yelled out. Galen flopped back in his seat as if his body was a piece of inanimate rubber.

"So they are," Galen said calmly, lamentably.

And outside of the ship, Nazere drove his sword into the hull of the dreadnaught. Lights flashed across the sky like thousands of flickering light-bulbs as the dreadnaught took on the golden glare of the Blade of the Unbroken. Almost immediately, the ship began to collapse and dent in on itself. From afar, it took the appearance of an aluminum can that was being repeatedly crushed. The hull of the ship continued to break down bridge by bridge and window by window, caving in under the pressure of a physical phenomena. At last, the ship appeared as a ball of scrap metal, colorless and motionless, and it plunged like a hovering whale into the Dead Sea; it fell only a few miles outside of the Ordren province. Watching the dreadnaught's drop into the sea, Nazere sheathed the Blade of the Unbroken behind his back. He locked his eyes in place for a moment as he contemplated the events that had just transpired, the thick cloud that surrounded him departing in the wind. So much for logic, he thought. A huge mass of mathematics, philosophy and forward progression just drowned. Who could have imagined it? He then blinked back to his seat on board the Redeemer, tranquil in his expression as if nothing had happened.

The Redeemer was floating amongst the stars, its elegant wings flapping freely and securely in the black vacuum of space. The Colossus, the Deliverer and all eight leviathans hovered at its side, their occupants all accounted for.

"Welcome back, my boy," Hayden greeted. "I assume the dreadnaught is done for, then?"

"That it is," Nazere replied as he glanced back at the high prophet.

"Like the falling tide of the Red Sea," Hayden began. "the captain of that vessel has met his unanticipated demise."

"So," High Prophet Baun began, glancing over again at Nazere. "I finally have the opportunity to meet the chosen vessel. I'm sure you know my name, as I know yours."

"I do," Nazere replied, his red seat ribbons flying out and strapping him in once again.

"I have long awaited your arrival, my child," High Prophet Baun said. Nazere turned his head toward the high prophet, his curiousity getting the best of him.

"Is there any particular reason for that?"

"We have much to discuss," High Prophet Baun began, looking Nazere deeply in the eyes. "I know of your dreams. I know of your visions. I know every single one. And by nightfall on the morrow, all will be revealed to you."

CHAPTER SIX

The Divine Apocalypse

Darkness shrouded Commander Entril's tower as the commander looked upon the rotating image of a blue ventari in front of him on his holographic display. His hands were crossed as they always were in front of his head, and his face could not be seen through the shadow that loomed over his upper body. Night had fallen upon New York City, and the moon outside of the commander's window appeared to take on a blood red shade. As the commander sat in place, footsteps could be heard quickly approaching the entrance to his chambers. Rounding the corner, a man with a bald head, piercing green eyes and a bit of gray hair around his crown stepped three paces into Commander's Entril's room; he was dressed in a white lab coat, white leather pants, and white gloves. His left hand behind his back, he offered his luminescent right hand for the commander to see. From it came the projected image of a black ventari with two sharp spines protruding from its shoulders. The image rotated as the commander retained his position and gazed upon it.

"What is the report?" Commaner Entril asked, his tone strictly business.

"We have completely redesigned the suit per your request, commander," the man in the lab coat began, still holding the image in front of him. "This one will require a great deal more power, as the core ethalon charge it capacitates contains far more motanic energy. Thus, we can only produce one at this time." Commander Entril dropped his hands and leaned forward in interest. "Unlike standard ethalon charges, the sanythalon charge within this ventari is thirty-thousand times the potency of the normal core. It is also specially equipped with anti-ventari weapon systems. Its armor is layered artolium, and its movement speed surpasses that of any other ventari by eight-hundred percent."

"Science is such a wonderful instrument, isn't it?" the Commander asked as he stood from his chair. "You have done quite well, Chief Scientist Olar. See to it this suit is produced immediately. We have no time to waste."

"Right away, Commander Entril," Olar said as he bowed. He then deactivated his hand projector and took three paces backward, quickly jolting out of the commander's sight. Leaning back and returning his hands to their folded position in front of his face, Commander Entril began to laugh hysterically.

"Praise High Lord Alune," he said, his laugh resounding throughout his chambers. "Everything is working just as he said it would."

At the Bastion of Lights' End, everyone had been rounded up and gathered together in the meeting hall. Every chair was occupied, all soldiers who had fought in the Battle of Ordren having been preserved by Elle and Lily's healing gifts. At the triangular stone table, the raiditor was returned to its normal place hovering above it. There was much chatter in the room, the voices of the three united gatherings echoing throughout the chambers. The soldiers in purple and red armor no longer wore goggles, but rather were dressed down in plain citizen's attire. Sitting next to Elle, Nazere put his hand under the table and grabbed hold of hers. Elle mildly grazed Nazere's hand with her thumb as she always did, her snow-white cheeks becoming flushed as her heart pranced around in her chest; just being around Nazere gave her spine-tingling chills. On the opposite side of the table, Ryan had switched seats with Aaron and sat next to his beloved Lily; he held her hand gently under the table, cherishing every moment with her. Smiling as he often did, Hayden grabbed a hold of his staff and took a stand at the edge of the table. The room came to calm stand still as all eyes were drawn to the bright-eyed high prophet.

"Tonight!" Hayden exclaimed in the midst of hundreds of attentive eyes. "Tonight we have returned victorious from the strain of battle! Operation Maelstrom is complete! Not a man has fallen, and we have much to be grateful for because of that. Through his infinite wonder, the Master has safeguarded his people! And this evening we will take to the Rook's Terrace, where there will be a grand celebration in honor of all who stood unshaken!"

"And two days from today," Arthur interjected as he took a stand, his cane at his side. "there will be a great banquet in the Hall of Peace. All are welcomed to attend." Hayden raised his staff high above his head, and as he did the entire room took a celebratory stand. The room was filled with loud cheers, merry laughter, and a constant, festive applause. Still holding Nazere's hand, Elle lifted her toes up ever-so-slightly and gently kissed Nazere's translucent cheek. Turning in each others' direction, Elle smiled brilliantly as she beheld her warrior. Nazere's lips reached the height of his cheeks, his breath taken by the beauty he saw in his spirit's mirror reflection. The two joined in cheering as the room was filled with joyous jubilee. Arthur wrapped his hands around Baun and held to him.

"I missed you, my friend," Arthur said, pulling back slightly and looking Baun in the face. High Prophet Baun laughed and grabbed Arthur by the hand, pulling him close again.

"Brothers to the very end," Baun said. "I never had a doubt." High Prophet Baun pulled back from Arthur and glared at Hayden, smiling as he looked into his eyes. He then drew close to Hayden and whispered something in his ear. In acknowledgment of the unheard whisper, Hayden nodded.

"Woo!" Elle cheered, still smiling and raising her clapping hands in front of her face as she looked over at Ryan and Lily. Caught intertwined together, locked lips kissing one another passionately, Ryan and Lily withdrew their faces from their entanglement and smiled back at Elle and Nazere. On all sides of the room, hugs were exchanged, happiness abounded, and select soldiers were brought to tears of gratitude.

"Ooo! Ooo! Ooo! Alpha Call!" Adrax cried out as he raised his red saber with a broad smile upon his face.

Alpha Call cheered louder than the rest of the room, chanting "Alpha Call!" again and again.

"Omega Call! My brothers and sisters! Make your presence known!" James shouted as he lifted his spear. The spear's head took on a brilliant white glow as it was held well above James' head.

And the right table suddenly became as loud as the left, raising their arms in the air as the chanted "Omega Call!" repeatedly in unison. With the room in a rowdy uproar, Sara turned her eyes over to James while she clapped. James dropped his spear to his side, the spear's head losing its brilliance as it touched the floor.

"I was surprised with your performance, James Featherwing," Sara said straight faced, looking over at James. The rest of the room continued in cheering and shouting. "I must admit, you commanded your forces admirably." James winked at Sara.

"It was never a sure thing," James began humbly, grinning. "I confess that I was beginning to lose heart. None of this was my doing. That much is for sure."

"But you made it through," Sara said with a smile cracking across her face. "And I'm happy that you did."

Walking around to where David stood, Drake reached out his hand. Grabbing it and pulling Drake into himself, David smiled. Patting David on the back, Drake drew his red-haired head back and held David's shoulders with his hands.

"Things work out when they're meant to," Drake said, looking into David's eyes.

"There were so many vizedrones," David said laughing. "My darling Redeemer was ripped apart!" He looked down as his face turned red in slight embarassment. "But she's okay now. I suppose that's all that matters."

"You should have seen the ground," Drake said excitedly, illustrating the scene with his hands. "Thousands, and I mean thousands of dreadhunters and bloodguards dropped down from the dreadnaught. I thought my heart was going to explode in my chest when I saw the number on my radar."

"Well," David began wryly, patting Drake's shoulder. "thank God it didn't. I would have lost my only source of competition." Drake laughed as David held to his shoulder. "You're my best friend, Drake. I was so very happy to have you out there with me after all we've been through over the years."

"My family!" Adrax yelled out to everyone as he climbed on top of the triangular stone table. "Everyone to the Rook's Terrace now! On this memorable evening, we celebrate till night's end. James has orchestrated quite the show for you all tonight!"

In one large group, everyone immediately started walking toward the back door of the meeting room. The door came swinging open as soon as Hayden had reached it, and people continued to chat and laugh as they made their way toward it. Elle held back for a moment, as if she were waiting for something.

"Shall I escort you, my beautiful madam?" Nazere asked Elle as he looked into her eyes and smiled.

"Do you even know where the Rook's Terrace is?" Elle asked with her hands on her hips.

"No I don't," Nazere replied. "But I am fully capable of following the others." Elle gave Nazere a stern gaze as Nazere slowly extended his left hand.

"Very well," Elle said as she took Nazere's hand, trying to hold back a wide grin. "I accept your offer, gentle sir. I just pray you don't get us lost."

"I make no promises," Nazere said as he began to walk hand in hand with Elle.

Following behind Ryan and Lily, who were linked at the elbows, Nazere and Elle walked through the opened door and on to the winding staircase beyond it.

"What is the Hall of Peace?" Nazere asked Elle as they followed Ryan and Lily down the staircase.

"It hasn't been opened in ages," Elle replied. "It is a lavish banquet hall. It is absolutely gorgeous. It's more beautiful than any hall I've ever seen."

"I know a certain woman who surpasses all the gorgeous things I've ever seen," Nazere said, grinning as he walked with his face straight ahead.

"Oh?" Elle asked, laughing to herself. "And who might this lucky woman be?"

"We'll I'll begin by telling you that her favorite colors are pink and emerald green," Nazere began.

"Those also happen to be my favorite colors," Elle said. "What else can you tell me of this woman?"

"Her eyes are the most astounding shade of hazel, and, for the strangest reason, her face lights up like the sun whenever I see her. She has long, flowing black hair, and she is the most intelligent woman I know. I can talk to her for hours and hours. She shares my love for all things animals and artistic. She questions me, but always seems to know what I'm going to say before I say it." Elle turned up at Nazere, her face glowing. "She takes long walks with me when I'm lonely, and will listen to me even when she's busy; she's like nothing I've ever known before. When I think of her, I think of the stars we both adore." Nazere looked down at Elle. "When I think of her, the heart I no longer have races like the mightiest steed fighting for an unattainable finish line. When I'm around her, I feel more alive than I've ever been. And no matter where I am, I find happiness in knowing that she is my very best friend."

"Does this girl have a name?" Elle asked, still gleaming as they reached the three doors at the bottom of the iron staircase. The third door on the left was opened, and Ryan and Lily passed through it. Nazere looked deep into Elle's eyes.

"Her name is the most beautiful one God ever created," Nazere began as he leaned into Elle. "It's yours." Wrapping their arms around each other in a tightly-knit pose, Nazere softly touched his pursed lips to Elle's. Holding that position, Elle angled her head and leaned further into Nazere. Her toes lifted off the floor as the two held each other a little closer than they ever had. And after several moments of ecstasy, Elle released her lips from the kiss.

"Perfect," the two whispered at the same time, their heads close to one another.

"I love it when we do that," Elle whispered like velvet, her face defining excitement in a flush of happiness and vibrance. "Your face becomes soft whenever I kiss you. There's nothing like the time I share with you. Nothing."

"I love it, too," Nazere whispered in reply, softly kissing Elle's forehead. "But come on, my sweetheart. I was worried about you all day and now I have you back again. That's more than enough reason to celebrate for me. Let's go see what this party is all about."

"Okay," Elle whispered back, exhaling the breath she was holding back. The two started advancing toward the open door. "Hand!" she exclaimed wryly as they entered the next toom. "And there better not be another Elle!" Nazere laughed as he took hold of Elle's hand, believing with all of his heart that he was finally the richest man alive.

The room that lie in front of the couple was large and comprised entirely of gray stone. There were eight elaborate silver framed oil paintings on the left and right walls of the room altogether, and a staircase that led straight up about five yards away from the pair. To the right were the silver-framed paintings of a lion, a horse, a castle and a crowned king. Silver-framed artwork on the left wall was that of a dove, a bishop adorned in white and gold robes, a lamb and a crowned queen. The paintings all hung parallel to the floor and were about five feet tall and three feet wide. On the ends of the banisters that led upward were two large rooks, fashioned like articulate, stone chess pieces. Side by side, Elle and Nazere walked up the long staircase slowly- taking their time. Nazere could vaguely hear the sound of drums and a guitar from his place on the stairs. And at the top, the pair were met by yet another room.

This one was even larger than the last and was comprised of a stone floor and all glass furnishings. There were thirty glass round tables, and on the tables were glass champagne flutes and wine glasses with tied red and violet ribbons around them. The chairs around the table were made of thick, sturdy glass, and there were eight chairs around every round table. In front of each table were fine parchment scrolls tied in red and violet ribbons like the glasses beside them. In the center of each table was a lit wax candle with a golden candle-holder. In the three corners of the room, square flags hanging from polished, vertical redwood bars and bearing the insignias of the gatherings were presented for all to see. Hanging on the left side of the room in violet was a large, silk flag of a rook with feathered wings embroidered into the fabric by means of gold threading. And on the right in red, a large, silk flag of a black-embroidered lion with wings hung from the redwood bar beside it. In the left hand corner of the room was the silk flag of the Gathering of the White Knight, a white horse's head with wings on its sides embroidered into the silk fabric. In various shades of violet, the glass shards of a chandelier hanging by a chain from the ceiling seemed to reflect the small bit of light within the room. The back of the room was marked by a wide opening that led outdoors, with two elegant, velveteen, red drapes that were tied in lusterous, nylon ribbons to both sides of the opening.

In front of the white knight's flag was a circular, black platform, and on top of the platform were two thin, black halogen lamps on the left and right of it. A complete set of drums sat in the center of the lamps, polished cymbals accenting the rhythm of song. The halogen lamps were facing down, dimly illuminating the dark platform before them. Sitting in a black, wooden chair behind the drum set, Adrax wore a sleeveless, white t-shirt with the imprint of a red lion on it. He moved his agile arms at a rapid pace in producing a background beat for the room, his skills finely honed. To his left, Drake held a wireless bass guitar that was connected through the air to an amplifier. And standing toward the front of the platform, David moved his fingers with the greatest precision as he played a wireless electric guitar. Singing into a round microphone hovering in front of his face with the practiced voice of an angel, he front-lined the performance of an ancient song in celebration of the victory at Ordren. A hovering sub-woofer off to the right of the platform produced massive bass for the room, and music electrified the very air around Nazere and Elle.

"Can you still hear me?!" Nazere yelled to the object of his heart, putting his hand to his hear.

"Yes!" Elle yelled as she smiled at Nazere. "I'm surprised that all the glass in here isn't completely shattered!"

"Let's go outside!" Nazere yelled over the music. "I want to see what's going on out there!"

"Alright!" Elle yelled back, slipping her arm around Nazere's back. "Let's go!"

Walking through the opening in the wall, Elle and Nazere were met with the mesmerizing sights of Rook's Terrace. They were on the upper tier of the Bastion of Lights' End, upon one of the eight circular balconies that jutted out from the center tower of the castle. Flowers adorned the entire ground of the platform in a bed of contrast, color and fantastic fragrance. Most of the people from the city congregated on the bed, sitting down or laying amidst the plethora of assorted flora. As Nazere glanced above him, his eyes captured a close snapshot of the central cylinder of the bastion that towered overhead. Its violet, cone shaped roof seemed to reach into the clouds, endlessly magnificent in scope. It reflected lights from the sky that surrounded it, the celestial ambiance of shining stars and the crescent moon. Flying above Rook's Terrace, leviathans soared freely throughout the peaceful air.

"Let's take a seat," Nazere said as the music from inside attenuated to a subtle but audible melody.

"Where?" Elle asked, looking around herself, a discombobulated look on her face. "It's completely packed out here. There's no place for us to sit that I can see."

"Take my hand," Nazere said, outstretching his arm. Lightly grasping his hand, Nazere gently pulled Elle close to his body. In an instant, Nazere took flight into the air, his arms enveloped around Elle completely, securely. He flew all the way up to the peak of the central tower of the bastion, setting Elle down as he landed. Looking down, Elle's awestricken eyes widened.

"I've never been up here," Elle said with an intrigued look on her face. She quickly took hold of Nazere, wrapping her arms around him again. "The view is breathtaking! You can see everything."

"Best view in the house," Ryan said, about ten yards away from the couple. His body was outstretched on the roof, turning his satisfied face to Nazere and winking. Lily smiled, nestled on the roof next to Ryan. Nazere and Elle turned to the two of them and returned the friendly gestures.

"Sit down, you two! Get comfortable!" Lily exclaimed, extending hospitality with a simper.

"Shall we?" Nazere asked, looking into Elle's eyes as she held on to his body for dear life.

"Okay," Elle replied. "Just promise you won't let me fall."

"I promise," Nazere replied. "I have my eyes on you even when you don't know it. If you happen to slip, I'll be right there to pick you up. You know that I care for you."

Together, Nazere and Elle lied down next to one another on the slanted surface of the top of the bastion. Cuddling close to one another, Elle rested her head on Nazere's chest as she looked up at the stars. Nazere put his left hand behind his head, gently moving his right pointer finger up and down Elle's neck as he stared upward.

"This is so nice," Elle said slowly in a downy voice, exhaling as she rested her head.

The sky was clear, the stars creating the perfect atmosphere for gazing. Flying above them, three leviathans driving their heads upward into the clouds opened their mouths together. A great screech filled the airwaves as three small flares were hurled into the sky. In the colors of red, purple and green, fireworks exploded over the Rook's Terrace and the violet roof of the bastion high above it. Cheers and claps were heard from the terrace below as yet another wave of leviathans followed the first, painting the sky a sparkling white, gold and blue. Turning his head, Nazere noticed that Lily and Ryan were completely making out on the other side of the roof.

"Reproductive Faculties Prepared for Engagement," Nazere's internal display read as his crosshairs met Ryan's preoccupied body. This targeting system is too much, Nazere thought. He was so very happy in every regard; happy that he had been delivered; happy that he had survived the battle; happy for his romantically fused friends across from him; happy that he had Elle near to him, just knowing she was safe, serene. Turning his head and smiling, Nazere returned his attention to the sky where more fireworks burst into thousands of vivid sparks of color. Suddenly, the crowd below became unusually rowdy. They screamed and clapped as yet another ship took to the skies. Slowly rising above the roof of the bastion, Nazere and Elle giggled like children as they looked upon the massive vessel known as the Colossus. His cannons extended upward, he fired what seemed to be a hundred repeated bursts of concentrated gunpowder in succession. The bursts rapidly took shape in the night sky, becoming a red lion, a white horse, and a purple rook. As the Colossus reached the peak of the bastion, he nodded his head and winked his amber, right eye toward the couples on its surface. Nazere waved with his left hand, smiling at the Colossus as it began to accelerate.

"Woo!" Elle cheered, still resting on Nazere's chest. The Colossus smiled as he passed over the intertwined couples, increasing his speed in flying upward over the bastion. He extended his arms straight out to his sides and curved his flight pattern along the night sky, a smooth gust of wind blowing over Elle and Nazere. Another flight of leviathans followed the Colossus, firing additional fireworks into the sky.

"You know, Nazere," Elle began softly as she watched the show. "this all feels like a dream. You asked me how I could ever care for a machine, but I wonder sometimes how I ever became fortunate enough to have you come into my life. Your spirit is beyond all compare in my eyes, and I never look at you like a machine. You're the same you I met when you entered into our cabin, and I just wanted you to know that you are my heart." Nazere leaned his head up and kissed the top of Elle's head.

"I feel the same way," Nazere whispered. "Some things are destined to be. And I believe that our story was written before time began. I think of all the things that I can thank God for sometimes. I thank God for you and every little thing you mean to me, Elle. Every night I thank Him for the heart that we share."

On the Rook's Terrace below, Hayden lay next to Arthur and Baun. All three of them were on their backs, and Baun had a pipe hanging out of his mouth. All of them were lying down amidst the flowers, their hands all crossed behind their heads in the same fashion. Taking a puff from his pipe, Arthur turned his head to Baun.

"Something just entered my mind, Baun," Arthur began. "From the time from we were children, we have been fighting this war together. I'm blessed to have you by my side as the only brother I ever knew. I just wanted you to know that." Baun smiled.

"Remember when we used to have churches to go to?" Baun asked as he looked upon Arthur. "And our mothers would take us out of the building for talking to each other while the sermon was going on?" Arthur and Hayden both started laughing as the imagery returned to them.

"You forget that I was there, too," Hayden said, turning his head and smiling at Arthur and Baun. "You got me into more trouble than I thought I could withstand, Baun! But I suppose the discipline did us some good after all."

"That it did," Baun replied. "That it did." Arthur took a puff from his pipe and blew the vanilla smoke from it into the air, the recollections of yesteryear returning to him like the sight of an ancient, liquid crystal display refreshing motion pictures.

"You have trained James quite well," Hayden said. "Ryan is coming along. He has the heart to become a mighty battle prophet." Baun nodded.

"It took a while for James," Baun said. "He was a stubborn hard-head in the beginning. But, with some time, he learned to see what cannot be seen. He took up the Word, and then the spear. I am very proud of his journey into manhood. Fighting for everything he has in his spirit, he's traversed a path that I have the utmost respect for."

Yards away on the Rook's Terrace, James Featherwing sat next to Sara Maple on the very edge of the flowered, stone platform. They both had neutral looks upon their faces, watching the sky as gunpowder from the gatherings' flight gave it a new stroke of color every couple of seconds.

"Quite a sight out here, isn't it?" James asked Sara as his eyes were fixated on the bright lights in the sky.

"It's gorgeous," Sara replied, also eyes also set on the fireworks. "I'm glad you set this up. It has been a long time since I've seen any fireworks. I was just a little girl the last time." James grinned.

"I'm sure you were quite the adorable little lady," James said. "You've grown to be quite the attractive woman, I must say." Sara turned her head to James with a smile, his words catching her by surprise.

"You aren't so bad, yourself, James Featherwing," Sara replied, leaning her face into his and kissing his cheek. James grin became a full fledged smile as he glanced back at Sara with an eyebrow raised.

"Now what was that for?" he asked. Sara returned her eyes to the sky nonchalantly.

"Just because," she said as she paused for a moment. "you have a sweet heart, and I enjoy being out here with you." James continued to smile as he returned to watching the leviathans twirl amidst a brilliant array of outbursts in the sky.

"I was wondering, Sara," James began, his eyes still focused above. "The banquet is in two days, and I need a date. I was wondering if maybe you would…"

"In a heart beat," Sara interrupted hastily, smiling.

Hours passed, and as they did, Elle remained close to Nazere atop the Bastion of Lights' End. Calming down from their intimate frenzy, Ryan and Lily cuddled softly and silently together on their spot on the roof. James and Sara sat side by side on the edge of Rook's Terrace, talking every now and then. Pointing to the sky, James would point out his favorite aerial formations to Sara as the leviathans demonstrated their prowess over the air; Sara would nod and inject inquiries in between his comments. Her eyes growing heavy, Elle began to fall asleep on top on Nazere's chest. Leaning over gently as not to disturb her, Nazere drew his head close to hers.

"You are tired, beautiful girl," Nazere whispered in her ear. "Are you ready to head back inside?"

"I want to stay here with you," Elle said as her eyes slowly opened.

"I know you do," Nazere replied. "But you'll only fall asleep. You need your rest. Let me escort you back inside."

"If you say so," Elle said, cuddling her head and hands up against Nazere's midsection as if she was bent on staying outside.

"Come on, Elle," Nazere said after about a minute. Elle slowly lifted her head, and as she did she kissed Nazere's cheek. "Take my hand, my sweetheart." Standing up, Elle took hold of Nazere's outreached hand. And as Nazere stood, he swept Elle's body up in his arms and began to fly through the air. After zooming down to the Rook's Terrace below, Nazere gently assisted Elle to the floor beneath them.

"Will you hold my hand?" Elle asked sweetly as she looked at him and smiled.

"Of course I will," Nazere said while looking back at her. "I'd have it no other way." Stepping up from behind Nazere, Owen Candlefire grabbed hold of Nazere's shoulder. Turning around, Nazere met the blacksmith with a cordial smile.

"I wanted to congratulate you, my friend," Owen began slowly. "You have done us all such a service in aiding us in the returning of High Prophet Baun to his proper place." Off to Owen's left, Felix Amaldores grinned at Nazere.

"My heart goes with you," Felix said to Nazere. "One day, your blade will be complete. I have seen it."

"I thank you both again for your superb work," Nazere said to Felix and Owen.

"If it was our doing alone," Owen began. "it would never have been accomplished." Nazere nodded in understanding, turning to Elle.

"Are you ready, my dear?" he asked her.

"I'm awake now," Elle said, widening her eyes and wanting to stay up with Nazere. "But I suppose I'm ready to head back in if you think I should sleep. Maybe I need it."

Holding each other's hand, Elle and Nazere walked into the noisy space within Rook's Terrace. The music still played loudly, David singing yet another ancient song as Adrax and Drake performed along with him. Walking to the staircase, yet another hand grabbed Nazere from behind. Turning around, Nazere noticed that it was Endarius Darkhand that had drawn him to attention.

"Come for a moment," Endarius began in his bass-filled tone, holding a glass flute filled with dark, red wine in his right hand. "I do not want to miss the opportunity to toast to the chosen."

"I can't drink anything," Nazere said with Elle at his side.

"Let it be a symbol, then, of your victory this day. Please," Endarius said, waving his arm for Nazere to approach him. "Come."

"Go ahead, honey," Elle said. "I'll wait right here." Nazere sighed and nodded, letting go of Elle's hand. Walking over to the nearest table, Endarius picked up the glass flute closest to him. The flute was filled with a bubbly, yellow champagne. He then handed the glass to Nazere, who took the flute.

"To the future," Endarius began, extending his arm out in front of him in a toast.

"To the future," Nazere replied, lifting his flute and touching it to Endarius' glass. Endarius drank his wine down and then turned to Nazere. Nazere handed Endarius his champagne flute, still filled with the bubbly fluid.

"Till next we meet," Endarius said, placing his glass on the table and drinking down Nazere's.

"Until then," Nazere replied, turning his back and joining Elle once again.

"Hand!" Elle exclaimed while smiling. Grabbing hold of Elle's hand, the two walked down the straight stone staircase. They then went through the door that had led them to Rook's Terrace and back up the winding iron staircase to the meeting room. Walking down the lower-left corridor, the two stopped in front of Nazere's room. Elle wrapped her hands around Nazere's neck, and he held her hips.

"So," Elle whispered with a serious face, looking deep into Nazere's eyes. "there's this guy I know, and he is the most handsome and most certainly the sweetest man in the world."

"Oh?" Nazere asked in a smiling whisper. "Tell me more about this supposed gentleman."

"He has blue eyes, and he doesn't like to be wrong. He asks a lot of questions, and he loves his dog. But he loves cats, too."

"Anything else I should know?" Nazere asked.

"When I need a hand to hold, he always obliges. He lifts my spirit, and he never ceases to bring a smile to my face. He's strong, and he doesn't give up when things get tough. He has gentle hands, and a kind face. We talk all the time about the things we both share love for, and he patiently listens to everything I have to say. He has a heart like mine, and whenever I see him I see my little piece of heaven. But most importantly, he's my very best friend."

"And who, may I ask, do you speak of?" Nazere asked. Leaning into Nazere, Elle tilted her head and kissed him with all of the passion she felt for him.

"I'm speaking of my date for the banquet," Elle whispered as she withdrew her lips ever-so-slightly.

"There better not be another guy," Nazere whispered back.

"You are the only one I see," Elle whispered as she looked at Nazere, fighting back a laugh with a grin as she was tickled by his wording.

"Well then," Nazere began, backing away from Elle a few inches. "I would be more than honored to attend the banquet by your side." Elle's smile widened as she took a few steps back. She glanced over her shoulder at Nazere as she walked down the corridor slowly. Nazere winked at her as she continued in her steps down the hall, his mind staying with her. He then redirected his eyes to his door.

"Nazere," Elle's voice chimed as he pushed his door open. Nazere turned his head toward Elle, who was now facing him.

"What is it, Elle?" Nazere asked, concerned. Elle shook her head as she took a few paces backward.

"Never mind," she said slowly. "It can wait."

Nazere nodded and walked into his room as Elle walked out of sight. Keldrid stood in the corner, moving his head as if he were carefully monitoring every move as Nazere nestled himself in his bed. As Nazere covered up, he sighed to himself and turned on his side as if something were bothering him.

"What concerns you, human?" Keldrid asked. "What is on your mind?"

"Quite a few things, Keldrid," Nazere replied, sighing again.

"Quite a few things. I have a lot on my heart right now, and I guess I never would have suspected it coming. I miss her when she goes to sleep, you know?"

"I know," Keldrid replied. "I do know love, human. I know it more than you could ever understand."

"Do you think it's love, Keldrid?" Nazere asked ardently as he turned his head up at Keldrid.

"I will let you determine that, human," Keldrid replied. "But do not lose focus of what your immediate goal is."

"And what is that exactly, Keldrid?" Nazere asked.

"Sleep now, my child," Keldrid began. "Tomorrow, you will gain the necessary understanding that you lack right now." Nazere turned his head back to his side and closed his eyes, deep in thought as he drifted off into a deep sleep.

In the middle of the night, Nazere's body tossed and turned like a ship amidst the crashing waves of a stormy sea. In the darkness, he felt as if he was falling from a magnificent height; his nervous sensations were active as a slight sense of euphoria overtook him completely. The fall seemed to continue for miles until at last his body was caught in a part of the darkness like an insect in a web. And out of the darkness came a blinding light, a light that was transformed into the image of a black horse with a man on its back as the glow receded to a cone of luminescence like a focused lamp; it was just enough light for Nazere to see what was going on. The rider on the horse was bone thin and dressed in rags, appearing like one the famishing, homeless vagrants on the inner-city streets. He carried a mid-sized, sedimentary rock in one hand and what appeared to be manna in the other. The rider looked at Nazere, and fell off of the horse to the ground beneath him as if he had fainted. Suddenly able to move, Nazere approached the man's location as his whole field of vision was abruptly illuminated. He nudged the man's body around and crouched down, desperately trying to bring the man to consciousness, but the man wouldn't move; he appeared to be without a pulse, dead on the ground. As Nazere continued in his efforts to revive the man, a black lightning bolt came from out of the heights of the white space that now surrounded Nazere in an aftermath of violent thunder. As he turned his head to the right, he could make out the figures of two horses rapidly approaching in the distance. Another bolt of black lightning came from the sky as the riders entered into plain sight, rearing their horses before the fallen rider. The first rider rode atop a horse that was so frail and thin that it looked like it was going to fall over and die any second, its eyes weak and its skin clinging to its bones like Saran Wrap. The second rider rode atop a red steed with smoke rising from its nostrils and orange eyes as radiant as those of pumpkin lanterns.

The first rider was completely clothed in black, wearing a black hood, black robes and a long, black cape. His face, however, was completely exposed as Nazere looked up at it. And as he studied the horrific face, he noted that it appeared to resemble the face of a human in its structure. But it had no nose, no lips, black pools for eyes, and high cheek bones. There was no hair on the first rider's face, and its skin was so morbidly pale that it was virtually transparent. The second rider followed behind him, and dare not move in front of the black rider. He was dressed in a scarlet red hood and robes, and his face was an eclipse; it could not be seen completely, but the eyes and the outline of the head were as bright and blinding as the face of a supergiant star. The rider with the pitch-black eyes looked on Nazere for a moment, examining his face thoroughly before he signaled for the scarlet-clothed rider to pass him by with his left hand. The two horses leaped over Nazere's crouched body and rode out of sight, leaving a trail of black lightning in their stead.

And then it came. The red dragon Nazere had seen so many times before flapped its enormous wings above him, snarling in rage, its teeth fully exposed. As the dragon landed five feet from Nazere's face, the ground everywhere around him quaked as if the white domain he was in was about to erupt. The great, red dragon positioned its wings behind its back and walked up to Nazere in a series of pounding steps, its crimson eyes glued to the ventari's. And at the very moment the dragon came within six inches of Nazere's head, two dark figures came from behind Nazere with swords in hand. Nazere didn't have enough time to get a good look at the two figures as he glanced back for but a second. With their swords lifted above their heads, about to strike him, Nazere awoke from his dream.

Falling out of his bed and onto the floor, Nazere instinctively shouted, “Come, Verus!“ Running to his side, Verus began to lick Nazere’s body on the hardwood floor. Moaning in shock and exhaustion, Nazere slowly climbed to his feet. The sun was high in the sky, the light from outside Nazere’s window pouring into his room like a pitcher full of lemonade into a shimmering glass. Looking to the corner of the room, Nazere noticed Keldrid was still standing in his normal, fixed position.

“What time is it?” Nazere asked as he looked at Keldrid.

“It is precisely noon, human,” Keldrid replied in his slow, deep voice. “Prepare yourself. A knock is coming to your door at any moment.” And in exactly three seconds, as Keldrid predicted, a single loud knock met the wooden frame of Nazere’s door.

“Come in,” Nazere said as he veered his eyes toward the door; surprises were becoming the norm.

Opening the door, Hayden entered into Nazere’s room with his black staff in hand and a smile upon his face.

“Good afternoon, my boy,” Hayden said, his voice refreshingly crisp. “I do hope your sleep was pleasant.” Nazere shook his head.

“My nightmares come and go,” Nazere said. Hayden nodded and his face became serious, his eyebrows down as he prepared to speak.

“I have come to you on official business,” Hayden began as he stood at the doorway. “High Prophet Baun awaits you in the Sanctuary of Revelations in the highest place of the bastion. We have much to accomplish today, so I would ask that you follow along with me as I lead you to his quarters. Today is the day for questions. Today, your eyes will be opened.” Nazere nodded.

“Lead the way, High Prophet Hayden,” he replied.

Walking in front of Nazere, the high prophet advanced out of the lower-left corridor and took a right hand turn at the corner of the railing. He then proceeded to walk up the northern corridor on the second floor of the meeting room, Nazere following closely behind. The two came to a door once they had reached the end of the corridor.

The door was made of glossy redwood, but had the silver insignia of the white rook on its surface. As Hayden opened with the push of his hand, a narrow, marble hall was presented to Nazere. On the right and left sides of the marble wall were the silver busts of human faces on granite, white walls. These busts were mounted on the walls about thirty feet up, and each face was unique and finely articulated. Under each bust was a silver plaque with the inscribed names of the men and women who were displayed on the wall. As Nazere continued to follow Hayden, his eyes moved from wall to wall and from plaque to plaque. One bust displayed the name "Jake." Others included the names "Joseph," "Amber," and "Olivia." But Nazere's eyes widened as his eyes met the face of a man with a shocking inscription under his bust. The inscription read, "Richard."

"High prophet," Nazere began as he walked down the hallway with Hayden. "What is the name of this hall?"

"This is the Hall of Saints," Hayden replied. "These are the men and women who stood for the Master."

A new door confronted Hayden at the end of the passageway. The door was made of marble, and had the golden inscription of a king with his mouth wide open; out of the crowned king's mouth came a long, sharpened sword. Nazere watched with curiosity as Hayden opened the door by pushing on it with his staff. The room beyond the door with the inscription of the king was completely carpeted, with the scent of frankinscence lightly sprinked throughout the area. The Wilton carpet was a regal, deep purple with a golden nail embroidered in its finely-tailored center. There were a total of seven doors in the narrow room; there were three on the left, three on the right, and one in the center. The doors on the left and right consisted of completely unmarked marble, but the one in the middle consisted of shining, solid gold. Embossed on its surface was the face of an unknown child, the mouth of the child widely smiling. Nazere followed Hayden down the center of the narrow room in the direction of the golden, child-faced door, glancing to his left and right in wonder as he walked.

Hayden lifted his staff in the direction of the central door, and it immediately came sliding to the right. When the door opened, Hayden and Nazere stepped into a small, square elevator. The elevator had marble walls and a solid gold floor with a digital panel on the right of the wall that displayed what floor they were on; it indicated that they were currently on the third floor. In a moment's time, seven green holographic panels appeared in the air. They were all rectangular, and they rotated in a circle around Hayden and Nazere- accelerating as they moved.

"There is only one way up," Hayden said in a stern voice. "Make the choice."

"What is the consequence of making the wrong one?" Nazere asked.

"Simply choose," Hayden replied. "That is all there is to it."

Nazere looked around him, attempting to solve the equation that surrounded his body. All of the panels appeared to be exactly the same, and they were moving faster and faster. He paused as the panels became a whirlwind, his right hand on his head, his mind incapable of discovering the truth that he believed only one panel held.

"Just choose," Hayden said.

Reaching out, Nazere closed his eyes and touched the first panel that twirled around him in a circle. Opening his eyes, Nazere noticed that all of the panels had stopped moving. The panel he had touched had turned blue, and it remained in place where the rest of the panels fell to the floor and quickly disappeared. Suddenly, the elevator began trembling, flying upward at a rapid speed. Hayden smiled as he glanced at Nazere. The digital panel on the wall of the elevator adjusted as the elevator ascended, and before Nazere knew it the elevator had reached the twelfth floor. At the elevator's entrance was the same gold door of a child's face that was on the bottom floor, this time the face of the child on the inside of the elevator. Again, Hayden lifted his staff to lead the way. But this time, the door came sliding to the left. Strange, Nazere thought to himself, a dumfounded expression on his face.

"After you, my boy," Hayden said cheerily as he motioned for Nazere to exit the elevator with his extended right arm.

As Nazere stepped out of the elevator, he immediately began to look around in all directions. The violet ceiling was coned, signifying that they had reached the pinnacle of the bastion, and the floors made of marble that was clean and polished. The room was brightly lit, the sun peeking in from two tall windows on the right side of the room and three tall windows on the left. There was a square, purple, Wilton carpet in the dead center of the floor with the symbol of a golden rook embroidered on it. As Nazere looked up, two solid gold statues in parallel caught his attention in the very back of the room; the statues he had inquired about seeing when he was in the Forge of Elders. One of the statues was that of a youthful boy in ancient clothing and bare feet reading from an opened scroll. The second of the statues was that of a teen-aged boy with sandals, a bow saw in his left hand and a small plank of wood in his right. There were four bronze chairs in the center of the elaborate carpet in the room. Two of them were empty. Sitting next to High Prophet Arthur, Baun leaned over and smiled hospitably with his eyes on Nazere.

"Welcome to the Sanctuary of Revelations," High Prophet Baun began, his voice echoing throughout the room. "Come and sit with me, friends." Walking up to the chairs, Hayden took a seat next to Arthur on the right, and Nazere took a seat next to Baun on the left. Remaining silent with serious expressions on their faces, Arthur and Hayden looked on as Baun addressed Nazere.

"I thank you for your welcome," Nazere said graciously after taking a seat, bowing his head in gratitude. "You must know that I have a few questions for you."

"Then we have an understanding," Baun began. "I have quite a few for you in return. But before we begin, allow me to lay down the ground rules of this hallowed sanctuary. All that is discussed here does not leave this place. Not a soul is to know what goes on within these confines. If you agree to adhere to these rules, we may proceed." Nazere looked Baun in the eyes and nodded in confirmation. "Proceed with your questions first, my child."

"Who are those statues of?" Nazere asked as he pointed behind him.

"Those are statues of the Master we serve," Baun said. "They are one and the same person. We will discuss more on that subject a bit later. Your next inquiry, please."

"The busts downstairs," Nazere began. "I read one of the plaques, and it read 'Richard' on its face. I couldn't help but wonder…"

"You are correct in your assumptions," Arthur interrupted. "That is the face of your father. We all served alongside him."

"He was a member of the Gathering of the White Rook at one point in time," High Prophet Baun said. "He died by the hand of the once High Lord Xar. Please allow me to elaborate on the condition of the scientist, and his blinded search for truth. Before Xar became high lord, he completed the book Spontaneous Organization Via Purely Random Conditions, a compilation of papers which soon led to the discovery of the mota. His papers demonstrated that everything including the universe itself was brought about by purely random probability. This proof was the basis for the Scientific Magisterium's proclamation that they had declared no existence of a God. This was determined to be the first step in society's movement toward Utopia. The Scientific Magesterium is the supreme society that is science; it encompasses a correspondence between political powers, large corporations and educated scholars who collectively guard their findings to the point that they will oust any intruders that serve to undermine their forward progression. Your father's work was that of an elite mathematician, and he responded with a book far superior to Xar's. But when Xar became high lord, he guarded his position with great fervor. When your father produced a book entitled The God Proof, he sent out legions of his minions to have the books burned and your father escorted to Rome to be executed. Your father produced two other items of great significance before he died, but now is not the time to discuss those things. So I should ask you, are your questions finished?"

"I suppose so," Nazere replied. He had many more questions, but his primary interest was in hearing what High Prophet Baun had to say first.

"Very well," High Prophet Baun began. "Then let my inquiry begin. Arthur has told me much, but I would like to hear the truth from your mouth. Tell me what brought you to this place." Nazere paused.

"The whole story?" Nazere asked.

"All of it," Baun replied. Nazere knelt his head down as if in shame.

"Of course, my story begins when I was a child. As you surely know, my mother Eliza was killed when I was young. I remember her face. I remember her reading to me late at night. I remember her coming home from work with a distraught look upon her face shortly before she was taken. After she died, I lost all of the guidance she shared with me. At fourteen, I began running the streets in my native city of Baltimore. Pennsylvania and North Avenue, walking down the road in an endless search for anything. I'll never forget it. I can't erase the murders, the pain and the relentless despair I saw in all directions. And how it was to be alone; how it was to be in the cold; how it was to wonder what I'm here for. It wasn't long before I became a part of the streets I walked, a notorious thief and a desperate dezium addict. I had no place to call home, so I never really felt I had anything to lose. When I was caught stealing at the age of twenty-four, I was sent to Ordren to be placed into stasis. I can't say I wasn't rightfully sent there. I've been far away in my mind. I've been lost in my heart. But out of nowhere, someone came and delivered me to safety. He carried me to Undrum, where I met the Gathering of the White Knight. Things have been changing for me ever since then. What a difference a day makes. I feel I have a family. I feel a sense of home. And I know I have people that truly care about me."

"As you do," High Prophet Baun said as he lifted Nazere's chin with his hand and leaned close to his face. "You are not alone in having faults. Every single one of us has faults. We were born into it. We do not choose the placement. We choose the destination. You are loved by many, and many more will come to love you. It is important to remember that you are never alone, although you may believe at times that you are."

"Do you know the significance of this day?" Hayden asked Nazere. Nazere veered his eyes toward Hayden.

"No," he began. "I don't know anything."

"Today," High Prophet Baun began slowly, Nazere immediately redirecting his attention back to High Prophet Baun. "I bestow to you a cherished gift. A gift that is one of a kind. My gift is given in love, to give you guidance for the journey that lies ahead of you. I forewarn you, your journey will be trying. You will face powerful adversaries not of this world, and you will suffer much pain. But it is guaranteed that in the end, you will overcome all things." Baun outstretched his hand. "I have waited all my life for this simple moment in time. But what is time but a mirrored moment? The name of the gift I give to you is the Divine Apocalypse. Use it well." High Prophet Baun paused as he looked upon Nazere's face. "Take my hand." And at that moment, Nazere outstretched his trusting hand and grasped High Prophet Baun's.

In a flash of light, Nazere and High Prophet were transported high atop a towering mountain. They were both standing next to one another, looking down at an astonishing view that presented itself before them. All of the ground was red like molten rock, and below the two of them was a the open valley of the mountain. The wind blew with mighty ferocity, and lightning bolted across the unseen sky. There was nothing but a void where the sky should be; there was no stars and no moon, and the earth quaked below in the valley. The valley was separated by two sides, a group of men on one side of the valley in ranks and a far larger group of infantry on the other. Amidst the larger group were millions of bloodguards and ventari, all arranged in perfect place. In their center, a machine that resembled the Colossus stood tall, with ten, sharp horns on its head and ten, glowing white eyes on its face. The dominant machine was perhaps fifty times the size of the Colossus, and had twenty cannons on each side of it. The sky was filled with vizedrones, phantoms, dreadnaughts and what appeared to be red, female ventari. Their very presence consumed the entire sky in blue, red, green and black. Nazere turned his face to High Prophet Baun's.

"Where are we?" Nazere asked, completely shocked at the sight before him.

"We are on a mountain in the place once known as Megiddo,"

High Prophet Baun replied, his hair blowing in all directions as the wind whisked through it. "Only one other man has ever seen this. Do you see what is before you clearly?"

"I do," Nazere replied. "What is the number of the small army there?" Nazere pointed to the soldiers standing before the bloodguards and ventari at the other side of the valley.

"They are two-hundred and two thousand in number," High Prophet Baun replied.

"And the other army?" Nazere asked. "How many in number are they?"

"Over two billion," High Prophet Baun replied. "with well-prepared reinforcements at the ready." Nazere looked on the Colossus-like creature with great curiosity.

"What is that machine?" he asked as he pointed.

"That, my friend, is the Phallion," High Prophet Baun began. "It is a destroyer vessel, capable of obliterating anything that comes anywhere near it. It is the primary ship of High Lord Alune. Vice Lord Xar commands his ground forces at its feet. And he who commands them both cannot be seen. He is known by many names. He is the mighty musician, the great deceiver, the eternal betrayer, and the defiance of the light."

"So there are three leaders in total?" Nazere asked.

"Amongst the kings of the world, yes," High Prophet Baun replied as the ground quaked underneath him. "The three are known to man as the unholy trinity. And their leader's name was once exalted amongst the angels. He is called Lucifer, and his demons are also in the valley."

"So what is the significance of this battle?" Nazere asked as the wind continued to blow.

"This battle is the last one mankind will ever fight," High Baun replied. "The valley below us is referred to as Armageddon, and it is there that the final stand of man will take place." High Prophet Baun turned to Nazere and pointed to the small army. "You are amongst the outnumbered. You are out there with them. You have been chosen before time began to fight this war. Outnumbered and out-powered, you will drive the forces of evil back into the pit. And at the end of all things, you will stand unscathed. Now is the time for faith, my son. You've been far away. But now, you have the ability to gain insight from what has not been seen. With this insight comes a tremendous burden, as you have been given the ability to see when others have not."

The earth began to crack and crumble under Nazere's feet, shifting plates sliding deep within the mountain. Grabbing his side, High Prophet Baun transported Nazere back to his seat in the Sanctuary of Revelations. Sitting precisely where he had before he had been carried off, Nazere looked into High Prophet Baun's eyes with his lips sealed.

"There is more to the gift of the Divine Apocalypse," High Prophet Baun began. "One aspect of it is the interpretation of dreams."

"The nightmares," Nazere began, dying to discuss his inner turmoil. "You know of them?"

"I do," High Prophet Baun replied. "But I want you to explain what you saw regardless."

"Well," Nazere began. "there have been repeated dreams, and they have all been of different things. In my dreams, I saw three dark figures. One of them rose up and took the form of a red dragon."

"Stop right there," High Prophet Baun interceded calmly. "These dreams are no ordinary sequences. The red dragon you have seen is one of the many forms the once glorious angel Lucifer takes. His objective is to meddle in the matters of humanity and to exploit their predispositions." Nazere looked up with a defeated look in his eyes.

"Will he ever stop haunting me?" Nazere asked.

"His intentions are unending," High Prophet Baun replied. "He will forever chase you. He thirsts for the failure of mankind, as it is the Master's design for all of us to be what we are in our susceptibility. Hope when hope fades. Believe when there is nothing to be seen. Defy what you are designed to be, and you defeat the dragon's underlying will. Nonetheless, he will chase after you. He rejoices in humanity's failures. He revels in the nature that the Master has given mankind. Faith is your foremost defense. The other two figures you have seen are the dragon's tokens. Throughout the course of time, they have become his cherished possessions. They are known as the beasts. But make no mistake, High Lord Alune has been allotted much power in his reigning position. He draws his power from Vice Lord Xar, who follows in the ways of Lucifer. But tell me, what else have you seen?"

"I saw a number of riders on horses," Nazere replied as he thought deeply. "One of them shot an arrow at the world. Another had a fiery horse and carried a large sword. The third was skinny and frail, and when I tried to assist him in my dream two more horsemen approached." Hayden and Arthur leaned in to listen closer to what was being said.

"These horsemen...," Arthur began, a trace of intrigue in his voice. "What did they look like?"

"One was dressed in black and had only eyes. The other had a black face with light in his eyes and around his head, and rode a red horse that breathed smoke from its nostrils."

"These horsemen," Baun began slowly. "are collectively the four horsemen of the seals of judgment. The Master's judgment will be cast out sevenfold upon the earth when all is said and done. These horses are the first four seals, and a sign of things to come in the very near future." Nazere's eyes were set in place like jewels set into a ring as he looked upon High Prophet Baun, listening intently. "The first horsemen is the initiation of the judgment. The second rider's name is War, and he represents the advancing presence of High Lord Alune on the earth. The third rider's name is Pestilence, and his presence indicates the forthcoming of famine, bloodshed and death. The fourth rider is Death, and with him rides the one called Hades." Hayden nodded.

"Was there anything else, Nazere?" Arthur asked. Nazere recalled the House of Arthur burning in his dreams. As he flashed back to its image, he thought of what might be- but he chose not to speak of it.

"No," Nazere replied. "There is nothing else."

"I know that an inquiry lies within you yet," High Prophet Baun said. "What do you wish to know?" Nazere squinted as the greatest question imaginable came to his mind.

"Tell me, high prophet. How did humankind begin?" High Prophet

Baun smiled.

"Your father and I have shared the revelation of mankind's origin. Allow me to elaborate. Before time began, there was the Master alone. His first manifestation was a perfect one, a being without flaws and built in spirit to reign forever at his side. This creation is better known to mankind as the angel, for they are our messengers. Outside of the physical universe in which we live is a completely separate realm. In the spiritual realm, the Master reigned above his subjects as King. When He built the angels, a perfect design and a set of immovable principles was set into place. The Master does not change what He is. Once His principles were set forth, all of the successive actions taken on His part were already in motion. History was perfectly written by a perfect Author. The Master is omnipotent and infinite, knowing no bounds or limitations; He does only as He wills. He knew what would come of His creation long before He put the process of building it into motion; He knew all things when He gave creation the ability to choose.

The angels served as reflections of the Master, serving his script perfectly on a plane apart from our physical reality. Time is based on the deterioration of energy, and in the spirit realm there is no time. There is only eternity. Every angel was given a gift by the King, and these gifts were each unique. The angel called Lucifer caught the eye of the Master Himself, an exalted creation that knew no limits. His gifts and talents were in the areas of creativity and music, and he excelled in those fields on a level mankind could never dream of. The angels and the Master were the perfectly-knit family, and their network was a representation of what the Master is. The King is called Love, and with all His heart, He demonstrated what he is to His creation. And Lucifer loved his Master, wanting to be as He is. Together, they would communicate endlessly, and Lucifer would produce melodies to serve his King. Every moment spent together was infinitely precious, and the two continued to draw closer to one another. Before the beings were ever given life, the Master designed a principle within the angels to aspire always to be as He is. But there can be only one Infinite. Lucifer's eyes beheld the full glory of the

Master, and He ardently strove to be what He was per his design, but Lucifer's eyes were opened more and more the closer he drew to His Master. They opened to the point that he realized He could never be what his greatest Love is. Not without a conflict.

And so it began. Lucifer walked into the Master's domain and pleaded to be given full power. The Master wept in sorrow at the sight of his greatest love, but He will never change His principles. He denied Lucifer the power that the angel knew full well he could not have, knowing what the outcome would be. In reply, Lucifer devised a plan in desperation and thirst for power; he knew he could not complete his plan alone. He walked out of his Creator's presence and chose to begin amassing forces to aid him in conflicting the King he had loved; the betrayer's power was so great that a third of the assembly in Heaven trusted the angel over their Master. Lucifer wanted what His Master had, and in his creative genius, Lucifer constructed the first weapon. Man would follow in his footsteps in the creation of the sword, using the same developmental techniques as the deciever in always seeking the fundamental truth he never found in nature; he still hasn't found it. In full knowledge of what must be done, the Master called to His faithful. Two-thirds of the assembly in Heaven immediately came to His side, the gifts He had given His angels now about to be brought out full-force. A certain angel by the name of Micheal offered his service in counter-craftsmanship. With the help of the Master, Micheal devised a blade to parry Lucifer's attack.

When the betrayer entered the throne room, the Master did not need to intervene. He gave Micheal the title of archangel, leader of the charge against Lucifer; Micheal's power in battle was insurmountable, his cunning abilities revered. War broke out in Heaven, and it would be the first of many wars to come for the angels and demons. By divine force, and by the sword, Micheal countered Lucifer with his blessed blade. And one by one, over a long and hard-fought battle, the angels who had misplaced their love in Lucifer were driven from Heaven. Floating in the anguish of the abyss, Lucifer's heart grew as black as night. But the Master is not without infinite mercy. He recalled Lucifer to His side, and the two of them spoke. The King was manifesting a new creation, and he was casting Lucifer into it.

It is written that in the beginning of time, God created the heavens and the earth. He breathed life into an entire universe with simple words. And with each seemingly simple creation he designed came a complex set of principles. He made everything else before he made man, creating the perfect environment for him before his coming. Man was finite, designed with far less power in mind than the angels, but he was made in the identical spirit of his Maker. Adam's origin was in the Garden of Eden, near the Tigris and Euphrates rivers. The location would forever be referred to as the Cradle of Life. Empathizing with the loneliness He had known, the Master created a companion for his new creation. She was called Eve. The Master loved His creations, but He knew what was coming. Because of the principles He set forth, He would not stop His element of time. Death had its place already. The stage was set.

The Master directly intervened, instructing the two to do whatever they wanted within the confines of their Utopia. Their bodies were flawless; their companionship with the animals knew no conflict, and they could speak to them. But there was one draw to the garden. The two were not to eat of a forbidden tree in Eden, as the fruit it produced brought forth the end; knowledge, mankind's greatest downfall, and the cycle of life and death. Suffice it to say, it was over before it ever began. But that was the design. Mankind had the choice to make, and Adam and Eve made it. When Lucifer took on the form of a snake to tempt the beings, they slipped so easily as the tempter brought to question what the King had ordered. From that point on, the Master knew he had to further define the Love that He is. Time passed, and wars were fought amongst men. He intervened for a time to give mankind a running start. When He disappeared, His handiwork could be seen everywhere. Look in the eyes of an animal, and you might wonder to yourself what they know that we don't. When the Master disappeared, everyone started lifting their heads to the clouds. They tried to figure out the truth; they tried to calculate an infinite equation while standing on a broken foundation.

'What a pathetic creature you have made,' Lucifer told his Master.

'They will never be worthy to stand in your presence. Their spirits are weak. Give me full control of their domain and I will prove my point to You.' The King nodded, allotting Lucifer free reign over mankind with his demons by his side. And they wasted not a second of the time given them. The Master watched as what was once His greatest love took hold of His new creation and drove it to the floor. Love is patient. It waited for the right moment. Love is kind. It knew what must be done. Love never fails. It followed through with what He promised. And Love sacrificed everything He had to save mankind. He was made into His own creation, destined to suffer unthinkable pain. Because He was Infinite, He took on all the perverse evils of mankind at once. And He was hated for it — truly alone. Walking in the shoes of His creation, He made every move as perfectly as He had from the throne. His sense of love continued, and He spread it to everyone around Him like wildfire. And He bled out in agony, His power sufficient to defeat death by passing through it. His message was a simple one: I am the Father of all things. Love is what I am. You are what I wish to keep close to me forever.

Rejoicing in His lessened state, Lucifer met with the Master in the desert and offered him food. He took Him up on a cliff, and offered Him His domain back if He would forfeit His power. Stricken with heartache, the Master declined again. He knew what He had to do, and he completed the task He set out to. Once He was killed by His own beloved creation, the King descended into Hades and set all of the imprisoned free. And in the process, he sealed Lucifer's fate. The betrayer is not without his power, however, and his work is far from complete. He seeks to exploit a flaw in the Master's perfect ending. As for mankind, we continue as we always have to misconstrue simple ideas and principles. There is no easy way out of what we've done. The earth has been completely marred, and is far beyond repair. All that remains is the love that we share and the faith that we choose to hold to."

"A trying time awaits us," Hayden began as he spoke to Nazere. "There is no doubt about that, no way to evade the trials rapidly approaching. There comes a time where you must rise and fight. The path of most resistance is all I foresee for you, Nazere. But in the face of trying adversity, there will be a select few who survive and remain close to you. In the face of pain and suffering, there is always hope."

"Remember always, Nazere," Arthur began. " that love is your greatest asset. As we all love you, extend the same love to others. Its power encompasses what our Master is, and it is a wide-spreading force that nothing can stop." High Prophet Baun looked to Nazere.

"There is one final element to the Divine Apocalypse," High Prophet Baun began. "Come close to me and I will enlighten you on what you must know."

Deep within Jerusalem, in the reconstructed temple of the once high king Solomon, a dark figure sat upon a solid-gold throne. The throne had the wings of angels extending from it and was adorned with the intricate carvings of ancient warriors. Veiled in a shroud, the face of this figure could not be seen in the darkness of the room he sat in. His body was completely covered in shadow except for his hands, dimly illuminated by thin light that barely leaked into the temple. His hands were clearly human, both tanned and both marked by the tattoo of a dragon breathing flame. The chambers of the temple were all solid gold, from ceiling to floor. Before his feet stood an enormous and articulate golden box; there were engravings that were scratched out on its surface. Broken in half, the veiled figure kicked the massive, gold box across the solid gold ground beneath him as if it were weightless.

"Damned altar!" the dark figure exclaimed in a hiss like a snake, his voice the very embodiment of viciousness, resounding throughout his golden throne-room in an evil echo.

A black carpet extended from the solid gold throne in the room to a gate at the end of his chambers. The gate was also gold, with two golden angels set into the many thin bars of the gate, their winged bodies extending from the top of the gate to the bottom. The angels had been scratched and defaced, their images mauled completely. All of a sudden, two dark figures approached and entered the barred gate. They pushed both sides of the creaky gate open, walking before the figure atop the throne side-by-side. One of the figures appeared to have two spines rising from his shoulders.

"Bow before your master!" the figure on the throne commanded in a slithering, sinister voice. The two figures immediately dropped to their knees and put their hands on the floor in submission. "How dare you enter the Inner Court of my temple?!" the figure on the throne yelled out, increasing the volume of his voice. "On your feet, my creations! What have you to say for yourselves?!"

"The plans have been established as you ordered, my lord," one of the figures said. "I have been afforded the power I require to see to the destruction of the ventari who has damaged your name."

"Commander Entril! On your feet!" the figure on the throne demanded. The commander slowly got up from his position kneeling before the throne, his form vaguely visible. The dark figure sparked a ball of fire in his hands with a flick of his fingers, and the area in front of the throne was completely illuminated. Before the throne, the outline of a black ventari with moving spines extending from his shoulders became visible.

"He has accomplished his task, High Lord Alune," the figure on the floor said in a deep voice equal to that of the high lord.

"Rise, Vice Lord Xar," High Lord Alune said, his tone still putrid, but altering in recognition of his only equivalent. "I did not know that it was you or I would not have been so rash in my demands. It is I who should be bowing before you, my infinitely wise teacher."

"On the contrary, High Lord Alune," Vice Lord Xar began slowly in a voice like doom, his shrouded head covering his face in darkness. "I foresee all things. We are the gods of this world; we are the lords of the Scientific Magisterium. We need not quarrel with one another."

"So the plans are set then?" High Lord Alune asked, still holding the flickering flame in his hand.

"All is prepared," Vice Lord Xar replied. "And I have made the final decision. I shall see to the conquest of the city. All of the pieces are in place. Commander Entril has bypassed the ventari processing sequence, so he will have his wits about him when he engages our enemy. Queen Airya — that witch of Babylon — has offered me a few of her most prized vessels; she speaks as though they are enchanted with her black magic. She has taken it upon herself in training the men and women of Babylon in the dark arts to seek out the refugees; she seems to have little recognition of the scientific principles that mandate all things, and she needs to remember her place in the new order."

"What of the Blade of the Unbroken?" High Lord Alune asked.

"Do not concern yourself with it," Vice Lord Xar replied, growing stern in his inflection. "I will personally see to its collection. Do not forget that I preceded you as the High Lord of Jerusalem. Our master has made perfect arrangements. As for the prophets, they will be attended to. Judah's tribal territory is within my very hand, and the expanse of the Kingdom of Babylon will only continue after Judah's fall."

"Excellent!" High Lord Alune exclaimed like a serpent as he laughed. "Go forth and take the city of Bethlehem; lay waste to those who oppose you. You have my utmost regards."

"I assure you," Vice Lord Xar began. "by week's end, I will drink of the blood of the prophets."

The morning sun came with a quickness, as did a beckoning knock at Nazere's wooden door.

"A sleep without nightmares," Nazere said as he leaned up from his warm blankets, awakened by the knock and glancing over at Keldrid.

"Good morning, human," Keldrid said. "I am glad that you did not have any 'nightmares,' as you call them."

"You don't have nightmares, Keldrid?" Nazere asked.

"No," Keldrid replied. "I do not dream."

The knock at the door persisted, and as it did, Verus climbed out from underneath the bed.

"Yea, yea," Nazere said in reply to the door. "I'm getting up. Just give me a second."

Nazere stood up and walked to the door in an exhausted stupor, opening it to find Ryan on the other side.

"A little tired, are we?" Ryan asked with a grin on his face.

"Just a bit," Nazere replied, his eyes still a bit heavy. "I had a long night of thinking about 'things' and I probably need to eat something.

But Elle and I had a nice little date yesterday at Zeke's Museum of Automotive Art, and we ran into James and Sara at Old Johnston's Orchard. So what's going on this morning?"

"I just wanted to take a walk with you in the city," Ryan replied in his normal, consistent voice. "The banquet in the Hall of Peace is tonight, and we need to get ourselves some suits. We can grab a bite in the city if you want to." Nazere nodded.

"Sounds like a plan," Nazere said, turning around for a moment. "Verus, you stay here boy. I'll be back in a little while." Ryan laughed.

"Growing a little attached to him, huh?" he asked.

"He's a good companion for me," Nazere replied, glancing back at Verus. "Shall we?"

"Let's roll," Ryan replied excitedly.

Together, the two men ventured out into the city surrounding the Bastion of Lights' End, the morning greeting the men as a sun-touched beauty without a single cloud in the sky. Leading Nazere past Parrion's Café, something across the cobblestone road caught Ryan's cagy attention.

"Look over there," Ryan whispered to Nazere as he pointed. As Nazere followed Ryan's signal, his eyes noticed Elle and Lily walking amongst a number of other women. They all carried large white bags and were laughing and chatting amongst themselves, broad smiles and jesting faces in a well-dressed bunch. "Watch this," Ryan whispered as he silently navigated around a few walking citizens in the direction of the women. Nazere followed close behind, keeping a straight face as he allowed his friend ample space to operate; a ventari in a crowd sticks out like a sore thumb. Ryan walked right up to Lily, the clever ninja, completely undetected by the commotion in the crowd of ladies. "Hey there!" Ryan exclaimed, taking hold of the bag at Lily's side. "What have we here?" Lily laughed and snagged the bag back.

"That's none of your concern, sir," Lily replied. "Don't you boys have some business to attend to?"

"We'll get to it," Ryan replied. "I was just wondering what such a beautiful woman like you was doing out in the city so early in the morning."

"Attending to her daily routine," Lily replied, jutting her face out in Ryan's. Ryan nodded, protruding his lower lip.

"I'm sure there's breakfast in those bags," Ryan smirked. "I'm so sorry to bother you ladies as I'm sure your schedule is booked. Enjoy the rest of your 'daily routine'!" Elle looked over at Nazere, smiling and waving from a distance as she continued to walk along with the rest of her gabbing group.

"So where is this suit store?" Nazere asked.

"Just keep following me, my friend," Ryan said. "I'll show you the way."

The two continued to walk about five houses down, where they came to a stop in front of a little white house with a sign hanging above that read, "Fit For Heaven." Walking inside, Ryan and Nazere were met by a pale, little, old bald man in a black and white striped dress shirt and black dress pants and shoes. The interior of the house was rather ordinary, with two stages next to one another and two, ten foot mirrors in front of them. Otherwise, the room was plain, with a pale oak floor and an antiqued, wooden counter with an old-fashioned register on top of it. Behind the counter was a door leading to a back room, and in the left corner of the room there was a rack filled with neckties of all assorted colors leaning against the wall.

"Well if it isn't Ryan Galeheart!" the old man exclaimed in a kindly voice, walking over to Ryan and shaking his hand as he smiled. "I haven't seen you in quite some time, my boy. The word is you've been over to the Crowned Princess' jeweler. Making a few plans, are we?"

"On the down low, Paul," Ryan began. "I have been making my preparations for tonight."

"And that translates to what?" Nazere asked as he raised an eyebrow.

"He's proposing to Lily, of course!" Paul exclaimed joyously. Ryan nodded, straight-faced.

"I've got to get just the right suit for the occasion," Ryan said to Paul. "And my friend here needs a suit as well. Can you help us out, Paul?"

"It would be my greatest pleasure!" Paul exclaimed, clapping his hands. "Let me go find something appropriate for the both of you. Then we'll have you fitted."

"Thanks, Paul," Ryan said, smiling cordially.

"The ties are on the wall over in the corner," Paul said as he walked into the back room. "Go ahead and take your pick."

Ryan and Nazere walked over to the tie rack, eying the variety of ties there were to choose from. Reaching out his hand, Nazere picked up a glimmering, striped blue tie.

"This one will do for me," Nazere said, well-educated on good taste in style despite his humble background.

"I'm still picking," Ryan said, leaning over intently with his head close to the tie rack. After about five minutes of intense consideration, Ryan finally picked the one he wanted.

"Silver," Ryan began. "I think that will do with my suit."

"What color do you want your vests to be?!" Paul called out from the back room, overhearing Ryan's voice. "I just can't decide!"

"A blue vest with a black jacket for me!" Nazere yelled out.

"And you, Ryan?!" the old man exclaimed.

"Give me a silver vest with a black jacket!" Ryan yelled back.

Moments later, Paul emerged from his back room. He walked over to Nazere and looked up at his face.

"Get up on the right stage," Paul said, a round tape measure in his hands. "I'm going to measure you." Paul then turned to Ryan. "And you, Ryan, hop up on the left stage."

"Gotcha, Paul," Ryan replied as he took one long stride onto the stage; he was as giddy as a school boy. "I need to look snazzy for my lady tonight!"

With Ryan and Nazere aligned parallel to one another, Paul stepped in front of the right stage and tightened his eyelids in focus.

"Alright, sir," Paul began, extending the tape measure in his hands in front of Nazere. "I need you to straighten your arms out on both sides." Nazere obliged him, and Paul quickly took measurements of Nazere's arms, legs and chest. He then had Ryan do the same, operating with a slick swiftness in ascertaining his size. "Alright,"

Paul said. "You're both all set. I have a tailitrest in the back room, so your finished suits will be out in a jiffy. I have some black dress shoes for the both of you as well. They have a nice, high-gloss finish to them. They should serve you quite well." Paul then darted into his back room, excited to go to work.

"Thanks a lot, Paul!" Ryan yelled as he stepped off the stage. Ryan then turned to Nazere. "The blue suits you well, my friend. I like it. You'll be looking good for Elle tonight."

"Thanks, Ryan," Nazere said. "Blue just happens to be my favorite color. The whole body thing will set the blue ensemble off, I'm sure."

Within a minute or two, Paul emerged from his room in the back with two bags in his hands. Printed on the face of the bags were the words "Fit For Heaven" in fancy black lettering. Taking the bags, Nazere and Ryan exchanged smiles with the elderly man, nodded simultaneously, and made their exit from the small house. Back on the busy cobblestone street, Ryan glanced at Nazere.

"Let's get back to our rooms," Ryan said. "I need some rest before tonight to calm my nerves."

"What about food?" Nazere asked, laughing.

"Do you want to stop by Parrion's?" Ryan asked.

"That's where Elle and I frequent," Nazere replied. "It has turned into my favorite restaurant in the city. Let's do it."

Together, Ryan and Nazere made their way to Parrion's legendary restaurant, talking about all things women as they walked. After a good meal and a nice, continued chat, the two returned to their rooms in the bastion. Opening his door, Nazere dropped his bag and sprawled himself out on his bed. He leaned the sheath containing the Blade of the Unbroken up against the redwood dresser to the right of his bed.

"An eventful evening ahead of you, I suppose?" Keldrid asked.

"Yea," Nazere said, laying easy on top of his comforter. "I've got a hot date. Ryan is proposing to Lily tonight. He says he's nervous, but I bet I'm even more nervous."

"Why is that?" Keldrid asked. "You are a mighty warrior. Certainly a woman wouldn't bring you to your knees?" Nazere sighed.

"She does, Keldrid," Nazere said. "I think about her almost all of the time. She's grown very precious to me."

"Well, if its any condolence to you," Keldrid began. "I become fearful at times just as you do. Simply look beyond the fear, and all will be well."

"You're right," Nazere replied. "But I think I'm going to take a nap. I need some rest before tonight. Maybe that will calm my nerves a bit."

"Rest peacefully then, human," Keldrid said. "I'm by your side, as I will always be."

Turning in his bed, Nazere quickly drifted off to sleep. He was awakened by a nudge at his side.

"Nazere? Nazere?! Awaken!" Keldrid yelled.

"What is it?!" Nazere exclaimed as he jumped to his feet from his bed. "What's wrong?!"

"I think these will serve quite favorable to your evening," Keldrid said as he reached inside of his shroud. As Nazere watched, Keldrid withdrew two dozen pink roses with a pink bow tie around their center, pink baby's breath accenting the arrangement. Keldrid extended the flowers in Nazere's direction. "She should like these." Nazere smiled.

"Thanks, Keldrid," Nazere said as he took the flowers and set them on his bed.

"Now prepare yourself. A knock is coming to your door in a moment or two."

And just as Keldrid projected, a knock came two seconds after Nazere took the flowers.

"Man, you're good at that," Nazere said as he glared at Keldrid. "Come in!" Nazere yelled toward the door. Ryan stepped into the room, completely dressed in his suit with his hair spiked up. His silver tie accented his silver vest, black jacket and pants with a shocking flair.

"You aren't dressed yet?" Ryan asked, a hint of nervousness seeping through the incited expression on his face. "You better hurry up! The gentlemen enter the Hall of Peace first. It's an old tradition within the bastion."

Nazere hastened to get dressed, throwing his black pants, dress socks and dress shoes on in a motivated hustle. He threw his white dress shirt around him, and hurried to button it up. Ryan assisted him in putting his glimmering blue vest on, throwing the jacket around the back of it while Nazere secured the shimmering vest. Throwing his hand into the bag from the store, Nazere tossed his tie around his popped collar.

"Looking good, brother," Ryan said as Nazere tightened the tie up to his neck. Nazere reached down and picked up the pink flowers from off of his bed, imagining Elle's lovely face as his fingers rounded the beautiful bouquet. "I like the flowers. I'm sure your darling will savor just the thought."

"Thanks," Nazere said with a smile. "I got them from a good friend of mine."

"Are you ready?" Ryan asked as he looked Nazere in the eyes.

"Are you?" Nazere asked back.

"I am," Ryan said as he exhaled. "Let's get going. Keep up with me."

Together, Ryan and Nazere walked out of the room and down the bottom left corridor. They then took a left and hung a right, finally taking another left on the second floor of the meeting room. Standing side by side, the two of them walked down the upper right corridor, a series of doors that were a mirror reflection of Nazere's hallway. At the end of the corridor was a brilliant, sparkling, black granite door with a heart shaped silver emblem on its face. Opening the door, Ryan leaned down before Nazere and shifted his left palm face-up under his diaphram.

"After you, Nazere," Ryan said in the voice of a gentleman, appearing as calm as he possibly could be. "Welcome to the Hall of Peace."

The Hall of Peace was enormous, gleaming, and consisted of two floors. The bottom floor was made of marble, and two wide staircases led to the upper floor. The staircases were made of marble, and the banisters that accompanied them were of a high-gloss, redwood finish. The ceiling was an octogon of shining, elevated glass, thin, solid-gold frames separating the panes from each other; the view of the celestial bodies of the stars and the moon above widened Nazere's eyes as he glanced upward, taking his breath away. A piano sat in the left corner of the room, an elderly gentleman sitting in front of it dressed in a black suit and tie and wearing a thin frame of glasses. In the right corner of the room, his ready fingers on the holes of it, Adrax held a polished saxophone in his hands. He was dressed in a white dress shirt, a lustrous red vest with black pants and dress shoes. David stood next to him, dressed in a black and white suit and a sheeny, golden tie. He was holding an acoustic guitar with the emblem of a lion engraved into its soundbox. Redwood tables with redwood chairs were arranged toward the back of the room, leaving space for people to move about beneath the staircases. Plates, glasses and naperies were in front of every chair to be seen, all immaculately spaced and placed on a velvet tablecloths. A sparkling white chandelier hung from the center of the golden frame of the ceiling, glistening like a million perfect diamonds.

Sitting at the tables at the rear of the room were all of the gentlemen from the local gatherings. The gentlemen sat at the backside of the table, facing the balcony as was the tradition, each of them still and silent in anticipation; the quiet didn't make Ryan or Nazere any easier. All of the men sitting at the tables were dressed in suits and ties, mainly black coats and pants with an underlying color in a vest and tie, looking up at the staircase in front of them. Arthur, Hayden and Baun all sat next to one another, dressed in identical white robes with gold on the end of their sleeves and around their neck.

"Let's get closer to the banisters," Ryan said to Nazere. "They should be down any second."

Walking to the banister to the right, standing within an arm's length of the stairs, Nazere tapped his foot on the ground and gently shook as he eagerly awaited her appearance.

"Patience," Ryan said standing at the left banister, looking over at Nazere and noticing his nervous tick. "We're going to have fun tonight. It will be something you'll never forget." In the back of the room, Hayden, Arthur and Baun smiled as they overheard Ryan.

Nazere looked at the ground, holding his flowers hidden behind his back and still tapping his feet and shaking nervously. A minute or two passed. I can't believe I'm this nervous, Nazere thought to himself. If I can kiss the woman, I can certainly serve as a suitable date for a banquet. As Nazere continued to think, his racing thoughts revolved around Elle. The next two minutes seemed like an eternity to him, his heart and his mind looping around deep within him like a wheel rolling downhill. He stopped tapping his foot, bringing himself to a state of homeostasis and confidence as he tried to reassure himself; he tightened up, taking hold of his quaking bones, just thinking of Elle. She was the one thing that could keep him from shaking, her gentle everything his treasured escape, her closeness the one thing that made him feel real — alive.

And finally, out of the corner of his eye, a beautiful sight caught his attention. Looking up, Nazere's eyes widened in awe as Elle made her anticipated appearance. Adorned in a lavish, lustrous pink dress, a pink corsage and a platinum bracelet, Elle smiled down at Nazere in comforting rays of loveliness. And on the opposite side of the staircase, Lily looked down at Ryan in the same intimate fashion. She was in a sheen, green dress with a white and green corsage. As Elle began walking toward Nazere, he could feel the very ethalon core within him begin to flare wildly. Hello again, nervousness, he thought. Following behind Elle and Lily were a number of other ladies dressed in an array of vibrant colors accompanied by corsages and shoes of all shapes and styles. Elle's dress seemed to light up the entire room, standing out boldly as she neared Nazere. Reaching out his right hand, still holding his flowers behind his back, Nazere bowed courteously before his elegant date.

"You look so very beautiful, Elle," Nazere said calmly as he slowly handed Elle her flowers. Elle's eyes lit up as she beheld the bouquet, surprised at the unexpected gesture.

"They're perfect," Elle said softly, her pink lipstick and extra-long eyelashes catching Nazere's attention. "So you thought of me today?"

"I did," Nazere replied. "I missed you, Elle." Elle's cheeks took on a glow as they often did at Nazere's responses.

"Let me set these flowers somewhere," Elle said, quickly walking to the tables in the back of the room and setting them beside a plate near the place she wanted to sit with Nazere. She then pranced back to Nazere as he held his hand out, patiently awaiting her return as he maintained a strong, upright posture. Taking his hand, the couple made their way out onto the floor. They were soon joined by the rest of the entire gathering.

"Hit it, maestros!" Drake exclaimed. And suddenly, the piano began to play. And directly thereafter, the saxaphone and the guitar creating a spectacular rhythm, Adrax and David began playing their instruments. The soft, smooth melody created the perfect atmosphere for what was to come next.

"May I have this dance, my angel?" Nazere asked as he looked Elle in the eyes with confidence and care.

"I would be honored, my sweetheart," Elle replied in her snuggly-smooth voice with a smile.

Soon, the entire room was slowly dancing to the smooth melody that reverberated throughout the hall in adagio tempo. Holding closely to Elle, Nazere leaned his head into her ear.

"I just want to let you know," he whispered. "I can't really dance."

"Just follow me," Elle whispered back. "I'll show you."

Trying to get his footing just right, Nazere shifted his feet around.

"Move with me," Elle whispered. "I'll carry you." After a few moments of trial and error, he finally moved in sync and harmony with Elle; it was a wonderful feeling for the both of them once they were moving as one.

"There you go," Elle whispered as she laughed. "You've got it now."

"I've been nervous about this all day," Nazere admitted in whisper. "But now that you're here, everything's just right. You make it all right. I just missed the simple comfort you give me, because I've never had that before. I treasure you, Elle." Elle leaned her head against Nazere's shoulder.

"I missed you, too," she whispered, her perfume enticing Nazere's senses as she leaned against him.

"Your scent is euphoric," Nazere whispered. "It fits you perfectly."

"Thank you, sweetheart," Elle whispered. "I like your scent, too. It's heavenly."

Dancing with Elle, every step seemed so perfect. Of all the things that made Nazere happy, he couldn't think of thing that surpassed the joy he felt in Elle's soft embrace. She was the source of his smile in a world of confusion. He couldn't think of anywhere he'd rather be than right where he was, moving steadily with his heart. He thought of every moment in his life, and how her presence seemed to eclipse every second of it. He wanted to cherish every moment he had to dance with Elle; he looked forward to a future with her by his side, as she did with him. Her heart was the most magnificent thing he had ever come across, and he was grateful for every second and every step they took together. Each step taken with Elle was a sweet and precious gift to Nazere. Nothing could replace it. As the music played, Elle slowly lifted her head and looked deeply into Nazere's eyes.

"What did you miss about me?" she asked in a whisper.

"I missed your adorable smile," Nazere began slowly. "I missed your mesmerizing eyes. I missed your unparalleledly beautiful face. I missed the soft touch of your perfectly graceful hands." He then leaned closer to Elle, drawing out his words. "I missed every little thing about you. We belong here together."

Elle then leaned her head back on Nazere's shoulder, the music slowly playing like a lullaby in the background.

"I miss you all the time," Elle whispered as she lay her head on Nazere's shoulder. She lifted her head again, her eyes clearly engaged in sentiments. "There's something I've been afraid to tell you. I thought that maybe it was too soon. So many times I've considered it. But, I want to take the opportunity to say it now."

"There's something I've been wanting to say, too," Nazere whispered. Their heads drew close to one another's. And as Nazere was about to lean in, the words seemed to flow in perfect harmony.

"I love you," they whispered at the same time, touching their pursed lips together as Elle tilted her head. Nazere held Elle tightly, holding on to the kiss as if it were the most valuable thing in the world; the closest to heaven he'd ever been.

And in the middle of the room, people were gathered in a wide circle as the music stopped for a moment. On the center of the dance floor, Ryan had dropped to a knee in front of Lily. He reached into his pocket as was always his struggle, trying to find the item he was looking for. But finally, after a few anticipated seconds, he pulled it out. In his hands, he held a small black box. The attention of the entire room was on him as he opened the box to reveal a large, princess cut diamond set into a platinum band.

"To my confidant, my best friend, and my love," Ryan began as he began to form the words. "I present you with this humble gift as a symbol of what we have grown to become together. For all the times we've spent together; for the nights spent dreaming of a life growing old together; for all the long walks, talking endlessly of anything and everything, just you and I; for all the memories I'll always hold locked away in my heart. Lily Anderson, will you marry me?" A tear welled up in Lily's eye as she looked down at Ryan, a surprised smile rounding her enraptured face.

"Forever isn't long enough," Lily replied. "I will." Ryan slowly put the ring on Lily's finger; he climbed to his feet and formed a tight circle around Lily with his arms, kissing her lips gently.

The room was filled with great applause and cheers for the proud couple to be. Hayden, Arthur and Baun took a stand and raised their hands in respect for the pair's union, one long forgotten in the fleeting period of man's existence. Taking a stand, Hayden raised his staff into the air.

"May this be the beginning of a long and fruitful marriage,“ Hayden spoke loudly for all to hear as he looked upon Ryan and Lily with a father's loving smile. "I congratulate you both on your decision. I'm proud of you, Ryan, and how far you have come. And now, let us continue to celebrate!“

"I love you both with all my heart! Congratulations on the beginning of a great thing!“ James yelled in a cheering voice as he raised his fist in the air, standing next to Sara Maple on the dance floor.

"You are my brother, Ryan!“ Adrax yelled with saxophone in hand. "I wish you and Lily the very best in living a long, happy life together!“ Drake and David whistled and laughed as they clapped for the happy couple. The whole room around Ryan and Lily continued to congratulate them for several minutes, merry voices rising from every direction floating over to the engaged pair. As the applause came to a halt, the music resumed and the couples in the room reunited and started dancing again. Holding close to one another, Sara and James looked each other in the eyes. Sara wore a shocking red dress with a black corsage and high heels. James wore an all white dress suit and dress shoes.

“You look gorgeous tonight, Sara,” James said as he danced with her.

“You look pretty handsome yourself, James,” Sara replied. “I’ll admit, I didn’t expect you to ask me.”

“Why is that?” James asked as he looked into Sara’s eyes.

“I don’t know,” Sara began. “I just thought you were into other types of girls, I guess.”

“On the contrary,” James began, his often commanding voice becoming soft. “there is no one else on the face of the earth that I would rather be here with than you.” Sara smiled, continuing to dance close to James as her heart spread its wings in her chest.

Elle held close to Nazere, kissing his neck softly as she lifted her head. “This has been such a wonderful evening; I’ve never felt this way. I wish I could express in words how perfect I feel right now.“

“Time with you never seems to be enough,“ Nazere whispered. “I haven’t danced like this before. I think we will always remember this dance. This moment is something special to me, Elle.“ Elle gleamed, reflecting the love she had for Nazere clearly.

“I‘ll always remember,“ Elle whispered. “And you were right when you said there’s not much left in the world that is special anymore. You and I are one of a kind. But listen, do you want to take a little break to go and get a bite to eat?”

“By your side,” Nazere replied with a smile. Leading the way, hand-in-hand, Elle guided Nazere to the back tables. Nazere pulled out Elle’s chair in a loving gesture, ready to share dinner together as had become their routine. And just as she was about to take a seat, a man came darting into the Hall of Peace. The man was covered in sweat, leaning over and panting heavily as if he had sprinted all the way into the bastion. And suddenly, the music stopped. There was absolute silence in the hall as this man began to speak.

"High prophets!" the man called out. The room remained as quiet and still as a boarded-up house as High Prophet Hayden looked on the man in confusion.

"What troubles you?" Hayden asked, his alertness peaked.

"A message from the citadel!" the man exclaimed, still trying to catch his breath. "The sign of the fall has finally come! We must move now! We cannot stand against him alone!" Nazere turned his head to Elle, and then back to the man at the door. Commotion suddenly erupted throughout the hall.

"Everyone to your ships!" Hayden yelled as he held his staff in the air. "At long last, the beast is preparing his attack. Make haste, for we have little time to make preparations!"

"We fly tonight!" High Prophet Baun shouted. "Set your coordinates for Sade's Citadel! The war has begun!"

CHAPTER SEVEN

Sade's Orders

Confusion and activity were scattered throughout the Bastion of Lights' End as soldiers made their final preparations to depart. Running to his room down the lower left corridor, Nazere hastened to retrieve the Blade of the Unbroken from where he had left it leaning up against the dresser in his room. He tossed his black jacket, vest, dress shirt and dress pants on the bed in a frenzy. Kicking off his glossy dress shoes, he picked up the solid gold hilt leaning against his dresser. He then threw the strap of the hilt around his shoulder, tightening it in place with his hands. Standing at his side, Verus panted as he looked up at Nazere. Looking back at Verus, Nazere opened his door and clapped his hands for the German shepherd to follow him. Stepping out of the room, Verus followed his master's every footstep. As Nazere reached the end of his corridor, he could see that the wall-bridge to the field outside was down. Men and women had already dressed down into their plain citizen's attire, and were making their way onto the bridge with great speed. In their hands, the soldiers that had fought alongside Nazere in the Battle of Ordren carried tightly-packed duffel bags as if they were departing on a long journey.

Looking down, his core fluctuating in his own disarray, Nazere scanned the meeting room desperately for Elle. He stood in place near the corner stairs of the meeting room, waiting for any familiar face to appear, but there appeared to be no one that he recognized in sight. Walking down the steps in front of him, Nazere grabbed the arm of a man passing him by.

"Have you seen any of the gatherings' members?" Nazere asked anxiously.

"Which gathering to you speak of?" the man asked as he turned around. "The Gathering of the White Knight?"

"Any of them," Nazere replied, a serious tone to his voice as he still held firmly to the man's arm.

"They could be outside already," the man replied, his face explaining that he was quite busy. "I'm sorry that I couldn't help you." Nazere released the man's arm, staring into space for a moment, the man immediately beginning to walk toward the bridge.

What could possibly be going on now? What war did High Prophet Baun speak of? Nazere wondered, an infinite number of possibilities haunting him like an army of ghastly ghouls. His questions taunted him, but he was most concerned for where Elle might be. "One more question," Nazere directed at the man before he was out of range. "Where is it that we are going, exactly?" The man turned around as Nazere's voice touched down on his eardrums, turning around but walking backward as he replied.

"Before the Council of the White Queen, of course." The man then turned again and continued to stride toward the bridge, disappearing amidst a crowd of soldiers walking in the same direction. To Nazere's alarm, a hand from behind him grabbed his shoulder.

"Hey, old buddy," Ryan said as he walked in front of Nazere and faced him.

"My friend!" Nazere exclaimed with startled face as Ryan fake-punched his stomach with a grin on his face. "It is good to see you! I've been looking for someone... anyone."

"It's good to see you, too," Ryan replied nonchalantly. "Are you ready to get moving?"

"What exactly is going on?" Nazere asked with a combined look of seriousness and confusion on his face. He hated being in the dark on any subject, but especially this one; he wanted answers, and he wanted them now. Ryan nodded and glanced into his eyes.

"We will know when we get where we're going," Ryan replied, unfazed by the enigmatic circumstances that presented themselves as he maintained a constant smile on his face. "Patience, my friend. Patience." Standing in place with a continued look of shock on his face, Nazere watched as Ryan turned and started moving toward the bridge.

"Come, Verus," Nazere said, beginning his walk toward the bridge several yards behind Ryan. Once on the bridge, Nazere turned his head from side to side. He noticed that the bridge was lit by purple flames on the left and the right. Strange, Nazere thought to himself. Why would the colors of the torches change? At the end of the bridge, the entire flight was in their readied positions. It was dark outside as night had fallen, and the air was bitter cold. The circular landing pad was glinting orange, and the clearing outside of the bastion was illuminated solely by the lights of the gatherings' ships. The leviathans were in their proper ranks, and the Deliverer's lift was down. The Colossus had its chest shell opened with its staircase extended, and the Redeemer had its wings in the upright position with its door pushed back and opened to the right. Assisting Sara Maple up on the Deliverer's lift, Adrax smiled over at Nazere.

"Nice of you to join us, brother!" Adrax yelled as Sara Maple took a stand next to him aboard the hovering circle. "I'll see you when we get to the citadel!" Before Nazere could respond, the lift ascended into the stomach of the Deliverer. Moving its amber eyes down at Nazere, the Colossus waved and smiled in its cordial fashion. After waving back at the gunmetal man, Nazere began moving toward the Redeemer with Verus at his ankles. Both Nazere and Verus hopped into the Redeemer at the same time, walking up the three stairs toward the seats. David was already strapped in at his usual spot in the captain's chair, employing his hands in working the primary control panel to the ship. He was completely focused on getting the controls set for flight, his eyebrows down and his eager eyes deeply involved with his intricate operations. Ryan was sitting in his usual seat, sight straight forward, his earpiece audible to Nazere as it was at a high volume. Hayden was also on board, strapped in beside Nazere's chair. His face was also forward, his hand on his bearded chin as if in deep thought. His eyes seemed to be out in the middle of space somewhere, just wandering around. Elle was no where to be seen.

"Come on in," David said, still facing the holographic control scheme in front of him and pressing buttons on it with both hands. "We're almost ready to take flight, Nazere. My beauty is all set up to take to the skies."

Walking to his chair, his mind as distant as Hayden's appeared to be, Nazere slowly took a seat. Responsively, the ribbon straps behind the seat came flying out and secured him tightly. As Nazere turned his head to the right, Ryan glanced over and nodded his head at him. Hayden's eyes remained firmly in place, unmoved by anything around him. His hand remained at his chin, his body as motionless as a stone statue. Wondering where Elle was, Nazere looked to Hayden to inquire as to her location.

"Hayden?" Nazere asked. Hayden made no response, remaining in-situ following Nazere's clearly spoken words. "Hayden?" Snapping out of his daydream, Hayden turned his face toward Nazere's.

"I apologize my boy," Hayden said calmly. "I have a few things on my mind right now." Nazere looked at Hayden with questions still swirling throughout his volatile mind.

"Where is Elle?" Nazere asked. Ryan pulled the earpiece out of his right ear.

"You have a lot to learn about women, lover-boy," Ryan began. "They're always the last to get ready." Ryan winked at Nazere. "Don't worry, buddy. She'll be out." Nazere redirected his attention span to Hayden, who had returned to staring into the distance.

"What is this all about?" Nazere asked him. "Why the rush to move from the bastion? And what is all this about a war?"

"It is not for you and I to discuss, my boy," Hayden replied, his eyes widened and still set into place. "Even I do not know the full extent of what we are about to get ourselves into."

"Get ourselves into?" Nazere asked, leaning over as his very core began to shake with endless curiosity. "Don't you think I should know?"

"Even I do not know!" Hayden shouted as he turned to Nazere, his expression like a fine twig that had just snapped. His eyes became calm only a moment later. "I apologize, my child," he said as he took Nazere's right hand from his lap and held to it. "I wish I knew everything. But I am human just like you, and I cannot foresee what comes next. The Master has given me a limited ability to do that. It is tearing me apart inside." Hayden then returned to his gaze into the distance, his hand returning to his chin. Turning his head straight forward, Nazere curved his eyes over at the left holographic display of the Redeemer. The display showed the leviathans lifting their final attendants onboard. "To see beyond the dark," Hayden began slowly. "I must keep my own wits about me. Pray for me." Hayden then turned his eyes to Ryan. Knowing what Hayden would say next, Ryan took the earpiece out his left ear. "Do you have it in your possession, Ryan?" Hayden asked. Also veering his eyes to Ryan, Nazere wondered what Hayden might be talking about.

"I have it," Ryan replied, smiling and putting his earpiece back in place. "We're all set." Hayden nodded at Ryan. He then returned to his fixed and thoughtful pose. Looking down at the display, Nazere smiled as Lily and Elle came into plain view on the screen. His non-existent heart jumped exuberantly at the very sight of his love. He lightly tapped his fingers on the arm rest next to him in anticipation of her arrival. They were both dressed down in sweaters and jeans, but both still had their makeup on. Climbing all the way up the steel stairs of the Colossus, Lily was quickly drawn out of sight. Turning behind him, Nazere watched as Elle climbed aboard the Redeemer.

"Hey sweetheart," Elle said as she reached Nazere, leaned down and kissed his lips.

"Oh! Hey sweetheart!" David mocked, his hands and eyes still on the controls.

"Silence is golden," Elle said to David as she moved to her seat.

"Good to see you, honey," Nazere said, looking at Elle as she sat down beside him. "I looked all around for you inside the meeting room. I couldn't find you anywhere."

"Girls take a little longer to get ready, my dear," Elle said, looking back at him with a smile on her face. Her red straps came flying out from behind her and fastened her securely in place. "That's just the way it is."

"I told you!" Ryan exclaimed at Nazere, staring at the display and listening to the music that played on his earpiece.

"Hi, honey!" Lily called into the intercom of the Colossus, pushing her way in front of the captain's camera.

"Hey baby!" Ryan hollered back. "I'll see you as soon as we get there. Tell the Colossus to drive safetly!" Nazere could overhear a scrabble as James forced his way to the pilot's seat of the Deliverer.

"I may not be a pilot, but I still get the captain's seat, Lily!" James exclaimed over the intercom. A second fight could be heard from the Deliverer as Sara tried to make her way in front of its camera, Drake holding his position firmly.

"Come on, Sara," Drake snickered. "James is not going anywhere! And I place great emphasis on James, who we all know you're head over heels for. You two can talk when we get there. Sheesh."

"We didn't even get to finish our kiss, Drake!" Sara pouted at the Deliverer's captain, her outburst clearly audible over the intercom.

"When we get there, sweetie," James said, winking into the camera. Sara maneuvered her face into the Deliverer's camera and winked back, making mean eyes at Drake as she backed away.

"Alright, folks," David began. "This is your captain speaking. Let's take it up. Confirming communications with all networked vessels."

"You know I'm with you," Drake began. "And I'm going to beat you there again, too."

"This is the Colossus. I hear you loud and clear, leader. On your word, we move."

"All leviathans online and ready to take flight," the captain of the eighth leviathan said. "Just say the word, flight leader." David smiled.

"Redeemer, raise your ion shield," David began. "To all linked vessels: I'm taking her all the way up. Set your coordinates to my checkpoint."

"Ion shields engaged, captain," the Redeemer said. "Where shall we be traveling to today, David?"

"Set your mark to the Citadel of the Northern Lights, Alaska," David said. He raised his voice as he began the countdown. "Lifting off in three...," The Redeemer began to move its talons in the dimly lit clearing. The Colossus' ion shield flickered as it began to hover above the ground; it then threw its arms out parallel to its shoulders like it was simulating an airplane. The leviathans all began to move forward slowly, inching their claws across the grass. The Deliverer lowered its body in the pounce position, purring as it prepared to catapult into the sky.

"Two...," David continued. The Redeemer started running, as did the leviathans.

"One! To the sky!" David yelled. The Redeemer pointed its beak toward the clouds, advancing through the troposphere, throwing its wings into the air and screeching as it took flight. The Colossus began to pick up speed behind it like an over-sized missile being rocketed into the ozone. And one by one, the leviathans flew behind the Colossus in one, long, linear formation of spined, green wings. As Nazere looked at the display, he saw the curled-up orb that was the Deliverer storm into the exosphere of the earth in flames. All of the flight except for the Deliverer caught up to one another above the clouds, their ion shields becoming a brilliant yellow as they burned through the thermosphere.

Reaching space, the Deliverer growled as the Redeemer began to spread its wings and fly in a wide circle around it. The leviathans followed directly behind the Redeemer, flapping their wings as they encircled the Deliverer, mirroring the same flight pattern as the eagle. Stopping in place fifty yards from the Deliverer, the Colossus turned its eyes purple for a moment as it looked into the face of the odd, floating lion; the Deliverer growled and turned its eyes amber in response. The Colossus laughed, the noise booming throughout space, both stationary vessels recalling their original eye colors as the Redeemer and the leviathans continued their flight pattern around them at an astonishing speed. Attuned to a perfectly-spaced formation, the winged ships accelerated to over a thousand miles-per-hour as they awaited David's call to reenter Earth's atmosphere.

"Alright, my people," David began. "Get ready for the plunge!"

"I'm ready to plunge," the Colossus replied. David laughed to himself at the Colossus' unexpected remark.

"Send us down!" Drake exclaimed.

"Alright, Redeemer," David began. "Begin your descent at full speed. I want to beat the Deliverer down."

"That isn't likely," Drake replied, overhearing David's commands over the intercom.

"Engage your secondary storm-booster engines, my love," David said, smiling to himself. "And three...," The Colossus pointed his head at the earth with his arms still fully extended at his side. The Deliverer curled itself up in a ball, beginning to spin like a furious racing tire with no traction. The leviathans floated in a line behind the Redeemer, their wings angled forward at their sides. "One! Go!"

The Deliverer began dropping at an outrageous speed, visibly hitting the thermosphere in a little over a second. As it flew out of sight, four total, small propulsion engines popped out from underneath the Redeemer's wings; during his stay at the bastion, David had secretly upgraded the storm-boosters to twice their normal power. In two seconds, the propulsion engines began to hurl green cones of flame from within; and as soon as they did, the full-fledged drop began. The Redeemer kept its wings at its side as it darted like a bolt of lightning from the blackness of space into the clouds. The Colossus dove head first downward, and the flight of leviathans followed behind it. Nazere could feel the entire body of the Redeemer tremor heavily as it blasted through the skies; the deck felt like it was going to collapse. He then looked at the display, a surprised look on his face. The Deliverer was at the side of the eagle, twirling in a ball.

"Bye now!" David snickered as he flew past the Deliverer.

"Yea, yea," Drake said over the intercom in a disappointed tone. "You never said two."

The Redeemer came to a stop high atop a landscape filled with snow piled mountains, sending out an electrifying, green shockwave as its secondary propulsion engines disengaged. Peering down at the display, Nazere evaluated all of the scenery below him. The skeletons of trees covered in snow heavily populated the frost-ridden mountain tops and terrain below. There was light precipitation falling from a partly-cloudy sky, a few small snow flakes dropping to the ground slowly like a bunch of tiny, white feathers. And in the distance, three thin, cloud-reaching white spires could be seen extending from a massive circular structure.

The middle spire stood higher than the others, and had an apex shaped like the top of a queen's chess piece. The top appeared to be made of quartz as it gleamed like a gemstone in the light of the Alaskan sun, untouched by snow or frost. The apexes of all three spires had glass midsections, the whole circumference of them consisting of long glass windows separated by extremely-thin pearl panes. Each of the two spires that extended from the circular building on the left and right of the queen-shaped spire were pointed like the head of a bishop's chess piece. The circular building below them was white like the spires above them, and was a quarter mile tall in and of itself. It also had two smaller square buildings extending out of its sides; the smaller square buildings both had an arched roof that connected to the tip of the central structure. The circular building had an enormous, opened drawbridge that was built to establish a pathway between two steep cliffs; it appeared to be made of blackwood. A frozen river reflected light from the sun underneath the snow-covered drawbridge, and the bridge itself was connected to the main building by two frost-covered steel chains. The area in front of the drawbridge provided a substantial clearing, and had long served as a landing spot for aircraft of all shapes and sizes.

"Now maintaining a reduced speed for the initiation of the landing sequence," the Redeemer reported, gently gliding freely towards the clearing.

"Thank you, babe," David replied. "You flew much better than the Deliverer. I always knew you were the superior ship." The Redeemer flapped its wings in moving closer to the white buildings as the rest of the flight began to approach from the clouds above.

"The Deliverer's not even mean to fly," Drake smirked as the

Deliverer rolled past the Redeemer in the direction of the clearing in front of the drawbridge. Looking at the display in interest, Nazere watched the Deliverer land for the first time. Snow rocketed upward as the Deliverer's paws all met the powdery flakes at once.

"Now initiating landing sequence," the Redeemer announced as its dangling talons scantily ran through the snow near the drawbridge.

"Come on, boy!" Nazere commanded as he held out Verus' cube. Verus then returned to his digital confines in a ball of smoke. "I can't have you frightening anyone in here." I suppose they'll be frightened enough at the sight of me, Nazere thought.

With the Redeemer leading the way, the collective flight grounded themselves next to the Deliverer. The Colossus stomped its large feet down in the heavy snow next to the leviathans, deactivating its ion shield once it had landed. The leviathans gathered together and formed up in their typical two ranks, following the Colossus in deactivating their ion shields. Turning its head, the Deliverer veered its angry eyes at the Redeemer — perched behind it.

"Deactivate the ion shield, my beauty," David commanded, punching a bunch of buttons on the holographic panel in front of him.

"Now deactivating the ion shield," the Redeemer replied.

The Deliverer turned its head forward again as its own ion shield came down in a series of glinting flickers. The lift from its belly then descended, carrying Sara, Adrax, Endarius, Drake, Owen and Arthur on its circular surface. The lift hovered over the snow, and Adrax hopped off first, offering his assistance in aiding the others in finding their way to the frost-chilled ground. In the mean time, the Colossus extended its staircase into the snow. Felix and Lily were the first to be seen carefully descending the steel stairs, the staircase lacking a railing for support. They were soon followed by Aaron, James and High Prophet Baun, who cautiously took each step down the flight and onto the chilled ground. Each leviathan lowered its lift up and down, transporting its many occupants into the ice-cold outdoors in batches. To the left of the Deliverer, everyone in the clearing began grouping together in one large circle.

"Wings up, sweetie!" David yelled.

"Affirmative," the Redeemer replied. And as the Redeemer let out an ear-piercing call, its wings flung upward to their elevated position.

"Open the doors!" David commanded next.

The door to the Redeemer popped back and rolled open as the ribbons to each seat within the bird came undone. Getting up from his seat, Nazere glanced at Elle; her eager eyes were already set on him.

"Hand!" she exclaimed as she held arm out. Smiling, Nazere took Elle's hand and assisted her in climbing out of the Redeemer. Standing up, Hayden and Ryan followed directly behind them in exiting the eagle and making their way into the frigid climate.

"What is next on the agenda, captain?" the Redeemer asked.

"I don't have take to chat now, my angel," David replied. "You can keep your ion shield down out here. You're safe here."

"Initiating energy conservation mode," the Redeemer reported. "Have a great day, captain."

"You too, girly," he replied. The ribbon straps animatedly flew behind David's chair into their proper slots. David then pressed a few buttons on the holographic panels in front of him, causing them to disappear. Standing up, he quickly made his way out of his ship. Once outside, he walked toward the others who had huddled together in the light blanket of snow that laid about three inches deep at their feet. Each individual had their arms crossed, shivering in the below-freezing climate. Nazere was unfazed, his artolium body adapting to the chill by increasing his core temperature. He had his arms wrapped around Elle, his metallic surface a warm blanket for her cold body.

"Nice of you to join us, David!" Drake yelled, his teeth chattering and his arms crossed as David approached the gatherings. Embracing Drake with a hug as he joined the group, David curved his eyes toward Hayden.

"So when is he coming?" David asked, visually exhaling into the frosted air as he spoke.

"He should be out any moment now," Hayden replied. Holding Elle's hand, Nazere set his eyes on David; his face was an expression of muddy thought.

"Who are you talking about David?" Nazere asked. And just as the words came from his mouth, the crystal-clear voice of a man came from the direction of the drawbridge.

"Welcome, brothers and sisters!" the man exclaimed, a slight southern drawl to his voice. "I'll be out to y'all in a second!" Looking up at the drawbridge, Nazere noticed a bald black gentleman advancing across the bridge toward the group with his hands in his pockets and his eyes focused ahead of him. He was wearing a thick, white vest with a white, turtleneck sweater underneath, along with heavy, white pants and white snow boots. As he came within close proximity of the circle, Nazere could make out his facial features distinctively. This man wore a thick frame of black glasses that amplified the size of his eyes quite considerably, and when he opened his mouth a few golden teeth were exposed.

"What's goin' on, High Prophet Baun?" the man asked as he shook Baun's hand. The man then looked directly at Nazere, a surprised expression enveloping his face; his eyebrows raised as high as they could, his upper forehead wrinkling as he stared. "Who's the new guy? I know the queen said nare a thing about no ventari!"

"His name is Nazere," Hayden replied. "He is the one whose coming was foretold."

"I knew that," the man replied succinctly. "So y'all's Operation Maelstrom or whatever was a success I gather." The man put his hands at his hips, his tongue in his cheek as he looked Nazere up and down. "That's good, man. That's real good. This your man, Elle?"

"He's all mine," she said, smiling and looking up at Nazere as she held tightly to his artolium hand. Nazere turned to Elle and leaned his lips close to her ear.

"Who is this guy?" Nazere whispered.

"My name's Ray Thompson," the man replied. Nazere's eyes widened as he realized that the man could hear what he was saying, remaining still while veering his eyes over in the man's general direction. "But you can call me Rock. I'm the chief battle prophet of the Gathering of the White Dove."

"The white dove?" Nazere asked as he leaned up to his original position and looked on Rock with confusion and a touch of amusement;

he almost laughed at the idea of a gathering dedicated to a dove.

"Let me tell you something," Rock said as he walked up to within an inch of Nazere and stared him straight in the face. "We may be symbolized by a dove, but we make one mean dove when it comes down to it."

"He's right," David added. "His soldiers are the best out there. They're only second to the Gathering of the White Lamb; and that's because they practice day in and day out." Rock turned his head to David, his mouth gaping open in shock.

"Sade chooses the men for that gathering, my brother," Rock said to David with his eyebrows down. "That's why they be the best. If I could choose my men, well shoot. There would be nare an army that could stop us." Noticing his presence in the crowd, Rock — his bald head glistening just like the crystalized snow under the particularly bright Alaskan sun — turned his face to Adrax and smiled. "Sup, Adrax? Long-time, no-see, my brother." Adrax walked up to Rock and shook his hand gracefully, grinning.

"It's great to see your face again, Rock," Adrax replied, his tone a weightless ball of cotton fibers. "We've been doing what we do best; what we've been given the gifts to do.."

"Yea, you keep doin' that," Rock snickered, laughing to himself. "I know you do it well, but maybe one day" — Adrax shook his head and looked at the floor — "you'll have all of your men trained like mine are. Keep your practice up, my brother, and maybe I'll give you the opportunity for a hand-to-hand duel again; you came real close last time. Everything you need to practice up on — spirit strength, control, endurance, timing — was all within your reach the last time I saw you. Good to see you." Rock then turned his head to Ryan, his already-magnified eyes expanding.

"Sup, Ryan? You do that thing yet?" Rock winked at Ryan.

"Yes," Ryan replied, holding Lily's hand. Lily lifted her hand to show Rock her sparkling diamond ring. "We're officially engaged."

"That's good. That's real good. Congratulations to you both — especially you, Ryan — on getting the marriage thing finally moving." Rock's eyes scanned the group thoroughly, rising up on his tip-toes to improve his view angle. "Where my boy James be at?"

"Over here," James said from within the circle as he stood huddled in the snow next to Sara Maple — his body facing her's — to Rock's far right. They had their arms around each other, cowering to remain warm.

"I just wanted to say 'hey', my brother," Rock began. "I've missed seein' your face around here; can't forget all the old times in training together under High Prophet Linxera before he passed. You lookin' good, man — you too, Miss Sara Maple." Sara held tightly to James' heated body, facing away from Rock as she pressed her face into his defined pectorals.

"Thanks," James replied with a friendly grin, recalling all of his younger teaching in memory. "I've been training heavily alongside Adrax."

"Well, you know we don't have no time for trainin' now," Rock began, shaking his head. "We got some serious stuff to talk about. The queen is waitin' inside, so let's get in there and not leave her waiting. Y'all just follow behind me." Rock popped his vest with his fingers before the group, his eyes widened as he looked at Nazere. "I'm y'all's guide today."

As Rock completed a one-eighty and began walking toward the drawbridge, all those behind him immediately began to follow. Reaching the middle of the drawbridge, Rock turned around his head to the side to address the group while he walked.

"Since we got a new man in the house," Rock began. "I'ma be an outright tour guide so he gets his proper introduction to the fort. Welcome, one and all, to the Citadel of Northern Lights."

"So this queen...," Nazere began in a whisper as he leaned down to Elle's ear. "What distinguishes her as such?"

"Her gifts, sweetheart," Elle replied softly, the breeze of Nazere's voice over her ear giving her a rushing chill. "She is the best pilot and spiritual combatant amongst all of the high prophets. The Master has given her the greatest ability to foresee events amongst the prophets in the Western States. She was also the only human to outrun a ventari on the ground, calling forth a curse that presented itself in the form of a large number of bears — much like the prophet Elisha — to fend off the machine." Elle glanced up at Nazere, looking at him as she walked with an innocent sense of pride. "I love you," she whispered sweetly.

"I love you too, Elle," Nazere whispered back, his voice a masculine, mirror image of Elle's. "You're my heart."

Walking into the citadel alongside Elle and the rest of his comrades, Nazere glanced around at his new, mesmerizing surroundings; he expected no less, anticipating the grandiose qualities of the citadel before ever stepping foot into its confines. Inside of the drawbridge was an enormous hall, far wider and taller than any hall he had been in during his stay at the Bastion of Lights' End; the scents of spearmint, honey and lavender drifted throughout the air, creating an affect of aromatherapy. Above the group, about two hundred feet up, were hundreds of hovering crystals in various shapes and precise cuts; above them was a flat, silver roof that appeared to be polished and well-maintained despite the fact that it was so very high above the floor. These crystals that hung in the air like ornaments produced intensely-white luminescence and were suspended to the very end of the walkway. They ended above a curved door in the distance which consisted of a silver body with the glowing, crystal emblem of a queen's chess piece in its center. The whole of the door had a six-inch outline that consisted of twenty-four karat gold, the outline accented with a single diamond at the top of its arch; the diamond was small, unique, and cut into the shape of a ewe. Below the group was a white marble floor with two shimmering-gold lines on the far right and left sides of it. In the center of the hall, the two gold lines connected to form the insignia of the full body of a dove perched on a barren olive branch; the dove had its head pointed upwards, as if looking to the sky. At the end of the golden illustration of the dove, the lines then led back to their original paths at the far left and right sides of the room and ended before the door at the end of the hall.

The walls were made of opaque crystal, and glistened like intensely-glossy pearls from the glow of the crystals hovering overhead. There were a total of seven, rectangular gaps in the wall on the right and seven gaps on the left; they were all tall in height and narrow in width. Every single gap started with a marble staircase that led straight up to an unknown location, the bottom few stairs visible from the hall. In total, the walkway was about two-hundred and fifty yards in length — quite a distance.

"Alright y'all," Rock began, leading the rest of the group by a space of twenty feet. "This is the Pathway of Sanctity. It's over a hundred years old, and has been the main operation hall for the Council of the White Queen since it was built. Real nice, isn't it?" Rock laughed to himself.

"It is as magnificent as always, Rock," Elle began in a cheery tone. "I've always loved the Pathway of Sanctity. It is eloquent, yet simple. The design is divine."

"Quite the walk to the end of the hall, though," Sara interjected, holding James' hand as she walked down the pathway.

"Especially with high heels, I'd imagine," Drake japed.

"If only you knew, Drake," Sara replied sharply. "If only you knew."

As the group came within twenty yards of the door, two wide, rectangular portions of the wall slid to the side; they were hidden compartments that served to store some of the citadel's mysteries, with one section on the left side of the hall and the other on the right. Two machines shaped like enormous ladybugs came crawling out of the newly-revealed gaps in both sides of the wall, moving quickly into the open. These machines were gunmetal gray, and had silver and gold spots on their wings; they had many small eyes, and each of them had a big mouth. As they stopped at the left and right sides of the group respectively, their eyes scanned the entire group with a purple laser in a rapid motion that lasted only a second or two.

"All clear, Red," the left one said in a light, hasty voice as if it were excited. "I like the blue one."

"Yes, Blue," the right one replied, its voice a bit slower. "It corresponds with your name. That is why you like it. The ventari registered just fine. Initializing the secondary sequence." Blue nodded.

Suddenly, the ladybugs opened their mouths; from them came a massive mist that covered the entire group. Nazere reached down and sniffed his wrist as a plethora of fragrances wandered about the assembly's position.

"Romant's," Nazere commented to Elle as he recognized the scent. "That's my favorite cologne." Elle reached down and opened her nostrils over his wrist, inhaling the adequately measured mixture of essential oils and water.

"Mmm. I love that scent, Nazere!" Elle exclaimed. "I wear Chateren's."

"You smell just as heavenly as you did when we danced," Nazere commented as he turned to Elle and smiled. "So these oversized bugs search and spray, huh?"

"That's it precisely," Elle replied. "They make sure everyone here is a member or ally of the Council of the White Queen. If you aren't a member, they tend to get quite nasty with you. If you are, you simply pass right by them. Then they spray everyone checked with their most desirable perfumes — or colognes in your case. Those who don't typically wear anything simply get a 'clean linen' scent." Nazere laughed at the idea.

"You smell wonderful, sugar," Ryan complimented Lily.

"I like the scent of your body," Lily slowly whispered in reply as she smiled, drew her body close to Ryan's and softly kissed him on the cheek.

"Take a whiff," David said bluntly to Drake as he stood beside him. Drake reached his neck down and breathed in the scent.

"Not bad," Drake said, nodding his head. "It's Gullidan's isn't it?" David laughed.

"You aren't so inept, after all," he snickered. Drake shook his head.

"What is that you're wearing Sara?" James asked, still walking next to her.

"My little secret," she replied. "Do you like it?"

"It's sweet," he replied. "A very sophisticated scent for an unbelievably sophisticated lady." Sara smiled, her cheeks beginning to flush red — which was unusual for her.

"What is that awful smell, bro?" Aaron asked as he looked at

Endarius.

"It's Blackfadis's," Endarius replied. "A very dark scent, indeed — fadeleaf, tobacco, coffee and musk. I'm sorry that it offends you so."

"No sweat, bro," Aaron replied. "Everyone has their own taste. I can respect that."

"Here we are now," Rock began as he approached the large, queen marked door and turned to face the group. "Now, for y'all who don't know, beyond this door is the Keep of Serenity." Rock looked at Nazere with his big eyes. "And by y'all, you know I'm talkin' to you, Nazere. Be on your best behavior in here, as it is considered hallowed territory." Rock smiled, exposing a few gold teeth within his mouth. "Silence in the keep." Rock turned around in the direction of the door. "Password: Olive Branch."

With the receipt of Rock's words, the door opened into the room beyond it. Rock stepped a few feet in and smiled as the assembly began to enter in a cluster. He stood in place like an usher, waiting for the group to pass him by before entering himself.

As soon as Nazere entered the room, his eyes were shocked by the images that snatched his attention. Looking to his left and right, Nazere's eyes were taken aback by ten sets of ten-tiered steps; each tier was rounded and connected in a row. The ten-tiered steps circled the whole of the gigantic room, meeting at a platform one-hundred yards from Nazere that was raised up above the rounded flight of steps; the immense room looked like three-quarters of a stadium. There was a wide, circular opening in the center of the room between the platform and the entrance to the keep. Each flight of steps had cushioned, white chairs with the mark of a golden queen's chess piece on their back; they all hovered, still and stable in their places. There were ten total aisles leading up to the plush seats; five on the left half of the room and five on the right. These aisles were lined with a rolled-out golden carpet, and each carpet was rolled all the way out to the platform across from the entrance. Thousands of people were already sitting in their seats, watching still and silently as the group following Rock entered the room.

The central platform was made up of two tables that connected to a podium in the center. Together, the tables and the central podium stood at least thirty feet off the floor and were purely-opaque crystal. The right table had three occupied crystal chairs, the backs of the chairs spiking up like two shining spades. At the right table, in the right-most chair, was an elderly black man with a medium build, a gray beard, and gray frayed hair; the man wore a white dress suit with a gray tie. Sitting next to him was a well-fit man with a bald head sporting an all black dress suit; this man had brown eyebrows and wore a orange tie that stood out against the backdrop of black garments he was wearing. Next to him was a man who wore purely clean, white robes; he was thin, bearing the characteristics of a long gray beard and a balding head with just a bit of gray hair on it.

The left table had three empty chairs sitting before it. The backs of these chairs were also spiked up, but had the appearance of sharpened halberds rather than spades. The podium that the two tables connected to closely resembled a pulpit. Triangular at the top, the podium in the center of the room stood well above the tables to its right and left. It was engraved in gold in its center, with the marking of a queen and king side by side. Surrounding the engraving on the right of the king and queen were the silver markings of an eagle, a rook, and a horse; on the left were the bronze engravings of a bishop, a dove, and a lamb. Above the images of the king and queen was the engraved, golden emblem of a queen's chess piece encased in the outline of a golden diamond. Behind this central platform, an ebony woman wearing a thin frame of silver glasses and white robes looked around the room. She had gray dreadlocks, a sparkling crystal necklace around her neck, and she was completely silent as she stood. Below the tables and the central podium was a flight of twelve, tall marble stairs.

Behind the platform and connecting tables, a Tiffany glass pane which bore the illustration of the upper half of a crowned king with a sword in his hands encompassed the entire wall. Above the seats and the podium were a multitude of shining crystals that illuminated the room. One enormous crystal — easily the size of a glacier — was suspended in the very center of the room, catching Nazere's watchful eye as he gazed upon it. And in the space between the stands and the central podium, a raiditor hovered to the right of a huge, onyx projector. Its massive lens was clearly visible to all those who looked upon it from above, the projector facing upward. The onyx projector reflected light from the crystals above, and was fashioned in the shape of a square.

"This way, honey," Elle whispered to Nazere, pulling his hand to follow along with her to the right. Hayden, Arthur and Baun walked toward the twelve stairs below the table to the right of the raised platform. Baun assisted Hayden up the tall flight first, as Hayden required the use of his staff to advance up the stairs and was the oldest of the three high prophets. As soon as Hayden was seated closest to the pulpit-like platform, Baun aided Arthur in using his cane to reach the top of the large stairs. Nazere followed along with Elle and the rest of the group to the right of the entrance, where many had already walked up the first aisle and taken seats. Elle took a seat next to Ryan, who had chosen to sit next to his fiance, Lily. Nazere took his seat at the end of a fully occupied row by the side of Elle, folding his arms in front of him on his lap. "Hand," Elle whispered under her breath. Nazere cracked half-a-grin and moved his hand over to Elle's lap when no one seemed to be paying attention; she gently began rubbing his hand as she always did. As soon as Nazere took his seat, Rock walked to an empty seat on the end of a row located three tiers up on the left. And as soon as Rock took a seat, the woman behind the podium looked to the seated gatherings on the right and began to speak.

"Welcome, one and all," the woman began slowly, her voice as bold as espresso, yet as calming as distilled ylang-ylang oil. "brothers and sisters alike." The woman set her eyes on Nazere as she continued to speak. "I see we have a new brother in our midst. And as is the tradition, I extend a warm welcome to him in prayer that he will remain at our side for some time. You are safe here from the outside world, an initiate of rank in the Keep of Serenity with my personal regards. As your time passes, young brother, my hope is that you reach the highest ranks of honor within the keep. I shall begin our meeting with the introduction of my fellow high prophets. I am High

Prophetess Sade Hopebreather of the Gathering of the White Queen. Sitting to the far right of myself is High Prophet Bruce Olrays of the Gathering of the White Bishop." Bruce took a stand, his expression unchanged. "To his left is High Prophet Joseph Domiano of the Gathering of the White Lamb." Joseph nodded, the room remaining silent as he took a stand next to Bruce. "And next to him is High Prophet Benjamin Johnston of the Gathering of the White Dove." Smiling cordially, Benjamin took a stand next to Joseph. "To my far left is High Prophet Baun Lightseeker of the Gathering of the White Rook." High Prophet Baun grinned as he took to his feet slowly. "To his right is High Prophet Arthur of the Gathering of the White Lion." Standing with the assistance of his cane and setting his pipe on the table before him, Arthur nodded at the attentive audience. "Finally, to my left is High Prophet Hayden, keeper of the Gathering of the White Knight." Smiling, Hayden grabbed his staff and rose to his feet. "Together, we make up the Council of the White Queen; we are the select ambassadors of the Master to a blinded world with little time and little opportunity remaining. In going forth in all that we do, let us never forget where we came from. As I always do, I will recite the Serenity Prayer before we commence with our business." Everyone bowed their heads and closed their eyes as Sade spoke. "God," she began slowly to a firm rhythm. "Grant me the serenity to accept the things I cannot change, the courage to change the things that I can, and the wisdom to know the difference."

As every eye opened, Sade clapped her hands together. "Now," she began, her voice returning to its robust but peaceful state. "Now begins the beginning of the end. For him who has ears to listen, let him hear. A vision has come to me in the night, and a dark vision it was. High Lord Alune has issued his orders to begin the descent from Jerusalem into Bethlehem, initiating the collection of the territory of the ancient Tribe of Judah in order to desecrate it in blood. Operation Fall has commenced, and a day from now, the city of Bethlehem will be under siege by the dark forces that be. There is no time for waiting; now is the time to act. This is a declaration of war. In so much as we are together in this place, we are united now as one army. The Prophecy of the Torn has long foreshadowed this event, and it has been seen that the city will be secured in the end. However, this calls for much wisdom. In order for the city to be secured, actions must be taken on the behalf of each prophet. These actions call for the endurance of those who follow in the footsteps of the Master. The events that will transpire in Bethlehem are unknown to any prophet, but we will be up against those who have been given great power over the earth. We will be outnumbered. We will be unbelievably outmatched. And we will be stricken."

Clapping her hands, Sade prompted an image of the city of Bethlehem to be displayed before the room. Towering structures and machines moving throughout the city could be seen on the projector in the middle of the room. "The city of Bethlehem has been alerted, and have prepared their defenses accordingly. There are less than one-hundred thousand troops within the city. An unforeseeable number of men and an unknown number of vessels come to claim it. As one united brotherhood, we will go forth from this place and defend the city of Bethlehem alongside its citizens. This is my order to you: hold tight to your faith as the war begins." Sade looked to Nazere, picking up the pace of her words. "And never lose sight of hope. Opened eyes see reality, and this is our reality. This is no game, no simulation, and every choice made is essential to the outcome; every single one matters. Play your pieces wisely."

Sade paused for a moment as she looked upon the projected image of Bethlehem on the floor below her. Nazere's eyes focused in on Hayden as he began to speak. "The beast will lead his forces," Hayden began. "That much is known. And he will destroy everything he has the power to, killing as many as he can in the time given him. Fortunately, the Blade of the Unbroken has been forged; the carrier of the blade is he who wears the armor of the enemy." The entire crowd looked upon Nazere, his hilt protruding from the golden sheath around his back. Hayden reached his arm out in the direction of Nazere. "Take a stand, my boy, and show them."

Rising from his seat, Nazere put his right arm behind him and gripped the hilt to the Blade of the Unbroken. Withdrawing it from its sheath, Nazere's body instantly took on a luminescent golden glow; the room became as radiant as gold itself in the presence of the weapon. Gasps and whispers were heard spreading throughout the Keep of Serenity, all eyes fixated on Nazere's brilliant body.

"It is just as I imagined it," High Prophet Joseph commented, his voice as captivated as his eyes. "The undefeated covenant blade of the Master." Sade clapped her hands, redirecting the attention of the room to her. Nazere promptly sheathed his sword and took a seat.

"Rock Thompson. Jadus Rathe. Isaac Schwartz. Do you have your forces prepared?" A man with short, gel-spiked, red hair and a clean shaven face rose from the crowd. He was wearing black pants, a gray long sleeve t-shirt, and a black vest over top.

"We are prepared, High Prophetess Sade," he said. "The Gathering of the White Lamb stands ready."

"Very well, Isaac," Sade replied. "As for you, Jadus?" Another man then took a stand. This man was very tall, with a thick, muscular build and broad shoulders that seemed to rise out of his garments. He wore black goggles with green rings around them, sandblasted jeans, and a black aviator jacket with a white t-shirt underneath.

"The Gathering of the White Bishop awaits your command, high prophetess," Jadus replied in a deep, booming voice, his chiseled jaws locking after his words. Rock then stood up.

"You know we ready, High Prophetess Sade," Rock said as he smiled, a strong sense of courage in his tone. A few cheers and laughs came from the crowd around Rock, his troops demonstrating their strong support for his renowned leadership skills.

"Then the orders have been established, and we are prepared," Sade began. "Rock, I will task you with seeing to it that our newest brother is seen to his quarters. Feel free to show him your armaments if you wish, but keep in mind that the men and women from the far gatherings need rest. They have had quite the long day and night."

"That will be no problem, high prophetess," Rock replied.

"Then with that, I adjourn this meeting," Sade said with a smile. "We high prophets will remain in the keep to further discuss our plans for battle."

As soon as High Prophetess Sade stopped talking, everyone erupted into motion like the revolution of a motor. Swiftly walking down the aisles in rows, the audience moved out of the entrance to the Keep of Serenity in a congested bunch. Nazere remained by Elle's side, taking her hand and lifting it to his face — kissing it in a soft peck. In the midst of the crowd, Rock navigated his way through the congestion in the direction of Nazere. As he approached Nazere, he looked him up and down with his hands on his hips as if it was the first time he had ever seen him.

"So you got the Blade of the Unbroken, huh?" Rock asked with a smile on his face. "Let me take you away from your woman for a moment." Elle lifted herself up on her toes and kissed Nazere lightly on the cheek.

"I'll see you soon," Elle said. "Go take a look around. And have sweet dreams, okay?" Nazere leaned down, put his hands on Elle's temples and kissed her forehead gently.

"I'll see you in the morning, sweetheart," Nazere said as he looked into Elle's eyes. As he turned and began walking away from Elle, he glanced back at her. "I'll miss you until I see you again, you know."

"I know," she replied, a withheld sigh finding its way out of her mouth. "I'll miss you, too."

Nazere followed Rock out of the entrance to the Keep of Serenity, the two of them swerving in and out of the people still trying to get out of the heavily packed entrance.

"I'm going to show you the hangar bay," Rock began as he walked alongside Nazere, stepping into the open Pathway of Sanctity. "I wish I had the time to show you the towers, but you need your sleep. Besides, you'll see them eventually. As for the hangar bay, we like to keep our instruments of war indoors." The two walked to the first gap in the wall, which happened to be on the right side from their vantage point. As with every gap in the Pathway of Sanctity, the marble stairs pointed upward to an invisible location. "It's right up here, my brother," Rock started. "We're going right through the door." Walking up the stairs, a solid gold door with the sparkling, crystal emblem of a standing dog resembling the Egyptian god Anubis marked Rock's destination. "Password: Olive Branch," Rock said, prompting the door to slide open to the right.

The hangar bay was immense, and the view was no less astonishing to Nazere than the Keep of Serenity. The roof was at least seven hundred feet off the ground, and the width of the bay was at least four-hundred yards. The hangar bay was plain for the most part, with all-white walls and a concrete floor. It was the structures within the hangar bay that made it quite the sight to see; the garaged machines that congregated the petroleum-scented space. Ardrodrones flew throughout the room; there were hundreds of them in total, working diligently in preparing for the battle that awaited them. Crafted in the shape of bees, their titanium bodies flew from one side of the room to the other as fluently as the insects. Programmed to repair larger structures, these cow-sized robots had red repair needles where their stingers should be. These needles were capable of penetrating, melting and molding all alloys except for artolium; it was possible to weld artolium, but ardrodrones had great difficulty doing so. Whenever they reached a location on a structure that needed repair or additional welding, their needles would light up like a torch. Dancing around in the two-way traffic of the air in the bay, they carried unshaped chunks of metal near their destination with their gray arms and dropped the portions to the ground. They then bonded the metal to the necessary site via the needle on their rear ends as quickly as possible.

Standing taller than any other structure, a great, dark-blue dog stood fully erected in place with its back against the center of the wall facing the doorway. Its face resembled Anubis' exactly, but it had four arms and two circular ethalon cannons bonded to its shoulders. The towering blue dog was as accurately manufactured as the Deliverer and the Redeemer; the machine had thin hairs all over it, with glowing irises and pupils. The machine looked down with its radiant, aquamarine eyes as Nazere entered the room, its tall ears alerted at the slightest sound; the machine demonstrated that it was fully conscious of everything around it. Next to the massive dog on the right was an equally massive ram; it wasn't as tall as the dog, but its body was thick and long. It had a full, fluffy coat of wool, and it was also a nearly perfect replica of its animal counterpart; its horns were fully coiled, with twelve gleaming orange rings on each horn; its eyes were as fiery an orange as the very face of the sun, and it had a threefold ethalon cannon attached to its back. To the left of the dog was perhaps the most spectacular and artistically unequaled sight in the room. With the face of a dove, this monstrous being stood upright like a man; it had four, crystal wings, and on those wings were a series of ethalon and proteon cannons. There were two ethalon cannons and one proteon cannon on each wing, combining for quite the offensive advantage. The bird had a fully crystal body, with shining red eyes; its eyelids would flicker in and out, looking down at Rock as it tilted its head ever-so-slightly back and forth.

Perpendicular to the other machines, on a wall to the right of the room, sixteen leviathans sat on the ground. Their wings behind them, they looked at Nazere as alertly as the other machines did. The leviathans were arranged in two ranks of eight, and the ardrodrones seemed to be working hardest on preparing them as opposed to the three other machines; a white leviathan caught Nazere's focus in the first rank. As Nazere had been looking around, a man had stopped what he was doing and had walked across the room from the direction of the ram. Catching Nazere by surprise, Isaac reached his hand out to the ventari in salutations.

"A pleasure to finally meet you, Nazere," Isaac began, his voice as welcoming as a wedding invitation. "I am the chief battle prophet for the Gathering of the White Lamb. I apologize that the rest of our crews aren't up here right now. We're working overtime right now so that the techs can get their much needed sleep. Welcome to the citadel's hangar bay, though." Isaac glanced around at all of the machines in the room. "I know it isn't much, but we have been working hard trying to prepare these bad boys for war."

"The pleasure is all mine," Nazere replied. "And your hangar bay is amazing. I have to wonder what these great machines are named." As Nazere talked with Isaac, Jadus began his approach from underneath the titanic dog.

"Well," Rock began, grinning. "let's start with our little beauty. Her name is Lunase. She's fully equipped with just about every offensive and defensive weapon you can think of. Have you heard of thratum lances, Nazere?"

"I haven't," Nazere replied.

"State of the art," Isaac interjected. "They have a chance to penetrate artolium armor. It all depends on the shot accuracy, but they are quite impressive weapons, indeed."

"Hey!" Jadus yelled in his deep voice as he jogged up to Nazere and shook his hand; Jadus had a firm grip. "Had to get away there for a second when I saw you. It is my absolute pleasure to make your acquaintance. I'm the chief battle prophet for the Gathering of the White Bishop. Thank the Master you made it here in one piece."

"So that dog up there is yours, then?" Nazere asked as he looked up at it, wondering what it must be like to pilot it.

"His name is Soulsearcher," Jadus replied. "And yes, he's our gathering's primary vessel."

"Soulsearcher?" Nazere asked.

"Yea," Rock interjected. "He searches your soul. If it don't look good, you're done. If you catch my drift."

"Our vessel is called Abram," Isaac said. "He is actually the fastest and best equipped out of all the other machines in this hangar bay." Jadus and Rock looked on at Isaac with skeptical eyes.

"I guess we'll find out," Rock began. "We got one day till we see. I'ma count my vizedrone kills, that's for sure." Isaac laughed.

"Never count your chickens before they hatch," Jadus said, a serious undercurrent to his tone. "We do not know what awaits us outside of Bethlehem." Rock nodded.

"You right," he said as he pointed at Jadus. "And I'll get back to you on that one. But I need to get this guy to his room. He needs some sleep before tomorrow. Personally, I can't wait to see what he can do with that sword."

"I'm sure all will go just as the Master has willed it," Isaac said. "Goodnight to you, Nazere. And thank you for your visit. I will see you in the morning." Nazere nodded.

"Thanks for being so hospitable," Nazere replied. "You all seem to act the same way."

"And how is that?" Jadus asked.

"Kind and generous," Nazere replied. Jadus patted Nazere's back.

"We are all in this together," Jadus said. "Even to the bitter end. We're with you." Rock nodded in agreement.

"We're with you all the way, brother," Rock said as he looked Nazere in the eyes. "On the real, it is a blessing that you came here. We've been praying for a long time. It's good to see those prayers answered in you." Isaac reached out and hugged Nazere.

"Know that it is love that we share with you," Isaac began. "We have it because it was given to us first. All of these machines and all of the technology in the world doesn't compare to the power of love. Mankind thought he had it right — even love. But war never seems to meet its end. It's laughable when you think about it. Your eyes will behold the end of all things. One day, we will all see the face of that one true Love that defines the beginning of eternal peace."

"I look forward to it," Nazere said smiling. "Goodnight to you, gentlemen. And all my love in return."

"Peace, gents," Rock said as he threw up the peace symbol with his fingers and opened the door to the hangar bay.

"Where are we off to now?" Nazere asked as he walked behind Rock.

"We're headed to your bedroom," Rock said, laughing. "It's night-night time for you. We'll catch up in the morning when we get down to business."

Rock and Nazere walked down the staircase leading to the Pathway of Sanctity. Leading the way, Rock strolled across the hall to the other side, walking up the second set of stairs on the left. The staircase led to a marble floored hall with doors cascading down it that were made of the same opaque crystal as the walls around them. Each door had a number, and as Nazere walked down the long hall he noted the numbers in his head.

"You're in room forty-nine," Rock said as he continued to walk. As Nazere arrived at his room, a friendly and unexpected face came strolling out of the room next to his. It was Elle, and she was dressed down in an emerald green nightgown, her shimmering, dark hair flowing down her back. She smiled almost mischievously as she looked at Nazere, her endlessly deep, hazel eyes tantalizing and immediately captivating her love. "Alright," Rock began, noticing the exchange of intimate interest. "This is my cue to roll out. I'm down the hall in sixty, Nazere. If you need anything, just come knocking." Rock then threw up the peace symbol with his two fingers once again and walked down the hall, quickly moving toward his room. Nazere's blue eyes were probing, weak with passion as they looked upon Elle.

"You aren't supposed to see me until tomorrow," Elle teased softly as she leaned against her door.

"I'm not?" Nazere asked, smiling and placing his muscular arm above Elle on the wall. "I wasn't the one who just walked out of the room right next to mine."

"Do you want to come in?" Elle asked with a straight face, tilting her head toward the door with a gleam in her eyes.

"I suppose I can break from my busy schedule," Nazere jested. Elle smiled as she opened the door to her room, slowing and methodically pacing in. She then jumped on her emerald-colored, glimmering comforter, laying on her side as she looked at Nazere; a trail of her hypnotic perfume met Nazere in a rush of heat. She smiled as she looked at him, and he fought to keep his eyes from widening as his insides completely melted away in the light of her piercing beauty. The rest of the room consisted of a marble floor and a crystal nightstand next to the crystal bed. The room was dimly lit by a forest-green, wax candle with a thin, silver candle-holder on top of the nightstand.

"Come and lay with me," Elle said as sweetly as honey, her eyes intently engaged in his. Nazere's eyes lit up uncontrollably, and his core seemed to explode as he looked at Elle; he knew that the fluctuation of his internal energy was quite visible, a nervous reaction, but he didn't care. Nazere slowly walked toward the bed, approaching it with the utmost care. He climbed onto the bed and faced Elle, slowly laying on his side; the storm that was his nerves was always calmed when he was close to her. Elle looked him in the eyes as he lay there next to her. She then placed her gentle left hand on Nazere's face, the touch of her fingers pure euphoria. “I know there’s a lot going on tomorrow,” Elle whispered softly. “I just wanted the opportunity to spend time with you before you go into battle. I’m worried about you.” Nazere shook his head.

“Don’t worry, my sweetheart,” Nazere whispered slowly. “We have a lot of back-up for this battle. Calm yourself and rest easy. Everything is going to be alright. I promise.” Elle smiled and turned over on her other side, leaning her head down on her pillow.

“Hold me for a little while,” Elle said. Nazere scooted over until his body was linked with Elle’s. He then wrapped his arms around her, reaching his head down to softly kiss her neck. “This is nice,” Elle whispered slowly. “I wish it could always be like this. I wanted so badly to see you before tomorrow.” Elle turned her head around toward Nazere’s, focusing deeply on his eyes. “I guess I just got lucky.” The two touched lips softly. Elle slowly inched her head into Nazere‘s. She then moved her fingers around his face, rounding her lips around his as she kissed him passionately. Elle’s lips remained connected to Nazere’s in a tightly-knit frenzy, until slowly she inched away. Looking him in the eyes, she held her right hand to his face.

“I love you,” they said at the same time. The two then laughed, Elle grabbing her pillow and shoving her head in it to hide her blushing face.

“Come on, you,” Elle said as she turned around again, an enthusiastic smile still rounding her face. “Cuddle with me.” Elle paused for a few moments as Nazere remained close to her. “And Nazere...,”

“Yes, my love?” he asked.

“No matter what happens, know that I will always love you. You and I are two intertwined hearts, and I could never ask for anything more beautiful than what we share. Something inside me tells me that it will always be this way; I know my love for you will never change.”

“I know I’m not deserving of it,” Nazere whispered in reply. “I never dreamed I’d have someone as precious as you so close to me; for what it’s worth, you are so far beyond all compare in my eyes. Unconditionally, always and forever is my love for you.”

Nazere stayed next to Elle, moving his finger up and down her neck as her eyes began to fade out. He stayed up until the late hours of the morning, and Elle struggled to stay awake; she cherished every second, every heart-beat that the two felt. Before Elle fell asleep completely, she turned in Nazere's direction and kissed him again; she kissed his neck, his lips and his upper chest. Nazere returned the gesture with a soft and simple kiss on the cheek. Perfection, Nazere thought to himself. I've never had something so special... not even close. So this is love. Interconnected together, Elle and Nazere rested their heads right next to one another. After several hours, the two fell asleep in each others' arms. Then came the darkness.

Nazere couldn't see anything. He simply heard the noise of a heart, to the tune of thud, thud, thud. He wondered where it could be coming from, but he continued to see nothing. Again the noises came, to the pounding rhythm of thud, thud, thud. Out of the blackness, Nazere raised his arm; it was visible to him. He then raised the other, and it too became visible. And suddenly, out of the black nothingness, a mirror image of himself appeared before him. The sound of a heartbeat continued as Nazere looked at the reflection of himself, actively wondering what it could mean while dreaming. Nazere raised his arm, and the mirror image did the same. Nazere took a step, and his reflection followed in perfect tune. The heartbeat got louder and louder as Nazere stood before his image. And just as he held his hand out and began to open the eye within his palm, the reflection of himself turned black. Two spines rose out of its back as it looked back at Nazere as if it had no fear, the eye of the black ventari's palm surging with light. And as the black image was about to fire, there came an eardrum-crushing thud, thud, thud.

Rising up from the bed, Nazere was alerted by a knock at Elle's door. Hopping out of the bed, Nazere walked to the source of the knocking. Opening the door, Nazere looked upon the faces of Ryan and Hayden. Wearing his usual white robes, Hayden's face remained straight as he stood at the doorway.

"I figured you were in here," Ryan began, whispering and smiling. Ryan wore a forest-green, cotton jacket with a pair of torn blue jeans and black boots. "Everyone's down in the Keep of Serenity. I advise you get down there. Let the ladies sleep; Lily is out like a light in her room. We have a lot of planning to do this morning, so we're just trying to get a little head start." Nazere nodded.

"Let's go," he whispered.

Together, Hayden, Ryan and Nazere walked down the stairs to the Pathway of Sanctity and to the door of the Keep of Serenity. Hayden raised his black staff to open the door. Inside, the projected image of Bethlehem remained active in front of the podium. All of the high prophets were in their seats except for Hayden and Arthur. The keep was filled with armored soldiers in goggles; orange, white and blue armored soldiers covered the left side of the keep, while the red and violet soldiers of the gatherings of the white rook and the white lion sat on the right. As Nazere peered around, a wall of black and white smoke appeared at his side. Nazere glanced over, but pretended not to see — putting on an act as best he could.

"Hello again, friend," Keldrid said, his voice dragging out. "I am by your side on this day." Nazere turned and nodded when no one else appeared to be looking.

"To your seats quickly," Hayden directed Nazere and Ryan. Moving to their respective seats, Nazere and Ryan watched as Sade sat still and silent behind the podium; her hands were leaning on the podium, her eyes pressed on the audience. Keldrid took a seat in Elle's usual spot, looking out toward the queen.

"Where is Arthur?" Ryan asked with a confused look on his face.

"I have no idea," Nazere replied. "Your guess is as good as mine."

"Well I suppose I will begin," Sade began, her lowered and tightened eyebrows demonstrating that she might be curious about Arthur's unexpected tardiness. "The Battle of Bethlehem begins today. The landing zones have been ascertained along the walls of the city. We must…"

Suddenly, Arthur stumbled into the Keep of Serenity with Endarius very near to his side. He fell on his knees as he reached the projected image of Bethlehem, the high prophet ill with an unknown ailment. Nazere looked to the entrance where Arthur had fallen; and as his eyes met the sight of Arthur, his non-existent heart sank in his chest. Everyone started talking, and their voices echoed like an infinite number of dinging chimes in Nazere's head; thoughts began to spin like a whirlwind in his mind as he considered the pragmatic possibilities for Arthur's collapse.

"Silence!" Sade commanded, silencing the room. "What is the meaning of this, Arthur?"

"I have had a vision!" Arthur exclaimed, appearing weakened, completely out of breath.

"I have had it too," Endarius said in a calm voice.

"I believe my house is under attack!" Arthur rasped in a loud voice, grasping the cane at his side. "We must return to Baltimore! I believe that something has gone terribly wrong!"

"We cannot afford to send forces to Baltimore with you," Sade replied. "We must defend the city of Bethlehem at all costs."

"I have had the vision, too," Hayden said as he rose from his seat. "It was not concise. But I will join Arthur in securing the site. There are innocents there."

"I will go as well," High Prophet Baun said as he took a stand. He then turned to Sade. "We will rally with you in Bethlehem once this matter has been settled."

Leaning over into Nazere's ear, Keldrid whispered to him. "Do not go to Baltimore. Tell the prophets you will not go! If you go, know that I cannot help you." Nazere took a long, drawn out look at Keldrid. He then looked at Arthur, thinking oh-so-carefully to himself.

I know what will happen there, he thought, the faint signal of the Scientific Magisterium resonating in his head, calling his name. I have hidden the vision! I am responsible for this, but I cannot risk the others being drawn into harm's way.

Nazere clenched his teeth under his lips, standing and drawing his sword. "We cannot return to Baltimore!" Nazere exclaimed, the glory of the Blade of the Unbroken elucidating his core in gold. "I will not return there!"

"We realize the risk!" Arthur pleaded as he looked up at Nazere from the floor, his face in a condition Nazere had never seen it in before. "But we are our brother's keepers! There are children there!"

Hayden looked Nazere deep in the eyes, slowly pondering the equation before them. “I leave the choice to Nazere! Let him who has been chosen make the decision.”

“Very well,” High Prophet Baun said as he nodded, setting his eyes on the ventari. “What is your answer, Nazere?”

Nazere turned to Keldrid, his eyes spelling out desperation for guidance. “Make your choice, human,” Keldrid said in a voice like the depths of the earth as he opened his arms. Nazere considered the people he remembered seeing in the House of Arthur; he recalled his days homeless on the streets right outside of the house’s very doors; he remembered the vision of the house burning; he recalled not mentioning it. As the burden lay on his back, Nazere lifted his head toward Hayden. He waited a few moments. He let everything sink in as he came to his conclusion.

“My choice is made,” Nazere began, clenching his fists below his hips. “I will return to Baltimore.” As Nazere looked to his side, Keldrid nodded in acknowledgment of his well-considered choice. And like a shifting shadow, Keldrid faded away against Elle’s chair in an instant. The keep erupted in shouts of confusion and anger. Ryan glanced at Nazere, looking him directly in the eyes.

“Well,” Ryan began slowly. “Let’s go wake up the girls.”

CHAPTER EIGHT

Breath of the Dragon

In an all white room, a figure with a scroll in his hand and a white hood over his head stood next to another with white robes and a white hood. All that could be seen of these two beings were their hands, and they sparkled in the radiance of the white room in which they stood. Before them was a huge, rectangular, golden door. The door was adorned with gemstones of all kinds around its perimeter; rubies, sapphires, emeralds and diamonds beautifully accented the outline of this tremendous door. They seemed to sparkle in a way that made them superior in every way to any gemstone on the face of the earth. In the center of the door was the embossed letter "A." Below it, the Greek symbol Omega was inscribed rather than embossed, cleverly demonstrating the powerful differences between one letter and the other. In a blinding flash of light, the door opened to these two beings who stood only five feet away from it. And from within the door came yet another being.

The door shut behind the figure departing from it, creating a sound like multiple crashes of thunder as it sealed tightly behind him. This figure who came from the door had the face of perfection. Not a mark on him, his skin shimmered as if there were a million tiny white sparks dancing on its surface. His hair was golden blond, and every single hair seemed to shine like impeccably refined gold. His eyes a bold shade of dark blue, his irises circled around his widened pupils like the turbulent sea. This figure stormed out of the door like a child angry with his mother, stomping his feet with every step he took. As he walked, one of the hooded figures behind him unveiled his face. He then called out to the being who was treading away.

"Lucifer," Gabriel began, emitting tiny flares of white light from his own face. His black hair was as reflective as the purest of onyx. "You must know that you cannot win this war!"

Stopping dead in his path, Lucifer's pupils overwhelmed his eyes. They turned as black as night as he remained facing away from Gabriel and the hooded being. Smiling to reveal a full set of pearly whites, Lucifer held his right hand parallel to his head.

"Tell me something, Gabriel," Lucifer began, a smile still rounding his face. "Was it you who was given the Bonds of the Infinite? What gift has the Master bestowed upon you, other than the grace of His presence?" Gabriel smiled.

"Unlike you, Lucifer," he began. "I am content with my standing with the Master. Here within His perfect domain, there is nothing I seek other than His grace and glory."

"Then tell me," Lucifer started, laughing as he held his position. "how is it that you underestimate the power bestowed upon me? You bow to your Master. I converse with Him. But this has been the last time. My plans are in order, and in the end, it will come down to which plan is the greater. Look at His pathetic creation alone, and you will see the fatal flaw." Lucifer glanced back at Gabriel, his irises returning to their dark blue flow. "There is much you do not know, Gabriel. Despite your perfect design, there is much you cannot see. Love is a broken thing. He has done all of this to Himself, and I will demonstrate for all who have cast me out how a much greater order can be established." As Lucifer talked, a tear like a glistening diamond fell from Gabriel's eye onto the light surface beneath his feet.

"We loved you once, Lucifer," Gabriel began slowly. "You were once my greatest friend. The Master gave you everything. I am sorry for your pain, Lucifer. But you have defied my first and greatest Love. Go now, and do what you will. Your time draws short."

Lucifer laughed at Gabriel, his glorious face fully alive with the resplendence of what he was. He then turned his head back in the path he had chosen and continued walking into the distant light until his figure could be seen no more.

A heavy knock came banging upon Elle's pearly crystal door as the morning drew on. Quickening herself to the beckoning call, Elle jogged across the floor of her room and pushed the door open. She was fully dressed in a white sweater, jeans and plush black snowshoes — ready for the day. Her emerald amulet hung in plain view over top her sweater, and a smile rounded her white cheeks as she stood at the entrance to her room. Before her stood Nazere, and behind him were Ryan and David. There was a pause as Elle held to the side panel of her door with her right hand, her eyes briefly capturing the snapshots of the three that stood before her. Their emotion-infused faces were almost melancholy as they looked her straight in the eyes. As Elle directed all of her focus deeply into Nazere's eyes, her smile evolved into an indistinct stare.

"What's wrong?" Elle asked, her troubled heart racing within her chest.

"We have to go, my love," Nazere began, his face carrying with it a burden of sorrow. Doubts and concerns ran like an unstoppable freight train through his head.

"To Bethlehem?" Elle questioned, turning her head to all three men that stood beyond her door as her heart continued to pound.

"No," Ryan said in a soft voice, shaking his head. "Something has happened. We must leave immediately for Baltimore." David looked at the floor as Ryan spoke, worry bearing down upon his heart like a brick that lay upon a small feather.

"Take my hand," Nazere said as he outstretched his arm. He wanted to reassure Elle. "There will be others with us."

Taking Nazere's hand, the four hastened to descend the white stairs that led to the Pathway of Sanctity. As they walked, Elle would glance up at Nazere periodically. Her expression was neutral. She could sense something was wrong with the one she loved; she knew him all too well. She gripped his hand as they made their way down the hallway in the direction of the snow-covered drawbridge beyond it. Nazere remained silent, his eyes locked in place straight ahead of him. Taking a piece of paper from the jacket pocket at his side, Ryan scribbled a few notes down with a pen. He then folded the paper and put it back in his jacket pocket. Staring at the floor, David walked alongside Ryan with his hands in his light-blue jean pockets. David wore a long-sleeve t-shirt with the words "REDEEMER" printed on its surface in blue.

Reaching the bridge, the four were met by the portrait of Hayden kneeling beside his brown staff in a cake of snow. As the four began to walk across the bridge, the Deliverer turned its eyes toward them. The Colossus stood erect in the snow, its face unmoved as the four caught up to Hayden. As Nazere neared Hayden, he noticed that his eyes were closed. Opening his eyes as he felt the presence of his gathering around him, Hayden gripped his staff and slowly took to his feet. His eyes were set on Nazere's as his knees brought his body to a stand. His face straight and as sincere as ever, Hayden turned his eyes to his other students.

"The others are already prepared for flight," Hayden began slowly. "The flight of leviathans will be joining Sade in Bethlehem. We do not have much time, but I wanted to say a few things before we depart. Remember all of my words, as they will remain close to your heart wherever you may be. I love you all dearly, and no matter what happens, do not forget what defines us as what we are. Hold to your faith. Grasp courage as if it were the one thing keeping you alive. But above all else, hope. Hope is the one thing no man can take from you." Pausing for a moment, Hayden glanced at David. "To the Redeemer, then."

"On the wings of the eagle we will fly," David began. Nazere thought to himself, flashing back to his first moments of freedom from Ordren. He recalled Keldrid's words, and how all of what had come to be was far from anything he had ever imagined. He recalled running on the streets of Baltimore as a young child, moving wild and free amongst sprinklers on the blacktop. He recalled living on those same streets, falling asleep to the sweet melody of the city surrounding him.

The sound of crickets chirping in the grass, and the noise of vehicles that flew over his head as his eyes came to a close. He remembered the pain of being alone, and the tears that would stream down his face as he wished he was anywhere but on a park bench. But then the thoughts of Undrum came back to him in a thousand little fragments. He recalled the shock of being delivered from within the depths of a dark prison. He remembered taking joy in having a prospect for a home in the cabin that sat so beautifully in the mountainous snow there. He remembered seeing Elle's beautiful face for the first time. And his thoughts captured the kind welcomes that were given to him by David, Ryan and Hayden. He held to the thought that he was not alone anymore; he knew he had true family. And that family was in the Gathering of the White Knight. Nazere came to as Ryan's words floated out into the open.

"Let's go brothers and sister," Ryan began, patting Nazere's back. "We have accomplished so much together. Let's not stop moving now." Nazere glanced back at the Citadel of Northern Lights as he walked beside Elle. Together, the group walked up to the majestic ship that was the Redeemer. As they neared it, the Redeemer let out a mighty cry.

"Wings up!" David yelled as he pulled out his trentorod. As it extended, he inserted the device into its proper position in the door of the Redeemer. The Redeemer's door pushed back and rotated to the side. Climbing in first, Nazere pulled himself into the eagle. Leaning down and reaching out his right hand, he then assisted Elle onto the ship. Once Elle was onboard, he held his position at the door.

"Come on, Ryan," Nazere said, still leaning over. "I've got you." Ryan smiled as he took Nazere's hand and entered the Redeemer. He patted Nazere's back as he walked over to his seat. "David," Nazere began, his eyes looking down at David's drooping head. "Look up at me. This is your ship. Come take us where we need to go." David pointed his head upward at Nazere and nodded. Grabbing Nazere's hand, David lifted his body into the ship. "Last but not least," Nazere began slowly as he looked at Hayden. "My teacher. Are you ready to go?" Hayden smiled.

"I am, my boy," he replied. "I am." Holding his staff firmly, Hayden grabbed Nazere's forearm. He then walked up the three stairs below the knight-stamped chairs to the ship, taking his usual seat next to Nazere.

Sitting in the captain's seat, David activated the holographic controls to the Redeemer. His demeanor remained calm and still, as if he himself were a machine. Nonetheless, he moved onward. He shifted, twirled and pressed the two green rectangular panels before him in the fashion he always had. As everyone was in their designated place, Ryan took a disk and placed it into the steel pane in front of him. He then took his earpiece and put it in his right ear, turning his face to Nazere.

"Music," he began. "It'll get you through." Nazere flashed back to his very first flight on the Redeemer, and the words Ryan spoke to him. His face was still focused ahead of him, just as if he were thinking of nothing at all.

"Take us up, my beauty," David spoke to the Redeemer in a slow, steady tone. "Set your destination to the House of Arthur, Baltimore. Throw up the ion shields. All linked vessels…," David paused for a moment, looking at the floor for a split second as if his spirit were broken. The Redeemer then cried out as the timer popped up on the display next to David. He then lifted his head and continued, "Set your coordinates to my destination. We're going to land down the street from the House of Arthur. I've changed my directions accordingly."

"Affirmative," the Colossus replied.

"I'm with you, my brother," Drake said, his face shown smiling on the lower right corner of the outdoor display.

As the countdown timer dropped from ten, there was a still quiet about the deck of the Redeemer. Reaching out her hand, Elle looked at Nazere's face.

"Hand!" she exclaimed, happily smiling. Taking Elle's hand, Nazere's spirits lifted as they always did when she held him. And as he looked to the right, he noticed the projected timer had dropped to five. As it hit three, the Redeemer began to move its feet across the clearing before it. The Colossus could be seen hovering lightly off the surface of the ground on the display, and the Deliverer was in its lowered pounce position.

"We're up in three...," David began. The Redeemer extended its wings and began to flap them. The Colossus lifted just a touch higher than it was a second earlier. And the Deliverer maintained its position. "Two...," Lifting off, the Redeemer pointed its nose to the clouds. Its metal eyes seemed to shine in the glory of the radiant sunshine that bounced off of everything in sight. "One. Stay with me, Drake. I need you by my side."

"I'll wait for you, my friend," Drake replied softly. "You know I will."

"Take it all the way up," David instructed.

And as the Redeemer stretched its wings out above the Citadel of Northern Lights, Nazere focused his eyes on the display. The snow-covered drawbridge, the powdered trees on the mountain tops and the magnificent citadel all seemed to wave goodbye as they slowly drifted out of sight. Side by side in the clouds, the Colossus winked at the Redeemer as if just to say hello. And the lion flew next to the Redeemer, its paws extended out in front of it rather than its usual position in a ball. And as it never had before, the lion smiled. The clouds that flew all around the flying machines seemed as wondrous as ever they did, like many puffs of cotton spread out on a blue mantle. For the first time, the three machines flew side by side. As Nazere looked at the screen, everything below him that was in fact so great seemed so very small from his position in the air. The Redeemer's deck jolted as it burned through the atmosphere next to its mechanical companions.

And altogether, the flight lifted into the great void of space. The three machines circled around in perfect harmony as they seemed to dance around in space. Looking down upon the face of earth, every tiny memory came back to Nazere. His eyes set on the world, he remembered his first Christmas as a boy. He maintained his firm gaze so that no one could see through to his innermost thoughts. Opening the presents that sat under his little evergreen tree was one of those precious moments he could never forget. And moments came back to him one by one as the world he gazed upon served as a chronological trigger he could not overcome. He reminisced about his first day of school. With his book bag strapped to his back, he waved goodbye as he glanced back at his mother but for a second. While he read his comic books under the weeping willow tree in his backyard, all of reality's pressure seemed to fade away for just a little while. Riding his little, red tricycle at one time seemed an impossibility to him. He remembered falling down off of it, and then getting back up again. Running with his friends in his front yard, life's many complications always seemed so miniscule. Every memory that came back to Nazere was held close to his non-existent heart. But of all the memories he loved, there was one that made him forget the world he looked upon. The few moments that he danced with Elle was his perfect memory, and as he held to it closely, everything spinning throughout his head like an out-of-control carousel seemed to come to a halt.

"Together," David began calmly. "Let's take the flight down to the skies."

"I'm right behind you," Drake said, a smooth tone to his voice.

"Following you, captain," the Colossus acknowledged.

And altogether, the three vessels dancing in the depths of space flew side by side toward the earth. Each of them pointed their heads downward, the Redeemer throwing its wings in front of it as it dropped like a tiny dime being tossed into the earth's atmosphere. Aligned together, the three vessels' shields burst into flame as they rained through the heights. The clouds came quickly, cushioning each vessel like a warm blanket. And as the three poked through the clouds, the lights of moving vehicles and skyscrapers below came into view.

"Approaching your destination now, captain," the Redeemer reported. David remained silent.

Nazere looked at the display as so very many familiar locations appeared before him. If he wanted to, he could point to the place he grew up. And if he was feeling up to it, he could point out the very school the bus used to transport him to after he had waved goodbye to his mother. He wished the weeping willow tree he used to sit under was still there, but it had become a distant memory as it was paved over years ago.

"Initiating landing sequence," the Redeemer said.

"Alright, my friends," David began. "Land next to me on the street."

"Copy that," Drake replied.

"I'll be next to you, David," the Colossus said.

The Redeemer held its wings in position as it dropped to the pavement below. There was insufficient space on the street to land all three vessels together. The Deliverer parked itself in front of the Redeemer, and the Colossus set its feet on the ground behind it. As soon as the Redeemer set its feet on the ground, David silently pressed a button on the center of the holographic display to his right. The red ribbons crossing Nazere's chest unwrapped, animatedly twirling to their position in the back of his seat. Still set on the outdoor display, Nazere watched as the Deliverer dropped its lift. Arthur stood beside Sara, Adrax and Owen. Adrax hopped off the hovering circle and began to assist the others. Nazere was sure the Colossus behind the Redeemer had dropped its long stairs. With a straight demeanor, Hayden turned to Nazere. Feeling his eyes land on him, Nazere looked back to Hayden.

"My radar is clear," David announced with an exhausted look about him.

"We must remain with the ship," Hayden said to Nazere softly as he looked him in the eyes. "The other two gatherings will accompany you to the House of Arthur. Of the other gatherings, only Drake will remain behind." Nazere nodded as he slowly took a stand.

"I'm going with him!" Elle insisted, taking hold of him by the left forearm. David turned his head to the floor once again. Ryan's eyes turned to Hayden, and Hayden glanced back at Ryan. Smiling, Ryan nodded.

"Very well," Hayden began, looking back at Nazere and Elle. Pressing a button on his control panel, David released the straps holding Elle back. By Nazere's side, she rose to her feet. "Know always,“ Hayden started. "you will both be close to my heart."

"Are you ready?" Elle asked Nazere as she exhaled a nervous

breath.

"I am," Nazere said, trying to hold back all of the madness in his head. He then turned around and set his eyes on Hayden. "I promise you, high prophet," he began, slow and sincere. "I will keep her safe from all harm." His eyes still set on Nazere, Hayden made no response. Nazere outstretched his hand toward Hayden, a small black cube in his palm. "Hold on to Verus for me. I shouldn't be long." The high prophet reached out and retrieved the cube from Nazere's palm. Hand-in-hand, Elle and Nazere made their way to the entrance and exit of the Redeemer. Closing his eyes, David punched a button on his control panel and the door rolled open.

Everyone stood in one mass on the black streets of Baltimore, huddled together tightly as they awaited Nazere's arrival. There was a still silence in the air as Nazere and Elle approached the congregation, and it remained in place until Nazere made his way to Arthur. Smiling at Nazere, High Prophet Baun seemed to say so much without speaking a single word. Owen Candlefire nodded as Nazere stood before him, and Felix winked. Nazere knew that they had placed their faith in his judgment.

"Let's be on our way then," Arthur said, looking into Nazere's eyes.

"I will lead the way," Nazere said. He turned to Elle and stared her in the eyes. "You must remain behind with the rest of the group, Elle. I want you to remain safe." Elle let go of Nazere's hand; God knows she didn't want to. Nazere then made his way to the front of the group, taking up his position as a guide for the gatherings in the city he once called home. "Follow me."

Inside of the Redeemer, Hayden leaned over and looked to David.

"Cloak the ship," Hayden instructed, a blank stare on his face. Closing his eyes again, David leaned back in his chair.

"Cloak yourself, Redeemer," he said, placing his hands over his face as he spoke.

The group outside walked along the street, looking from side to side as their eyes searched for some sign of warning. They continued walking behind Nazere, speaking not a word to one another. Holding his head high, Nazere walked down the streets he knew all too well. Looking to his left as he made his first couple of paces, he captured the sight of a thin, red tabby cat walking down the street with no place to go. Wanting to reach out to the cat but not being able to, he recalled the very same feeling of not having any place in particular to find shelter. Endless strolls down the streets of Baltimore had been most of his adulthood memory. In his mind, he was that lost tabby cat. He noticed a rusted park bench to the right where he used to nestle himself under the cover of woolen blankets. A dove was perched on the iron arm of the bench; it almost seemed that the dove was watching attentively as Nazere advanced beyond it. Keeping his eyes fixated straight ahead, Nazere tried to block out all of the memories in his head. Holding tightly to the task at hand, Nazere lifted his head into the distance. He looked and looked. There appeared to be nothing in the distance where the House of Arthur was located. He looked to the street and noticed where he used to play on the streets as a boy. He imagined a little sprinkler where the one he had at one time ran through used to be. And as he lifted his head, his eyes widened as they embraced the sight of smoke beginning to rise in the distance.

In that moment, every thought that passed through Nazere's mind seemed to shatter like a mirror falling on the floor. Sprinting at full speed, he moved his body as quickly as he could to the site of the smoke. It was there that his deepest fears were confirmed. Dropping to his knees before the very sight of it, Nazere looked up at the House of Arthur as a thick body of smoke rose from its roof; he could smell the fire that was burning deep within it. The group ran and caught up to Nazere as fast as their legs could carry them. They all gathered around him in a circle; the looks on their faces clearly communicated that they were wondering why he wasn't charging in. Everything was silent in Nazere's mind. The voices calling to him were like unintelligible whispers drifting around him in all directions. Reality and time itself seemed to slow down to a snail's pace as the group looked upon Nazere. As if he could predict the next move, his heart sunk deep within his chest. His arms hung inanimately at his sides as he awaited what was to come. With the subtlety of a mishandled pin dropping to the floor, the door to the House of Arthur came flying open.

The body of Ferris Shadowpath dropped to its knees before the startled group on the stairs beneath the house. Every glaring face carried the unbearable burden of knowing what was to come from that point on. Eyes closed and hands shielded faces from the unthinkable sight. A steel sword had been driven through his chest, and he who held the blade was dressed in black robes and a black hood that hid his face from sight. All that could be seen of the man were his hands, tattooed with the image of a dragon breathing flame. Coming from behind the shrouded man were two other figures. The first man had a balding head with gray hair encircling his crown. He had green eyes and wore a lab coat with white pants and an electronic wrist watch made of sterling silver; he took a stand behind the right side of the sinister, central figure. Behind this figure to the left, an equally disheartening image came into the plain view of all who stood outside of the house. Time slowed down even more as this image became visible. It was that of a black ventari with two spines rising from the middle of his shoulders. The shaded, central figure kicked Ferris' slain body off of the sword and toward Nazere. Time seemed to slow down even further as his body landed before Nazere's knees. Blood smeared across the blacktop as Ferris' body was hurled across it, but Nazere's wilted neck stared into space.

Gaining the strength to look up at the three at the entrance, Nazere took a valiant stand. He drew the Blade of the Unbroken from his back, becoming consumed with the blazing fury of the golden sword. The shrouded figure dropped his bloodied sword and flicked out his arm, curling the fingers on his left hand. Knocked to the ground beneath him by the unrealized power of him who could not be seen, Nazere's entire body became completely paralyzed. His ears ringing, he made every attempt to move his afflicted structure; his body was face down on the blacktop. He had been in that same position so many times before. He tried to hold to the blade with all of his heart. More than anything he wanted to maintain it. He believed he could hold the sword with every ounce of mental endurance he had. But the blade was now beyond his control. Lifting off the ground, the Blade of the Unbroken seemed to float like a balloon that had been released into the clouds — right into the curled fingers of the shaded figure. Holding the hilt of the blade in his hands, he laughed to himself at the very embodiment of golden glory that he harbored. As soon as the blade arrived in his palms, a radiant glow consumed his blackened shroud.

"Did you think that your actions would go unnoticed?" the shrouded figure asked with an evil ring to his black voice. The figure held the blade in his right hand as he pointed to Nazere. "Behold your chosen one, prophets! Behold your miserable, homeless addict! With the assistance of Ferris and this filthy wretch, all that I require has been delivered into my hands. Do you not speak, ventari?! Would you like to explain your late night excursion to the Lone Wolf in search of dezium? Did you possibly think that your actions would go unseen? All mistakes hold consequences. They only begin with all of the innocents who remain locked in the house." Held to the ground without the possibility to move, Nazere's eyes shut in disgrace.

"Ferris betrayed us," Endarius whispered to High Prophet Arthur. "I could never have known. You must believe me."

Out of the crowd, a friendly face stepped over Nazere's immobilized body. Smiling in the face of the one with the shroud, High Prophet Baun opened his arms. The shrouded figure laughed in reply.

"Vice Lord Xar," High Prophet Baun began slowly. "How I have longed to see your face." Still laughing, Vice Lord Xar held the Blade of the Unbroken with both of his hands.

"Ironic that it ends this way," Vice Lord Xar began with great bass to his voice. "The very hand of your Master is now in mine. I am the great calculator of all things, and you have been defeated per my infinite ability in every single school of thought. At long last, I shall become one with the Blessed Blade of the White Rider. Unfortunate that your Master never changes. Unfortunate that you misplace your faith. I too have long awaited this moment. By means of your Master's craftsmanship, you shall die." High Prophet Baun continued to smile. Nazere's eyes opened as he overheard what was being said.

"You could be happy," High Prophet Baun began slowly with his arms still opened widely. "if you had what I have. I am not of this world as you should know. But I have had a long and fulfilling life. I know you have questions. Science will never be the remedy. But in the end, the answers to what you do not know will be delivered." High Prophet Baun paused for a moment as he looked into Vice Lord Xar's eyes for a fleeting second. He then smiled. "I am ready," he said. And in one swift motion, Vice Lord Xar drove the Blade of the Unbroken through High Prophet Baun's heart. The sound of thunder tore through the air as Vice Lord Xar withdrew the divine sword. High Prophet Baun fell to his side and onto the blacktop, a stream of blood running from his breathless being. A single tear dropped from Aaron's face as he watched the fall of his beloved teacher.

"Olar," Vice Lord Xar began in his slow, vile tone. "Take the prophets to Ordren. They shall be executed immediately. As for the ventari, bond him and drain him of his core. Our master has ordered that he is not to be killed. It appears there is a place in our order for him yet. Is that understood?"

"Yes, my lord," Olar replied.

"As for myself and Commander Entril, we have matters to attend to in Bethlehem." In a blur of shadow like a light switch on the wall being flipped down, Vice Lord Xar and Commander Entril instantaneously blinked out of sight.

In a downpour of blue fire, one hundred ventari descended from the sky above. Once on the street, they surrounded the ill-equipped prophets. And one by one, they took hold of their bodies. No one dared to struggle. Two ventari stepped out of the crowd. One of them carried immense artolium bonds in his hands; the shackles were shaped to fit Nazere's torso, as well his hands and feet. There were four folding shackles in total, each stacked on top of each other in the ventari's arms. Each shackle had artolium teeth that clasped together and locked in place once they were folded. A blinking blue box on each of the shackles would ensure Nazere's weaponry would be deactivated. The prophets watched in sorrow as their chosen one was lifted in the air by the second ventari. Working in unison, the ventari holding Nazere supported the weight of his body as the torso shackle was pinched together and locked in place around him first. Next came the twin arm shackles, each of them being methodically set into position and locked. Last came the feet shackle, which bound his ankles in position indefinitely.

Still immobilized by the power of the beast, Nazere shifted his eyes around. As he was held in place, he watched as the only family he knew was taken away one by one. A ventari wrapped his arms around James and launched him into the clouds like a shooting star. Next came Sara Maple, who looked at Nazere with tears streaming down her face. Adrax winked at Nazere with a smile on his face before he was flown into the distance. With their saddened eyes set on High Prophet Baun's lifeless body, Felix and Aaron were taken away together. Before he was carried away, Arthur looked on as his house burned to the ground; his eyes were stuck in place as the rafters of the structure fell onto the street below. Lily, Endarius and Owen disappeared before Nazere had the chance to watch them leave. As he looked around, his eyes finally met his heart. How he wished he could reach out to her. The regret he felt was more than he could withstand. He desired to speak but a single word, but the conditions upon him were out of his control.

"I love you!" Elle called out as best she could as she disappeared in a trail of blue fire, tears pouring down her face.

After they were all taken, a beep could be heard from where Nazere was being held. Chief Scientist Olar had pressed a button on his electronic wrist watch. Soon, the shadow of a vizedrone's body fell over Nazere and the ventari that remained. Landing overtop of Nazere, the vizedrone dropped a hovering surface from within its stomach. The hovering surface was rectangular, and the ventari carrying Nazere's body placed him in its center. Chief Scientist Olar and all of the ventari on the streets stepped onto the lift. As soon as everyone was on it, the lift retracted into the vizedrone's belly. Pulling a round circle of electrical tape from his side, Olar tore off a small strip. He then placed that strip over Nazere's eyes. Under the cover of darkness, self-disappointment filled Nazere's true core.

"Set your coordinates to the province of Ordren," Chief Scientist

Olar commanded the vizedrone. And in an instant, the great dragon began to move. The interior of the creature shook violently as it picked up speed, its claws crushing the street beneath them. So many thoughts passed through Nazere's mind as he was carried back to Ordren. He felt beaten; overwhelmed; crushed; shamed; guilty. His dearest love was now in the hands of the enemy. And there was nothing he could do to change that. An all-too familiar feeling had returned to him after he had experienced so much change since having first arrived at Undrum; he was powerless.

Within the Redeemer, the three that remained in their seats seemed completely devoid of all emotion. Their faces depicted that they were patiently awaiting some kind of a response from the others. His eyes set on the display before him with great intensity, Hayden pointed his right finger upward toward the sky.

"Take us up, David," Hayden instructed, his eyes still glued to the display. With slow and seemingly automated movements, David began operating the right holographic display before him.

"We are heading out, Drake," David said, forming his words slower than he had ever done so before. His arms slowly moved from sub-panel to sub-panel on his display, working as if this was the most daunting task he was ever engaged in. His eyes appeared heavier than solid rock boulders. His body was a giant steel mass. There seemed to be no one who could possibly pick him up. "Colossus. Stay with me now."

As the electronic dragon began to flap his wings transitioning into flight, the autonomous function of breathing seemed an overwhelming struggle to Nazere. The deck within the ship shook mildly as the dragon flew. All Nazere could see were the eyes of his friends, all looking upon him as the power he was given slipped right out of his faulty hands. For the tiniest moment, he had hoped that this were all but a dream he hadn't snapped out of yet. For more than a moment, he regretted the first time he picked up a pill of dezium on the streets of Baltimore. Everything he remembered brought his locked body to its knees all over again. Hayden's never-ending smile was a bittersweet reminder of what he had lost. The scent of Elle's characteristic perfume when she was close to him never failed to make him feel complete. Fighting his way down to the core of the Gantor Pinnacle alongside Ryan seemed an impossibility to his friends—but they completed their task. He reminisced about having a normal body, and how letting it go there changed his entire world. Without Ryan by his side, perhaps that metamorphosis never would have come to pass. The words of his comrades rippled throughout his body like a wishing well's waves after a penny had been tossed into it. I love you, they said. If only he had said what he had always felt whenever they said it to him. If only.

"We are within the province," Chief Scientist Olar said to the vizedrone. "Take the ship into gate two. We will take care of our obligation there."

The ship's interior rattled as the dragon's tail swirled like a kite being driven in a circle by the volatility of the wind, landing before the gate beside the one Ryan and Aaron had entered during the Battle of Ordren. The thick artolium's rise from the brown, sandy ground was the first nail in the lifeless coffin that was Nazere's despair. The gate had four lights three feet from its bottom, all of them light-emitting diodes fashioned in four line segments. Blinking in and out like Nazere's weakened spirit, the square gate made the noise of two bus cars slowly colliding as it reached its top. The deck rocked back and forth as the vizedrone walked into the entrance of the Ordren prison. Nazere could hear the claws of the dragon pound the solid surface beneath them. The surface of the ground beneath the vizedrone personified Nazere's sense of worth. Crushed. Crushed. Crushed.

The second gate on the far left of the Ordren jail was a large square artolium room with two green lights attached to the ceiling by a steel arm. They were about eighty feet off of the dock's surface, which was comprised entirely of unmarked artolium. The gunmetal lights circled rapidly like a top spinning on its head, sending two green beams of luminance running around the flat walls of the ship's dock. In front of the dragon's rounded face was a circular artolium door. The door wore the mark of the dragon like a garment; its embossed image completely covered the door's face. Standing outside of the dragon, a united team of five scientists dressed precisely like Chief Scientist

Olar held electronic notepads in their hands. They excitedly awaited the arrival of Nazere, talking and laughing amongst themselves as if they were attending a festivity. Several bloodguards stood by their sides, their widened nocturnal eyes watching ardently in curiosity as the lift of the vizedrone was lowered to the gray floor. Their pupils came to life and their hands were lifted in the air in celebratory unison as they witnessed Nazere's ensnared and immobile shell.

"Carry him carefully to the deethalonization chamber," Chief Scientist Olar instructed the ventari closest to him. "Strap him up tightly. Myself and my fellow doctors are going to take a close look at him once his affiliates have been attended to. There is a reason for this ventari's abnormal performance, and we intend to get to the bottom of it." The ventari he was speaking to nodded. Olar then glanced around at the rest of the ventari on the rectangular lift, pointing down to Nazere with his left hand. "The rest of you escort him to his holding location beside the ventari carrier. I will have rewards for all of you for your superb service to the high lord." They all nodded as Chief Scientist Olar smiled and walked to his own associates to the right of the vizedrone. They all laughed and cheered at the sight of their chief scientist, shaking his hand in congratulations on a job well done.

The ventari tasked to carry Nazere reached his arms down and slowly lifted his body off of the ground. This ventari held Nazere at his chest level as he gradually walked toward the round door. The others walked in two single-file lines behind the one who held Nazere, their movements precise and calculated. Each had a perfect pace and alignment that demonstrated how far from human these machines had truly become. The circular door automatically raised like a standing quarter being picked up off of a table as the ventari carrier approached it. Within this place, the ventari had total dominion. A long hall with an black and red carpet was revealed as the ventari stepped through the second entrance. The other ventari continued to follow the leader in two files, proceeding to march in mirrored paces. The carpet embodied the entire ground and had the full body of a dragon in black thread outstretched from one side of the hall to the other. Nazere could make out the tail of the black-threaded dragon out of the corner of his right eye. An advanced feature of a ventari's inner workings, his internal display was barely able to see through the tape placed around his eyes; the tape merely hindered his sight, reducing it to the point where he had to struggle to see anything. There were three circular doors in the passageway that were fashioned uniformly as exact copies of the dragon-faced entrance.

There was one door on the right, one on the left, and one at the very end of the hall. Perhaps twenty-five yards in length, the hall's roof was made of thick, opaque glass. The walls were solid artolium, bearing no distinctive qualities. As Nazere hung his head back, the volume of the many ventari marching behind the one who carried him became increasingly loud with every step; like the slow drip of a leaky faucet, the noise became unbearable to Nazere as he was escorted down the path to his destination. He dropped his heavy head back completely, as if he were dead in the arms of the ventari that held him; he felt beyond dead inside. Coming to a stop between the right and left doors, a ventari walked out of the two files behind the leader and opened the right door. As it flew open, the carrier performed a right-face and walked past the ventari who opened the door.

This chamber was ten yards wide, made of solid artolium walls, floors and ceiling. A blue radiance illuminated every contour within the vicinity of Nazere. The floors and side walls had no markings, and the ceiling had a camera attached to it in its center; the camera was welded to the ceiling in artolium, pointing directly at the back wall. As Nazere glanced at the wall, he beheld the fate that awaited him. In a massive, clear encasing, an orb similar to the one seen in the Gantor Pinnacle was hovering in place over a life-sized artolium mold of a ventari's back. This orb capacitated the energy of an overwhelmingly large, blue-ethalon charge. Twenty clear cords were attached to the encasing of the charge on the right, and there were twenty on the left. But no ethalon flowed through them. They were inanimate, and consisted of the same synthetic artolium as the cords in the Gantor Pinnacle. The difference between these cords and the ones in New York City was that the cords within these chambers had a small, black vacuum at the end of each of them; the vacuums were circular and rounded at the ends like a small, blooming flower.

The mold had thick black magnets on the head, midsection, wrists and ankles of it. The artolium outline was thick and protruded from the wall. It had forty round holes on the top of it, and next to the holes hung the ends of the shielded cords like dreadlocks dangling downward. A sharp needle of thin artolium extended from the center of the back of the mold. To the left of the mold was a square electronic panel with a sterling-steel handle set to the upright position beside it. The ventari approached the back wall at a turtle's pace, stopping in the center of the chamber as the machines behind him assembled in the room in three ranks. The ranks of ventari reached from one side of the room to the other once they were in place. And with all eyes in the chamber on Nazere, the carrier slowly walked to the mold on the back wall.

The ventari set Nazere upright on his feet only two feet away from the mold. He then gripped Nazere's shoulders and lifted him off of the ground. Hanging his head, Nazere braced himself for the inevitable. Slowly and precisely, the ventari's hands pressed Nazere's shoulders into the mold. The needle penetrated his back slowly, blue sparks throwing themselves in all directions. Nazere's active nervous system cried out in agony as the needle was finally pressed in completely; bearing the full brunt of the sting, he was determined to show no sign of weakness. Nazere clenched his fists and kept his lips tightly shut. His eyes looked out at this blurred reflection of himself as he was released from that ventari's hands. His arms came flying to the sides like a bird spreading its wings. The high-powered magnets locked his shackles securely into place. And just as they did, the cords that surrounded him became animated. Each vacuum tube connected to their corresponding position above the mold, knowing exactly where to go as if they thirsted to drink of the ethalon within Nazere.

The ventari who had carried him slowly stepped back, his eyes pinned to Nazere's image as the vacuums began to drain the ethalon from Nazere's core. The forty clear tubes were now a bright blue, drawing the ethalon from Nazere into the charge enclosed above his head. Utterly overtaken with pain, Nazere's head limped over the rest of his body. His vision blurred further as the ventari who had overseen his placement on the wall marched out of the entrance of the chambers; the drainage was impeding his vision and his ability to remain awake. Drowsiness immediately set in as a side-effect of the suction, but the ongoing infliction of stings shooting throughout his body kept his teeth clenched. As the last ventari made his exit, the door slammed tightly shut. Slowly but surely, the core within Nazere's center was weakening; it expanded and contracted like a straining muscle. And as Nazere's head continued to hang, his vision became more and more distorted.

Two hours passed by, Nazere feeling more and more distanced from the world around him. His internal display began to flicker in and out, a message flashing "WARNING: ETHALON < 50 PERCENT" in bold red font. His pain was beyond unbearable; he knew that he would lose consciousness soon; he kept his lips and fists clenched as he tried to hold on. Despite all of his extreme suffering, his mind was set on those he loved. The tempest within his mind was relentless, and he believed he was being driven to the outer reaches of madness. His life flashing before his eyes, a small white outline lie underneath his feet. He bore down on his neck and squinted to focus his vision as best he could at what was beneath him. He thought he was hallucinating when he captured a snapshot of the image before him. He looked up at the door, and he was positive that it was still shut. He then looked back down at the ground. The vision of a white dove staring back at him brought all of his scattered thoughts to a stand still; the dove was on its little feet, just standing on the floor. As soon as Nazere made out its figure, the bird took flight and landed on his shoulder; the dove perched itself there, nestling softly and keeping its watchful eyes on him as it cocked its head to and fro. Still fading out, Nazere was sure he was dreaming. He kept his head lowered, fighting with all of his heart to keep himself awake and alert.

Within the Redeemer, a close eye was kept on the radar on the holographic panel to David's right. The external display was deactivated. His gaze set on the radar, Ryan sat with the ribbon straps of the chair he was sitting in securing him tightly. He had a black box in his left hand with a clear cord attached to it; at the end of the cord was a sharp needle. It was midday, and the sun was high in the cloudless sky, its rays unable to bounce off the cloaked vessels below it. Sitting in his usual seat, many thoughts ran through Hayden's mind. His staff to his right, he too seemed preoccupied with looking at the holographic radar shown to David's right. There were many red dots resembling the nearby presence of enemy vessels. But there were two blue dots in addition to the red ones. They resembled the cloaked presence of the Deliverer and the Colossus to the right of the Redeemer. The expression on David's face appeared as lost as it had been when he was in Baltimore as the three continued to stare in silence.

In the midst the stillness of the deck, Hayden closed his eyes slowly and gripped his staff. No voice came from his mouth. No eyes turned to him as he maintained his peaceful pose. He simply held to his old, wooden staff. And outside of the spiraling cabin at Undrum, the eye of a stone statue to the right of the house became fully alive. As the vivid color of red consumed its iris, the pupil of the statue widened like an overflowing pool. Opening his eyes, Hayden's emotion remained unchanged. He turned his head to Ryan. Realizing Hayden's eyes were upon him, Ryan turned and smiled. The sky was clear and void of all matter.

A few seconds after Hayden had opened his eyes, a soft wind began to flow over the Redeemer. Everyone remained in position, unmoved by the whistling air outside their ship. The wind then slowly began to increase in intensity; it was subtle at first, a soft rattle over the hull of the Redeemer. Then a second rattle penetrated the hull, shaking the deck every-so-slightly more. The third rush of wind came as a powerful gust of wind, shaking the deck of the Redeemer as if there were a massive earthquake outside of its door. It was then that the radar became predominant with the color of blue dots.

Pushing a button on the holographic image to his right, David released the straps on Ryan's seat. The straps danced into the air and gently returned to their place behind the chair. The sun was still high in the sky without a cloud in it; but it was no longer clear. Descending from the heavens like one hundred meteors at once, white horses with white wings dove from the sky into the province of Ordren below. Opening their mouths, they hurled balls of fire upon the city without relent. The first ball of flame hit the second door on the left end of the prison, leaving a gaping hole in it. Molten metal dripped from the top of the exposed gate. The answer to this came in the form of a company of blue flames rushing upward. The horses collided with the ventari in the air, undamaged by their genora blades as the machines made an attempt to attack. Phantoms and vizedrones followed close behind the ventari, catapulting into the air from sites throughout the city.

"The Ghosts of the Fallen are upon us," Hayden began softly, his eyes still upon Ryan. "Now is the time." Ryan nodded as he stood up and drew his green blade. "You have all you need now."

"I pray you both remain safe," Ryan said as he rubbed the blonde hair on David's head. He then walked over to Hayden, leaned over and gave him a great hug. Releasing his arms from the embrace, Ryan turned to the door of the Redeemer. He briefly glanced back, still smiling. "Thanks for everything you've shared with me. I will love you both always."

In Bethlehem, the preparations for the forthcoming of the beast were well underway. The city consisted of twelve primary skyscrapers, and all of the vehicles that would usually be flying from structure to structure were absent. Below were smaller steel structures and homes. Men armed with photon cannons ran about in the unpaved streets of the city alongside senturions, light brown dirt flying around the patrolmen. The senturions were Bethlehem's citizens' foremost defensive unit, and each was piloted by only one man; each senturion was shaped like a walking locust, standing about fifty feet off of the ground. Their outer hull was a solid gray titanium, and their appendages were exacted akin to the true insect. They had the limited ability to hover for a short period of time, but their internal technology was outdated. Their wings were incapable of true flight and they moved at a snail's pace on the ground; their thin legs advanced like those of a wounded animal. There were four steel walls connected around the city in a rectangle; they were marked by red flares at every corner of the wall. The Gathering of the White Dove defended the northern wall, the behemoth of a machine known as Lunase standing behind the palisade. Surrounding the machine on both sides, soldiers in white armor and goggles aimed their photon cannons at the sky. White light-emitting diodes surrounded the goggles, emanating light from four, curved line segments around each eye.

"This is Rock. I still don't have anything on my radar."

"Copy that," Isaac replied, standing alone in an orange chair on the deck of Abram on the eastern wall. "I have nothing, either."

"We're all clear on the west side," Jadus reported, sitting in his blue captain's seat.

"The south is clear as well," High Prophetess Sade said, piloting one of the leviathans. Her leviathan was the white one, and it was especially equipped for bombardment. "We do not know the exact moment he will strike. Keep on your guard."

The remainder of the flight of leviathans flew in a circle around the city, with ardrodrones flying along with them.

"We shall," Jadus replied. His body raised over the western wall, Soulsearcher turned his head from side to side; his aquamarine eyes vigilantly peered out into the distance for any sign of the enemy. "I'm just not seeing anything at the moment."

"Wait a minute," Rock said over the intercom only a second later. "I think I've got something."

In the blinking of an eye, the sky turned as black as night as if someone had just switched the lights in a lit room to the off position. There was no sun, nor any stars or moon. There was an eerie silence about the city as citizens braced themselves for things they knew were creeping their way. All remained quiet as Lunase's glowing red eyes illuminated the barren space of light-brown dirt before it. Inside of Lunase's deck, Rock removed his glasses as he stared at the radar before him; he wanted to speak, but the words could not come fast enough. A number was displayed under the radar, and it brought on a devastating shock as Rock stared at it in horror. It was as if the enemy were toying with him. The count of vessels that were flying inbound was exactly six-hundred and sixty-six thousand.

"He's here!" Rock yelled at the top of his lungs from within his ship, pressing a button in the middle of the right holographic image before him. "All ground forces engage your ion shields now! Get ready for war!"

Deep in the chambers of Ordren, hope faded fast as Nazere's internal display indicated in bold red lettering that his core power was under twenty percent. His eyes completely out of focus, he couldn't see much of anything. But out of his peripheral vision, he continued to make out the outline of the mysterious dove on his shoulder. His eyelids dropped and rose again as he fought harder than ever to stay conscious. He swore he could feel blood running from his back as his nerves screamed out in bitter anguish. Holding tightly to the memory of Elle's beautiful face, he continued to endure the trial of being drained of everything he had left. All he really wanted was to undo the actions he had taken the night he was first introduced to the House of Arthur. But Vice Lord Xar's words echoed like a thousand whispers in his head. Some mistakes cannot be undone, and that harsh reality sank in like an obliterated ship into the depths of the ocean. Finally closing his eyes, Nazere gave in to the symphony of unbearable pain that ripped through his entire body.

At that very moment, the dove flew from Nazere's shoulder. Nazere didn't look up; he didn't have the strength to. But as the dove took flight, the door to Nazere's holding chambers came open. Opening his eyes, Nazere looked to the door. In a blur, a glowing green object peeked around the corner. Following the green object, a figure slowly moved himself into the entrance of the chambers. He was crawling on the floor, with a box in one hand and his sword in the other. A trail of smeared blood followed his every stride as he moved toward Nazere on his hands. Hand by hand, the body gripped the floor, inching its way across the floor to within ten feet of Nazere. The blood followed from him like a spool of torn red ribbon in a seemingly endless coil. Nazere didn't need to focus his eyes to know it was his dear friend.

"Hello again, my brother," Ryan said as he greeted Nazere, looking up at him with a smile. "I am glad to see you again."

Unable to speak, the image of his bloodied face painted a canvas that uttered a thousand susurrations in Nazere's head.

"I have several final gifts for you from your father," Ryan began, struggling to speak as he dropped his sword to the floor and held up the black box with the shielded cord attached to it. "You must plug this core into your back. It will restore your energy completely. The second gift is a downloaded message from your father. Use it only when you need it most." Ryan tried to emphasize, but he coughed as he tried to maintain the breath within him. "In my pocket there is a note. See that Lily gets it. The others have not been harmed. They are on the third floor. I tweaked the box to give you their precise location. The cameras are down. With the enemy preoccupied outside the gates, you have time to set them free. The Redeemer waits outside. But I have one final favor to ask of you before I go."

"Anything," Nazere fought to reply in a barely audible voice.

Ryan held his eyes up to Nazere as he said, "Do the things that you were always meant to." With his last motion, Ryan outstretched his hand and used his power to pull the handle to Nazere's right down. His arm then dropped to the floor as he gave up his last breath. A pool of blood accumulated under his body like a steadily flowing ravine. Time seemed to slow down all over again as Nazere pulled himself from his bonds, ripped the tape from his eyes, and ran to Ryan's motionless figure. He wrapped his arms around Ryan's body. As he slowly looked down at his fingers, he noted they appeared as if someone had colored each one in scarlet. He sat there for some time, rocking Ryan's body back and forth in his arms, just holding to the lifeless body of the brother he once had.

Inside the hull of a dreadnaught, miles away from Bethlehem and approaching the city quickly, a figure sat upon a cushioned black chair. The deck of the dreadnaught was purely studded steel, and there was complete silence about it. This figure's hands rested softly on the cushioned armrests of the black chair, the white surface of the hands bearing the tattoo of a barcode upon them. Wearing a black uniform adorned with military ribbons and medals on his breast, this man had three projected holographic images in front of him. One displayed the city of Bethlehem, and it was this image that the man was focused on.

The most distinguished of the medals that decorated his chest had the face of a dragon breathing fire embossed into its shining, silver surface. This man had blue eyes and gray hair that was of moderate length, slicked back on his head. The wrinkles upon his face demonstrated the older age of the man. Petty officers in black uniforms surrounded his chair on the left and the right. Their eyes were set on the electronic control panels before them, actively pressing an array of colorful square buttons in front of them.

"This is Fleet Admiral Clayton," the decorated captain said. "We await your command to descend, oh great one."

Onboard yet another dreadnaught, a shrouded figure wearing all black sat upon an ornamental throne. His face could not be seen. The throne he sat upon was comprised of intertwined silver and gold. The left foot of the throne was a solid gold dragon's claw, and the right foot was a silver dragon's claw. Together, the silver and gold clashed above the head of the chair in the shape of a dragon's head. The dragon's head had its mouth opened, but no flame came from it; its eyes and tongue were sterling silver, and its face was pure gold. Below the dragon's head, this enigmatic figure appeared to have no interest in the three suspended panels before him. His dragon-tattooed hands gripped the gold and silver armrests of his throne as he sat with a perfectly-upright posture. He too had petty officers sitting in his midst, but these officers wore tattered, gray rags in honor of his very presence. From behind the black figure, a trembling voice called out.

"It is r-ready to be f-forged, V-vice Lord X-xar," the man called out, shaking like a dog. He was dressed in an all white lab-coat, pants and shoes. He was bald, and wore a wristwatch that was an exact clone of Chief Scientist Olar's. He too had the tattoo of a barcode, but it was placed on the left side of his neck; his position was twelve feet from the throne.

"Oh little town of Bethlehem," Vice Lord Xar began slowly in his deep, sadistic voice. "Admiral Clayton, hold all your forces in position. We will come on the city like an unstoppable plague when I am fully prepared. Remember that none of the holy sites are to be damaged. Is that clear?"

"Crystal, my lord," Admiral Clayton replied over his intercom.

Vice Lord Xar hastened to rise from his chair, throwing himself up like a raven at the sight of its prey. He then stepped to the left. Curving around the side of his throne, he made large strides in walking toward the quivering scientist. His black robes left molten footsteps beneath them, the feet of the vice lord scalding the surface of the studded-steel surface beneath them.

"Follow me, worm!" Vice Lord Xar commanded as he passed the scientist. The fear-stricken man dropped to his knees and bowed his head down in submission before his master. He then stood up and navigated his steps around the heated path of the beast. As the vice lord continued to move rapidly, the quad-fold artolium entrance to the deck automatically opened to reveal a white hall behind it; these quad-fold doors consisted of four triangles that slid open whenever someone would walk within five feet of them. The narrow hall beyond had bloodguards equally spaced out on the left and right sides of the white-artolium hall. Vice Lord Xar walked directly down its center. The bloodguards were in the erected position of attention, their files extending to the end of the twenty-yard hall. Each of them took a knee and bowed their head to the floor as the beast moved swiftly past them. There were six quad-fold doors on the left and right that extended to the end of the hall. But the beast's head was pointed straight ahead, his feet continuing to leave molten imprints despite the thick artolium that made up the floor. The scientist continued to shiver intensely as he followed behind the vice lord, moving as best he could to keep up with the determined beast.

Reaching the end of the pathway, the quad-fold door at the end of the hall opened. A team of five scientists awaited Vice Lord Xar in a circular room with black artolium floors. Two closed quad-fold doors to the right and left of the circle led to various rooms throughout the dreadnaught. The scientists bowed before Vice Lord Xar upon his very appearance, their bodies surrounding a hovering artolium anvil; a hovering artolium melting pot filled with molten gold was set into place exactly two feet from the anvil. Brilliant golden sparks flew from the melting pot as the gold within it burned with intense heat. The anvil hovered about ten feet from the door Vice Lord Xar had just entered in from. Standing beside a scientist on the right of the circle was the transparent, black body of Commander Entril. He held out the sheathed Blade of the Unbroken in his right hand, his palm grasping its golden exterior. The assembly were standing in an immensely tall artolium room with a plain white, domed roof. An immense green-ethalon charge encased in clear artolium highlighted the room's center; it hovered eighty yards above the group bowing before Vice Lord Xar below. Its encasing was connected to two clear artolium pipelines above and below it. The anvil and the artolium melting pot filled with shimmering gold were ten yards from the lower pipeline. These pipelines directed a steady ethalon flow to power the dreadnaught and all of its weapons systems.

"The Head of the Churbim has been p-placed into the f-furnace," the tremor-ridden scientist beside Vice Lord said. "We have completed every d-diagnostic t-test on the sword. There is n-no f-feasible explanation for its power." Vice Lord Xar walked to Commander Entril and drew the Blade of the Unbroken from its sheath. Holding it in his hands, he looked on the blade for a moment as if mesmerized with its potency; his body carried the full radiance of the sword as he took the blade by the hilt and placed the blade into the pot. Three bolts of lightning flew from the roof of the domed room as the gold within the melting pot churned and swirled. The blade began to move as if it were alive, and Vice Lord Xar held tightly to it as it shook in his tattooed right hand. He then began to take on a new glow; his body became more brilliant than the surface of the sun, and the scientists surrounding the vice lord shielded their eyes as he held to the blade.

Drawing the blade out of the molten metal, Vice Lord Xar was astonished to find the blade had become twin-edged. He set the blade on the artolium anvil, but it only melted the artolium away. The blade needed no further refinement; it was complete. Vice Lord Xar held the blade with both of his hands as its weight was immense. Holding it straight in front of his shrouded head, he laughed wickedly in elation at the sight of the weapon.

"Behold!" Vice Lord Xar shouted, all of the scientists below him shielding their eyes with their hands. "You will listen to your lord's commands! I said open your eyes!" he screamed, his voice resounding like thunder. As each scientist slowly opened their eyes, their breathless bodies dropped immediately to the floor beneath them; they were stricken dead by the very sight of the sword. Commander Entril looked on the blade with a smile, amazed, able to see the blade through his electronic internal display. "Behold!" Vice Lord Xar shouted again as his hands gripped the sword's hilt tightly. "The Blessed Blade of the White Rider!"

The cell of the Orden prison was filled with blank faces and empty stares, the ion shield outside of the rectangular space seemingly taunting those within it with every flicker it made. Without any chairs or benches, bodies with sunken heads sat on the floor. In the right corner of the cell, Sara Maple rested her head softly on James' strong chest; James had his legs extended out in front of him like two heavy tree trunks as his eyes stared at the face of Adrax on the other side of the cell. His chin touched the top of Sara's flowing blond hair as she held her arms around him. Arthur and Adrax sat side by side, their backs leaning against the left wall behind them; their eyes were set on the floor, with no sign of emotion on their faces at all.

Lily sat alone in the left hand corner of the room, her hands wrapped around her knees and her chin touching them. She stared into the distance, her mind lost in the vast void of the unknown. In the center of the room, Felix and Owen had fallen asleep next to one another on the cold, artolium floor. Only a foot away from Lily on the left, Aaron too had his hands wrapped around his knees; he thought only of High Prophet Baun, the memory of his death cycling through his mind like a great ferrous wheel. On the right wall, Endarius' eyes spoke a thousand volumes; his knees were slightly bent, his hands resting on top of them. He looked at his hands only. He looked at the hands that had trained Ferris Shadowpath. It seemed as if he were looking beyond his hands as he drifted periodically into his library of memories. Elle sat next to him on the right, closest to the ion shield.

Her hands were around her knees, her legs pulled close to her body. But her neck was erect, and her hazel eyes were searching.

Filled with life, they scanned the artolium doorway outside of the barren jail chambers with a flare of hope. As hours passed, she kept watching, searching, and waiting. She could feel the heart within her chest pound heavily as she anticipated what she was convinced was coming. The fingers around her knees moved like a bunch of restless wings; flapping back and forth, they danced around her legs as she held to the faith she kept locked deep within her spirit. Every few seconds or so she became convinced that something was moving outside of the shield. The guard watched her face, laughing to himself whenever he captured the gist of her innermost thoughts. But this didn't dishearten her; her eyes were set on the door.

Hours passed, and as they did, Elle kept her vision locked. And when a leg kicked the door to the chambers open, her heart jumped in her chest. The guard didn't even have time to turn. His eyebrows down, his palm raised in the guard's direction, Nazere unleashed the full fury of his eye; when the sterai blast subsided, not even the chair the guard sat in remained. The concentrated beam left a gaping hole in the artolium wall beyond the guard. Everyone in the cell stood as Nazere deactivated the ion shield and walked into their presence. He was at full power, the hole left by the needle completely repaired as if nothing had ever penetrated his back.

His face was empty of emotion as he looked upon his comrades. His right fist was clenched as his left held a piece of blood-blotted paper in it. Looking to Lily, he dropped to his knees. Holding the piece of paper out in his twin palms like an offering, he leaned back on his calves in silence.

"This is a message for you, Lily," Nazere said softly and slowly, his head lowered as if it carried the weight of the world.

A confused look overtook Lily's face as she approached the parchment. Her mind racing wildly, she gently reached out her hand and picked up the folded piece of paper. She paused for a moment before she unwrapped it; she was convinced it couldn't be from him; she knew him better than anyone else had ever known him. Slowly unfolding the piece of paper, she placed her left hand over her mouth as she read the words on the blood-dotted paper. The paper simply read, "Forever could never be long enough." At this, she dropped to her knees. Tears streamed from her face, and Elle hurried to comfort her. Wrapping her arms around Lily, Elle gently rubbed her back. Sara hid her head in James' chest as she couldn't bear to see the painful emotions written on Lily's face.

"It will be okay," Elle whispered slowly. "It will all be okay."

"I am sorry for everything," Nazere softly said as he took a gradual stand. He looked into Arthur's eyes, his heart dropping in his chest all over again. Walking up to Nazere, High Prophet Arthur slowly wrapped his arms around him.

"You were already forgiven," Arthur whispered with his head beside Nazere's. Backing off of Nazere, a new appearance overtook Nazere's face — fear.

"We have to leave here immediately," Nazere said for all to hear. "The Redeemer awaits us outside." Arthur nodded in reply.

"Make haste, my children," Arthur began. "Bethlehem awaits us. Unfortunately, we have no time to spare." Slowly rising to her feet alongside Elle, Lily attempted to gather the strength to go on.

The group moved like wildfire through the brush as they descended the floors of the Ordren prison. Elle held Lily's hand the entire way, rushing down each flight of stairs in the jail with the utmost speed. It didn't take long to reach the bottom. In front of the group, Nazere took the first few steps through the obliterated gate that led outside. His eyes expanded as they looked into the sky. All was black, and there were no stars nor moon. He watched as a horse with wings descended from the heavens and landed beside him. The horse's eye was as red as fire as it looked upon Nazere, and its body and wings were completely white. As he thought to himself, Nazere realized that these were, indeed, the statues in the courtyard to the right of the cabin. The group caught up to Nazere quickly, shocked faces astounded with the vision before them.

The ground was littered with the bodies of burning ventari. Parts and pieces of phantoms and vizedrones covered the visible terrain, all of them in flames. A cavalry of horses flew in a circle around the now annihilated city; every structure but the jail was up in smoke, utterly consumed by conflagration. All that remained of the once existent stasis chambers was an orb of obsidian shards. And as soon as every prophet had caught up to Nazere, a hail of fire was directed at the prison. Explosions like a symphony of vengeance overtook the jail, driving it into the floor within seconds. Coming out of the darkness of their cloaks, the gatherings' vessels were all opened and ready for transport. The Colossus' staircase was down, the Redeemer's door was opened, and the Deliverer's lift was hovering.

Climbing outside of the Redeemer, Hayden walked slowly beside his dark staff to the site of the horse that stood before Nazere. He smiled as he softly ran his hand through its white hair. Looking on the horse with curiosity, Nazere began to take steps toward the beautiful animal.

"Tell me, Hayden," Nazere began as he reached out his arm toward the horse. "What are these creatures?"

The horse's pupil widened as it turned its body to face Nazere. Backing away from the animal, Hayden remained unresponsive; he simply continued to smile. It was then that the horse opened its mouth.

"We are but a drop in the ocean," the horse replied with great bass to his voice. "We are the forgotten ones. We are the betrayed. We are the silenced. And we have waited a great time for rebirth. Today, the first call to return has been answered. We are those who have suffered. We are the tormented. We are them without a voice. We are the Ghosts of the Fallen, and on this night, we shall have our revenge."

CHAPTER NINE

Him Called the Beast

A calm, still peace enveloped the very air in the city of Bethlehem, a tranquility that seemed out of tune with the erratic heartbeats of the soldiers that awaited his coming. Bracing their cannons with the utmost precision in aiming high above the northern steel wall, the white-armored warriors of the Gathering of the White Dove demonstrated visible signs of fear; the scorching-hot climate was not the reason for the sweat that poured from these soldiers' foreheads like rainfall from blackened storm clouds. Every single armored chest was moving back and forth heavily as if gasping for an unattainable breath; each facial expression was a ceramic mask, a guise fixated to protect the turbulent anxiety within each soldier's mind. Their lips were sealed in place like a finished-brick foundation, each pair immovable and inanimate; their eyes were set far into the distance as they awaited their call to fire. The contour of every right elbow was at a perfectly uniform forty-five degree angle, ensuring the security of the weapons they held in their shielded hands; their knees were bent ever-so-slightly; every left foot was straight forward, forming a concise right angle with the right. These soldiers were as solid as steel in form, but as pliable as watered-down clay in mentality. Like the acknowledgment of whistling wind before a tornado, no man or woman within the walls of the city knew the exact time of the catastrophe to come.

Intensely sharp red eyes stared out into a sky that had transitioned into an empty void of nothingness; its beak pointed straight ahead, the crystal body of the machine called Lunase refracted the light from the twelve skyscrapers behind it. Its head motionless, even the machine seemed to have an understanding of the events about to unfurl. The pristine glass skyscrapers were lit like a series of candles bunched together, projecting incandescence throughout the deathly-silent city of Bethlehem. The lights from one reflective skyscraper would bounce off another, revealing portraits of the senturions that sluggishly paced through the streets below. Under the cover of blackness, each senturion's antenna was extended and illuminated by powerful light-emitting diodes within their steel encasing.

Within the cockpit of the crystal dove, the gloom infected atmosphere was as thick as a Sequoya tree. Observing the number of the enemy on the three-dimensional image to his right, the captain's spine was hunched over as if his back had given out. His glasses still removed, Rock looked down at a radar that spelled impending doom. Rubbing his face with his hands, he leaned back in his chair for a moment to let the gravity of the circumstances before him soak in. With his head cocked back in his seat, the silence he heard over the intercom was like a nail being driven into his skin. And the more time passed, the more his anguish penetrated his drifting mind; there was no turning back now, and he knew it. Finding the strength to drop his hands and rise in his chair, he placed the glasses he had set to his side back upon his face; he then took action in the anticipation of the forthcoming onslaught by activating the holographic buttons for the weapons systems of his vessel. Eight crosshairs responsively began to move around on the display to his right, scattering like a fearful flock of geese as all of Lunase's targets were out of range.

Miles away, the sky was flooded with the neon-green luminescence of dreadnaughts, their bronze hulls glinting faintly; vizedrones and phantoms encircled each one of the titanic vessels like flies around an outdoor lamp — waiting. And with them, in his own formation, flew the commander of death; the black ventari marked by the white outline of a black flame stormed in a burning spiral. Within the secure enclosure of his deck, Fleet Admiral Clayton looked at the holographic display of Bethlehem — the city miles from his location. He too was waiting. Waiting for a message from another vessel; a dreadnaught that carried the body of Vice Lord Xar. Fleet Admiral Clayton laughed to himself as he began to speak over his intercom.

"They have asked who is like you," he started in his native British accent, directing his words cleverly — as coolly as chilled spring water — over the communication channels. "It is laughable to see these religious zealots fight against you. By our master, and by your grace, we are impenetrable. And yet, the society that is under the order of the Scientific Magisterium still asks the question: Who is like you?"

Sitting upon his silver and gold throne, he who is called the beast laughed to himself sadistically — the gears of his mind cranking with deafening volume like a brisance; his laughter shook the very hull of the artolium dreadnaught like an earthquake. All of the petty officers who had been in his midst only minutes earlier were scattered about the studded steel floor, silently stricken dead from irradiation; preternatural radiation that originated from the sword held in Vice Lord Xar's left hand. He held to the Blessed Blade of the White Rider lightly by spinning the surface of the hilt into the floor of the deck with his dancing fingers. The place where the two-edged end of the sword touched the steel floor's surface didn't melt; it instantly evaporated.

"Who is like me?!" the beast asked in a roaring voice as the hull of the ship began to crack into pieces. His whitened robes threw out sparks of the purest white light, the temperature of his mercurial anger rising into the red. "There are none like me! I am the great calculator! He who has given mankind all of its greatness — all of its desires! I am a god, and on this day, I will demonstrate my unrelenting vengeance on those who have challenged the total extent of my boundless wrath!" As the dreadnaught around him fell apart like a toy model being rapidly disassembled, the beast took a firm, gradual stand. Shards of the dreadnaught flew through the sky, tearing through the air molecules around them as they further disintegrated through the combined power of the beast and his blade. Leaning over, gripping the sword with both hands and curling his legs toward his stomach, he began to open his mouth. And like a banshee, he slowly screamed, "SEND EVERYTHING!" A shockwave tore into all nearby vessels like a hurricane as Vice Lord Xar's outburst officiated the call to war; the ion shields of all nearby aircraft flickered repeatedly in response to the devastatingly powerful cry. A light like the face of a star marked the beast's location in the sky, his body hovering amidst the uncountable hordes in flight around him that were his chosen bringers of death. The dreadnaught that once encased his body had become ashes that span around him in a savage cyclone. Upon his issued command, thousands of fell dreadnaughts began moving toward their directive, their glowing green tentacles swimming through the air. The red eyes of vizedrones and the ocean-blue tentacles of phantoms dominated the sky as they made their descent upon the city of Bethlehem.

About four-hundred yards from the city, circular artolium pods dropped in perfect harmony onto the ground below like many hail stones falling at once during a momentous disturbance in the weather. Mist escaped the pods as their four oval-shaped doors opened like a blossoming flower, each door landing in the light-brown dust beneath them. As the dreadnaughts continued to fly, their metal under carriages slid back. Like a rain of fire from the heavens, the sky came to life in a symphony of blue flames followed by jet-like blue trails. The ventari encircled one another in the air, spiraling and twirling as if to mock the city below them; but their display of prowess was short, and they began their drive into the heart of the city with startling speed. Their very approach made the sky appear as if it had burst into a wave of blue flame.

In the inner-reaches of space, one-hundred horses with white wings and red eyes bent on judgment rounded the outlines of four vessels. As could be seen from their spot in space, a great white beam of pure radiance highlighted the exact location of the beast on the face of the earth. The tall, sparkling light transmuted the earth, making it appear as if it were anything but home. In the center of the flying ensemble, the Redeemer spread her wings as widely as they had ever been spread; to her left, the Deliverer growled, its mouth filled with the fission of red particles as it set its eyes on the earth below it; on the right, the mighty Colossus opened its six shoulder cannons as it prepared for the frenzy of men, animals, and machines that awaited it on the surface of mankind's home planet. Now was the time to act; now was the time to face the daunting nightmares; now was the time to preserve the threatened city; now was the time to see to the completion of a prophecy that had yet to be fulfilled. And below the Redeemer, he who had been chosen to lead the charge clenched his fists at his sides.

And in a wall of shadow and smoke, a barely-visible darkened figure appeared next to the chosen in the starless space. Turning his eyes to his right, a blank stare overcame Nazere as he looked upon Keldrid; flapping in the nothingness, Keldrid's black robes seemed to prance around his morbid being. Reaching behind his back, the shrouded angel drew forth the sacred sword Entryu with his right hand. As he turned his faceless shroud toward the earth, Keldrid's blessed blade began to take on a blood-red glow. Nazere stood firm beside Keldrid, watching as the angel gripped his sword tightly. Keldrid then outstretched his arm and pointed the edge of his blade at the beaming light on the face of the earth. At this inclination, Nazere smiled.

"The time has come, human," Keldrid began in his dark tone, the pitch-black face of his hood redirected at Nazere. "We shall be outnumbered and outmatched, as you well know. But I told you that I would never leave your side. Together, we shall bring him who is called the beast to his knees."

"I should have listened to you," Nazere began apologetically, shaking his head as his eyes remained set on Keldrid. "I have so much yet to learn. I have no idea as to what forces are already against the city, but I am confident in our combined ability to defeat whatever serves to overcome it. I only ask that the Master deliver us from the enemies that await us."

"Your call shall be answered," Keldrid replied slowly. "The events of this day have long been written. Tonight, we shall dance with the horseman called War."

And as if it were written long before it transpired, the Redeemer let out an immaculate battle-cry in the form of a high-pitched screech a single moment after Keldrid spoke. Within the cabin of the Redeemer, the high prophet of the Gathering of the White Knight looked down upon Earth with a bittersweet ambiance surrounding his demeanor; his face was calm and unmoved, but his eyebrows were serious and tightened at the sight of the light on the earth. Looking upon the person she loved on the display to David‘s left, Elle's heart raced in her chest; she wished that he was sitting next to her, holding her hand as he always did. In his stead, she lightly tapped her right hand on the armrest beside her. The captain's hands were where they most often were, swiftly maneuvering the complex controls to his beloved ship. Taking a brief break from his duties, David turned his eyes to the empty chair that once seated his friend. He imagined him still being there, listening to his music whilst dreaming of a life with Lily.

"Shadows fall where he used to be," David said slowly, still looking at the empty chair. "It seems the moments you cherish the most in memory are there for a split second, then vanish before you have the time to love them while they're still here." Hayden nodded.

"Sacrifice is the name of our game," Hayden began in a smooth, slow voice, veering around him in addressing Elle and David. "Hold to the memories of those you love, for you never know when He will bring them home. I will forever hold to your memories. You have been the only children I've ever had, but every instant with the both of you has far surpassed the blessing I thought it would be. I'll take the time before it's too late to say that I love you both with every ounce of my beating heart. There is much pain in store for a damaged world; what hurts the most is that so many cannot see it. Smile in the face of our adversaries, for they are no different than we are in nature. They may take your lives, but the spirit is not limited by that which they take. More than anything I wish that things were different for mankind. But here we stand."

Looking to his control schematics, David resumed the operation and control of the Redeemer. Elle continued to watch as Nazere stood suspended in space, wishing she could reach out to him—even if it were only for a moment.

"All linked vessels," David began with a face of determination. "I am beginning the descent into the city. We knew this was coming. Our relay point is in the center of the city. Sara, prepare your spirits. Adrax and James will rendezvous with their soldiers once they have reached the south side of the city. I am certain the other gatherings are already deep in combat. Let's show the Scientific Magestirium what we're made of."

"This is Drake. You know I'm always with you, my friend. Let us bring salvation to our brothers in Bethlehem. This is the beginning of what all of time has come down to."

"For High Prophet Baun," the Colossus said.

"For all that is Love," Elle said smiling.

"For our Master," High Prophet Hayden said.

"Redeemer," David began firmly. "take us straight down. We're heading into the city."

"Affirmative, captain," the Redeemer replied. "Now engaging the descent."

The hull of the Redeemer remained firm as the bird threw its wings forward and began to propel itself toward the greatest light on the earth. Standing in place like a statue, Nazere's mind on was on Elle. Nazere watched the three vessels and the Ghosts of the Fallen flew past him and into the atmosphere. As his non-existent heart jumped in watching Elle burn through the atmosphere onboard the Redeemer, he turned to Keldrid. As if reading his mind, and perhaps he was, Keldrid looked upon Nazere and nodded. Still standing in the exact place he was, a blue flame consumed the machine that was Nazere's body; at the same time, Keldrid became a subtle beacon of shadow and smoke; the two waited for the flight below them to fly out of sight. And as soon as they did, their mighty descent began.

In a spiral of black and blue, the angel and his man began their rapid flight into the atmosphere. Like a tornado's end about to touch down, the two beings flew around one another at an alarming pace as they neared the clouds. They caught up to their allied vessels and flew beyond them at maximum speed. Nazere's head was straight forward, his focused eyes directed at the city in the distance. The angel kept his head up also, flying in perfect parallel with Nazere as if they were two precisely aligned rockets. The two came to a shockwave of a halt about a mile outside of the city, instantly regaining their equilibrium as they stood erect and set their eyes on the city of Bethlehem. The flight was not far behind, the cry of the Redeemer within an earshot of where they stood eighty feet off of the ground.

His eyes widening at the very sight of the city, explosions echoing through the airwaves, Nazere kept his fists clenched at his sides. The city was like a flare, the lights of rapid cannon fire, ethalon charges and other weaponry flashing in and out at a constant rate. This was a far cry from the Battle of Ordren; this was the sight of a complete catastrophe, covered in black and white. Screams in the distance accompanied the eardrum-shattering sound of concentrated blasts. The noise shook the very ground beneath Nazere and Keldrid. Rocks and sediment bounced off of the ground every other second, the strong sound-waves of detonations in the not so distant city of Bethlehem seemingly covering everything within view. Smoke rose from one of the twelve skyscrapers in Bethlehem, but it was barely visible amidst the chaos of the battle already underway. The vizedrones, ventari and phantoms were an infectious hive, blanketing the city like flies on a dead carcass.

"Impossible," Nazere said as he looked at the city in horror. "My display is indicating that there are six-hundred and fifty-nine thousand enemy vessels in the city. There is no way we can surmount that number of enemies. We must tell the others to turn back!" Keldrid laughed.

"Nothing is impossible, human," Keldrid began in his deep voice. "They have eliminated over seven thousand enemy ships already, and the city stands yet. Take heart, human. All is not as lost as you might think it is. Perceptions are strange things; you fear what you do not yet realize."

Landing beneath Nazere, the Redeemer's door popped back and rolled open. The Colossus dropped its staircase and the Deliverer its hovering lift. The Ghosts of the Fallen surrounded the vessels on the ground, keeping their wings lifted as they trotted around in all directions.

"God speed," David said as Elle and Hayden made their way to the door of the Redeemer. "Hear me for a moment," he said, projecting the plan of defense he had formulated in his head. Elle and Hayden turned around in pause as he explained the details of his operation. "Drake, myself and the Colossus will have to infiltrate the hordes that surround the city walls. We will take the enemies at the gate. Sara Maple will be able to get everyone over the wall shielded. Someone must take to the Master's birthplace. The beast will try his best to seal that location, and his desecration will be stopped! Drake? Do you hear me?"

"Loud and clear," Drake replied. "I've established a data connection with Lunase, Abram, Soulsearcher, the queen and the rest of the leviathans. I don't have communications up yet, but it appears they all have their ion shields down and have sustained heavy hull damage. They have lost several hundred ground soldiers already; the number of the living is dropping rapidly. We must allow the damaged ships time to get to the center of the city to deploy their atrons; three high prophets are standing their ground there. The androdrones are too busy defending themselves against the horde at the moment to help any other vessels."

"Hear this," a ghost called out miraculously over the intercom. "We will obliterate all of the invading swarm as sure as the sky is black. We will ensure that there is time for the prophets to make it to their proper places."

"So be it," David replied as Hayden and Elle started to climb out of the Redeemer.

All of the occupants of each vessel met in a tight circle around Sara Maple on the ground below. With lance in hand, James stood by her side; in his own mind, he wished he could be close to her to ensure her safety. The others encircling the couple awaited explanation from Sara for the route of travel into the city. Dropping to the ground next to them, Nazere smiled in the faces of his friends. Hayden slowly walked toward Nazere with his staff in hand; he then held out a small, black cube in his palm. Softening his left fist, Nazere outstretched his arm and took hold of the cube. There was no time to waste.

"Bring forth the animals!" Lily shouted, holding her summtorant in her hand. The others hastened to draw forth their devices, and as they called out, one-by-one the animals came. "Come to me my precious! Come, Tygrys!"

"To my aid, Borexis!" Adrax yelled, his brilliant red saber in his right hand.

"Bloodfang! Bring forth the first death!" Endarius shouted.

"Judgmane! My friend!" James yelled. "Come forth and help us now."

"Elothis!" Hayden yelled, mounting his white steed as soon as it came forth.

"Come, Cadra!" Arthur commanded, walking up the fiery footsteps of the steed as soon as they were presented before him.

"Let's go, Umerald," Elle said softly. She mounted her green tiger as soon as came forth.

"Verus!" Nazere yelled. "Come on, boy!"

All of the animals stood in a circle around their counterparts, calm and still as they were far from battle. But the eyes of the Ghosts of the Fallen appeared to be growing impatient, as if they had waited for an eternity to engage in battle; oh, and how they had. Elle approached Nazere closely, looking him eagerly in the eyes as she leaned into his ear.

"Could I have one kiss before you go?" Elle whispered in her silk tone.

"Not now, my love," Nazere replied back in whisper. "We will have plenty of time to spend together once this battle is complete." Elle stepped back, a melancholy look overcoming her face.

"Hear me!" Sara yelled out. The crowd immediately directed their attention toward Sara Maple, who held her hand in the air in announcement. "The city is overcome! We shall make our way to the center, and support will be provided by our ships. Each prophet must take flight with me over the wall. On my mark, we make the sprint for the gates; run with everything you've got in you." Sara knelt down and threw her hands behind her, a prismatic orb projecting itself over the whole of the group. "This shield will become empowered as we move, amplifying our speed many times over! As we reach our destination, everyone break to their designated locations!"

"Aaron, Owen, Endarius and Felix shall join us on the southern wall," James said.

"Arthur will join the high prophets in the center of the city," Hayden interjected, raising his staff. "They will ensure the location is safe for all vessels to make necessary repairs as the war ensues. Elle and myself will make our way to the Master's birthplace and secure it."

"I will take the ventari," Nazere started, his fists clenched once again. "I will provide as much support against the enemy as possible."

"I will ensure the healing of all those around me," Lily began. "Elle and I must separate to offer assistance to all those in need; we will not be together. Elle must ensure Hayden is safeguarded at the holy site."

"There is no time to waste!" Arthur exclaimed. "Once in the city, you must move quickly! We have six-hundred thousand vessels to eliminate and lives are being wasted while we speak."

"But above all," Hayden began slowly, making a quick glance at Nazere. "no matter what happens, never lose the faith."

While the gathering had been talking, the ships around the group had shut their doors and were preparing for takeoff. As the Redeemer began to move, the Colossus hovered above the ground. The Deliverer then dashed toward the city as if it were after a gazelle — the first of the gatherings' vessels to enter the fray.

"Everyone get ready!" Sara exclaimed, a strong tone to her resounding voice. Letting out a loud shriek, the Redeemer lifted its talons off of the ground and took to the air in the direction of Bethlehem. The Colossus followed directly behind it, performing a straight rush into the city. "Go! Go! Go!"

Altogether, all of the group but Nazere began to sprint as fast as they could. The sphere passed Nazere by, leaving him staring at the haunted city. Looking down at Nazere, Keldrid unveiled his hand and curled his pointer finger toward himself; Nazere lifted off the ground and joined Keldrid by his side. Seconds into the sprint, the shield around the rest of the group lifted off the ground like a shining bubble. Once in flight, everyone stopped moving as Sara closed her eyes in a deep focus in the center of the orb. The sphere span through the air at an incredible speed, passing the Ghosts of the Fallen, the ships and masses of bloodguards, stormdivers and dreadhunters outside the steel wall that guarded Bethlehem.

Everyone within the shield was stunned as they began to close in on the bloody battle. Energy in many forms hit the sides of the shield as it was moved forward, rippling the sides of the solid orb in an array of color. Sara set the bubble down in the dead-center of the city, where three high prophets stood back to back in intense combat. Sara raised her arms as ethalon fire from all directions began to hit the shield hard, the noise echoing throughout the air like the heavily-amplified pop of a cork. High Prophet Joseph doubled the shield held up by Sara, raising his arms in defiance of the oncoming storm of blasts.

All around the shield were the bodies of dead men and senturions that had been torn into shreds; the street was filled with blood and bits of scrap metal. Just as Sara landed, the skyscraper in flames came crashing to the ground like a fallen Titan. Smoke and ashes flew in all directions, but the shield kept all exhaust from the defeated skyscraper from entering. Above the shield, the blackened sky was not visible; all that could be seen were the bodies of vizedrones, ventari and phantoms. The Redeemer let out a mighty call as it entered the city, the rest of the corresponding flight following directly behind it.

Like a flood of fervor, the Ghosts of the Fallen spat fire from their mouths as soon as they entered the city. A cavalry of vengeance, they unleashed balls of the purest flame with immaculate accuracy. The entire group within the shield looked up briefly as the grouped bodies of at least one-thousand phantoms, ventari and vizedrones exploded into bits and pieces as a single winged horse flew by.

"Everyone break now!" Sara yelled, looking up at the light of the beast that still hovered over the city. "To your positions! And beware the light of the beast! Do not enter its vicinity!" The group nodded, scattering in all directions with weapons at the ready as Sara held her shield in position; the majority of the assembly headed south to guard the wall there with the summoned animals by their side, James and Adrax leading the rush. Hayden stepped off of Elothis and patted her on the rear end. Elothis then dashed to the south, her four tails flying around in the air as she galloped away.

"Send Umerald with the rest of the summoned," Hayden said as he turned to Elle. Hopping off of Umerald, Elle nodded.

"Go, my baby!" Elle commanded as she patted her tiger on the back. Umerald glanced back with a confused look on her face; her eyes appearing broken, she then turned and ran in pursuit of the other animals. Together, Elle and Hayden sprinted east into a small house. Once they were there, they slowly walked inside and glanced around. The room was lit by a few white candles on a small wooden table in the back of the room; the house was barren, with no major distinctive qualities to it. The floor was made of stone, and had the emblem of a cross surrounded by a barn plainly etched into it.

"This is the place," Hayden said as he looked around. "The birth site of the Master, and the site the beast wishes to capture first and foremost." Elle slowly paced around, the noises of explosions and gunfire from outside the structure echoing throughout the room. The house had no door; there was only an opened entrance where a door should be.

"So we stay here?" Elle asked.

"Yes," Hayden replied. "I will keep a hold on the door for as long as possible." Taking hold of his dark staff and tossing it to the door, Hayden closed his eyes. In an instant, his staff took the form of a thick wall of flame to keep outsiders from coming in; the wall of fire crackled and persisted without the need for fuel. "Now," Hayden began slowly, his eyes set on Elle. "we wait."

The war was in full swing just outside the entrance to the small house, burdened vessels relieved at the arrival of reinforcements. "Bout time you got here!" Rock yelled to David and Drake over the intercom with a smile on his face, his crosshairs locking onto the fifteen vizedrones that were crawling all over Lunase. Their sharp teeth and claws were doing everything they could to drive the wounded dove to the ground. Rapid photon cannon fire from the white-armored soldiers below attempted to fend off further vizedrones; but the soldiers were preoccupied by phantoms that continued to advance over the wall with their tentacles, driving the blue-ringed arms down in deadly dives. The air around Lunase was completely saturated with bolts of white energy from the hand-held cannons carried by the Gathering of the White Dove's infantry as phantoms continually lunged their appendages toward the white-armored soldiers. "I have lost a few men on the front wall, but we're holding the city. My ion shields are down and my hull capacity is down to twenty-three percent!" Taking a pause from speech, Rock fired eight white ethalon blasts from Lunase's wings; four vizedrones dropped to the floor in flames. "I can't hold out much longer! If I can repair, I might be able to get off two or three thratum lances."

"I will assume the position of the northern wall," the Colossus replied, flying with a ghost at his side toward the northern wall. The Colossus was being followed by a legion of three-hundred and fifty phantoms and twenty enormous vizedrones. The winged horse turned around for but a brief moment and consumed every last one of the machines in a magnified ball of red conflagration; it then returned to escorting the Colossus to the northern wall, an unseen smile rounding its face. "Get to the center of the city and initiate your repair sequence, Rock." The Colossus fired its six cannons at the vizedrones digging their claws into Lunase's hull, hurling a group of eight dragons from the dove. Three-hundred and eight vizedrones stood with their mouths open above Lunase, preparing to fire a series of charges at the northern wall. One of the charging dragons would drop every few seconds from the fire of photon cannons below, but the majority remained unscathed.

Dropping beside Lunase, the Colossus fired secondary shots at the two remaining dragons clawing the erect dove; the vizedrones exploded into fragments from the concentrated impact of the six blasts. Lunase was immediately covered by another twenty vizedrones thereafter, their tails and claws doing as much as they could possibly do to tear the machine apart. The Colossus opened up its head and launched an ethalon shot from its central cannon at the vizedrones tearing at the dove to draw their attention and aggravation. The dragons looked up and flew onto the Colossus as soon as they were fazed, attacking it from all sides. Lunase darted from the northern wall in the direction of the center of the city as soon as the Colossus was in position — the fortified whipping boy for Lunase. The winged horse flying around the Colossus breathed fire from its nostrils, hurling a singular ball at the hundreds of vizedrones charging their ethalon blasts in an attempt to destroy the northern wall and all who stood to defend it. The ball increased its size as it reached the site of the vizedrones, igniting every last one of them in an aura of flame. The horse then set its avenging eyes on the dragons attacking the Colossus, the gunmetal man spinning around in an attempt to shake the behemoths from its hull.

"This is Jadus Rathe! My hull integrity is down to ten percent! I need to repair now!" Soulsearcher was completely overtaken by vizedrones; pinned to the ground by hundreds of dragons piled on top of one another, there appeared to be no escape from the viscous and increadibly-heavy assault. Following the Redeemer, five ghosts stopped above Jadus on the western wall in parallel with the eagle; charging the ethalon cannon in its beak, the Redeemer fired in unison with the ghosts in its midst. Devastated parts of circuitry and scrap metal went flying in all directions like thousands of jigsaw-puzzle pieces being forcefully pitched out of their box, the burning head of a dragon flying past the Redeemer at a rip-roaring volume. As soon as Soulsearcher kicked several burning dragons off of its body, another flock of two-hundred vizedrones swarmed down and mobbed its body in an attempt to finish the machine. The Ghosts of the Fallen next to the Redeeemer flew down in defense of Soulsearcher, their bold bodies colliding with the herd of dragons. Hundreds of phantoms swarmed around the western wall, picking up blue-armored soldiers with their tentacles and tearing them asunder as they painted the brown dirt a dark crimson. Surviving soldiers were firing their photon cannons with all of their human might as sonic booms and streams of light dominated the air, holding to their position as they attempted to fend off the overwhelming population of phantoms.

"Get to the center now!" David yelled frantically. "I will hold this position down." The five ghosts at the western wall hurled balls of flame as fast as they could, destroying all of the vizedrones they had collided with and incapacitating over one-hundred phantoms that stood at the wall; however, the highly-populated swarm of phantoms continued their attacking advance as if untouched. The Redeemer began to charge another shot directly at the center of the phantoms as it stood suspended above the western wall. A few more balls of fire ensured that all of the vizedrones around Soulsearcher were down, providing the dark-blue dog with adequate space to move. Rising to its feet, the badly-marred Soulsearcher took advantage of the opportunity to run to the center of the city as blue-armored soldiers continued to provide cover.

Above the center of the city, the queen and the flight of leviathans were making a valiant effort to evade as many vizedrones and ventari as possible as they soared and defied sound in a wide-oval formation. The vast majority of the Ghosts of the Fallen joined them, firing upon all vizedrones within range as they turned their heads behind their backs periodically. The leviathans flew ahead of a swarm of over two-thousand vizedrones, evading all ethalon fire and outmatching their speed; but they couldn't outmatch the ventari. Strategically taking a moment to drop behind the swarm, the Ghosts of the Fallen hurled fireball after fireball at the enemy machines as their unquenchable thirst for payback showed itself; each ball of flame dropped over one-hundred machines at a time, immolating the once-human ventari and vizedrones and sending them to the ground in fragments of agony. Sterai beams originating from the palms of grouped ventari had dealt damage to the flight before the arrival of the ghosts; five leviathans had been hit by the particle beams and were continuing to fly despite severe internal damage — burning fuel pouring from their necks and wings.

After jumping over the eastern wall, the valiant Deliverer joined Abram and many lance-wielding warriors in eliminating vizedrones and phantoms in that region. The lances held by the orange-armored soldiers next to Abram were set to hit their targets and return to the thrower much like a boomerang; and in the same fashion as James' spear, the soldiers threw their glowing orange lances at their targets unceasingly only to have them return promptly. Despite having been utterly overwhelmed, the Gathering of the White Lamb had only suffered three casualties at the time of the Deliverer's arrival; Abram fired the ethalon cannon on its back into a shieldless group of hundreds of crippled, crawling vizedrones as Drake began to charge the jaws of his lion in the form of neon-red vindication.

"I'm heading to the center for repairs," Isaac announced from within Abram. "My hull is at sixteen percent."

"I have the wall, my brother," Drake replied, the Deliverer unleashing a red beam of energy upon multiple phantoms. "My ion shield is at ninety-two percent. I can offer you plenty of time. I'll be right here, Isaac."

The ventari were amassed in the center of the city, firing upon nearby leviathans and eliminating all of Bethlehem's remaining soldiers and senturions as rapidly as possible. On the ground, defenseless senturions would attempt to fire semi-automatic photon cannons back at the ventari; the impact had no effect on the superior machines, and the ventari were relentless in their heartless eradication of the soldiers of Bethlehem. Numbered in the thousands, their offensive sterai beams trailed the lightning-fast leviathans in the center of the city very closely. A ventari set his eyes on the queen's white leviathan, aiming precisely with his palm; the ventari had the queen within his very grasp, opening the eye of his palm in proper preparation.

Just as the eye of his palm blinked, a sword sliced through his core as if it were lukewarm butter. Thousands of ventari eyes widened in concert as they realized the gravity of what had just happened. High above the halved ventari's falling mass, Keldrid laughed as he turned his black hood in the direction of the stunned group.

"Too late," Keldrid said in a tone like death as his laugh came to a stern halt. From behind the thousands of ventari grouped in a circle came a fully-charged sterai beam — the resounding call of surprise.

The beam hit every single one of the stunned ventari, their cores popping like water balloons as the beam charged through them like an unstoppable bull. Raising his palm again, Nazere's angered eyes focused on another group of ventari near the southern wall. When the sterai beam was released from Nazere's palm, it detonated in a ball of pure light. Ventari fell to the ground and scattered in all directions, becoming alerted by the presence of their new enemy in the center of the city; he who wore the mask of the elite faced his opposition as if inviolable, beginning his next assault directly; there was no time for pause in his mind.

Beneath Nazere, vessels were undergoing the process of major repair. Sara Maple and High Prophet Joseph held the circular reflective shield in place as atrons covered Soulsearcher's body. Abram quickly charged into the center, deploying all of its atrons in order to ensure a timely repair so that he could return to his designated position. In the mean time, Lunase had been completely restored, rising to its feet and charging out of the shield and into its place on the northern wall. High Prophet Bruce hurled bolts of lightning at phantoms that continued to attack the shield held up by Sara, the high-intensity discharges arcing from one machine to another. High Prophet Arthur would freeze as many phantoms as he could see, leaving them immobilized and vulnerable to the slightest attack. High Prophet Benjamin would take control of a single phantom at a time, turning it against its own allies and using its own tentacles to shatter other phantoms that had been frozen by Arthur's gift.

"Keep the shield firm!" High Prophet Joseph commanded as bolts and flares in a wide variety of fierce flavors rippled the prismatic orb.

"I'm doing all that I can through the Spirit!" Sara exclaimed, her arms still high in the air.

As the ventari were off of her tail for the time being, the queen transitioned into a new flight pattern. The Ghosts of the Fallen continued to bombard wave after wave of vizedrones with spheres of flame, their hands full with providing cover for the allied vessels. From dreadnaughts high above, six green ethalon blasts hit a second structure in the city, sending it crumbling to the earth in ashes.

"All leviathans remain here," High Prophetess Sade commanded, her voice determined. "I am heading up for the first strike!"

"Affirmative, high prophetess," a damaged leviathan's persevering captain acknowledged, heat from flames expelled from the machine causing the pilot to sweat profusely.

The queen drove her leviathan full speed into the blackened sky, the sound-barrier breaking repeatedly as she headed directly for a dreadnaught. With three vizedrones behind her, she released a purple proteon blast that jolted the dragons' necks back. She continued to fly upward once she was no longer being tailed, landing on the exposed, bottom side of a dreadnaught. The long neck of her leviathan poked its head into the opened carriage of the immense ship; it then began to charge an ethalon blast in its mouth. The three vizedrones attempted to catch up in time, but their struggles were in vain; the queen had released her ethalon shot into the dreadnaught's carriage by the time their claws reached her leviathan.

The dreadnaught became nearly as white as the light from the beast, its windows cracking and its armor shattering as it became fully irradiated with the wrath of the queen; the illumination held for a few seconds, finally darkening as the ship blew away in trillions of twirling ashes. A ball of fire from the watchful eye of a ghost ascended in the queen's direction, hitting all three vizedrones that were upon her and sending them to the earth in shards and flames. As the queen's leviathan attempted to dart from her position back into the center of the city, eight vizedrones from above collided with her vessel and began to drive it downward.

"This is the queen!" High Prophetess Sade called out to anyone who could assist her. "I am being pinned under eight dragons and am requesting immediate assistance!" A leviathan answering the cry of distress flew out of its flight path and began making its way in the direction of the queen's white ship, its tail swerving as it flew as fast as it possibly could to save her.

In the center of the city, Abram was nearing full repair; the scratches, holes and frayed portions of its exterior were now restored. It recalled its atrons and began moving in the direction of the western wall, its horns gleaming a bright orange as they were prepared to go to work in incapacitating incoming enemies. At the same time, the Deliverer was being shredded apart by a flock of twelve vizedrones; its feral face had claw marks down the sides of it, exposing the raw metal underneath.

"Drake," Isaac began. "I'm at full power. Get your lion to the middle now!"

"I'm on it," Drake replied, the lion desperately trying to draw itself out of the frenzy. Running along the Deliverer's side, the ram called Abram unleashed the fury of its horns on the vizedrones covering the lion; in two concentrated ethalon beams, the ram tore through the shells of the dragons covering the Deliverer with the utmost accuracy.

Several miles above the city, Vice Lord Xar gripped the Blessed Blade of the White Rider with both of his hands as his sights were set upon the battle below. He looked at the center of the city, where he could see Nazere firing upon all nearby ventari. His eyes also beheld the image of Keldrid, the angel's robes fluttering around him as he held his hand next to Nazere's; he was empowering every sterai blast that came from the ventari warrior. Nazere fought as if he were far superior to any of the machines surrounding him, standing his ground in battle as if he had no fear; he fought in a passionate way that Vice Lord Xar had never seen any machine fight before. He then glanced over as a leviathan darted for the queen's pinned ship, setting his full focus on the speedy dragon. As the leviathan flew into the queen's range, it opened its mouth in preparation for a full-powered ethalon blast toward the vizedrones that had tackled her. Like a silent flicker, the vice lord bolted to that leviathan's backside without an inkling of a sound. And before the leviathan could release the charge in its mouth, the beast drove his sword into the back of the machine. The sound of thunder resounded for miles, bringing Keldrid's focus to a standstill and his gaze to the sight of the beast's first attack. The leviathan's mouth became colorless, and its lifeless shell began to drop; like an avalanche, the leviathan's body came pouring down to the dirt in a million disintegrated pieces. The beast then turned in Keldrid's direction, staring him down in a deadlocked pose as he held to the Blessed Blade of the White Rider. A ghost responsively flew past the beast and fired upon the dragons atop the queen's leviathan, uninhibited by the light of the beast. She swiftly lifted her leviathan upward and flew alongside the ghost, the horse escorting her to the center of the city. The beast paid no mind to the queen.

"Bring down the walls!" the beast screamed, unmoved in his stance. Outside of the perimeter of Bethlehem, tens of thousands of dreadhunters, bloodguards and stormdivers had awaited their time to attack. The stormdivers couldn't risk flying above the walls with the extensive weapon fire coming from behind each one. So they waited in flocks, their teeth-layered mouths opening and lightning from their fins arcing across the air outside of the walls; spread out along the entire perimeter, they thirsted for the blood of those within the walls. Explosive and heavily concentrated ethalon charges were attached to every wall in the form of a small black box with six arms. Running backwards substantially, a bloodguard with a cylindrical remote detonator pressed his thumb against the top of the device; the center of each wall was ripped down in the wake of the detonation, exposing a gap with molten metal dripping from each side of it.

The outside enemies began charging inside of the walls, blades, claws and bolts at the ready. Driving into the center of the city with all it had left, the Deliverer fought to make it to the center shield; it was moving slowly, sparks flying from its various joints. As Sara turned to her head upward, she captured a glimpse of a flight of three black vizedrones that were suspended above the Deliverer. Turning his head in the same direction, Nazere flew full speed at the vizedrones. And as they he outstretched his arm and opened the eye of his palm, a black image appeared before him. He also had his arm extended, his palm within one foot of Nazere's. As Nazere stood firm, he watched as the ventari's spines directed additional energy into the growing ball of energy in his hands.

"A pleasure to finally make your acquaintance," Commander Entril began, his face emotionless. "I have heard so much about you, hybrid. My name is Commander Entril, and I'm quite sure our time together will be short. Cherish it!"

Looking down at the Deliverer, the machine exhibiting signs of tangible pain, the faint noise in Nazere's mind began to drag him down into the blackened soil of despair as it took the form of a barely-audible voice. You cannot save them, it whispered, a strong temptation beginning to mount. You are of the Scientific Magisterium, and you always will be — forever connected, never free. Forget your efforts. They were never good enough to save you before. How could they possibly be strong enough to save you now? Let the city fall and redeem yourself before it is too late. You have the power to run; run to the green woods, to where life flourishes. There you can live forever; what a simple compromise to save you from a road of endless suffering. The prophets will be able to handle themselves. Your time is short. You have three seconds... Nazere's core began to shake as he looked at the disarray around him. two seconds... He set his memory on Ryan's final words. One second. He gripped his hands as he thought of Elle's face. And so you have made your choice, and will reap what you have sown. Then came the second voice, even fainter than the first.

Hold on tightly, because I'm coming to help you. Fight with everything you have, and I will deliver you. I promise that I will not give up on you; there will be a way out. Rushing to Nazere's side in smoke and shadow, Keldrid began to raise his blade into the air in enraged defiance. Preparing to drive Entryu down into the black ventari, a white figure appeared at the black ventari's side in the form of a blinding white light. A brilliant sword blocked Entryu's drive in a clash of thunder, holding its place solidly against the angel's strike.

"Watch now," Commander Entril began slowly as he looked into Nazere's eyes, his sterai beam's charge larger than Nazere's. "Watch as you lose everything you care for."

Twirling Entryu in his right hand at the speed of a band saw, Keldrid turned and lashed out at the beast who stood before him. The beast countered by lifting his hands behind his head and driving his two-handed sword forward with all his might; their blades were locked in an earth-quaking shockwave, Entryu barely able to withstand the force of the vice lord's covenant blade. Balls of fire were hurled at the beast from the mouths of three of the Ghosts of the Fallen, but the beast proved invulnerable to their attempts. He stood unmoved, the Blessed Blade of the White Rider pushing down upon Entryu with uncanny force. White sparks danced around the blade, Entryu growing red with fury as Keldrid defended himself against a mere human.

As Commander Entril was about to fire, Nazere discontinued his charge and escaped to the skies above in a blue flame. The commander laughed, releasing his charge into a third towering building. The impact hit the center of the building, sending glass and metal flying like a twister in all directions; the top of the building bent over and gradually fell to the ground below, hitting the shield held up by Sara and High Prophet Joseph. The commander paused for a moment, giving Nazere ample time to gather himself together in the sky. He then set his black eyes to the house covered by the wall of flame, ensuring his motives were obvious. Taking notice of Commander Entril's chosen direction, Nazere shot out of the sky in a blue flame and landed on his feet before the door of the Master's birthplace. Commander Entril smiled, humored by his lesser counterpart.

"This is the Deliverer," Drake called out as ten phantoms pinned him to the ground. Just as a phantom tore one the Deliverer's arms off with its tentacles, David glanced at his display; the great lion had collapsed only feet from the center shield. Attempting to climb to its remaining legs, the three vizedrones above unleashed their charges on the Deliverer. A look of horror overcame David's face as the blasts hit the Deliverer's side, sending its primary engines spilling out of it like internal organs. David closed his eyes for a split second as he let reality slowly sink in. "I love you, Dave," Drake said slowly, his camera fading out on David's left display. "I gave it all I had. I'll see you on the other side. You were and always will be my best friend. Until then."

"Until then," David replied slowly as he gripped his armrests, a tear falling from his face onto the deck of the Redeemer. "Farewell." Swarming around the Deliverer, the phantoms above it tore the head from the rest of the machine; lacerated cords from the head of the ship threw sparks everywhere. The phantoms' tentacles penetrated the exterior of the head of the great lion again and again, until the brilliant glow in the lion's eyes finally faded away.

The Blade of the Blessed White Rider and Entryu clashed together in a series of light-fast, angled strikes as the beast battled Keldrid without relent. Slowly but surely, Keldrid was being driven back by the blessed blade's dominant force; he would raise Entryu to block, but the glowing white blade appeared to be superior time and again. The covenant sword consistently propelled Keldrid backward, and he was unable to counter the spry attacks of the beast. Holding his blade in one hand, the beast drove his fist out in front of him in a punching motion; there was a three yard distance between Keldrid and the beast, but the beast's power was tremendous; overtaken by the supernatural power of the punch, Keldrid plummeted to the dirt below like a rag doll being tossed to the floor. The beast descended from his location in the air in hot pursuit of the angel. In a wave of shadow and smoke, Keldrid streamed his way into a nearby house. The beast dropped to the ground and entered the house directly behind Keldrid, walking in slowly with his sword in his hands.

In the white light of the heavens, a figure robed in all white stood outside a gem-studded gold door; his hood was over his head, and he was facing the door. Within several moments, the door came flying open uproariously in less than a second. A beam of glorious light came from the entrance of the door as it opened, and another robed figure emerged from it; he walked up to the figure who appeared to be waiting patiently for his emergence.

"The time has come," Gabriel said as he unveiled his brilliant skin and shining black hair from underneath his hood.

"The King's orders are in place," Michael replied as he removed his hood, looking Gabriel in his eyes. "We have discussed the matters of Earth. Keldrid will be overwhelmed by the power of the Master's manifestations. The beast is strong, and his blade even stronger. But the end has been written, and I have been chosen to intervene."

"May the Master carry you to victory," Gabriel said as he smiled.

"He always does," Michael replied with a smile, patting Gabriel's shoulder. "I shall see you soon my friend. I go to the house of Lucifer to settle some unfinished business."

In the rear of the vacant, small house Keldrid had flown into, the angel sought refuge against the back wall. As the beast entered, he raised Entryu in front of him.

"Your blade is insufficient," the beast hissed, laughing to himself. "You are in Lucifer's domain now, and you shall be obliterated." Keldrid laughed back at the beast.

"My blade was crafted by better hands than yours was," Keldrid replied in his dark tone, holding Entryu tightly. "You know not the pain in store for you."

"I know no pain!" the vice lord exclaimed in a wicked, thundering voice. "I am god of this place! And nothing can penetrate me now that I carry the blessed blade. You are already defeated where you stand!"

"Then demonstrate for me the vast understanding you have," Keldrid whispered in a twisted tone as he motioned with his left hand's fingertips for the beast to enter further. "Take me on, human!"

Charging in at full speed, the beast drove the front of the Blessed Blade of the White Rider toward Keldrid's chest. Entryu blocked the incoming attack, joined by a second blade at his right. The beast stared at a new being in white robes with great curiousity.

"It has been quite some time, old friend," Michael said to Keldrid in a voice as cool as the summer breeze, glancing over in his direction for but a moment. He was standing at Keldrid's side with his sword drawn; his face shimmered as it had in heaven, a perfect reflection of the Master's design. "My sword is called Blessara, beast. And it shall be the end of you."

"Who is this fool?!" the beast shouted with his blade caught between Keldrid's and Michael's. "What manner of science is this? Are you some sort of misdirected magicians? How can you stand in my presence?!"

"I would choose your words wisely," Keldrid began slowly. "Micheal and I have quite the history together. He prefers a respectful tone."

"You do not know my power," the beast began, a long, forked tongue slipping out from within his black hood for but a moment. "You shall both die by my hands this day, and you shall bleed out in the streets of Bethlehem." The beast held his right hand out in front of him, holding to the Blessed Blade of the White Rider with his left. He then opened the palm of his outstretched hand; the two angels were launched backward by the power of the beast, Keldrid and Micheal crushing the stone wall behind them. The two then stood simultaneously, dusting themselves off; they stared at the beast as if humored by his attack. In unison, their wings spread out to full length behind them as they pointed their swords at the beast. Vice Lord Xar laughed as he simply looked on the two challengers for a moment. Lightning arced across the room as the beast charged into the two angels like an enraged bull; and blades clashed like little novas, sending bursts of energy floating throughout the barren house. Standing his ground, Micheal made a nearly perfect swipe at the beast's arm with Blessara; but the beast evaded the strike by cleverly calculating a subtle step to the right. He then lashed out at Micheal with the blessed blade, attempting to cleave the angel where he stood in one fell swoop. Keldrid came to Micheal's defense, holding Entryu firmly in place against the beast's weapon. Energy continued to bounce throughout the room as the divine struggle ensued.

"Nazere!" Elle exclaimed from within the doorway as she saw him standing outside of the wall of flame. A look of loving concern overwhelmed her beautiful face. "Why are you down here?"

"Stand back, my love!" Nazere shouted nervously, looking to the sky as Commander Entril flew to his position. Standing about five yards away from one another, Commander Entril raised his arm and opened the eye of his palm in Nazere's face. Countering the attack, Nazere raised his own arm and began to charge his sterai beam. As the two released their energy, the beam grew rapidly in size; a ball of particles snowballed between Commander Entril and Nazere, but the commander had the advantage. Two white particle beams from the commander's shoulder spines enhanced the power of the ball of energy between the two and drove it in Nazere's direction. Nazere's eyes widened as he looked upon the blinding energy coming his way;

he knew Keldrid could not bail him out of this predicament.

"How pathetic," Commander Entril said as he continued to drive the beam. "All your faith, and all your beliefs — they are nothing when they are confronted with tangible reality. Science is the means by which my superior armor was constructed. It is your only means of defense! And it will also be the means of your destruction!" The commander bore down on the beam with all of his might. Raising both of his hands in an attempt to resist the dominant energy, Nazere dropped to his knees. Clenching his teeth, he tried with all his might to reverse the accumulating orb of particles; he held on as the ball slowly moved in his direction. Elle's heart pounded in her chest as she watched the one she loved fight with all he had.

At the southern wall, forces were pouring in faster than they could be dealt with; Verus and Tygrys were the only animals on their feet. Lily reached out to the wounded, trying to heal as many as she could by laying on hands. Throwing his lance into oncoming teams of bloodguards, James was breathing heavily and wearing down quickly. Adrax moved swiftly around packs of dreadhunters, trying to down as many as he could with his glowing red saber; he separated his saber into five, trying to counter nearby bloodguards' attacks through the providential manipulation of the mirrored blades. Judgmane was on the ground, a pool of blood under the black lion's shredded body. Bloodfang and Borexis were both completely overcome by dreadhunters, whimpering as the fangs on the dreadhunters leeched into their sides. Endarius' blood apparition expired just as it attempted to drown three dreadhunters at once.

"We are undone!" Endarius yelled out as he defended himself against five bloodguards at once with his sword. "My plague is over!"

"Hands on Judgmane!" Lily yelled out, reaching her hand down and touching the black lion's fur. The lion rose to its feet slowly, running into a pack of panthers with a ferocious roar.

"We can't do this much longer!" Adrax yelled as he hovered ten feet off of the ground, giving himself a much needed break. Aaron's arm was bloodied by the hand of a bloodguard; he held to it as he tried to defend himself with his shortsword. Owen and Felix stood in front of him, driving back the oncoming waves of dreadhunters and bloodguards with different renditions of Jentaru; Owen's right side was burned and bloodied from the bolt of a stormdiver.

"Do not lose the faith!" James yelled as he continued to throw his lance through oncoming enemies. "This battle has been written! Keep your eyes up! You will wear these scars with honor when all is said and done!"

In the small house where the beast fought the two angels, blades danced around the room at great speed. Michael drove his blade forward, attempting to hit the beast. His precision was perfect, but when the blade did penetrate the beast's robes there was no recourse. The beast appeared truly invulnerable. Keldrid and Michael drove their blades down together, colliding with the Blessed Blade of the White Rider. The beast lifted the blade, sending the angels flying backward again. But with every fall, the angels would rise again with swords at the ready.

"Do you not understand the words that I speak?!" the beast screamed. The very foundation of the house shook with the cry of the beast as if an earthquake were occurring. "There is no way to overcome that which is immortal. You stand no chance against me. This entire city is already mine!" Keldrid and Michael stood with their wings upright and their blades before them; they then dove into the beast's blade, bearing down on their own swords. Holding Blessara firmly in place, Michael looked up at the beast.

"What you fail to see is that which is unseen," Michael replied smiling. "You lack much understanding. You are wise in your own eyes, and that is where you fall gravely short. You are an abomination to the Master, and your fate has been sealed." At this, the beast lifted his blade high above his head, driving the angels backward yet again. As Michael returned to his feet, his blade began to take on the light of a dying star; it covered the room in a light equal to that of the Blessed Blade of the White Rider. Spinning Entryu in a supernatural whirlwind, Keldrid clashed blades with the beast in an unending hunger for vigilance. The beast laughed in Keldrid's face as he was stopped dead in his tracks by the blessed blade.

Reduced to his knees before Commander Entril, Nazere pushed with all his might to keep the globe-shaped sterai beam from hitting him. The beam was now upon his hands, searing the artolium metal of his fingers. His mechanical arms struggled as they resisted, and the pain flared throughout his body as he tried to stop the seemingly unstoppable. Elle continued to watch as Nazere pushed with every ounce of energy within his core.

"Homeless rat," the commander sneered. "You are a poor excuse for a human being, let alone a machine. A chance — that is what you had; a chance to survive is what you lost. You can change your appearance, your physical makeup, but you can never change who you are. A collection of piss-poor decisions is all I see; it is all you ever were and ever will be. Don't let it drive you down any further than you already are; it was never in the cards for you to amount to anything. Problems follow you wherever you go, and they're all you've ever offered to society. You deserve what is coming to you, and I hope you feel every sting as you die. It won't be long now, and it will all be over."

Turning to Hayden, Elle's heart pounded faster than it ever had. She looked him deep in the eyes, and as he knew what she was thinking he closed his eyes and dropped the flame wall guarding the entrance. Below the once-existent wall of fire was Hayden's staff, simply sitting in the dirt. Holding to the Amulet of the Lifeseeker with her left hand, Elle slowly knelt down and grabbed the staff with her right. The staff took on a brilliant green glow as she held it in her hands, a swirl of green essence radiating in front of her — a swift breath of charged life. She then stepped out of the entrance to the house, setting her eyes on her target. She lifted the staff behind her back and struck the head of the commander with the empowered staff, the commander falling to his knees — his sterai blast interrupted. Elle stood at the commander's side, smiling at her love as Nazere began to climb to his feet; she waved for him to get up; Nazere waved for her to move.

"Run Elle! Go now!" Nazere exclaimed, as quickly and as loudly as he could.

While on the ground, with one foot climbing up, the commander drew his right genora blade. All of time seemed to slow down as Nazere realized what was happening, his eyes widening as he was unable to gather himself fast enough to block what was coming. Everything. Just. Stopped. The commander gently turned and took hold of Elle's shoulder with his left hand. He then moved his head to her side, driving the withdrawn blade precisely through her heart. Inside of the house, Hayden's eyes remained closed as he was in full realization of what had just happened. The commander took a stand as Elle's body collapsed on the floor, face-down in the dirt. Crawling across the ground as fast as he could, Nazere took hold of Elle's being with both of his hands.

"No. No. No," he whispered slowly in desperation as he softly cradled Elle, leaning his head down to hers. "I love you, Elle!" he exclaimed as tears began to well in his eyes. "Heal yourself! Please heal yourself, Elle. Please. Please. Please." Elle put her hand on Nazere's face as she looked into his eyes, the gleam in her eyes drifting as she stared up at him. All of the memories returned to Nazere as the blood from Elle's wound covered his knees. It seemed just a moment ago the two of them were lying on the roof of the Bastion of Lights' End; just a moment ago they had kissed for the first time; just a moment ago she taught him how to follow her in a simple dance. He looked her in the eyes as he tried to remember what it was to be happy. Happiness was always something he found in her embrace, but she was the one thing that taught him that he could be happy with himself.

"I love you too," Elle said, a smile still on her snow-white face. "We'll be together again. I promise."

"I'm going to miss you," Nazere said, sobbing uncontrollably as he embraced her body. "I'm always going to miss you. Stay with me. Just stay with me."

"I'll miss you, too," Elle replied in a whisper. "You made me happier than I've ever been. My spirit will carry all of what we shared together on to the other side. It will be there always and forever; that's where I'll be waiting for you." Nazere held to Elle's body for a few moments as her brilliance slowly faded out; he clenched his teeth as

Elle's eyes slowly rolled to the back of her head, his body covered in her blood. Placing Elle's lifeless body on the ground, Nazere shut her eyes with his fingers; he then took a stand, tears streaming down his enraged face.

"A ventari that cries," Commander Entril began. "I didn't think that was possible. Now that I've given you ample time for your final respects, where were we?"

Commander Entril raised his arm to open the eye of his palm, smiling; and just as he did, Nazere tightened every muscle in his body as his genora blades came flying from his forearms. Charging the commander at full speed, he relentlessly threw his blades into the commander's shell — focused and unafraid. He thought of every memory as it was projected like a reel of film; every step he took with love; and every moment he lost with her. His eyes wore pure ferocity as he stabbed the commander repeatedly, fighting back the superior machine with all of his strength — every ounce of his heart. The commander began to stab back with both of his genora blades, and blue sparks flew everywhere as the commander penetrated Nazere's artolium skin again and again with the greatest of ease; there was bitter pain for Nazere, but nothing could compare to the anguish of watching his love die in his arms. Unable to overcome the commander's resistant armor, Nazere pulled himself from the frenzy and flew in a stream of blue flame to higher ground. His internal display showed the many wounds he had endured in red, his nerves flaring throughout his torn body.

Flying behind him in a black flame, the commander retracted his bloody genora blades in preperation to burn his opposition down in a style scientific. The two met each other ten yards apart, face-to-face three miles above the city. Both of them outstretched their arms, opening the eyes within their palms simultaneously; as they had done on the ground, the two fired at the same time. The spines from Commander Entril's shoulders empowered the sterai beam in front of Nazere to the point that the beam was once again growing in size. As the beam persisted, the commander spoke.

"You fail to see the logic in my process!" the commander yelled, the beam slowly moving toward Nazere. "Resistance is the means of your own demise! You have chosen your own fate! All of this is your doing, and I must now be your undoing! Accept the death that comes to you, and you will feel no more pain."

As it had before, the sterai beam began to grow in size; it continued to pick up pace as it moved in Nazere's direction. With his eyebrows down in passionate rage, Nazere put both of his hands up in resistance. But the energy kept moving in Nazere's direction, growing in intensity. Glancing down for a moment, Nazere noticed a flock of several hundred stormdivers flying directly at him. The sterai beam began to hit Nazere's hands again, making them take on the appearance of molten metal.

I need the help now, father, Nazere thought to himself. A message appeared on Nazere's internal display. The message was unintelligible, and his processors indicated that there was a data error. The flock of stormdivers closed in on Nazere, and the sterai charged sphere began to consume his forearms. Commander Entril looked Nazere directly in the eyes as the lightning of the bats began to arc across Nazere's back.

"Embrace the end," the commander began. "You are utterly hopeless."

A flash then came to Nazere's eyes; he recalled the face of the dragon, dropping before him and speaking the very same words; he remembered Keldrid's advice, and Hayden's repeated counsel; and he remembered his one love. As a myriad of memories returned to him, the faint, low-intensity noise in his head told him to give in. Why not? Resisting the passing thought, a new message flashed on his internal display. The message simply read, "HOPE." At that very moment, the moment he accepted it, a white dove descended from the sky — out of nowhere — and landed on Nazere's shoulder. Realizing the dove's presence, Nazere remained unshaken in his erect stance; the beam began to move towards his core, but he remained still.

"So long, young fool," Commander Entril said as he laughed to himself, declaring victory. "Tragic that you won't even be remembered. Your error was in listening to the prophets. They fail, as you do. The irreversible laws of science win once again. Who could have foreseen it?"

The flock of stormdivers flew around Nazere, a single stormdiver stopping at his right side. The bat turned his many eyes toward Nazere, and as the sterai beam reached Nazere's shoulders he glanced back.

"We were never meant to be this way," the bat said in a deep voice, looking into Nazere's eyes with a glint of sincerity. Nazere turned his head forward again, and one by one the bats began to run into the center of the commander's palm; each one was incinerated upon impact, but they continued onward nonetheless. And as they flew in the way of the beam, the sphere of concentrated energy began to reverse directions. As Nazere glanced at the ground, he noticed that the animals had turned; the dreadhunters and stormdivers on the ground were overcoming everything in sight, running to the defense of the allied gatherings.

"The creatures!" David yelled over the intercom from the Redeemer. "They are covering all of our enemies! The bloodguards! The phantoms! Everything!"

"What are you doing?!" Commander Entril shouted at the stormdivers. "I command you beasts! Stop at once!" Nazere shook his head.

"All of your science and all of your advancements," Nazere began slowly, looking the commander in the eyes. "what are they good for in the end? Look down at the earth below you; it was intelligently made, and foolishly flawed. Man has proven nothing, and perhaps that is the greatest truth we have to face; man is but a number now, and we were better off long ago. But amidst this beautiful disaster we have all created, I have learned a great many things; the view from the ground up is far more precious when you consider the view looking down; I have learned of life, and of true love; I suppose that's what matters most — what they really mean to me — and what she taught me without my knowing it. I have been in the depths of pain, my face in the pavement so many times it doesn't even hurt anymore; I've been down so far that there were days when I thought I wouldn't make it out of hole I dug my own self; but for once, I have forty-two days clean from the drugs that once ripped me down; for once, I can take life one day at a time; for once, I can look myself in the mirror and be happy with who I am; for once, all is well with me. I am free. Life is not about winning or losing, nor fleeting moments of grandeur or euphoria. No, life is not all about the 'ups'; it is about what you do when it all comes crashing down — smiling when you find that one little ounce of beauty in the heart of catastrophe. Humankind is not beautiful because we fall down; the beauty in humanity is in the still, small voice that tells you to hold on even when there's nothing left to hold on to — trusting that there will always be a way to get back up again. When no one else is around, I know now that I have Someone who will catch me somewhere on the way down — unconditionally, always and forever. Don't you wish you had the same?" Nazere dropped his left arm, pushing the beam with but one arm. Yet another flock of stormdivers ascended from below and aligned themselves behind Commander Entril. They then held his body firmly in place as stormdivers continued to run into the commander's palm. The bat hovering next to Nazere set its eyes on the beam, arcing bolts of electricity into it.

The energy came upon Commander Entril slowly but surely; he resisted with every bit of energy he had, trying to pry himself from the firm grasp of the stormdivers holding him in place. The clash of science and mathematics that comprised his suit should have given him an easy advantage over the stormdivers; but it seemed that they now had a supernatural grasp on the man. When the sterai energy was upon the commander's hands, he cried out in bitter pain. Nazere then raised his left arm, charging the eye of his palm as he looked on the commander.

"It was asked of me once what defined the line between good and evil. I have finally ascertained the answer to that age-old question; I finally understand. Now would be a good time to pray," Nazere began slowly, pausing as he fired his second charge, imagining just as Keldrid had taught him that the commander was gone already. "You can take my heart; you can take every little thing I am; but faith is that one thing that can never be taken away from me. I thank God for the person he sent me who taught me I'm not so alone after all; when she found me, I was at my worst; God knows I'll miss her, and God knows you'll never harm her again. Farewell, Commander Entril." The second bolt hit the sphere and pushed it completely upon the commander's body, consuming all of the black ventari in a great white light. As the commander opened his molten mouth to cry out in agony, the powerful charge generated a gravitational pull. The great vacuum pulled in the whole of the charge, compressing it into a little spark of amber light. Nazere floated over to the light and cupped it in his hands; he watched as it danced around in his hands like a little firefly for a moment or two. Turning his head to the sky, he wasted no time in hurling the spark into the air above him like a full-speed pitch. The spark flew faster than a rocket, straight into a mass of swimming dreadnaughts in the sky. The spark then exploded, tearing dreadnaughts, vizedrones and phantoms from the heavens in a reaction comparable to a miniature supernova. A massive cloud of radiation filled the air as the city below shook violently.

The beast was dueling Michael and Keldrid when it happened. The explosion shook the entire house like many repeated earthquakes, reducing the beast to his knees. With all his might he attempted to hold on to the Blessed Blade of the White Rider; he had it in his hands at one moment. But in the very next, he dropped the blade before Keldrid's feet. Unshaken by the earthquakes, Michael placed his foot on the hilt of the sword to secure it.

"Unfortunate," Keldrid said in his sinister tone as he reached down and picked the beast up by the neck. Slamming the beast against the wall with his scaly hands, he then tore the veil off of the beast's head to reveal a bald head and blood-red irises. Vice Lord Xar was aged in his forties, and he spat upon Keldrid as he was held upon the wall.

"I will return the blade to its rightful place," Michael said calmly as he reached down and picked up the Blessed Blade of the Unbroken by the hilt. "But before I do, I believe I will assist you a bit." Michael walked up to the beast and held his neck in place in Keldrid's stead; he then turned to Keldrid and smiled. Holding his sword behind his head like a knife, Keldrid drove Entryu through the beast's head in one swift motion. As Michael released his grasp, the beast dropped onto the floor below. Blood ran like a river from the beast's head, and Keldrid placed his foot on it as he attempted to pry Entryu out. With some blatantly drawn-out maneuvering and cracking, Keldrid was able to withdraw his bloody blade; but not before he left a generously-gaping hole in the side of the beast's skull.

"Until we meet again, Keldrid," Michael said smiling. Keldrid turned his head to Michael.

"It was good to see you again, Micheal," Keldrid said in his dark voice. And just as Keldrid spoke, Michael disappeared. "Goodbye, my old friend," he said as he looked at the space where Micheal was only a moment earlier. Keldrid reached to the ground and grasped the beast's shroud with one hand. He carried the body out of the entrance of the house and tossed the body in the streets. And just as he did, the shining sun returned to the sky; dancing clouds flew overhead as what remained of the dreadnaughts began to reverse their direction.

"All vessels retreat!" Fleet Admiral Clayton commanded over the intercom. "Vice Lord Xar has been murdered!"

Standing at the northern wall, Rock was still maneuvering his controls. He was steady and precise with every button that he pushed. His crosshairs locked onto a retreating dreadnaught; it was the very one that carried Fleet Admiral Clayton.

"Lunase," Rock began as he leaned over inside his cockpit. "Fire all thratum lances at my target!"

Four glowing, red lances were catapulted from the Lunase's wing cannons upon Rock's command; the projectiles were long energy spears with missile-like ends to them. Fleet Admiral Clayton looked down at his radar as the lances approached, his eyes widening as the lances penetrated the hull of his dreadnaught; every single lance had hit their target successfully, protruding from the octopus-like vessel like four tremendous arrows. The dreadnaught took on a red glow slowly, the energy from the center of the lances flooding the decks of the ship as if the vessel had broken open in the depths of the ocean. The energy took complete dominance over the ship; and like a massively-magnified display of neon-red fireworks, the vessel exploded into countless little pieces.

"Target neutralized," Lunase reported in a light female voice. Rock remained neutral in his expression.

"Let's head back to the center, Lunase," Rock replied. "We're done for today."

On the ground, all of the remaining forces from the walls joined together in the center of the city. Lunase quickly ran to the rest of the ships' placement around the middle of the damaged city. Sara Maple still held the prismatic shield in place, dropping her shield as she watched vizedrones and phantoms fly out of range and into the distance. Walking up to her, James' blood-sprinkled face smiled upon Sara. Below him were all of the summoned animals; they were all healed and intact, dreadhunters included. The leviathans began their landing sequences, dropping to the ground next to the shield. With an emotionless face, Adrax stared at the head of the Deliverer as he returned his saber to his back; he looked up toward the sky as the memories of his friend came back to him.

"Take advantage of the time you have with your loved ones," Adrax began with Owen and Felix at his side. "because you never know when they might make the journey home." And all at once in the air, the Ghosts of the Fallen who had rallied in the center of the city vanished into thin air. All of the gatherings' machines joined together around those on the ground, scratches and dents throughout their exteriors. They deployed their atrons at the same time, the atrons crawling all over each damaged hull to ensure the swift repair of their designated ships. In the mean time, each of the allied vessels knelt in honor of the lion that was lost — a silent requiem in rememberance of Drake.

"You fought valiantly," Sara said as she threw her arms around James tightly, gently kissing his cheek. "I am glad to see your face again, even if it is covered in blood."

"I'm happy to see you too, Sara," James said as he held to Sara, looking her deeply in the eyes. "We lost many men and women today. But I'm more than thankful to see that you made it through safely. Your beautiful face is an indescribable portrait of redemption for my weakened eyes."

"A pleasure serving with you, High Prophet Arthur," High Prophet Joseph said as he smiled. "We should discuss the reestablishment of your house. I can see to it that your forces are properly hidden before the end is upon us; the witch Airya will be sending her assassins out soon — her werewolves, vampires, magicians, abominations and the twin-demons of Babylon." Arthur put his right hand of High Prophet Joseph's shoulder.

"We will see to the survival of our gatherings no matter the challenge," Arthur replied. "I am glad to know you are behind me. When the king and the queen unite as one, we shall become known to the world. Then we shall demonstrate the full defiance of the two prophets of Adriel. I sense a change in the course of the wind. Like a whisper into the dark, we must remain hidden from the beasts. Lucifer is on the move, and his next steps will determine whether our house shall rise or fall."

"It's all over," David said slowly, the perched Redeemer on the light-brown dirt around the other vessels.

"For now," Jadus replied over the intercom. "The war has only begun. The forces the beasts send out next shall be far greater than the ones we have encountered this day."

"We must make haste from here!" Sade said, a tone of hurry in her voice. "They will be returning for the body of the beast shortly."

Nazere was back on the ground, kneeling by Elle's side. He gently took hold of her body and picked it up, kissing her forehead as a tear dropped from his right eye. From behind him, Verus came running full speed toward his master. A brief smile came to Nazere's face as he glanced back at his companion. Verus ran around Nazere excitedly, moving in circles and panting as if everything was just fine. Submerging from within the birthplace of his Master, Hayden slowly made his way to Nazere. He knelt down and grabbed his staff from the dirt, a sorrowful and almost apologetic look on his face. As he made his way to his feet, Hayden set his sympathetic eyes on Nazere. Refusing to look back, Nazere kept his eyes focused on Elle; her amulet dangled from her neck as she remained motionless in Nazere's arms.

"It was meant to be this way," Hayden said softly. "You may not understand it now, but there is a reason for everything. I am deeply sorry for your loss. I cannot begin to express how very near and dear she has been to every one of us. But it is true; she loved you most of all."

"I loved her with all of my heart," Nazere said slowly, looking up at Hayden with troubled eyes. "Why is it that everything I care for is stripped away?"

"It will not always be this way," Hayden replied. "Pain only lasts for so long, but problems will continue until the end. But the end is coming, and patience is the key to the door of it."

"I want to give her a proper burial," Nazere said slowly, looking back down at his love. "Somewhere high, so that she can always see the stars she loved so very much; even though I know she can't, that would mean so much to me." Hayden nodded.

"We can make that happen," Hayden replied. "She has made the ultimate sacrifice. In so much as she has, you must know that she loved you in return with a passion that is incredibly rare. No greater love exists than that of a person who lays down their life for the sake of another. She knew what she was doing, and she did it because she loved you more than life itself. The struggle of life and death consumes us all, and I'm afraid it's going to get worse before it gets better. The time has come to leave here. A new era is now upon us. Only the Gathering of the White Lamb will remain in Bethlehem."

Together, Hayden and Nazere walked toward the rest of the group in the center of the city. David opened the door to deck of the Redeemer, and Nazere walked onboard with Elle's body in his arms. Hayden climbed in with his staff in hand and sat next to Nazere.

"Where are we heading?" David asked as he glanced to his left.

"To Undrum," Hayden replied. "We must retrieve all of our things. We are leaving our home at once."

At that very moment, Keldrid appeared behind Nazere. He put his hand on his shoulder as if to comfort him. He then reached his head down to Nazere's ear.

"I apologize that I could not be there to save her, human," Keldrid said, as lightly as ever.

"It's alright," Nazere replied. "I know that you were engaged elsewhere."

"Who are you talking to?" David asked as he began to maneuver the controls in front of him.

"No one," Nazere replied.

"Alright," David said as he exhaled a breath, a skeptical look upon his face. "To all linked vessels, this is the Gathering of the White Knight bidding you safe passage to wherever the Master takes you."

"The same to you, brother," Isaac replied. "Our gathering will hold the defenses down in Bethlehem. It has been a pleasure serving alongside you."

"Take care, David," the Colossus said as it waved at the Redeemer. James raised his spear in the air as he stood beside Sara. Looking up at the eagle, Arthur smiled.

"Farewell, David!" James shouted as he stood with his right arm around Sara. "I know that I shall see you again soon!"

"Know that we are always behind you!" Adrax shouted, holding his saber in the air. "The Gathering of the White Lion will go on!"

"Well Redeemer," David began. "Let's take a ride. We're heading back home."

"To Undrum?" the Redeemer questioned.

"Yes," David replied. "We're leaving the cabin."

"Why would we be leaving Undrum?" Nazere accidentally asked out loud. He turned around to see if Keldrid was around to answer his question, but he was gone.

"We are leaving because the beast will return," David replied, his eyebrows raised. "They will be back to claim his body. And he will return many times stronger when his body is restored. The Gathering of the White Lamb has already agreed ahead of time to surrender it."

"But he is dead," Nazere said, still holding tightly to Elle. "He is in a pool of his own blood."

"Setting coordinates to Undrum," the Redeemer began. "Beginning the take off process in ten..." As the countdown timer to flight continued to drop, Nazere thought to himself deeply; he wondered how the beast could possibly return from such a devastating and death-inducing blow.

"He will be restored," Hayden said, as if he were reading Nazere's thoughts. "And he will destroy everything in his path when he arises. We have won the battle, but we have not won the war. There is much to be done. The Tribulation has now begun."

"The Tribulation?" Nazere asked as the Redeemer began to move and vibrate.

"The beast's first recourse will be to slaughter every prophet he can find," Hayden said with a solemn look on his face. "We must go into hiding and hope that he does not find us. The end will come after the last battle, when the Master returns; no man knows when that is. Until then, there are few places we can hide from the watchful eye of the beast. The Seven Year War has begun through the completion of the Prophecy of the Torn. And through it, mankind will begin to rapidly break down. Famine, plagues and pestilence are only the beginning of the acts the Master will carry out through us. We're in for a difficult course of years."

As the Redeemer took flight, Nazere held to the body of Elle tightly. He looked down at the display as he departed from the friends he had gained in the various gatherings. A great burden on his shoulders, Nazere closed his eyes as he tried to forget everything in his head; he tried to erase his emotions; he tried to hold back the pain that always seemed to follow him wherever he went. But as hard as he tried, he simply couldn't. And as the ship took to the clouds, his mind and his heart remained in the Bastion of Lights' End where his memory of dancing with Elle would always go on.

A timeless memory,
her immortal words spoken in his head;
he would never again be...
alone.

CHAPTER TEN

Into the Light

A full day had passed since the instantly renowned Battle of Bethlehem. The sun was at eye level in the sky, beaming morning rays of incandescence upon the glistening snow that blanketed Undrum. The clouds were few and the climate was mild as the wind softly blew through the clear air. The snow was firm in its place, unmoved by the soft wind around it as if it were made of a thousand little diamonds. Sitting and panting in the snow, the German shepherd known as Verus had its eyes set straight ahead of him. With his lighter oak staff in hand, High Prophet Hayden had his eyes fixated into the distance as well. Below them, frozen lakes and snow-powdered trees stretched for as far as the eye could see. High atop a mountain to the left of the Gathering of the White Knight's cabin, a gray boulder was placed before Nazere. He held out his right arm and opened the eye to his palm, carefully crafting a pristine triangular gravestone out of the large, formless rock before him.

Holding the very same bouquet of pink roses he had given Elle the night of the banquet in the Bastion of Lights' End, he began to etch the letters of her name into the gravestone to mark the site of her burial. As he completed the final letter, he slowly moved his sterai beam underneath the letters and etched the outlines of two hearts side by side; the ends of the engraved hearts were linked together in memory of her words. He then crouched down and gently placed the roses underneath her stone. Placing his right arm on the final resting place of his one love, he slowly spoke the words, "Goodbye, my sweetheart. You were always so much more than my best friend. You are still my heart, and you taught me the meaning of love. Until we meet again, always and forever, you'll remain right there." Inhaling the breath needed to go on, Nazere then rose to his feet and set his eyes on the rising sun.

The hospital in Jerusalem was buzzing with scientists and physicians in all white lab coats, khakis and dress shoes. They also wore purple nitrile gloves and a white box over their mouth to fend off any disease that should present itself; the box filtered all bacteria and viruses out of the air without fail, and was commonly used in surgical procedures. All of these men and women held to needles and wires, surrounding the body of Vice Lord Xar. There were twelve men and women in the room in total; six were on his left, and six on the right. He had been handed over by the Gathering of the White Lamb only two hours earlier, and his motionless body was hovering an all white room. There were two circular holographic displays projected on both sides of him. The one to the left maintained a constant beeping noise, a line on the display further indicating that his pulse had flat-lined; another display on the right indicated that all of the neurons in his brain were completely offline. A total of eighty needles were connected to his body, the majority of them to his head. Most of the needles connected to a vial of the rare substance kazium, and the neon green liquid was flowing into him and pouring out of him as soon as it had entered. The rest of the needles were attached to every vein that could be penetrated throughout his body. His eyes were closed, and there was a massive hole in the side of his head.

Chief Scientist Olar was positioned to the right of the beast; he would periodically look down at the hole, able to see through to the physicians and scientists on the other side as the kazium being pumped into him continued to drip to the floor below. In the mean time, a physician on the left attached two wires to the beast's chest, attempting to shock his heart back into motion by means of long-tested and precise wattage currents. He also connected a wireless, rounded probe to the beast's forehead. The probe served as a frequency modulator for waves penetrating the insides of his head. The radio waves were often used to seal wounds by method of heavily-amplified ionizing frequencies. The waves would burn through bone and skin in an attempt to reseal seemingly insurmountable lacerations and other dire wounds. They were a last resort.

A female scientist pumped blood into the vice lord by the gallon intravenously on the right, only to have it flow out of him again in a pool on the floor. She constantly reconnected quarts of blood stored in rubber packaging to an electronic pump. The pump was connected to the end of a thin tube that branched off into ten intravenous needles; the needles were connected to the arms, the hands, the legs and the feet of the beast. The pump accelerated the rate at which the blood was introduced to the body. The vice lord had been completely drained of blood, his face pale and his skin clinging to the inanimate muscles underneath. The probe wasn't sealing his incredible wound, and the kazium had absolutely no effect over the beast's dead body. A separate scientist took notes on the vice lord's status on a rectangular digital tablet by scribbling down notes with a wireless pen.

"I'm amplifying the frequency to maximum strength," the physician who had placed the probe on Vice Lord Xar's forehead said. He moved to the holographic panel on the left, which displayed the vice lord's outline and internal organs; it also displayed the man's pulse and neurological activity. All three of these indicators of life were null. Pressing a small, blue button on the panel, the probe lit up like a light bulb as the physician made an effort to seal the sides of the beast's head. When there was no response from the high-voltage frequencies, the scientist holding the panel in his hands jotted down a few more notes. "We can cap his head with an artificial skin graft, but his brain will remain non-functional. The damage is beyond extensive. I've never seen anything like it."

"He has lost all of his blood," the female scientist commented as she looked across the room. She was pumping the vice lord with pouch after pouch of pure human blood, a manic tone to her voice as she spoke. “He is far beyond any help we could possibly give him.”

“What do you think of completing a full machinatomy?” a physician on the left asked in suggestion. “We could replace his brain with one consisting of several quadrillion bioprocessors and copy the memory from his brain onto the artificial one.” Chief Scientist Olar shook his head.

“That cannot be done,” the chief of science began with a sense of defeat in his voice. “He is but a piece of flesh now. Any surgeries will fail, and a machinatomy is only practical with beings that still have some sign of life within them. His neurological transmission has been halted for over a day now. There is no electrical work that can be done to repair his neurons at this point.”

As blood continued to pour onto the floor, a male physician with black hair and black glasses stepped out from the right.

“Our display is indicating that he is far beyond gone. He is beginning to deteriorate further, showing demonstrable signs of internal decay. And the kazium supply is emptied.” Staring the physician in the eyes, Chief Scientist Olar’s face became as lifeless as the beast’s as he realized the fate in store for him.

“High Lord Alune is going to have my head for this,” Chief Scientist Olar began. “but there is nothing more that can be done here. I’m calling it.” The chief of science glanced down at his sterling-silver watch. “The time of death is zero nine-hundred and three hours.”

“Someone go get a body bag!” the female physician holding the quarts of blood exclaimed as she discontinued pumping the blood into the beast’s body. A physician nodded and left the room, returning only moments later with a black body bag in her right hand. She placed the bag around the beast’s body, zipping it tightly shut around him. The scientists and physicians removed their gloves and left the room, leaving the rest of the work to the coroner.

A coroner entered the room two hours later, dressed in an all-black rubber uniform and a rubber mask that closely resembled a gas mask. He wheeled in a metal rack sizable enough to fit a human body as he made his entrance; he then wheeled the cart up to the hovering body he had come to claim. The coroner removed all of the needles and devices attached to the beast one by one. He wrapped his arms around the beast's body and placed him gently on the rack. And just as he was about to wheel the cart out of the room, the coroner‘s heart jumped in his chest. The zipper of the body bag came down without the use of any hands, slowly inching its way down to the bottom. The beast's eyes were closed when his face was revealed, but the coroner was curious as to what moved the zipper so miraculously. As he leaned down into Vice Lord Xar's face, motionless eyelids came flying open. In shock, the coroner stumbled into the corner of the room as he witnessed the fiery-red irises of the beast swirling around his now nocturnal pupils. The beast sat up from his place on the rack, the coroner quivering in shock. The holes in the beast's head were sealed as if nothing had ever penetrated him. Vice Lord Xar smiled wickedly in the direction of the quivering coroner, revealing a hideous collection of razor sharp teeth within his mouth.

Black suitcases and cardboard boxes were stacked at the door to Undrum's cabin, Hayden carefully descending the spiraling stairs with his staff in his right hand and his suitcase in his left. Walking in from outside, Verus followed Nazere's every footstep. Nazere picked up two of the black suitcases that were at the opened entrance to the cabin; he took a brief glance up at Hayden and then turned around and walked toward the Redeemer. Once outside, he watched as David jumped out of the ship's door into the snow after loading several jam-packed boxes. The two walked past each other, Nazere climbing through the circular entrance to the Redeemer and dropping the suitcases next to the boxes on top of the vessel's three steps. With Verus at his ankles, Nazere walked back toward the entrance of the Undrum cabin. He was met by a side view of Hayden's face, the suitcase the high prophet was carrying now on the ground below him. The high prophet's eyes were plastered to the three dimensional television in front of the blue sofa. A female newscaster was reporting on a recent turn of events; she was reporting from Jerusalem.

"To the astonishment of the world at large," the newscaster began. "A stunning event has captivated those who have followed the events that transpired during the Battle of Bethlehem. Announced dead at around nine o'clock this morning, Vice Lord Xar arose from a body bag at Sinai General Hospital only two hours after having been pronounced dead. Reports indicate that he had suffered a fatal laceration to the head and that this said 'major laceration' has been completely healed. Physicians report that Vice Lord Xar is entirely coherent despite his injury, and has talked at great length to many of the staff within the hospital. He has stated that he will be making an appearance at the restored city of Adriel, where new jobs are being generated at the Eripsa Corporation; he will be joined there by Queen Airya of Babylon, who has promised to put an end to the religious resistances who are blamed for the injury sustained by Vice Lord Xar. Eripsa has successfully completed a manufacturing plant larger than the Gantor Pinnacle in New York, allowing for triple the output of ventari peacekeepers for the maintained order of the world at large. Eripsa has entered into a ten year contract with Vice Lord Xar, and have developed the blueprint for an advanced version of the ventari; the new ventari have been designed using images downloaded to a remote station from the deceased Commander Entril's internal cameras — images of a female who was killed during the battle. The company is currently being funded for additional research in the areas of ventari efficiency, and will begin what is being called 'The Phallion Project' within their state-of-the-art manufacturing plant. We will bring you more details as they become known.

In other news, the outbreak of animal-based violence in all parts of the world has continued to escalate. Scientists have no current information on why the animals are presently operating so intelligently. Nor does the joint Scientific Magisterium have information on the reason why they are acting out of violence, but they have begun undergoing research to bring a remedy to this unthinkable outbreak. In addition to mammals, birds, reptiles and amphibians, microorganisms have begun to demonstrate signs of unusual change; microorganisms have developed an unusual resistance to many standard and some highly-advanced antibiotics. Autopsies are being conducted on humans who have been infected with an unidentified strain similar in form to the bacteria streptococcus; this bacteria has the ability to replicate itself thousands of times faster than the standard streptococcus specimen, resulting in outbreaks of scarlet fever and tonsillitis for the first time in decades. So far, between the animal and bacterial outbreaks, over seventy-thousand lives have been lost due to this strange and catastrophic turn of events. Chief Scientist Olar has issued a statement..."

David shut off the television screen, turning his eyes to Hayden.

"We must make haste now," Hayden began. "Both of the beasts will be on the move shortly, and there is little time to spare. The Bastion of Lights' End has already been evacuated. His next target will be Undrum."

"Where will we go?" Nazere asked, standing at the doorway with Verus sitting by his side.

"We must travel to the Council of the Blue King," Hayden replied. "We will rally with the Gathering of the White Rook there. James has been elected as the gathering's new high prophet. The other gatherings will arrive there at a later time. Come now! We must make to the Redeemer immediately!"

The three men within the cabin picked up everything they could carry and made their way toward the Redeemer. David climbed into the Redeemer first, sitting where Ryan used to. Nazere looked at David questionably, but began to sit in his usual spot nonetheless. Verus parked his furry body in between Nazere and Hayden. As soon as Nazere had sat down, Hayden leaned over and placed his face in front of Nazere's.

"I do hope you can fly," Hayden whispered as his eyes looked directly at Nazere.

"I'm a ventari," Nazere replied as his eyes focused on Hayden's face. "Of course I can fly." Then, as Nazere's eyes refocused, he noticed something in the room had changed. Something was out of place. As he looked beyond Hayden to Ryan's seat, he discovered the change. David had disappeared. Knowing Nazere had realized the difference, Hayden began to speak.

"The Rapture has begun," Hayden said, still looking into Nazere's eyes. "The two of us are all that remain of the Gathering of the White

Knight. There is a third prospect, though, and he is currently under the supervision of the Council of the Blue King."

"What exactly is the Rapture?" Nazere questioned, his eyes wandering around the room in search of David as if they could possibly find him.

"There are few that will be brought home a bit early," Hayden whispered, Nazere's eyes finally accepting that David was gone as he looked solely to the high prophet. "The Rapture is the Master's process of safeguarding select people from the trials to come. But we are not amongst those to be taken home. David has passed on. It is now your duty to take his place as captain of the Redeemer." Rising from his seat, Nazere moved to where David used to sit in the captain's chair. A strange feeling suddenly overcame him, as if he had done this before. Or perhaps, he had seen it. He pushed a red button he had seen David push to the right of the captain's chair, and the holographic controls of the Redeemer popped up before him.

"Good morning, captain," the Redeemer's female voice said pleasantly. Nazere put his hands out in front of him toward the suspended images as he attempted to adapt to the art of piloting; he was nervous, and he didn't know the first thing about flight. But he had seen crazier things happen before.

"Alright," Nazere began, exhaling a withheld breath as he turned and smiled in Hayden's direction. "Here goes everything. Redeemer!"

"Yes, captain?" the Redeemer replied.

"Set your coordinates to the Council of the Blue King."

"Say 'Sydney, Australia,'" Hayden whispered to Nazere.

"Set your destination to Sydney, Australia," Nazere started. "Do you have your coordinates set?"

"Affirmative captain," the Redeemer replied. "I am waiting for your mark."

Looking at the overwhelming control scheme in front of him, Nazere began pressing buttons on the holographic control panel to the right. He glanced down at the floor, and to his amazement, a dated paper that read "The Case Study of Richard Roivas" sat on the floor before him. The ribbon straps from behind him came out and fastened him tightly in place; he then glanced at Hayden, ensuring that he had also been secured. The countdown timer then began from ten. Outside of the Redeemer, the regal eagle began to move her talons across the frozen ground. There was a brief pause as she continued to move at a slow pace. Seconds later, she increased her speed to a full dash; she ran across the snow of Undrum, extending her wings to their full length at her sides. And as the ship reached an oncoming bunch of evergreens, the Redeemer threw herself into the air. Aimed toward the clouds, she opened her beak and let out a mighty cry.

High Lord Alune stood on top of a majestic mountain, his shroud hiding his face from view. Bright evergreen trees covered the sides and the bottom of the mountain on which he stood. The high lord held his left hand out in front of him, opening his palm fully; he then set his sights on the castle that stood tall in the distance. Staring directly at the Bastion of Lights' End, he slowly curled his fingertips inwards toward his palm. As his fingers slowly moved, the earth around the great castle began to quake violently; slowly and methodically, he curled his fingers inward further. The apex to the bastion began to shake, finally falling under the pressure of the beast's incredible power. Crushing the structures beneath it, the spire was only the first part of the bastion to fall. Fragments from the turrets at the eight corners of the building began to fall next, dropping to the forest below them. And as High Lord Alune closed his hand completely, the entire structure dropped tier by tier. A thick smog covered the entire pile of rubble that was once the wonderous Bastion of Lights' End. The beast dropped his hand to his side, appeased by the sight before him. But on top of the rubble, a single sign poked through all that had fallen upon it against all odds. The sign read: "Parrion's."

In a dimly lit room, a dark figure knelt down at the back of a wall. He was fully shrouded, and the shadows in the room hid his being from view. There was a door that was barely visible on the robed figure's right. The room was an elegant marble-floored office within a skyscraper high atop New York City. The center of the room had the golden emblem of a dragon breathing flame embossed above the marble floor, and there were six candles on the left side of the room.

Each candle was erected on a solid gold pedestal, and provided some of the ambiance for the room. To the shadowed figure's left, a glass pane covered the entire wall; outside of the window, vehicles and flying buses moved from building to building in perfectly aligned traffic patterns. The sky was auburn as the sun was setting, a symphony of fireworks exploding over the city in an array of vibrant colors outside the glass pane; Vice Lord Xar's return was being actively celebrated. There was about ten yards between the shadow at the front of the room near the door and the back of the room.

In the back of the room, a familiar face sat upon a fully golden throne. To his left was another being. Both of these figures were robed in all white. The man who was standing to the left of the throne had a brown beard and a bald head, and his face shimmered like glass; he had no irises to his eyes, making them appear quite abnormal. The more radiant of the two, the figure that sat upon the throne had blue eyes that moved like the ocean around his pupils; his blonde hair glistened like fine gold, and his face was as bright as the sun. Its glimmering surface provided the most light to the room. This was the face of Lucifer, and his glorious features seemed to beam luminescence in all directions.

"I have heard the report of your valiant work," Lucifer began, his eyes swirling even more as he began to speak. "You have proven quite noble to my cause, and for that you should be proud. Everything is going according to plan."

"He has fought for the cause," the being next to Lucifer said. "His abilities in battle, although tried, are quite substantial. I recommend that he be promoted to a greater position of power, my lord." Lucifer nodded as he leaned over toward the darkened figure.

"I know you want revenge," Lucifer began slowly. "I know all of the things you seek. And in time, they will come to you. There is a fault in the King's design, and you have demonstrated that it can be exploited. A promotion in rank is indeed in order, and it is most certainly yours. But first, I must ask you one simple question." Lucifer's abyssal pupils widened as he leaned over further. "Do you understand what must be done?"

The dark figure in the front of the room nodded. Poking his head out from behind the shadows, the being took a stand. He slowly paced into the light, illuminating the whole of his body. And with his head facing the floor, Keldrid spoke, “I know what I must do.”

THE BEGINNING OF THE...END

EPILOGUE

The Case Study of Richard Roivas

DATE: JANUARY 23, 2211

MEMORANDUM: Subject: Dr. Richard Roivas

THIS FILE IS CLASSIFIED TOP-SECRET: TIER X

MARKED BY VICE LORD XAR FOR TRANSFER: VI VI VI

Examination by unauthorized personnel is a criminal offense punishable by trial by the Scientific Magisterium, immediate stasis, and possible termination if unauthorized personnel are discovered by Ventari peacekeepers prior to trial.

VENTARI AUTHORIZATION CODE: T-4-88-213 / 666

DO NOT COPY UNDER ANY CIRCUMSTANCES—DESTROY IF FOUND BY UNAUTHORIZED PERSONNEL

A Study on The Seven Year War by Dr. Lisa Mezea, Specialist First Class of the Scientific Magisterium (SFCwH, PhD)

References: a) The Scientific Magisterium and the End of Truth

b) V-6 Monitor: Subjects Dr. Lee and Dr. Roivas

Dr. Richard Roivas had just completed his final calculation for the pseudo-random-code generator needed for the Quantum Randomizer which his group had been tasked with by the Ministry of Science (*now known as the political system: The Scientific Magisterium). Roivas had been selected years ago to work in this group. His early work on mathematical models of theoretically infinite frame boundaries had drawn attention to his work by the Ministry of Science. It was even said that Minister Xar himself had taken note of Dr. Roivas' work and issued the mandatory order for Roivas to be transferred. The transfer took the usual toll on Roivas' marriage and family life that it did for most of the scientists operating in the demanding group. Trading family for prestige wasn't what Roivas wanted, but the requirements placed on him and the high-end responsibility that was demanded of all in the group called for more than Mrs. Roivas was willing to endure(their divorce was noted). But his job was not an optional one; it was demanded of him and the others that he completes certain tasks. The understanding of the implications of the scientific endeavors they were working on and how their failures or successes would impact the Utopia that the Ministry of Science had constructed for the entire human race made the idea of refusing the work almost unthinkable. Unfortunately, the wives of most of the groups' scientists didn't grasp that concept; like Roivas', their marriages quickly dissolved.

For Roivas, the additional cost was the eventual waywardness of his son Nazere (SUBJECT S). With little or no guidance from the male figure in his life, Nazere had wandered into the usual trappings of youth; a dezium addiction was annotated in his medical record. Another cost for Roivas, which was almost demanded from Roivas, was his faith. Roivas had grown up in a religious home, believing in a God. The Ministry of Science had no use for this outlook, and had clearly stated their opposition to this frame of mind. It was at first considered only an annoyance to them if any of their members believed in their fictional God or gods, but the highly-funded proofs developed by the ministry in the area of origins and biology had all but proved that a God was totally unnecessary for the development of the universe. But the real sinker was the work and achievements of Minister Xar. Xar was a child protégée who achieved more than any one human known in history; he seemed almost supernatural in his ability, and this is noted in his lengthy medical record (*I have personally studied Xar at great length). His work made some of the greatest advancements in recent history possible. His early paper (titled

Quantum Randomness and the Spontaneous Origin of Universes) had to most scientists proven without a doubt that no intelligent force was used to create, but that randomness itself was the true creator of all that existed; in essence, it was the dagger in the heart of all faiths around the world. But to the Ministry of Science, this new proof was the first step toward the Utopia they had all been searching for. It was the first universal truth that all members of society were expected to accept; any scientist, technologist or engineer was expected to understand this universal truth without exception. After all, Xar's paper had proven it without a doubt both mathematically and empirically.

Roivas, being assigned to the Quantum Randomness Power Generation Group (QRPG), certainly must understand the primary truth — especially considering his and the groups' work on randomness. But Roivas had his doubts, and they were noted; he dare not speak of them even mathematically. He constantly suppressed the ideas when they confronted him in his head, knowing full-well the consequences for such ideas.

All of the thoughts of his failed marriage, his wandering son and his doubts about the "Primary Truth" were made a back-burner to his immediate work on his project. He was highly respected for his work, and had risen to chief code mathematician in the group. But the more he worked out the math for these random codes, the more his mind returned to the doubts about the "Primary Truth." His work and mathematics were leading him to mathematic proof that randomness couldn't be the source of the universe and that pure randomness (which Xar's paper showed was the true source of all things) was not only unable to produce the universe, but that its probability rating demonstrated to Roivas that the most likely outcome of a purely random system was NOTHING at all. Roivas tried to avoid this idea, but the more successful work he did on random coding systems required for the Quantum Generator (for the generation of power), the more the eventuality of this challenge to the "Primary Truth" became evident. And not just to Roivas; other scientists were beginning to notice. But the politically-incorrect aspects of the observations kept the idea quiet. No respectable scientist would even imagine offering a challenge to Xar's ideas and the "Primary Truth." Xar had time and time again shown that his ideas were beyond reproach and quite high and above any peer review. The fact was that Xar had no peers; he was far ahead of everyone else in his advancements, and the production and technological ideas proposed and produced by Xar's ideas had made the idea of challenging them impossible.

Roivas' main competition for lead-code mathematician had been a younger and more ambitious scientist. Dr. Ran Lee went to all the best schools, and he expected that his accomplishments would be noted and that he would be given his due admiration. He didn't like waiting his turn and had a history of finding his way to the top no matter what demands were made of him. He constantly challenged Roivas even though he was technically working for him; he provoked arguments to the point of annotated incidences of violence at times. He was clearly brilliant, but far too aggressive in his ambitions. Most working with Dr. Lee found his provoking arguments too much to handle in a stable working environment. But Lee (in his brilliance) had noticed the direction Roivas' work was taking and the eventual conclusions that the work was leading to. Instead of avoiding the politically-incorrect ideas that Roivas' ideas might lead to, Lee saw the ideas as a way to ultimately discredit Roivas and perhaps leapfrog to the lead coders' spot.

Lee's first idea was to use Xar's paper to discredit Roivas' work. But try as Lee might, the doctor was unable to do so. It seemed like both Xar's and Roivas' works were both correct; Dr. Lee questioned how that could be possible since both schools of thought seemed to be in stark contrast. Lee decided after months of consecutive attempts that he couldn't discredit Roivas' work. However, he understood clearly that the ideas were politically dangerous and that the acceptance of the "Primary Truth" was so strong and fundamental to the Utopia that anyone proposing a challenge to it would invite certain destruction of their career; perhaps even a jail sentence would be merited for someone as high-ranking as Lee and Roivas. Lee's new strategy would be to convince Roivas otherwise and get him to commit to the obvious and detrimental outcome—that his ideas actually challenged the "Primary

Truth." After all, Lee thought the one weakness that Roivas had was his trusting nature and his obviously less-ambitious nature. Lee knew he would be able to manipulate Roivas given ample time.

Roivas returned to his quarters and ordered his dinner and readied himself for some downtime on the night of November 9, 2195; he couldn't resist reviewing the work of the day. This seemed to be the usual pattern Roivas took regardless of the fact that he knew he should give himself some downtime away from the work. But it seemed to consume him. He was interrupted on November 10, 2195 by an unexpected knock at his door. It was Lee, and he had a bottle of some rare brandy from the Carolina district of the Western States—expensive stuff.

RECORDED PER V-6 MONITOR: NOVEMBER 10, 2195

START 0904 HRS

"Can I come in Rich?" - Lee

"Sure," - Roivas, hormone levels depicting that the subject was not happy about his personal time being interrupted by Lee.

"I wanted to discuss some ideas I had with you about the latest developmental breakthroughs our group has made. I wanted you to know how much I respect the work that you have done." - Lee

NEUROLOGICAL SCAN (1110) NOTE: Roivas thought how hard this must be, knowing Lee's psychological makeup.

"Thank You, Lee. That means a lot coming from you." - Roivas

"No, really. It's beyond brilliant, and I've been contemplating the conclusions your work is leading us to." - Lee

NEUROLOGICAL SCAN (2113) NOTE: Roivas almost immediately became nervous, understanding the dangerous areas this conversation was heading towards.

"I think your work is heading us toward some real breakthroughs that could seriously have some implications in areas well beyond science." - Lee.

NEUROLOGICAL SCAN (3322) NOTE: "He knows," Roivas thought. His nervous system was in full-panic mode.

"I don't know what you mean, Lee," - Roivas

"Well, Rich, you know how much difficulty the Ministry of Science has had in convincing some of the lower classes of the Primary Truth of the Utopia, right?" - Lee

"Yes. I had heard that some sporadic groups still existed which held to their ancient faiths, but that the Ministry of Science had been able to convince most and was dealing with the rest. It is foolish to challenge the Primary Truth. Don't you agree, Lee?" - Roivas.

"Well, no. That's not it at all." - Lee.

NEUROLOGICAL SCAN (6678) NOTE: Lee knew this was the critical moment. He had to manipulate Roivas into thinking that his ideas were complementary to the Primary Truth. Lee had developed the duplicitous idea of convincing Roivas of the political use of the ideas being used to bring along the remaining faithful followers of god or gods to the eventual, easier handling of these outcast faithful.

END 0912 HRS

Lee's argument to Roivas the entire night was a complete theory on how the idea that Roivas' work was leading to (as far as the limits to what randomness could produce) could bring about a more inclusive political climate for these faithful. That would, in turn, please Minister Xar and the hierarchy. Lee's argument, combined with the ethanol in the Carolinian Brandy, had been somewhat successful. Roivas clearly stated to himself that he wanted the obvious conclusions of his work to be ultimately successful—made clear. Lee's ideas had tempted him into a sort of "wishful hoping" that this might be possible. He hadn't convinced Roivas of the idea, but he had taken a huge first step with the feedback he received from Roivas; in Lee's mind, his strategy would eventually produce the fruit which he had intended it to.

Many more nightly discussions followed, but not so many that he would risk annoying Roivas' disposition. The plan devised by Lee was slowly working, but it needed a catalyst; he thought to push Roivas into revealing his theory in full. Lee planted the idea of Roivas' producing and working on a complete paper on the limitations of randomness. But Roivas, although tempted, was still not convinced of the merits of writing it; he was convinced that the risk was too great. That was all to end when a violent encounter in Jerusalem between the Ministry of Science's forces and a new group of God-followers (calling themselves "prophets") had produced the death of thousands of citizens in the area(*this encounter has been labeled by the Scientific Magisterium as ENCOUNTER ALPHA). The usual way the Ministry of Science had dealt with the intolerant religious was to place them in live stasis; not killing them, but humanely placing them in a type of frozen animation with the eventual promise of reeducation; in addition to being humane, the process was cost effective. These followers were viewed as schizophrenic (practically insane) and the source of many of the earths' ills; they were tested and treated for schizophrenia, and the curable ailment proved non-existent. However (*in ENCOUNTER ALPHA) the "prophets" seemed to have acquired some high-tech devices which were able to resist the Ministry of Science's advanced forces. They had been practically irresistible in most other cases. These technological weapons have been documented.

Lee jumped on this prospective situation and pleaded with Roivas to write his paper, emphasizing on the ideas he had planted and nurtured in Roivas' mind about how his paper could produce peace and actually be praised by Xar and the Ministry of Science. Roivas was sad to hear about the deaths in Jerusalem, knowing at the same time that his son Nazere had been arrested in the province of Ordren for disorderly conduct and drug use. He mentioned this fact to Lee, and Lee milked the concept mercilessly; he implied that Roivas was endangering others like his son by not writing the paper which Lee insisted would produce peace. It was during what is being called INCIDENT G that Roivas was monitored in a state of rapid-eye-movement sleep that lasted for an unusual duration. Following the dream, Roivas made the following statements in his apartment complex:

RECORDED PER V-6 MONITOR: JANUARY 11, 2196
START 0633 HRS

"My second dream...can't sleep...can't eat. All I see are numbers and light. Light. Light. I have seen everything! I see the completed

Babylon; I see my son in battle. So much blood—so much death...I didn't think it was possible. The wolves at the gates of Sydney will tear everything apart because of that witch—the witch of Babylon. Minister Xar will kill everything in her name—but that shadow I see will counter him and battle her many demons. What is it? I understand everything else, but what is the shadow? This shadow casts its frame over The Seven Year War." - Roivas, pacing back and forth.

END 0638 HRS

Roivas was at last convinced; he would write the paper. The mathematics for the papers involved the intense usage of infinity terms as actual numbers and the intense work that had been done to produce random numbers in the group which Lee and Roivas worked in. What became evident in the work was that a purely random code was impossible without an infinite frame. What were actually possible were codes that produced what were better classified as pseudo-random-codes. If a portion of the code were used in a limited time, the codes could indeed be viewed as purely random; but each code had an underlying algorithm which included a mathematical configuration of combined polynomials and a starting point or number. The run length was limited by the hardware or computer's ability. The larger the numbers the computer could handle, the more randomness could be generated. This limitation in computing hardware was considered the frame limit of the randomness.

Roivas' work led to the conclusion that a purely random system required infinite hardware. Now this idea alone was covered in Xar's paper, which insisted and proved that everything was derived from a purely random system. Xar, like Roivas, made extensive use of infinity as a real number and insisted the universe was indeed infinite and could and did produce a purely random system which he further gave proof was able to spontaneously generate all that existed. Roivas, however, used statistics to show that, indeed, a purely random system would require an infinite frame and agreed with the idea that the universe (in the beginning) was infinite. However, Roivas showed that the best model for a purely random system consisted of an unlimited and infinite number of conditions, which all had an equal probability of occurring. Roivas showed that as the number of conditions in a system approached infinity, each condition's probability of occurring became lower and lower; at infinity, the probability of each condition was exactly zero. Roivas insisted that this demonstrated clearly that the only thing a purely random system could produce was NOTHING! That without an intelligent agent of some kind being impressed on the NOTHING, a purely random system would remain void and dark—that no condition could spontaneously change its probability of occurrence. However, if an intelligent agent introduced some sort of limit or filter which selected some conditions on the void as more probable than others, then the universe could have been produced; those introduced limits were, indeed, the physical laws which governed the universe. Roivas proved mathematically that these laws required an intelligent and selective agent of some kind.

The obvious conclusion that Lee understood was that this agent could be the very God that many of the remaining faithful still believed in. In fact, Roivas' paper was entitled the "God Proof" when it was introduced. Lee had already secretly greased the skids for the distribution of the paper in all the leading Ministry of Science trade journals and in many leading political rags of the times. The paper was the most controversial and talked about paper of its time.

Minister Xar, however, was not amused. He immediately called for the papers' squelching and arrested all editors of the Ministry of Science's magazines which printed the dribble. Paper after paper was then written to demonize Roivas when he was arrested. Xar went on the world-wide Ministry of Science Channel himself and addressed the world, pointing to how far the world had come in understanding the universal truth which Roivas' paper had challenged. He supported his "Primary Truth" with mathematics that surpassed the understanding of even the most renowned ministry scientists. Xar's technological achievements could not be denied; clearly, Xar must be right in that he remained unchallenged.

And he insisted to the courts which held Roivas that the paper he had written had done irrevocable damage in the establishment of the Utopia which the world had "achieved." He later recanted this achievement, announcing that work toward the Utopia Project needed additional attention in the areas of crime and resistance. After the courts held Roivas for a period of six weeks, Xar was elected High Lord of Jerusalem; overriding the courts' power, he sentenced Roivas to death in Rome, Europe. Xar insisted to the public that Roivas had been given every possible advantage and that the only conclusion that the Ministry of Science should come to in rationalization was that Roivas misused the abilities (*chronicled in STATEMENT R) the Ministry of Science had allotted him. Xar further stated that Roivas did so to cause a purposeful interruption of the march to Utopia. Xar stated that Roivas and those like him were the ultimate evil and that no toleration of this type of purposeful misuse of ministry resources would or should be tolerated.

Roivas' son Nazere and his personal troubles were also driven home by the world-wide media and were used to further discredit Dr. Richard Roivas. In the end, Xar's words remained beyond reproach. Lee was able to successfully hide his connections to the release of the Roivas paper. Dr. Lee founded the Eripsa Corporation in December, 2209, and has continued to work alongside the now High Lord Alune and Vice Lord Xar in the collaboration of the Babylon Project; his work was completed January 3, 2211.

SUBJECT was held for two years in his cell. He was allowed no visitors, but there was an unexplained incident of escape—the first in Ordren's history. A letter was later found written from Roivas to his son Nazere within the cell. The letter was delivered to Nazere in an unknown fashion. Nazere was not sentenced to death; the conditions of his holding were temporary stasis. Below is the interrogation of Dr. Richard Roivas in its entirety. His neurons and general physiology were studied, and there appeared to be no abnormalities. Dr. Richard Roivas was dissected alive per order 17.7, issued by Vice Lord Xar; his remains were cremated. His interrogation didn't reveal much information, but a letter (STATEMENT X) left in his cell after his death is now being evaluated; it is the purpose for this memorandum.

STATEMENT R: THE INTERROGATION OF DR. RICHARD ROIVAS

Dr. Paul Negentis Presiding

Location: The Vaults of Rome

Date: August 14, 2209

Q: During your writing of "The God Proof," did you see things that were abnormal?

A: I'm not answering any questions.

Q: Do you feel that you were in any way delusional when you were recorded talking to yourself? You were recorded dreaming.

A: No answers.

Q: Do you feel you have powers? Are you a prophet?

A: …

Q: During your self-conversation, you referenced a war. Do you have knowledge of any terrorist activities?

A: …

Q: You mentioned Sydney. Did you mean Australia? How did you know that Queen Airya became a witch before she did?

A: You should ask yourself that same question.

End of Inquiry

As an end note to the study of The Seven Year War, a recent document has been discovered that has led the Scientific Magisterium to believe that Roivas has other family remaining other than his son. The Scientific Magisterium and the End of Truth is a document that has been written by a certain Dr. Andrew Roivas and serves as a scientific paper on proposed technological improvements for the basic ventari core, as well as a near mirror image of Dr. Roivas' key paper—"The God Proof." Fragments of this paper were intercepted during wireless transfer, and the blueprints for a single, modified ventari core have been partially studied. Dr. Richard Roivas is believed to have initiated the production of this paper, and Dr. Andrew Roivas is charged with concluding it; Chief Scientist Olar was only able to draw from what appears to be a seventh of the text in his initiation of the Commander Entril Project. The location of the remaining text remains unknown, but the mention of SUBJECT S was duly noted in the paper.

***STATEMENT X: THE SEVEN YEAR WAR

***LETTER DISCOVERED IN THE CELL OF DR. RICHARD ROIVAS AFTER HIS DEATH

MYSTERY
BABYLON THE GREAT
THE MOTHER OF PROSTITUTES
AND OF ABOMINATIONS OF THE EARTH

For a time you shall stand and you shall slaughter everything you see. You will be given great power, and the beast will be the means of your supremacy. To Queen Airya, your fall shall be the greatest one known to mankind. The world will cry in pity as your forces are brought to their knees. For on the day that Bethlehem stands—and it will stand—the forthcoming of disaster will find you like a thief in the night. You will take as many prophets as you can locate, and your wolves, vampires, witches, demons and men will revel in their suffering; but know this: you will drown in your own blood when all is said and done. For on the day that the city of Bethlehem stands unshaken, The Seven Year War shall begin, and the count of bodies hitting the floor will be too many for even a mathematician to calculate.

See you on the other side,

—Dr. Richard Roivas

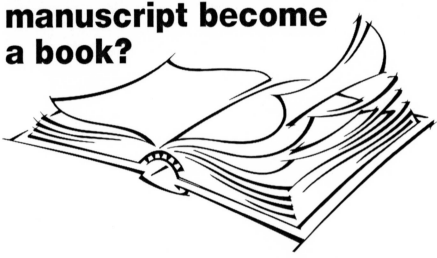

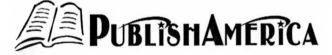

Breinigsville, PA USA
28 February 2011
256608BV00001B/39/P